THE

GUEST

COTTAGE

Books by Lori Foster

Too Much Temptation

Never Too Much

Unexpected

Say No to Joe?

The Secret Life of Bryan

When Bruce Met Cyn

Just a Hint—Clint

Jamie

Murphy's Law

Jude's Law

The Watson Brothers

Yule Be Mine

The Guest Cottage

Published by Kensington Publishing Corp.

LORI FOSTER

THE

GUEST

COTTAGE

KENSINGTON
PUBLISHING CORP.

kensingtonbooks.com

KENSINGTON BOOKS are published by

Kensington Publishing Corp.
900 Third Ave.
New York, NY 10022

All Kensington titles, imprints, and distributed lines are available at special quantity discounts for bulk purchases for sales promotion, premiums, fund-raising, educational, or institutional use. Special book excerpts or customized printings can also be created to fit specific needs. For details, write or phone the office of the Kensington Special Sales Manager: Attn. Special Sales Department. Kensington Publishing Corp., 900 Third Ave., New York, NY 10022. Phone: 1-800-221-2647.

Library of Congress Control Number: 2025930756

ISBN: 978-1-4967-5234-5
First Kensington Hardcover Edition: June 2025

ISBN: 978-1-4967-5235-2 (trade)

ISBN: 978-1-4967-5236-9 (ebook)

10 9 8 7 6 5 4 3 2 1

Printed in the United States of America

THE

GUEST

COTTAGE

CHAPTER 1

The miserable May weather suited the occasion. At least the eulogy was over, and she no longer had to talk with Dylan's friends and distant family, all of whom expected her to weep for the loss of her dear, adoring husband.

Little did they know she'd lost him months ago when she'd found out about the "other woman." For Marlow Heddings, everything had ended that day—the love, the commitment . . . the farce. Her plans for the future.

Her mother-in-law, usually an unstoppable force but now somewhat fragile, wouldn't hear of having Dylan's name tainted, not even with the truth.

Yet the truth was never far from Marlow's mind. He'd been a lying, unfaithful, deceitful bastard. He'd hurt her, then mocked her with a cruel lack of remorse.

The awful things he'd said, the hateful way he'd blamed her, continued to rage like a tornado in her mind.

As if to reflect her dour thoughts, the skies grumbled, dark clouds tumbling over each other. Soon there would be another deluge.

If it would end this farce, she'd gladly be soaked.

Despite her foul thoughts, all of them accurate, she maintained her composed expression. Let them think it was inner strength that kept her eyes dry, her emotions in check. In reality, it was numbness.

Soon she'd drive away from her loss, her oppressive memories, and the determination of her suddenly clinging mother-in-law.

"Such a beautiful memorial service," Sandra Heddings declared between her not-so-quiet sobs. "Everyone is properly honoring him."

Properly honoring him? In a bid to keep her thoughts to herself, Marlow flattened her mouth. She wasn't heartless enough to add to Sandra's pain. Whatever failings her mother-in-law might have, loving her son wasn't one of them. She'd cherished Dylan, making him her entire world.

Unfortunately, during the month that Dylan had been gone, it seemed Sandra had turned her sights on Marlow in some bizarre attempt to cherish his legacy.

"Come on," Marlow whispered gently, her arm around the other woman. "Let's get out of this rain."

"I don't want to let him go." Turning into Marlow, Sandra squeezed her arms tight around her as wracking cries broke loose.

Desperately, Marlow glanced around for help, but many had already moved on. Aston, Dylan's father, stood over the grave site, his head bowed and his proud shoulders slumped in pain. The few relatives still braving the weather were gathered around him, leaving Marlow to tend to Sandra.

Her wide black umbrella wasn't sufficient to shelter them from the endless drizzling rain. God, she wanted this day over with. She wanted, needed, to wrap up her duty, her social obligations, so she could escape it all.

Sandra had wanted to delay the service until the weather cleared, but Marlow knew if she'd put it off at all, she'd have broken down.

Because she was taller and sturdier than Sandra, Marlow was able to steer her back along the path. "That's it. One step at a time. You know how much Dylan loved you. He'd want you inside, warm and dry."

"Yes, he would. He was such a good son. So devoted to our family." Sandra's eyes slanted her way. "To the business."

Not always true. In many ways, Dylan had resented his mother. In other ways, he'd repeatedly disrespected her. His contribution to the business had been as a mere figurehead. He'd done very little actual work, even less after Marlow had caught him cheating.

With him and Marlow at odds, he'd repeatedly missed work, using the excuse that he wanted to avoid his wife's "volatile and hostile moods," even though she was always professional at work. Marlow had solved that for him by resigning her position and walking away.

She'd needed time alone to grieve the loss of her marriage and her future, and to start planning her next steps. The litigated divorce proceedings she'd begun almost a year ago had enraged all the Heddings—Dylan, his mother, and his father. None of them had expected her to fight, which only proved how little they'd really known her.

She'd given a lot to her marriage, and she'd helped to build the assets she and her husband had accumulated. Taking what she'd earned was fair; she didn't want or need anything of Dylan's. Yet he'd disagreed, and the battle had begun.

Just as it seemed they might get the divorce finalized, Dylan had died.

Now, none of that family antagonism seemed to matter anymore. Not to a grieving mother. Sandra had adopted a "let bygones be bygones" attitude.

As Marlow patiently urged her mother in law along, her gaze repeatedly swept the area. She half expected the "other woman" to show up. Wouldn't that be the perfect theatrical kick? A lone mysterious woman, dressed all in black, watching from afar?

But no, it was only Dylan's family and friends, all of them heartbroken that Saint Dylan was no longer with them.

Jaw locking, she lifted her chin a little higher and finally got her mother-in-law into the building. "Aston will bring around the car."

"This has destroyed him."

Yes, Dylan and his father had been close. Toasting each other at parties, golfing together. Dylan was supposed to inherit the family dynasty.

For the longest time Marlow had wanted children, but Dylan had refused, insisting that he wasn't yet ready. Now, she was grateful she didn't have a child that would tie her to these people. A decade of marriage had brought about familiar, if not openly affectionate, feelings, but she'd already decided that it was past time she cared for herself.

A while later, on the drive from the grave site, Marlow worked up her courage to set the wheels in motion. "I'll see you both home, but I'm not coming in."

Sandra had been weeping into her hands, but now her head jerked up and her tears miraculously dried. "What are you talking about? You're Dylan's wife. Of course, you're coming in."

In another few weeks, despite the way Dylan had fought her on everything, she would have been his ex-wife. Then he'd gotten himself killed in a car crash. Now she couldn't even make her grand exodus from the family. A divorce would have been the perfect exclamation point to her anger.

Instead, because she was a nice person, she was being forced to tiptoe away.

Nerves strung to the breaking point, Marlow shook her

head. "It's better that I don't. I have my own plans to finalize now."

In an expression reminiscent of his son's, Aston scowled darkly. "What *plans*?"

He practically growled the word, but she'd expected this. Anything that didn't comfortably coincide with his itinerary was an annoyance. "I'm moving away." To a different house, in a different community, in another state.

A fresh start, away from grief and heartache.

Somehow during the ten years of her marriage, she'd completely lost herself. Gone was the happy, relaxed young woman she'd once been, replaced by a staid, conservative-dressing, matronly businesswoman whom, honestly, Marlow didn't even like.

If she couldn't like herself, how had she expected Dylan to love her?

Because he'd made her the person she'd become. He'd made their major decisions as a couple. Where they'd live, how they'd live, and which social functions were advantageous. She'd *allowed* him to take the lead, to guide their marriage and their future. And in doing so, she'd morphed into someone different—an uptight, rigid woman who always followed the rules of etiquette and never caused a scene.

That nonsense was over.

"Don't be ridiculous," Aston said. "You'll reclaim your old job."

"No," she replied, softly but firmly. "I won't."

Sandra gave a shuddering sigh. "I understand why Dylan wanted you gone once you'd filed for divorce." Her look of censure showed through her sorrow. "I still don't understand how you could humiliate him like that."

Pride kept her voice even. "I will never settle for less than what I give."

Sandra waved her response away. "It was just a silly mistake."

"The woman meant nothing," Aston seconded with heat. "Less than nothing."

Their attitude no longer surprised Marlow. She'd had years of hearing his parents staunchly defend Dylan's every bad decision.

"She mattered to me. To our marriage."

Aston scoffed. "You were willing to throw away your life together because of one indiscretion? After Dylan gave you everything? After all *we've* given you?"

So many angry words danced through her thoughts. Things she wanted to say. Things she should have cleared up long ago. For her own sake, she held them back. "I wish you both nothing but the best."

They didn't return the sentiment.

Outrage overshadowing her heartache, Sandra narrowed her eyes. "You would actually abandon us now? When we need you most? When we're hurting so badly?"

Pointing out that she hurt, too, that she'd been hurting for months, wouldn't accomplish anything. "I'm sorry, but there's nothing more I can do for you."

Thank God, the limo driver had traversed the long curving drive to their sprawling home and stopped before the entry. Others had already arrived, and more cars pulled in behind them. Marlow scooted across the seat, not waiting for the door to be opened.

Sandra grabbed her arm, her small hand almost desperately tight. "When you filed for divorce, Dylan wanted you cut out of his inheritance."

"I know." Like a threat, he'd shouted his intentions at her. The sad part was that the need to avoid scandal and humiliation was what inspired him. Not love. He'd found it inconceivable that she, a plain businesswoman from an upper middle class background, would dare to walk away from the incredible Dylan Heddings.

"We talked him out of it," Aston said with satisfaction. "Stay with the business, and the money will still be yours."

What he meant was that she needed to go on playing the inconsolable wife. "It doesn't matter." She had her own accounts, in her name only. She neither needed nor wanted the Heddings' money. There were many things she'd let slide over the years, but she'd always protected herself financially.

Maybe she'd retained some survival instincts after all.

The door opened, and Marlow stepped out. It didn't matter that they were both hissing quiet demands at her. Or that she'd left her umbrella in the car and her upswept hair was immediately soaked by the downpour.

It didn't matter that others looked on in shock as she walked away, backbone straight and head held high.

Slowly, she inhaled. Fresh air. Freedom.

A new beginning.

It was time to return to her roots.

He answered on the second ring with a simple, "Hello."

"Mr. Easton?" Anticipation made her breathless as she loaded the last box of personal items into her Lexus SUV and closed the door. "It's Marlow Heddings."

"I recognized the number."

He had the deepest, darkest voice, no-nonsense and without inflection. She'd only called him . . . what? Five or six times over the past two months? Ugh, he probably thought she was stringing him along. *Please, please, please*, she thought. "The property I was interested in renting . . . Is it still available?"

"It is."

Breath left her in a whoosh. "I want it."

After the briefest pause, he said, "There've been two other interested parties, so I can't continue to hold it."

"No, I mean I want it *now*. Today." Sunrise turned the sky from dark purple to mauve. Sometime during the night, the storm had blown through, leaving everything wet and fresh, renewed. "I'll be on my way to you in the next few minutes."

"From Illinois?"

"Glencoe, yes. I think it's something like a six- or seven-hour drive, so I'll have to stop a few times, but it's barely dawn now. I'll definitely be there before the end of the day." She wasn't certain of the exact travel time because the town barely showed on the map. With no more than four hundred people living there, it would be an escape from everything familiar and just what she'd been looking for.

Mr. Easton greeted her news with silence. Whether it came of disbelief or surprise, she had no idea.

"Will that be a problem? When last we spoke, you said you had immediate occupancy."

"Same day is a little more immediate than I expected."

Marlowe stopped, her heart stuttering to a near standstill. The steady drip-drip-drip of rainwater from the trees mingled with the sounds of birds rejoicing and the distant bark of a dog. It could be a new and exciting day—unless he altered her plans.

The very idea got her talking fast. "Did you do the credit report? The background check? Is there something else you need?" She hadn't slept after the funeral yesterday. No, she'd finished packing everything she might need to begin anew, and nothing else. She meant to leave behind her old life.

A pre-arranged estate manager would sell the rest of the belongings in the house, including Dylan's things. The house had already been listed for a respectable sum, and the realtor could show it without her.

She was free and clear. All she needed now was a place to stay.

Ready to convince him, Marlow opened the driver's side door and got behind the wheel. "I'd like to pay you upfront for six months, but I'm happy to rent the place—" *Indefinitely.* Shaking her head, she amended her first, possibly overwhelming word choice, to the less ambitious, "For as long as it's available."

"Not just for the summer?"

God, she was botching this. "Is it only available in the summer?"

Another stretch of silence, and then, "It's available beyond that. You're sure you'll be here today?"

"Yes. Already in my car." She started the engine. "Pulling out of my driveway now."

"All right, Ms. Heddings. Everything in your application checked out. You have my number, so give me a call when you arrive, and I'll deliver the keys to you."

Gale-force relief rushed through her. "Thank you! Oh, this is wonderful. I can't wait to arrive." To start my new life.

Finally, things were looking up.

With a smile in his tone, he said, "Drive safely."

Thoughts of his new tenant played on repeat in Cort's mind all day. She wasn't what he'd expected. Her background check . . . her credit report . . . the photos he'd found of her online . . . her tone of excitement on the phone—contradictions, one after the other.

She was an accomplished woman, recently leaving a high-level job within a well-known, family-owned company . . . for an extended stay on Rainbow Lake?

For ten years she'd been married to the heir of the Heddings' Holding Company, but her upbringing had also been upper middle class, with a mother in education and a father who was a surgeon.

In her photos, she'd appeared dignified and serene, nearly untouchable in the way of valuable art. Cold, detached, under the spotlight.

On the phone, she'd damn near been bubbling over with

enthusiasm. She planned to spend all day in her car just to arrive for an extended stay in a modest home for rent in the "nowhere town" of Bramble.

None of it added up, but he was intrigued all the same.

Puzzles were meant to be solved, and he'd figure Marlow Heddings out in good time.

Spending the day working helped to distract him. He resisted the urge to check his phone. She'd call when she called, and if she didn't, he had two other renters ready to sign on for the summer.

"Much better," Herman said, giving the railing on the bar top a tug and finding it secure. "Good as new. Thank you."

"No problem." If he didn't stay busy, his mind would circle endlessly. Marines didn't slay their inner dragons—they made them work to their advantage. For Cort, that meant keeping his mind occupied with handyman jobs, which also built relations in the community and added to his savings. He didn't see a downside.

The early evening sun cast long shadows everywhere. If Ms. Heddings didn't arrive soon, she'd be getting acquainted with her new place in the dark. No sooner did he have that thought than she walked through the doors of the tavern.

Windblown fawn-colored hair hung loose to her shoulders. As she stepped into the dim interior, she removed large-framed sunglasses and glanced around with a smile of fascinated delight. Those eyes, velvety brown and heavily lashed, could get a guy into trouble.

She'd made an effort to dress casually in wide-legged faded jeans, with white Dior sneakers and a Dior sweater set. The outfit probably cost more than most people made in a month.

"Excuse me," she said to Bren Crawford, an eighty-year-old original who couldn't hear but refused to wear hearing aids. "I'm a tiny bit lost."

Bren squinted up at her, took another gulp of his longneck beer, and wiped his mouth on his sleeve.

Instead of intervening, Cort braced his forearms on the bar, content to watch and wait, and maybe be enlightened on a few mysteries.

Smile slipping, Ms. Heddings tried again. "I know I'm in Bramble, but I'm trying to find a specific address."

"What's that?"

Her lips parted for another question, but then the light dawned and she closed her mouth with a smile. Digging in her purse, she pulled out a slip of paper, presumably with the address, and showed it to Bren.

Of course, he couldn't see any better than he could hear.

Muttering, "What in the world?" Herman circled out from behind the bar and rushed over to her. "Can I help you?"

Giving up on Bren, she turned to Herman and said, "I hope so. I'm renting property on the lake, but I can't seem to locate the exact address."

"Keep going down this road and you'll run into the lake. To the left, the address numbers go down, and to the right, they go up."

"Oh." Resigned to finding the place on her own, she said, "Thank you. I'm close then?"

"You have to be, the town is so small."

"Of course." Flashing another quick smile, she stepped around Herman and headed to the bar.

Seeing that she was coming right for him, Cort straightened.

"Do you have food? Anything at all would be amazing. I'm *starving*." Hoisting herself onto a bar stool, she glanced around as if she thought she might find a menu. "I'd need it to go. I was going to stop for a few necessities, but I didn't see any grocery stores or markets on my way in."

"The Dry Frog Tavern has pizzas, burgers, and appetizers."

The name of the place sent her brows up, but she didn't comment on it. "Pizza," she repeated with a husky groan, "sounds amazing. How long does that take?"

"I usually have to wait forty-five minutes or more."

"You have to . . . ?" She shook her head. "It takes that long?" Her skeptical gaze skipped around again, seeing that the twenty or so customers in the bar were involved in drinking, not eating. "Do you have anything I could get quickly?"

By way of an answer, Cort bent to put the rest of his tools in the box, then started out around the bar. "I'll have my pizza any minute now. I'm happy to share it with you."

The tucking of her chin and straightening of her posture announced her thoughts without her saying a single word.

Herman reappeared. "Here you go, Cort." He handed over a flat box of hot pizza, along with some cash to pay Cort for his work. "Thanks for coming out on such short notice."

Cort gave his usual answer—"Not a problem"—and then made introductions. "Herman, this is Ms. Heddings. She's renting from me. Ms. Heddings, Herman Black owns the tavern."

She jerked around to face him, in the process ignoring Herman. "*You're* Mr. Easton?" Then to Herman, "But he was behind the bar. I thought—"

"Fixing a broken rail for me." Herman was happy to enlighten her. "Cort's not quite an original, but his mother lived here for years, and when she started ailing, Cort moved in. He's our local hero, you know, and a damn fine handyman. Got a problem with something, you call Cort."

She blinked at the outpouring of information. Cort was used to it. Some of the townspeople used any excuse to flaunt their association with him, regardless of how little it actually meant. He wasn't a hero, wasn't special in any way, but he was good with his hands and he'd done work, big and small, for just about everyone who lived in the quaint little town.

It helped that his mother had been accepted, and loved, by everyone who'd met her. During his time in the Marines, he'd moved her to Bramble—largely to keep her safe—and the locals had embraced her. In no time, she'd become one of them.

By extension, they'd accepted him, too.

"Come on," he said, holding the heavy toolbox in one hand, the pizza in the other. "We can talk outside."

She was halfway to the door before she thought to turn and say to Herman, "It was so nice meeting you."

Herman waved and got to work. During the week, the tavern wasn't overly busy, but tomorrow would bring the Friday night crowd, and he'd be run off his feet through Saturday.

Once they were away from eavesdroppers, Cort said, "I wasn't sure you'd make it."

"I got lost several times, and the traffic was brutal."

"It's always that way until you get here." He stowed the toolbox in the back of his truck and slammed the tailgate, then reached in through the driver's door to put the pizza on the passenger seat. "Here on the lake, it's quiet during the week. Bramble is a home rule city, and they don't allow crowds until the weekend. That means all the out of towners congregate nearby. Plenty of people live on the outskirts, too, then swarm in all day Friday and Saturday, and part of the day Sunday."

"Home rule what?"

Yeah, that had been his reaction at first, too. "Pizza is getting cold. Why don't you follow me? I can show you the place, give you the keys, and hand over a few slices. I already put drinks in the fridge for you, along with a few other necessities."

Color rushed to her fair cheeks. "I'm sorry. I didn't mean to put you out."

"Not a problem." He walked her to her car. "I'll go slowly, but you couldn't really miss me anyway. As Herman said, we'll continue along this road. When you see the lake, we'll go right about a mile." He opened her car door, noticing that it wasn't locked, then waited until she got in. "Ten minutes, tops." Closing the door again, he started off.

It was either that or continue staring at her.

When he'd done the background check on her as a potential

renter, he'd also gone through her social media. This windblown, blushing woman with incredible eyes was not what he'd expected. The fancy clothes, sure. The confidence, definitely.

That smile, though? The way she'd proclaimed herself starving?

Yeah, he'd be thinking about both for a while.

Now he just needed to get her settled, and then he could call it a night.

Honest to God, her face felt hot for the entire, too-brief drive to the guest cottage. Why had she assumed Cort Easton would be older? In her mind, the deep, dreamy voice belonged to a guy with reading glasses and graying hair, a retiree renting out property to help make ends meet.

She had not expected a tall, hard-muscled man in his midthirties with a stare that could strip a woman bare.

She'd worked for the Heddings family long enough to hold her own with anyone—family, associates, and business adversaries alike—but from the second Mr. Easton introduced himself, she'd lost the power of rational speech.

He had the bearing of a head of state . . . or an old-time warrior. He spoke only when necessary, wore an indecipherable expression, and carried that heavy metal toolbox as if it weighed no more than a basket of flowers.

She hardly noticed the passing scenery, and before she knew it, he was pulling into the short driveway to a house—*her house*—the incredible little cottage that she'd soon call home.

Suddenly, nothing else existed for her. Heart pounding, she parked next to his truck and stepped out of her SUV in a daze. Oh my, it was even more beautiful than it had looked in the photos. The setting sun was behind them, painting the front of the cottage with a soft golden glow. Three peaks—one over the stoop, another over the main rooms, and a third over the attic—were staggered off center to give the small home more character. Dark olive vertical wood siding paired beautifully with brown shaker shingles and natural stone. Matching the entrance door, double wooden doors at the right would open to a golf garage, and she knew a golf cart was parked inside.

"I love it." She'd meant to state the words, but instead they emerged as a reverent whisper. Her gaze briefly skipped to Mr. Easton, just long enough to catch what might have been the slight tipping of a smile, there and gone.

"How about I help you carry in your things after I've shown you around?"

"That's not necessary. I can do it." With renewed purpose, she headed for the front door, anxious to see the interior.

Somehow, he got there before her. He unlocked the door and they stepped into a foyer where the kitchen was visible straight ahead. Glancing to the left, she took in the small dining room, and next to the kitchen was a cozy sitting room.

"Along that back wall, behind the kitchen and sitting room, is the bedroom with a bathroom. From there you'll find the utility room and a laundry area."

She bypassed all that to head to the sliding doors all along the wall to the left. From the dining room and the sitting room—and maybe the bedroom, too—she could access a covered porch that had a wonderful view of the lake.

The cottage was so incredible, so perfect, that it overwhelmed her. Getting enough air became impossible, but she would not fall apart in front of her new landlord. No, absolutely not.

To give herself a moment, she went out to the porch, but damn, it was perfect, too. Sinking onto a soft padded chair, she stared blindly at the quickly darkening lake. All her focus was on holding herself together. She clutched her shaking hands together, breathed deeply through her nose, and did her utmost to tamp down the feelings of relief currently swamping her.

She was free of a bad marriage, away from her manipulative

in-laws, out of sight of prying eyes. The past no longer mattered. Here, now, was all about her future.

Silently, Mr. Easton slid a paper plate with two slices of pizza onto the small table beside her. He dropped a napkin into her lap, then offered her an open can of Coke, which she automatically accepted. "Be right back."

She stared at the can in surprise. It was cold in her hand, frosty on the outside, still foaming on the inside. When was the last time she'd drunk from a *can*? And that pizza . . . Heavenly scents teased her nose and made her stomach growl. She saw melted cheese, pepperoni, sausage, and ham, all perfectly cooked on a golden crust. She took a big drink, gave a quiet burp, then set the can aside and grabbed up the first slice.

Skipping breakfast and only having a protein bar for lunch were clearly not a great idea. As she ate, she watched the surface of the lake and serenity overtook all other emotions. The sun was nearly gone now, and the air cooled even more.

Breathing more easily, she wondered where Mr. Easton had gone. When she heard a soft thump, she knew.

Mortified, she jammed the last of the pizza into her mouth, washed it down with a big drink, and, napkin in hand, headed back through the house.

The front door stood open, giving her a clear view of her Lexus with the hatch open. Mr. Easton took out the last box and started her way.

"I'm *so* sorry," she rushed to say, stepping out to meet him halfway, looking back and forth from her empty car to the open front door. "I don't know what came over me. I swear, I didn't mean for you to—"

"Not a problem." He went past her as if she weren't standing there babbling, after eating his food and letting him wait on her.

Groaning, she launched herself after him. "Really, Mr. Easton—"

"May as well call me Cort. Everyone around here is informal." He went through the kitchen to the bedroom, a room she hadn't even seen yet, to deposit her last box.

Marlow hurried after him, then drew up short at the sight of all the right boxes placed out of the way against the wall. She'd passed others in the foyer and dining room. To make it easy on herself, she'd marked each box, and clearly he'd paid attention.

"Look around. Take your time. I'll wait for you in the kitchen." And out the door he went.

Such a remarkable man.

She couldn't think of a single time that Dylan had hauled a box . . . anywhere. He had hired people for that sort of thing. He would have complained if he'd had to step around a box, much less move it. Not that he hadn't been fit. He'd gone to the gym regularly and enjoyed golfing, sometimes pickleball, and occasionally tennis.

Though why she was thinking of Dylan right now, she couldn't say. There wasn't a single bit of resemblance between him and her new landlord.

A landlord who had put drinks in her fridge and shared his pizza *and* unpacked her SUV.

Putting a hand to her forehead, she took in the room. Of course, it was lovely, too. It did, indeed, open to the porch, but with French doors instead of sliders. Behind the full-size bed, windows gave a view of a wooded side lot.

The bed sat on a pedestal of white drawers for extra storage. An old-fashioned, floral quilt was topped with a beige knitted throw and fluffy white cotton pillows. After her sleepless night and long drive, her bones wanted to melt at the sight of that cozy bed.

The bathroom was all white tile with beige towels and rugs. Even the laundry room was pretty, with open wood shelving and a stacked washer and dryer.

Unwilling to leave Mr. Easton waiting any longer, she rushed back to the kitchen, and there he was, sitting in one of the chairs at the small square table, devouring his pizza and drinking his own cola.

Trying to correct the already miserable impression she'd made, Marlow retrieved her drink and empty plate from the covered porch, then sat across from him. "Mr. Easton—"

"Cort."

She paused, but he was correct. They had no reason to be formal. "Please call me Marlow."

He answered with a single dip of his head.

"Thank you. For the food and the unloading. I'm sorry I put you to the trouble. I'd love to repay you for the pizza."

"Herman gives me food whenever I work for him. It didn't cost me anything."

"Well, that was nice of Herman, but surely you'd planned to eat it, and here I've taken half."

His mouth lifted slightly again before he set another piece of pizza on her plate. "That slice gives you a fourth. As to the cola, I always stock the basics for anyone renting. You have bottled water, juice, and milk in the fridge. Also eggs and a few condiments. Sugar, flour, powdered creamer, salt and pepper are in the cabinet. I put two TV dinners in the freezer, just in case."

His consideration overwhelmed her as much as the house did. "I thought I'd be able to stop at a grocery store for all that, but then I kept driving and driving without seeing anything but houses. No restaurants or stores of any kind."

After wiping his mouth, he sat back in the chair, shoulders straight, chin held high.

He had incredible posture, and it spurred her to sit a little more properly when she really wanted to slump into an exhausted heap.

"Home rule-class city means Bramble can govern itself independently of the state constitution or statutes. As long as we keep things within reason, state power doesn't infringe on the local government. When I moved here to be closer to my mother, it kicked the population up to four hundred and one. That 'one' pushed them all over the edge." Another quick curve of his lips.

Why am I staring at his lips? Marlow lifted her brows and tried to look enthralled by the story, rather than enthralled by his mouth.

"Now the town doesn't allow any new building. I already had the guest cottage and the lake house, so I can rent them out, but new permanent residents aren't allowed. The only exceptions to population growth are children being born." This time he definitely wore a look of humor. "The town allows that."

They allowed births? She snickered, then laughed, then couldn't stop laughing. She wiped her eyes twice, pinched her mouth together, even shook her head hard, but it didn't help.

"Exhaustion," he diagnosed, as if he were an expert. "It's funny, but not that funny."

And for some reason, that only made her laugh harder. She covered her face, humiliated, even as she continued to make those obnoxious sounds.

"You need to get some rest." He scooted back his chair, regaining her attention. "These keys are yours. I have my own set, but each door has a dead bolt that operates from the inside."

Meaning she'd be entirely secure. "Thank you." Another snicker escaped, but she corralled it with a shuddering inhale. "You've been incredibly helpful."

"I'll stop by tomorrow around noon to go over anything else you might need to know. In the meantime, my number is on the fridge, along with some emergency numbers. Channel guide is by the TV."

"Oh, I need to give you your check." She reached for her purse, but he stepped away from the table.

"Tomorrow is soon enough." He stood in front of her, so tall and rugged, a pillar of strength, stealing her thoughts away before he stepped around her and headed for the front door. "Lock up behind me. And Marlow? Enjoy your first night in the new place."

Stretching awake on the supersoft mattress, Marlow breathed in the cool air and tried to orient herself to her new surroundings: well-worn quilt instead of a silk comforter, pale blue walls with pictures of birds instead of rich cream with original artwork. Everything was close and cozy in the twelve- by fourteen-foot room. She liked it far more than the bedroom she'd left, which was more than twice that size.

After all the driving yesterday and getting settled in, as well as her foolish behavior with Cort, she'd slept more soundly than she ever had in her life. She'd never taken a sleeping pill or drunk enough to knock herself out, but she imagined waking up after doing so would feel like this, sluggish and lazy, her thoughts blurred.

Stretching once more for good measure, she crawled out from under the covers and swung her legs over the side of the bed. Brrr, the hardwood floors were cold, and she hadn't yet unpacked enough to find her slippers. She located thick socks instead, then padded into the tiny bathroom. The tile was icy instead of heated, and the tub wasn't jetted but sat on four cast-iron legs.

She loved all of it.

Every new, different, and simpler aspect of it all.

Pulling a shawl around her shoulders, she went into the kitchen and started the coffeepot. Keeping the smile off her face was impossible as she tried to decide what to do that day. Exploring seemed like a good idea. After she unpacked, of course. And bought some groceries.

And met with Cort.

She wasn't sure why, but as she sipped a cup of coffee, she went through the kitchen to the sliding doors in the sitting room. One peek outside and the amazing sunrise over the lake captured her. Holy smokes, she'd never seen anything like it. It was as if a star had burst and poured brilliantly hued watercolors over the calm surface.

There was no hesitation as she opened the door and headed outside. The lake offered a stunning mirrored reflection of orange, yellow, and red.

The dew-wet grass immediately soaked her socks, and her sleep shirt and shorts offered little protection from the chill. Didn't matter. She couldn't resist trekking down the slight hill and onto a short dock to take in the view. Holding her warm coffee mug in one hand, cinching her shawl close over her collarbone with the other, she inhaled the crisp, fresh scent of country air. Even the early morning breeze that stirred her hair and set goose bumps over her skin didn't bother her.

This had to be heaven.

"Hey."

Nearly leaping out of her skin, she jerked around, spilling coffee everywhere and almost tripping off the dock.

"Careful. This early, the water is like ice."

"*Cort*." He stood on the shore with a fishing rod in hand, his line cast out.

"You're up early." His gaze took a two-second trip down her body, then deliberately focused on the lake as he began to reel in his line. "I didn't expect to see you this soon."

Mute. She'd gone entirely, ridiculously mute.

Without looking at her again, he said, "The sunrises are something to see. When I first moved here, they drew me out, and now I like to fish in the early morning. It's so quiet, even the frogs are sleeping."

The second he mentioned the frogs, she heard a deep-throated rumble begin and had to grin. "Well, they were. I think I woke them up."

"Maybe." He kept his gaze on the lake as he cast out again. "You should probably get a jacket. The mornings are still cold."

"I didn't think anyone else was around." She glanced beyond him and saw a tiny lake house and a larger house up on the hill. "That's where you live?"

"Yes."

Three houses. Mr. Easton was doing okay for himself. "No one is in the lake house right now?"

He shook his head. "I get weekend fishermen in it off and on, but with only one bedroom with an efficiency kitchen, it's not big enough for most people who want to vacation."

A comfortable silence spread over them. Marlow gathered her shawl around her and then carefully sat yoga style on the dock, avoiding the spilled coffee. Out of the corner of her eye, she watched Cort repeatedly cast out, then reel in, as the sun rose, shedding a golden gleam onto the water. The mist cleared away, and the air warmed. Her coffee cup, now empty, sat on the dock beside her.

In some indefinable way, it was the perfect morning for the start of her new life. Peaceful but not alone. Company that wasn't intrusive. No questions, no small talk.

And no pressure.

She'd just about convinced herself to get it in gear when she heard a splash and turned to see Cort reeling in a large fish.

Morbid fascination brought her to her feet. "You got one!"

"A bass," he said with no real inflection or expression, all his attention on the fish. "A big one."

Venturing closer, she asked, "What will you do with it?" The poor fish flipped around in the water, trying to escape.

"Dinner." He glanced at her, then away. "Squeamish about fish?"

"No." She could almost swear she'd made eye contact with that fish. "I mean, I love fresh fish." The second the words left her mouth, she wrinkled her nose. "Just not that fresh. Not . . . after watching it fight."

"They aren't grown at restaurants." There was no mocking insult in his words, just fact. "Every bit of seafood, meat, or fowl that you've ever eaten was once—"

"Ack." She covered her ears. "I know, I swear I do, but I like to live with the illusion that everything I consume just appears on my plate."

Again, without a single note of mockery, he asked, "You've never processed the food yourself?"

"Sadly, I was raised upper middle class and then married into wealth. No exposure to anything . . ." She searched for a word and settled on, "Earthy." The quick flash of his barely-there smile made her feel as if she'd just accomplished something worthwhile.

"I'm not sure a nice upbringing can be considered sad, but I get your meaning."

Naturally, she wondered about his upbringing, but as he pulled the fish from the water, she concentrated on not looking at it. If she did, she just might cry.

"He's in the basket," Cort said. "You can look now."

Oh wow, so he'd known she was cowering? Another humiliation. "Do you fish every morning?"

"Usually." His intent gaze, narrowed from the sunshine, moved over her face. "If you plan to visit the dock each morning, I can fish on the other side."

"I don't mind," she blurted too quickly, and then worried

that he'd see through her carefree façade to the chaos of her current emotional state.

Pasting on a false but hopefully convincing smile, she said, "It's so nice down here, I just might make it part of my morning coffee. Next time, with sneakers and a jacket or something, and hopefully I'll drink the coffee instead of throwing it." This smile, at least, was honest. "But hey, it's your property, and I definitely don't want you changing your habits for me."

He gathered up his rod, a tackle box, and the basket containing several fish before he spoke. "If I'm here, it won't bother you?"

"Not at all—as long as I'm not disturbing you." Marlow couldn't be sure, but it seemed the corner of his mouth gave another interesting little curl before he faced her again.

"You're renting the place, dock included. Make yourself at home."

That told her exactly nothing. So did her presence bother him or not? She was pretty sure she wouldn't get any answers today. "I should get going. I want to get unpacked and maybe explore the area a little before we meet this afternoon."

"Need help with anything?"

The man was far too helpful, but she knew it was important to reclaim her independence. She could and would get things done on her own. "Definitely not. You've been more than generous with your time."

As if he'd expected that answer, he nodded. "I should get these fish gutted, then. Enjoy the rest of your morning."

She watched him walk away, his posture military straight, his short, dark brown hair unmoved by the breeze. Such an interesting person. When she realized she was still standing there staring after him, Marlow quickly got it together. She retrieved her mug from the dock, peeled off her wet socks and used them to wipe up the rest of the spilled coffee, and then did a slip-slide climb up the dew-wet hill to the house.

Energized by plans and her pleasant visit with her landlord, she was anxious to get the house set up to her satisfaction. Not that it wasn't already incredible, because it was, but she was an orderly person who needed her things where she could easily locate them.

Fresh start, she reminded herself. This was her new beginning, and she'd do it on her terms every step of the way.

CHAPTER 2

Just before noon, Marlow got the last of her stuff put away. It had taken her far longer than she'd expected, but now she felt she had a good grasp on what was where, and it all made sense.

Donating the majority of her wardrobe had been a stellar idea. She'd owned far too much to move it all, and what use did she have for formal gowns or business suits? Her instincts, along with what she'd learned online, had been spot on. From what she'd seen of Bramble when she arrived, the townspeople weren't concerned with fashion.

Going forward, her clothes, like her life, would be simpler. Far more basic. She'd kept only a few of her Dior pieces because they were timeless favorites. She doubted anyone would even notice.

Because summer was just starting, she'd need to pick up more shorts, cotton slacks, and maybe a few sundresses. The problem was figuring out where to shop. Then again, she could probably just go online. In the meantime, she had some jeans, a few skirts, sleep shorts, and plenty of tops.

When she turned away from her closet, a wave of dizziness caused a misstep and she banged her hip into the side of the dresser.

She'd forgotten to eat again. Seriously, that was a bad habit she'd adopted during all the strife with Dylan. She'd put it at the top of the list of things she needed to get over.

Thankful that she had some padding in that area, she rubbed the aching spot and started out of the bedroom to grab food—anything would be fine for a quick snack to take the edge off. The ringing of her phone diverted her again. Was Cort delayed? She hurried through the house, unsure where she'd left the phone while sorting through her things, and finally, on the fifth ring, she grabbed it off the dining room table, swiping her thumb over the screen a split second before she realized it was her mother-in-law.

Almost at the same time, a knock sounded on the front door.

Biting back a groan, she put the phone on speaker and managed to sound pleasant when she said, "Hello, Sandra." No way would she let anyone, especially her mother-in-law, know that she was still adjusting to all the change in her life.

Once she answered the phone, she opened the door to allow Cort in.

"*Where are you?*" Dispensing with any polite greeting, Sandra snapped out the question, then didn't wait for a reply. "We went by the house and saw a For Sale sign in the yard. I know it has to be a mistake. Tell me it's a mistake, Marlow!"

Hoping to end the call quickly, she told Sandra, "This is actually a bad time for me. I could call you back in thirty minutes—"

"Dylan loved that house, and you plan to sell it?" she shrieked. "He worked with the architect. He chose the fountain in the yard himself. He put his heart and soul into that house."

"Sandra," she said gently, hearing that the older woman bordered on hysteria. "I'll call back in thirty minutes. I promise." Giving Cort an apologetic smile, she gestured him in.

"You can't be that heartless." And then with another snap, "Where. *Are*. You?"

"I'll explain everything when I—"

"It's a simple enough question!" she shouted.

Never, even on a good day, did Marlow allow her mother-in-law to use that tone with her. Oh, the woman had tried plenty of times over the years, and after Dylan's death, Marlow had given her a little more leeway.

No more. "I've relocated. The house is in my name, and I no longer need it. If it's important to you, you and Aston are welcome to buy it. Now if you want to discuss this further, we can do so—in thirty minutes." She disconnected the call.

Cort didn't ask a single question about the conversation he'd surely overhead, saying only, "Guess I've caught you at a bad time?"

"No, it's fine." She welcomed the interruption. Limping a little, she led the way to the kitchen. "My checkbook is in here."

"Did you hurt yourself?"

"Just clumsiness." Indicating the coffeepot, she asked, "Would you like a cup?"

For several seconds, he hesitated, then shook his head. "I just had lunch but thank you."

"Lunch," she grumbled, then had to laugh. Grabbing her checkbook and pen, she sat at the table and then indicated the opposite chair. "Join me?"

Another hesitation . . . and he sat. "You haven't eaten?"

"It's the most ridiculous thing, but before my life changed, everything was scheduled. At work, we always had business lunches and dinners, and on the weekends, there were arrangements with friends, Dylan's family, or other functions. I never had to think about food." That sounded pathetic, so she laughed to prove she saw the absurdity of it.

Still, he said nothing, and she just knew she was making him uncomfortable.

"I'm sorry. Not your problem."

"It's not that." Sitting back in his seat, he crossed his arms and gave her a long look. "Before my mother passed away, she got so sick that she wouldn't remember to eat, either."

How awful for him. Marlow wanted to ask him about it, about his life and his mother's illness, but she wasn't sure he'd be receptive. "I promise, I'm not sick. Just pampered and distracted by . . . things. But I'm getting over both, and so far, I'm not too disappointed with my progress."

He gave her a genuine smile. "My problem is that I want to grab a frozen dinner from the freezer, nuke it, and set it before you with a fork."

The question tumbled out of her mouth before she could censor it. "Is that what you did with your mother?"

One large, solid shoulder lifted. "It got her to eat, even when she didn't have an appetite."

Picturing this big, quiet man pampering his ailing mother turned Marlow's heart to marshmallow. The image was both endearing and appealing. "How long has your mother been gone?"

"Two years." He made an abrupt topic change. "You don't need to pay for six months."

"I want to be sure that I can stay that long." *At least.*

In fact, at the moment, she had no plans to ever leave. After only a single sunrise, she felt rooted here, as if this was where she'd been meant to land. She wanted to see the seasons change. She wanted to experience the people and the slower pace of life.

She wanted to find herself. Of course, she wouldn't go into any of that with Cort. "I'm a businesswoman through and through, and I like insurance."

"What if I already drew up a contract that gives you a month to month opportunity, ensuring you the option to stay but with no obligation on your end?"

"Wow." He'd surprised her. "You've put some thought into this."

"You told me your plans on the phone, so I thought I should be prepared." Lifting a hip, he withdrew a folded contract from his back pocket. "I have to run into town for a few hours. I can leave that with you to read, then grab it on my way back if you want."

"No need." It was only two pages, and she had plenty of experience with legal documents. "If you can spare two minutes, I'll read it now."

"No problem."

Her phone rang. She glanced at the screen, saw it was Sandra, and ignored the call. Standing with the document in hand, she went to her freezer, took out one of the frozen dinners he'd put there, and glanced at the instructions on the back.

She didn't know he'd followed until he said, "Allow me, while you read."

Assuming he was in a hurry, she murmured, "Thank you," and took her seat again. Everything in the contract was in order. As long as she paid on time, didn't damage the property in any way, didn't disturb the peace, and didn't move in anyone else, she'd have the option to stay. If she did cause damage, she'd lose part or all of her deposit. "Are you certain you only want a deposit and one month's rent?"

"Yes."

"A personal check is okay?"

"Sure."

No one would accuse Cort Easton of being chatty. She was about to make out the check when the scent of food hit her and she forgot what she was doing. "What is that?"

"Fettuccini Alfredo. It's not bad, but definitely not the quality of homemade." He glanced at her from his position by the microwave. "Or anything that you'd get from a nice restaurant. Still, it's edible. I have a few in my freezer, too, for when I don't feel like cooking. I add salt and pepper. You have to eat it while it's hot, though. Once it cools, it's not great."

"My goodness." She flattened a hand to her chest and said, tongue in cheek, "I think that's the most you've said to me since I arrived."

The corner of his mouth lifted. "I talk when I have something to say."

"Whereas I just talk. All the time. Sometimes endlessly." Her phone began buzzing again. One glance confirmed it was Sandra.

"Eat before you answer," he suggested.

"Yes, sir," she teased back. She signed the contract, made out the check, and set both on the counter beside him. "My mother-in-law. She's been needier since my husband died." Feeling she should explain but trying to keep it brief since he wasn't exactly gabby, she said, "We spent nearly a year going through a contentious divorce, but before it was finalized, he died in a car accident."

"Rough."

That single word didn't begin to cover the conglomeration of mixed feelings she'd had, the predominant one anger. "My in-laws relied on me to make arrangements. He was their only child and they both took it hard. I've tried to be there for them, and I guess somewhere along the way, they thought I'd forgotten about . . . other things." What a lame way to summarize infidelity, abusive words, angry outbursts, and ridicule. Not only from Dylan but from Sandra and Aston as well.

"You're here to start over?"

"Yes. I don't need to work to keep up with the rent, but I'd like to find a job, maybe open a small business . . ."

Cort shook his head. "Not here by Rainbow Lake. You'd have to head back to the city for that."

Amused, she asked, "No new businesses?"

"Afraid not. I sort of slid into being a handyman by working from home. They've accepted me, but if I tried to set up a shop, that'd be trouble."

"Understood. My point is that I won't miss paying my rent." She hadn't lied about the pampered part. She was what they called a person of means, and yet her life didn't have real meaning. At least, not the meaning she wanted.

She'd get there, though. Relocating here was the first step. Now she just had to keep up her momentum.

The microwave dinged, and he slid the hot entrée out to a plate, got a fork from the drawer, and put both on the circular placemat on the table. He gave a quick glance at the check and contract before folding both into his pocket. "I'll get going and let you eat."

She walked with him to the door. "After this, I'll find a grocery store and buy real food, but for now, I can't wait to dig in. Thank you again for being so considerate."

"Yes, ma'am. Around here, neighbors help neighbors. Keep that in mind."

Standing in the doorway, she watched him get into his truck, wondering if that last comment was mere friendly conversation or a statement to let her know not to get ideas. Ha! The very last thing she wanted in her life right now was another romantic relationship. No matter how appealing the man might be. It didn't even matter that he appeared to be the total opposite of Dylan.

But a neighbor, a friend . . . ? With a man like Cort Easton, she'd enjoy that quite a bit.

The next morning, when Marlow carried her coffee down the hill, she found an Adirondack chair on the dock. She started smiling and couldn't stop . . . until she glanced around and failed to see Cort. Had he skipped fishing because of her?

If so, why bring her a chair? Or maybe he hadn't. Maybe he'd planned to use the chair himself.

Unsure what to think, she walked out to the dock and soon became engrossed in the sunrise. It wasn't quite as colorful this time, but it was still beautiful. The birth of a new day, full of promise.

Stepping out of her sneakers, she settled into the deep chair, pulling her knees up and loosely draping the throw blanket around her legs and over her lap. Today she'd thought to dress more appropriately because she'd assumed Cort would be there.

The morning was less eventful without him, yet she rejoiced in it anyway. The sunshine on her face, watching birds swoop and hearing frogs awaken—she enjoyed it long after her mug of coffee was gone.

Deliberately, she'd left her phone in the house. After Sandra had talked her ear off yesterday, mostly attempting to bully her or coerce her into returning to her old life, Marlow hadn't wanted to chance another call until she was ready.

She wasn't naturally a confrontational person, but through business and her association with Dylan and his family, she'd learn to stand up for herself. Somewhat.

Tomorrow she'd bring the phone so she could take some photos.

Shopping had been an adventure. She hadn't planned out her own meals for years. Every ten minutes it seemed she found a new way that her marriage had changed her, and now life required a whole new skill set.

She embraced the challenge.

The most interesting part of her trip to town yesterday had been stopping back at the Dry Frog Tavern on her return. It had gotten late, and rather than cook dinner, she'd decided on more pizza.

Everyone had been interested in her, freely questioning her on her whereabouts, how long she planned to stay, and what she thought of the town so far. What she'd noticed most was the lack of artifice. There were no cultured manners, no snooty looks, but yes, plenty of judgment.

Outsiders, she'd heard more than once, always caused suspicion. The experience had been so unique, she'd stayed quite a bit longer than on her previous stop at the bar.

In fact, as her second full day in Bramble rolled on and evening approached, she decided on the same dinner plans, except this time she'd try a burger.

As she strolled into the tavern at exactly six o'clock, the first thing Marlow saw was a Help Wanted sign. Possibilities raced through her mind. Outrageous possibilities. She hadn't done that type of job since . . . well, high school, and it hadn't been in a bar but an ice-cream shop. The sign didn't specify the job, so she had no idea if it'd be janitorial work, waiting tables, dishwashing, or cooking. She stood there, staring at the sign until she heard a laugh.

That's when she saw the second thing—Cort at a table with three older people, two women and one man. Pen in hand, he wrote in a notepad while the three people all seemed to talk to him at once. One of the women laughed again, putting a smile on Cort's face even as he shook his head. He started to say something to the woman but suddenly paused and quickly turned until their gazes clashed.

Busted. Heat crawled up her neck and into her face, but she tried to play it off with a friendly wave and an immediate pivot to the bar. Sliding onto a stool, she prayed that Herman would notice her quickly, just to give her something to do.

No such luck. The owner was busy chatting with a customer and never glanced her way. Her gaze skipped around—avoiding Cort and his friends—until she found a dartboard toward the back of the room. She pretended an interest in it, when in truth, she knew nothing at all about throwing darts.

Even before Cort reached her, she knew he was walking over. The air around her changed, as did her heartbeat.

When he took the stool beside her, she tried, and likely failed, to look surprised. "Cort, hi. I hope I didn't interrupt you."

"Grabbing dinner again?"

That he acted so casual helped her to do the same. "Afraid so. I shopped the other day but forgot a few things so I ran back into town again. I won't be able to stay long because some of my groceries need to go in the freezer, but I've enjoyed the pizza here so much, I thought I might try a burger on the go this time."

"The burgers are good. Fries, too."

Peeking back at the table he'd left, she met the gazes of all three elders watching her with keen interest. With an exaggerated wince, she apologized. "Sorry if I was rude. I find everything about the tavern interests me, including the people here."

Leaning forward, he called down the bar to Herman. "You have a customer."

Herman hurried their way, and once he reached them, muttered, "Thanks, Cort. I couldn't get away. You know how Leo is. Doesn't even take a breath." He smiled at Marlow. "Back for more, huh?"

"I couldn't resist."

He puffed up with pride, then said to Cort, "She was here last night, too. Had everyone entertained. Girl knows how to tell a joke."

Cort's brows lifted.

And of course, that made her face heat again. "I was just getting to know the other customers, not really entertaining them."

Herman snorted. "She did a great impersonation of you."

Oh God. Fire burned in her face. Even her ears felt hot. "I didn't, that is . . ."

"Show him," Herman urged.

Someone ought to muzzle the man! "Oh, um . . . I have groceries in the car."

"Again?"

"Forgot a few things yesterday." She could handle CEOs, so surely she could handle one tavern owner. "I'd like a loaded burger, please. And Cort recommended the fries."

Laughing, Herman clapped Cort on the shoulder. "I'll get it going right now. Probably'll take twenty minutes or so."

As he walked off, Cort asked, "Will your food keep that long?"

She had no idea. She'd never left groceries in a car while she visited a bar and chatted with her landlord. New experiences were fun. "The few cold things are packed together, and it's not that hot outside."

"Should be fine." He left his stool. "Come on. I'll introduce you to a few other people."

Glad of the reprieve, she quickly gathered her purse. "You don't mind?"

"No."

Deciding to clear the air, she said, "That."

He paused to stare down at her. "That, what?"

"That's how I impersonated you. With one-word answers and teeny tiny smiles that only lasted a heartbeat. I swear it wasn't anything mean."

Light brown eyes seemed to warm before he said, "Sounds accurate." With that easy comment, he moved forward again.

Marlow couldn't tell if he was offended or not, and as he wouldn't say, she just let it go. At the table he'd left, he said, "Wade, Gloria, Bobbi, this is my new tenant at the guest cottage. Marlow, meet three originals, all siblings."

Glad that he hadn't given her last name, Marlow held out a hand. It might not be an issue here, but many people had heard of the wealthy Heddings family, and Dylan's sudden death had caused a stir in certain circles. She'd had enough of snoopy reporters and gossips to last her a lifetime. "Nice to meet you."

Wade immediately stood and offered his seat. "Here, you can sit with the girls, and I'll finish explaining to Cort what I want."

"No fair," Bobbi immediately protested. "You just want to dictate everything."

"And you don't?" Gloria asked. "This isn't a dictatorship, and Wade, sit down! Just because you're a guy doesn't mean you get the say-so."

"Don't I know it," he snapped right back. "You two always gang up on me."

They all ignored her hand, so Marlow withdrew it. She didn't feel slighted but rather as if she'd been dropped into a heated debate. "What are we deciding?"

Bobbi said, "The add-on to our house. Of course, it should be a great room for entertaining, but Wade thinks he needs a workshop." She snorted.

"I do need a workshop!"

"Then we wouldn't need to hire Cort, would we?" Gloria asked.

That quieted them all, which gave Marlow the chance to say, "I hope you're able to work it out. I'll leave you to your discussion so you can get to it." Not that they had let her interrupt anyway. She turned to go, but Cort was there, blocking her.

"Sometimes," he said loudly enough for his friends to hear, "they forget their manners."

"Wade always forgets," Gloria said. "But what can you expect of a man?"

Patiently, Cort pointed out, "I'm a man."

"Oh, don't we know it." Bobbi elbowed her sister and got Gloria's complete agreement.

Marlow turned back to them. "It must be wonderful to have siblings. I was an only child, and I never had anyone to argue with."

They all looked at each other, then cracked up.

Wade reached out, offering his hand. "You can have my sisters. You'll be singing a different tune in no time."

No sooner did she finish that handshake than Gloria was there, snatching Marlow's hand into both of hers. "Bobbi has her moments, but now Wade? Be thankful you didn't have a bossy brother."

"Or an older sister," Bobbi added, drawing Marlow into a hug.

"Better," Cort said, making them all smile.

Overwhelmed and equally entertained, Marlow smiled, too. "I think I'll check on my food now and then head home. Truly, it was wonderful to meet you."

With a touch to her arm, Cort kept her there while he spoke to the siblings. "I think I have a solution for your space. It would be a way to please all three of you. Tonight, I'll get my notes organized to make sure my idea works. Tomorrow, if possible, I'll get back to you with rough plans and a broad estimate, at least until we're able to finalize some things. Does that work?"

They all nodded.

On the way back to the bar, he glanced at Marlow. "For the record, that was far more than one word."

"Oh my, it was!"

When he gave her a big grin, she not only laughed, she also noticed that he had a dimple. Until that moment, she hadn't seen it, and now that she did, she also noticed how incredibly handsome he was in a quiet but very rugged way.

Not that any of it mattered to her.

Herman was back at the bar, so to distract herself from her gorgeous landlord, she asked about the job.

Both Herman and Cort stared at her.

"What?" They truly appeared bemused. "Is it for originals only?"

"Not exactly." Herman rubbed the back of his neck. "The thing is, you seem like a classy lady and your kind never work here."

Instead of taking insult, she said, "Thank you, Herman. I assure you, though, my kind also work."

"At a bar?" Cort asked.

She waved his question off. "This is more like a diner."

"Not on weekends."

Leaning over the bar top, Herman confided, "The weekenders are sometimes loud and a little rowdy."

That didn't scare Marlow. She'd dealt with cutthroat executives who would cheat their own mothers if they could. She'd have no problem handling a rambunctious weekend crowd. "What is the job? Waiting tables? For how many hours?"

The men shared another look, prompting her to say, "Gentlemen, your sexism is showing."

"Guilty," Cort said. "Plus, I'm not sure you realize what it's like to wait tables."

"Oh? And you know?" She crossed her arms. "Have *you* waited tables?"

"Yes, I have."

Hmm. She tried to envision that, but somehow Cort looked more like the guy who would not only own the restaurant but also the town it was in. Not like a slick wealthy guy; he wasn't what she'd call debonair. No, with his size and quiet air of authority, Cort was more like the man who gave orders and expected them to be followed. "I see. So tell me. What's so difficult about it?"

"Eight hours on your feet, heavy trays, irascible customers, whiny demands, drunks, guys who get grabby—"

"Here now," Herman protested. "I don't let anything like that go on."

"You," Cort countered, "can't be everywhere at once. Plus, that's why Cindy quit, right?"

"She was going back to school or something anyway."

Marlow's gaze ping-ponged back and forth between them. "Do you have the specifics? Pay, exact hours, that sort of thing?"

Resigned, Herman dug around behind the counter and produced a wrinkled sheet of paper. He slapped it down on the bar top, almost like a challenge.

Putting the paper in her purse without looking at it, Marlow asked, "My burger?"

Herman scowled, then left to check on the food.

Cort said nothing. Maybe she'd be crowding him by taking a job here, at a place where he obviously met with customers, but he'd get it over it.

The ringing of her phone seemed to change everything. Cort glanced at her purse, then at her face, before saying, "Enjoy your burger."

"I'm sure I will. Thank you for the recommendation."

With the briefest of nods, he headed back to the siblings. That's when Marlow realized every single person in the bar was watching her, or rather they'd been watching *them*, she and Cort together. Now that he'd walked off, their eyes mostly followed him but also kept checking back on her, maybe waiting for a reaction.

Smiling while resisting the urge to look at the paper in her purse, she pulled out her phone, already guessing who it would be.

Sandra again.

She may as well take it, otherwise her mother-in-law would

just keep calling back. Once she got her food, Marlow wanted a quiet evening to herself, not another debate with her mother-in-law.

Stepping toward the door and turning her back to the room gave her a modicum of privacy. She swiped the screen and put the phone to her ear. "Sandra, hello."

"I can't believe you're doing this. Disappearing without a word. It's unconscionable."

No, it was a necessity, not that she'd try to explain—again. Used to her mother-in-law's abrasive way, Marlow asked evenly, "Was there something you wanted?"

A moment of silence conveyed Sandra's frustration. "Tell me where you are. I have a few things I want to send you."

Though Sandra couldn't see her, Marlow shook her head. "I took everything I wanted with me." Including some memories, some feelings, that she *didn't* want. "Everything else, I left behind on purpose."

"There are papers from Dylan . . ." Sandra went quiet a moment before starting again, more crisply this time. "They were locked in his desk. I need to mail them to you."

Suspicion accelerated her heartbeat. "What are they?"

"Given your attitude, I think it'd be better if I just sent them."

Giving up, mostly because she wanted to get off the phone, Marlow recited her new address.

"Bramble? I've never heard of it."

"It's a small, quiet town in southernmost Kentucky." Well away from Illinois and everyone she knew. "I'm renting a guest cottage, but if I can find a way to make it happen, I plan to stay here." *Forever.*

"Dear God. A *guest cottage*?" She made it sound as if Marlow lived in a hovel. "You didn't buy your own home?"

"No, but I'm *not* returning." Marlow filled the words with firm conviction. "If it doesn't work out here, I'll find another place. Either way, I have no plans to return to my prior job or location." That was the nicest way she could phrase it.

"Many of Dylan's friends have asked about you."

Sure they had, the gossipmongers. His friends had not necessarily been her friends, but she knew them well all the same. They lived to uncover dirt on each other. For them, every scrap of knowledge was power to use for leverage or advancement, and if neither of those could be achieved, there was always the pleasure of ridicule. Once she'd filed for divorce, they'd come sniffing around, hoping to get the inside scoop. As if she'd willingly share that her husband found her lacking? Fortunately, she had the gift of gab and a formidable backbone when necessary. She'd shut down the first few people so thoroughly that others had decided just to talk about her behind her back, instead of approaching her.

That had been the least of her worries—she hadn't felt like socializing anyway. "Tell them I'm fine, not to concern themselves."

A note of excitement rang in Sandra's tone. "I'll let them know we've spoken. All will be forgiven, you'll see."

Incredulous at that attitude, Marlow half laughed, but without humor. Leave it to Sandra to think she needed forgiveness when it was her husband who'd been unfaithful. "I have to go." There, she'd said that reasonably enough, even though she'd forced the words through gritted teeth. "Take care of yourself, Sandra." Her mother-in-law was replying as she ended the call and dropped the phone into her purse.

Hoping her food was done because she was more than ready to seek real privacy, Marlow turned—and nearly ran into Cort's chest as he was about to step around her.

"Good God," she said, irritation and embarrassment crowding in. "How long were you looming behind me?"

Light brown eyes, rimmed with circles of darker brown, stared down at her with no visible reaction. "Just on my way out." Saying nothing else, he went through the door and headed for his truck.

Well, damn. She'd snapped at him for no reason. She was about to go after him when Herman stepped up with her meal.

"Here you go," he said with a broad smile. "I did a rush order for you."

A rush order? She'd hate to be hungry on a busy night. "Thank you." She read the receipt stapled to the bag, dug hurriedly in her purse, and handed a few bills to him. "Keep the change."

"Nice, thanks." As she rushed from the tavern, he called out, "I stuck salt and pepper, and some ketchup and mayonnaise packets in there, too."

"You're amazing, Herman." She gave an airy wave . . . and watched, disheartened, as Cort drove away. The day had not ended well.

Tomorrow, she'd do better.

On his short drive home, Cort's thoughts centered on Marlow and the frustration he'd seen on her face after she'd disconnected the call and turned, almost plowing into him. Clearly, she thought he'd eavesdropped when he hadn't.

Didn't need to.

Her body language alone made it clear that dealing with her caller had both annoyed and upset her. A few times her voice had gotten clipped, but most of the words weren't distinct enough to hear. Good thing, because he was pretty sure everyone in the tavern had been trying to listen in. It was always that way with newcomers, but especially with someone like Marlow.

Bramble didn't see women like her very often. An understated woman who attracted attention more for her poise than perfect looks. Not that Marlow Heddings was unattractive. Far from it.

She wasn't tall and statuesque, not delicate and petite, either. She was somehow more than that. More substantial, more real.

More woman.

Not just physically but in her strength of character and her convictions.

Her desires, too? He found himself wondering about that.

From what he knew of her so far, he'd bet yes.

She was in her mid-thirties, refined in a way that couldn't be faked, yet not condescending. Confident in every situation, even when the siblings had been rude to her with their bickering.

He enjoyed the way her soft brown eyes took in everything with interest.

She accepted her shortcomings with humor and faced new challenges with grit.

Her idea of casual style was still high class, but he doubted she could be any other way. Even barefoot and in secondhand clothes, she'd own any room she entered.

Would she take a job at the tavern? Of course she would, if for no other reason than to prove she could do it. He also got the feeling that, despite a self-confessed life of luxury, Marlow was not a woman who enjoyed too much idle time. That was something they had in common.

He had to remind himself that she was recently widowed, and not just in normal circumstances but with a lot of anger and hurt riding along with the grief. She was strong, but he knew well that even the strongest warrior had a breaking point.

Thankfully, Marlow seemed resilient, rebounding with iron resolve and a lot of good nature. She still needed time. Time to regroup, to recover. To grieve.

And in the meantime, he'd continue to get to know her better. Not a hardship at all.

She was a breath of fresh air, a woman full of wit, resolve, and charm.

After labeling her with all those complimentary traits, he realized he was smiling and didn't care. The town could use a breath of fresh air—and honestly, so could he.

CHAPTER 3

Over the next ten days, Marlow fell into an agreeable routine that, for the most part, kept her busy—or at least, busy enough. Her favorite part of each day was coffee on the dock watching the sun lighten the sky in varying hues. Some mornings were more pink, some deep purple, others transitioning quickly from dark starry skies to bright blazing sunshine.

It was especially nice on the days when Cort was there fishing.

On the day after she'd been rude to him, she'd found him on the shoreline when she came down. Not one to shirk responsibility, she'd walked directly over to him and said, "I apologize for snapping at you last night. I don't have a good excuse except that my mother-in-law is enough to frazzle anyone."

To which he'd replied, "No problem, I get it."

And indeed, it seemed he did, because he didn't hold a grudge.

Each time she saw him after that, he was the same friendly landlord, still laconic in his replies, but she understood that was just his way.

A week later, he surprised her by cutting her lawn. One minute she'd been online, searching for any available properties near Bramble, and then she'd heard the rumble of the mower. Her thoughts had immediately veered away from her future to land squarely in the here and now.

When she'd stepped outside, she'd found Cort on a big riding mower.

Shirtless.

That had arrested her attention for several seconds because, seriously, he looked *fine*. Muscular and firm and strong.

Intent on steering around the trees, he didn't notice her, but she couldn't take her eyes off him. His skin glistened with sweat beneath the sun. On his upper arm, she noticed a tattoo but couldn't make out what it was.

Perhaps she stared at him too long and hard, because he suddenly glanced her way, frowned, then stopped the mower and committed the awful crime of pulling on his shirt.

A moment later, he was striding toward her, and she couldn't very well duck away or pretend she hadn't been staring.

"Hope you don't mind the noise. I forgot to tell you I'd be mowing."

Thankful for the utterly mundane comment, she replied, "I hadn't thought much about the grass, but it has gotten longer, I guess." She'd noticed it tickling her ankles when she went down to the dock just that morning.

"It's not your job, so you don't need to think about it."

"That's a relief, actually, because I know absolutely nothing about landscaping—or even simple lawn work. That's the sort of thing we've always hired out." Saying *we* felt wrong, since she wanted no further association with Dylan, so she amended it with, "That is, I've always had landscapers who handled all the outside stuff."

"I get it." He looked up at the sky. "Looks like rain might be moving in, so I'd better finish up."

With that shirtless visual of him still crowding her thoughts, she nodded. "Thanks."

Unfortunately, after that, he left the shirt on.

Less than two hours later, a deluge rolled over, churning the surface of the lake into angry waves and keeping her entertained for a good long while.

Who knew a rainy day could be so impressive?

In her old life, she'd have grumbled as she fought with an umbrella to get from a car to a meeting or business lunch, and then back again. She wouldn't have noticed the turbulence in the skies, the wild wind, or how rainwater washed over every surface.

Now, here she sat on the covered porch, a throw over her legs, watching the graceful sway of the treetops and how the occasional leaf danced across the ground. The sounds were hypnotic, and all combined, it was better than a massage at what had once been her favorite salon.

Every day, it seemed she found something new to enjoy. And each day, she grew a little antsier for a real purpose.

At least three nights a week, she ate at the tavern, accustoming herself to the menu and observing the work patterns. On the ninth day she officially filled out an application, disconcerting Herman. The position hadn't yet been taken, and she had more free time than she wanted.

On the tenth day, she again drove out of Bramble to look at small-scale commercial buildings to use for a new business. So far, nothing was quite what she wanted. They were either too large or too rundown or too ordinary. She wanted something chic, a building she could enhance to make it one of a kind.

That was her strength, and if she could find the right place, a charming little spot that kept her close enough to Bramble so the drive wouldn't be a great chore, she'd jump on it.

She returned to the house and unloaded her few packages. Brighter shirts, a couple of hats to shield her face from the sun, pairs of Capri pants in soft fabrics, and new sandals. During an online shopping spree, she'd ordered three sundresses and three shirts, and then a bathing suit, too. Those hadn't yet arrived, but now that it was early June, temperatures were on the rise.

She'd just finished putting things away and was about to consider dinner when Herman called and grumpily asked, "You still want the job?"

Going stock still, almost afraid to move, Marlow considered the question and what it entailed. A job. At the tavern. She bobbed her head, convincing herself first, then burst out an enthusiastic, "Yes!"

"Then it's yours," he conceded.

To be sure she hadn't misunderstood, she asked, "I'm hired?"

With ill temper, he said, "No one else even applied, and we're short-staffed."

The job offer surprised and pleased her so much she wanted to dance. "When do I start?"

"Stop in sometime today or tomorrow." He didn't sound at all pleased. "I can give you some of the T-shirts you need to wear."

Oh goody, a Dry Frog Tavern T-shirt! Every time she was in the place, she admired the smart black shirts with bold white font and what looked like a thirsty frog. "I can come by this evening, if that works for you."

"That's fine. We'll go over everything, any limits you might have—"

"I do *not* have limits." The very idea insulted her.

"Oh yeah, smarty? So you can work anytime, any day, any hours?"

Hmm. Herman had a point. "I prefer to see the sunrise from my dock." Sometimes the sunset, too, but she could handle missing it since mosquitoes often came out in the evening.

Snorting, Herman said, "We don't open till noon anyway. Close at eleven during the week, and at one on Saturday. We take the Lord's Day off."

That made it official. She *loved* this town. "I'll be there, and Herman, thank you. You won't regret it, I promise."

With a sullen "We'll see," he disconnected the call.

Now she danced, all around the kitchen, through the sitting room, dining room, and into the foyer. She wanted to share with someone, to tell a friend that she, Marlow Heddings, formerly of Heddings' Holding Company had gotten a fun, somewhat funky job in the best small town ever. But she had no one.

That brought her to a halt.

For the first time, it struck her that she was alone. Utterly, completely alone.

Yes, she'd chosen solitude for herself, because really, Dylan's parents, his friends and associates, were never hers anyway. Her job, one she'd excelled at, was closely tied to his family. If she'd stayed, she never would have been free of Dylan, never mind that he'd passed away.

Still, the fact of her solitary existence suddenly settled on her like a dark, oppressive blanket, stealing some of her happiness.

She would not feel sorry for herself. Anything but that.

To escape her own realizations, she made the decision to grab her keys and go somewhere, anywhere. She was back at the door in thirty seconds, ready to walk out for God knew where . . . when Cort pulled into her driveway.

Her heart lifted—but *no*. She would not rejoice at the sight of a man, *any* man. Never again would she sink that low. And yet, her heart beat a little faster. Not with personal interest, she assured herself, but at the presence of another soul, a person to *see* her, someone to *hear* her.

She knew Dylan had stopped seeing and hearing her long before she'd discovered his deceit.

Composing herself, she stepped out, locked the door behind her, and met her landlord on the walkway. "Cort, hi. What's up?"

His dark brows rose as he noted the keys in her hand. "You're on your way out?"

"Just a little spur of the moment celebration." *Ha, what a lie.* Leaning closer, she shared, "Herman hired me."

One of those beautiful, dimpled smiles of his appeared. "And that makes you happy, I take it?"

He was so striking when he smiled, it was a good thing he didn't do it more often. Her heart couldn't take it. "I've been a slug, so yes. I'm ready to be busy."

"I won't hold you up. Mail is delivered to the post office, and this came for you. It was given to me because I own the property."

She finally noticed the thick packet in his hands. Since Sandra hadn't mentioned Dylan's papers again in her last few calls, Marlow had forgotten all about them.

When she hesitated to take the packet, Cort let his hand drop back to his side. "Where do you plan to celebrate?"

Biting her lip and feeling a little like a coward, Marlow looked up at him. He was so tall, and yet with him she didn't feel small. It had to be something about Cort, his ease and openness with others. "No idea. I guess . . . back to the tavern?"

He shook his head. "Now what kind of celebration would that be?"

"I don't know. I thought I'd get a drink, maybe something to eat."

"You know, we have an actual restaurant here."

"Here?"

"In Bramble. On the lake actually, and the fireflies are out."

"Fireflies?" That sounded dreadful, similar to the pesky mosquitoes. "As in bugs?"

He grinned again. "Have you ever seen them?"

"Maybe, when I was young?" Those memories were so vague that she sometimes felt seventy instead of thirty-five.

"You realize the lake is as nice at night as it is during the day, right?"

Honestly, she hadn't thought about it. Making a sudden decision, she asked, "Where is this restaurant? I want to check it out." And she wanted to see the fireflies, to see if they were as "nice" as Cort claimed.

"I could show you, if you wouldn't mind a little friendly company—or is it to be a private celebration?"

Did he know? Had he somehow looked at her face and seen that she was as lonely as a person could be? Playing it cool, she said, "I don't mind company, if you don't have anything else you need to be doing."

"I'm done for the night. Come on, you can ride with me."

Ride with him, in his big muscle truck? The idea gave her a thrill. She couldn't recall ever riding in a truck. "I also have to stop at the tavern later." With a good dose of glee, she boasted, "I'm picking up some uniform T-shirts."

This time, Cort actually laughed as he opened the passenger door for her to get in. "We can go by there, no problem."

The shiny black truck was pretty high off the ground, but she saw a step. Now how to . . . ?

"Foot there," Cort said. "Grip right here and pull yourself up. If you need help, I can hoist you."

Good God, he made her sound like a load of cargo, and in fact, maybe she was. "I'll manage, thank you." She had to hop twice before she got her backside into the seat, but it felt like another accomplishment, and she couldn't stop grinning. Trucks were nice, she decided. From the seat she had a better view, being higher up.

As Cort circled the hood, she tracked his every step with admiration. He had strong legs and a long stride that ate up the ground without his seeming to hurry. He, of course, didn't have to hop to get in. No, he just settled his large frame behind the wheel, and then placed the packet in a space behind the console.

Glad that he didn't expect her to look at the papers yet, she said, "This will sound absurdly uninformed, but I had no idea trucks could be so luxurious." Under her hand, the seat material felt like fine leather. "I thought all trucks were work vehicles."

"Mine is, but I keep it clean."

It went beyond clean to pristine. The two-tone interior loaded with gadgets gave her a visceral thrill. "I feel like I'm riding a wild bull."

His brows shot up. Then he rumbled a deep laugh that soon had her smiling, too.

"What?" she asked, enjoying the humorous exchange.

"The things you sometimes say."

"And the things I admit." She sighed with extra drama for fun. "I know it's silly, but it does feel that way to me. Being here, in Bramble, I've learned to appreciate things I never noticed before."

"Like the sunrise."

Oh, how she loved the sunrise. "And watching a storm." When he didn't laugh at that, only agreed with a small nod, she continued. "There's so much turbulence, but in an exciting way that's somehow also soothing." All that drama helped her to forget, taking her away from her troubles and hurt feelings and immersing her in the moment.

"I enjoy the storms, too," he said. "The way the waves jump around the dock and hit the shoreline. Sometimes I fish in the rain, but not when there's lightning."

Interesting. "Maybe I'll get a big rain poncho and watch from the dock the next time it rains."

His brows pinched together. "Just know that the dock can be slippery, and the lake has a wicked current. If you're not used to it . . ." His words trailed off.

"What?"

"Next time it rains, as long as it's not storming, we could sit on the dock together."

That sounded incredibly appealing. She, Marlow Heddings, liked the idea of sitting on a wooden dock in the rain. Astonishing.

"For safety reasons," he made clear.

Hoping it'd rain again soon, she nodded. "Sure. I'll order a poncho, so I'll be ready."

"What do you think of the tavern?"

Marlow didn't have to think about it. "There's a cozy vibe, like everyone is a friend."

"And no one is a stranger."

Not anymore, though they'd all given her the side-eye during her first few visits. "Know what else? I've learned that coffee tastes better outside, that the air here smells better than in the city, and that, at least for now, less is more."

With one wrist draped over the steering wheel, Cort sat half facing her, showing no real hurry to get going. "I've got one for you."

"My breath is bated."

Another grin, tempered this time, and he said, "Being alone and lonely are different."

She inhaled sharply, devastated that he'd read her so easily. "Am I that transparent?"

His expression softened, then he buckled his seatbelt and started the engine. "Actually, I was talking about me."

That one small confession, something he'd never admitted to another living soul, seemed to have an incredible effect on Marlow.

She lowered her guard.

This incredible woman who always appeared ready to deflect now showed her vulnerability. Not completely, because he knew she was hiding a lot of hurt, but she relaxed and let him in. He felt it in the air, saw it in the way she held herself, and heard it in the easy way she breathed.

It felt like a gift, the best gift he'd ever received.

He understood complicated emotions because he lived with guilt. It was as much a part of him as his need for privacy, his defensive edge, and his ability to handle any situation.

"What did you do today?" he asked her, just to give her a topic to focus on.

Like a lifeline, she grabbed it, chatting about her hunt for commercial property, as well as the continued calls from her mother-in-law.

"I've never dealt with a mother-in-law, so I can't offer any insights."

Sunlight caught in her golden-brown hair as she tipped her head to study him. "So never married?"

As if it would explain everything, he said, "I served in the Marines until my mother took ill. I'd be there still if she hadn't needed me home more often."

"Do you still have your father?"

It was the last direction he'd thought she'd take the conversation. Knowing he had to tread carefully so he didn't encourage her curiosity or risk her shying away again, he chose the vaguest explanation he could. "He was . . . gone by the time I was twelve." Not a lie, but certainly not the whole truth.

The seconds ticked by in silence before she spoke again. "I lost both my parents, too."

"Recently?"

She shook her head. "My father passed away when I was nineteen, my mother when I was twenty-two. They'd both been healthy one minute, then gone the next, Dad with a heart attack, my mother with a stroke." Brows tweaking together, she clarified. "Mom actually lived for a week, but it felt like a blink in time because she wasn't really there. The day before her stroke, she and I were working on my wedding plans, looking at gowns, talking about florists, things like that."

The urge to take her hand was strong, but Cort resisted. She might misconstrue the gesture, think he was coming on to her when he could tell she needed no-pressure friendship more than anything else right now. "You married young."

"No, the wedding was put off, and then put off again." Her mouth twisted to the side in a show of regret. "Not by me but by Dylan—my husband." Those words seemed to trickle into the next. "My deceased husband. I mean, that's why I'm here." She dropped back in the seat. "I'm botching this horribly."

"It's all right. You don't have to talk about anything unless you want to."

"I don't, not really, only because like much of life, it's absurd."

"Gotta tell you, Ms. Heddings, I don't think anything about you is absurd."

"Ms. Heddings." Her lips curled in a smile. "I know it's my name, but I'm trying to forget it."

"Trying to forget never works—trust me on that." Some things just stuck with you, no matter what. "Look at it this way, you own the name. And honestly, it suits you, same as Marlow does. It's a nice name."

Her smile bloomed into a grin. "I've always liked it. Cort is a nice name, too. Different."

"So the married name has been a hassle, I take it?"

"Ugh, afraid so. I already told you that the divorce was ugly, and then Dylan died in a car wreck. I wanted out, I thought I was out—mostly anyway—and then suddenly there were police at my door to bring me the awful news, and my in-laws to deal with, and a funeral to plan."

That was a lot for anyone, and yet look at her, sitting there with a smile, pleased to be in a truck, and willing to check out fireflies. "I bet you handled it all better than anyone else could have."

"I did my best, but I won't lie and say it was easy."

He hoped she'd never feel the need to lie to him. "Being here, in Bramble"—*with me*—"is your way of starting over?"

"Yes. The marriage ended months ago and hadn't been great before that. I have to take some blame for letting things get so far out of hand. I loved my job, and it seemed easier to concentrate on that, to pour myself into business meetings and lunches and projects instead of thinking about how distant he and I had grown."

"Path of least resistance," he said, totally getting her. "You have a comfortable place in life, and you hate to blow it up."

Those big, soft eyes of hers studied him. "Great summary, actually. Back then, the thought of starting over just left me breathless. Then I found out there was another woman, and when I confronted him on it, he wasn't apologetic. He was just hateful."

What a fool her husband had been. Weak and unscrupulous, too. Lack of honor was a pretty unforgivable sin to Cort. "I was already impressed, but now? A lot of people would sit down and suffer their misery for a year."

She made a choking sound, something between a laugh and a huff. "I was miserable until I decided on the divorce. Then I was just determined to get out without losing more of myself."

He understood that, too. It was so easy to let others define you. His mother had done that for far too long. "Then the guy died, and you were stuck."

Putting her head back, she closed her eyes. "There was so much to do, both personally and professionally, and my in-laws were understandably falling apart. Dylan was an only child, and to them he was pure perfection."

"Ouch. That had to suck."

"The eulogy with all his family and friends listening was the worst." Her mouth hitched to the side in a crooked grin. "I swear, I never wished him dead, but when it rained the day of the funeral, it felt so fitting."

To hell with it. He reached over and patted her knee, making sure to keep the contact brief.

Touching her was an eye opener. The gesture was offered in

solace, but damn, to him it didn't feel that way. To him, it brought a shock of awareness.

Returning both hands to the wheel, he pulled into The Docker, a restaurant literally on the side of the lake, positioned at the broadest part. Deck seating put customers right over the water. Many arrived by boat, parking at several docks along the shoreline.

Sitting forward, she surveyed the restaurant. "Enough of all that, though. I'm here to celebrate."

"New job and all."

Her laugh was light and sweet. "Another new experience. And you watch, I'll excel at this job, too."

As Cort parked a good distance down the lot at the only empty spot he could find, he said, "With you, Marlow, I don't have a doubt."

Marlow hadn't realized how much she'd missed real food until the waitress set a plate of appetizers before her that included crab cakes, chicken wings, and steak bites. She wanted to devour it all, but she remembered her manners and ate delicately—at least until Cort laughed at her.

He had the nerve to nudge the second crab cake her way, saying, "Go ahead. You know you want it."

And oh, she most definitely did. They were seated outside with the sounds of the lake lapping at the shoreline and the muted hum of conversation around them. The air had cooled, and she felt pleasantly relaxed.

In between sips of her white wine and comfortable conversation with Cort, she ate every last bite of the appetizers. She thought she was full until the server brought out her entrée. The wine paired perfectly with the citrusy, buttery marinade on the pork, and somehow she emptied a second glass.

All the while, it seemed Cort smiled at her.

"Have you been out on the lake?" he asked.

"No." She hadn't even thought of it! There was a big body of water she could be exploring. "I need to get a boat, don't I?"

Watching him fight a grin made her realize how outlandish it was to blurt out the fact that she could simply buy a boat.

Wrinkling her nose, she confessed, "I have a sizable savings account, and once the house sells . . ." She shrugged. "Plus, there are assets from Dylan . . ." No, she wouldn't talk about him anymore. "Did I tell you that my mother was a college professor? My father a surgeon? I inherited from them as well, and even when I married, I was careful to keep my finances separate." Damn it, that led right back to Dylan.

Searching for a topic change, she said, "I noticed the tattoo on your, er, biceps." Her gaze dipped to his upper arm, now covered by the short sleeve of his T-shirt, and still impressively . . . bulging. Shooting her gaze back to his face didn't help her composure. In a purely observational way, she noted that he was ruggedly handsome. Sinfully so. Cort reminded her of the lake on that stormy day. Remarkable, possibly dangerous, and mesmerizing because of it. He was a mix of strength and comfort.

Not that she cared. Of course not. Not interested.

She needed another sip of wine.

With his gaze teasing, as if he had a secret, he prompted, "You were saying?"

"Your tattoo." *I want to touch it.* Nope, she couldn't say that. "When you were cutting my grass, you had your shirt off. I couldn't see the details of the tattoo, so now I'm curious."

Casual as you please, he reached for the sleeve on that arm and lifted it. "Marine emblem. Eagle, globe, and anchor."

Leaning forward over her mostly empty plate, Marlow studied the image. "It's nice and manly."

With a shake of his head, he lowered his sleeve. "Not the purpose, but okay."

"How long have you had it?"

"Long time." Sitting back in his seat, one forearm on the table, he asked, "How about you? Any tats?"

That struck her as hilarious.

"Should I take your laugh as a no?"

"My mother would have perished if I'd done anything like that, and Dylan . . ." She groaned. "Bah, I don't want to talk about him."

"Then don't."

"But everything keeps leading to him." She rubbed her forehead, then crossed her arms on the table. "I never had any great desire to get a tattoo, but I would never have considered it if I had. Dylan liked things a certain way, and I never minded, so things like tattoos never came up. Manicures and pedicures, yes. Regular visits to the salon so I stayed polished from head to toe, absolutely. A refreshed wardrobe every season because God forbid I should wear the same thing too many times. You see, everyone remembers everything and there would be gossip."

"Not around here."

"Which is why I'm having so much fun."

Their server returned, and as he lit a candle on their table, he asked, "Did you leave room for dessert?"

The fact that everything struck her as funny told her she'd definitely had enough wine. "Decaf coffee?"

Cort spoke up. "You should try the cheesecake with fresh berries."

As soon as he said it, she immediately wanted it. "I will if you do."

"Bring us two," he told the server. "Same with the coffee."

The dessert turned out to be even better than she'd expected, but maybe that was the atmosphere and the company after so many days spent mostly by herself or chatting with total strangers. She knew Cort now, respected and liked him, and she felt she could call him a friend. A new friend, sure, a hot, sexy friend, but still, he was easy to talk to, even though he didn't say much. Best of all, he didn't seem to have any expectations of her.

Switching from wine to coffee had been a good call. She didn't want to get too tipsy when she still needed to go by the tavern.

As they rose to leave the restaurant, she realized that the sky had darkened all around them. Candles glowed from all the tables. Everywhere she looked, she saw the twinkling of fireflies.

In that moment, after eating scrumptious food and sharing her news with Cort, the fireflies were positively magical.

A perfect accompaniment to a wonderful day. She didn't want it to end, but she knew she couldn't monopolize Cort much longer.

As he led her to his truck, she said, "If I'd driven, you wouldn't have to go by the tavern with me."

"I don't mind."

She believed him. He struck her as a man who spoke his mind without a lot of nonsense tossed in. When a firefly got close, he carefully closed his hands around it, then opened them, palms up, in front of her. The little bug glowed, wings extended.

Inspecting it, Marlow noted the reddish head, the black body, and that soft light. "For an insect, it's really pretty."

"Most things are, if you look closely."

So very true. Until here, now, she'd never have considered getting up close and personal with a bug. Unable to resist, she lightly touched it. The light blinked a few times before the firefly took flight again. She watched it flicker away, lost among a hundred others.

The beauty of the night took her breath away. It was a moment she'd never forget.

Together, she and Cort strolled on, their progress marked by the crunch of their footsteps on the gravel lot. The quiet drone of conversation in the restaurant drifted on the cool evening air, barely audible and in no way intrusive. Stars twinkled in the purple sky, reflecting off the surface of the lake.

"It's wonderful here." She thought of all the exotic places she'd been, the luxury resorts she'd visited, and added, "Wonderful and peaceful."

"Weekends get more chaotic, when the area is open to outsiders."

"How does that work?" This time, when they reached his truck, Cort helped her up to her seat. As she buckled her seatbelt, she said, "I don't see any signs restricting people, and there's no one manning a gate to check addresses or anything."

Half grinning, he waited to explain until he'd walked around the truck and gotten behind the wheel. "You're right. No one tells outsiders to leave or anything like that. But the boat launch is closed, so no boats are put in. Bren Crawford, who rents out boats—paddle boats, rowboats, fishing boats, and a few pontoons—is closed all week until Friday evening. Butler, who owns the inn and is also the mayor, only opens on weekends."

"This town has a mayor?"

He ignored her question to say, "Basically, all recreation is shut down except the tavern and this restaurant, and that's not enough of a lure to bring in the crowds. If anyone does show up with thoughts of hanging around, there's no place for them to stay. Other than the inn, I have the only rental property in Bramble."

She looked at him in surprise. "But they let me stay here."

He started the truck, and his headlights came on, showing a startled deer that stared at them, frozen for a moment, before it bolted away.

"Oh!"

He drove forward slowly. "Where there's one, there are usually—"

Four more deer leaped across the road, their bodies incredibly graceful, their white tails the last thing she saw as they disappeared into the landscape. "It's a whole herd of them." This was something else she'd never experienced. The house she'd shared with Dylan, which would soon be sold, was remote enough for wildlife but fenced all the way around for security.

"They're all over the area. Always be careful when driving at night. They have a tendency to dash in front of cars. Just last year, one ran right into the side of my truck. Broke off an antler, too, but was otherwise okay."

Horrified, she asked, "You're sure?"

"After doing sizable damage to the driver's door and front fender, it ran off into the woods without a single limp."

"I'll remember to be careful." The thought of a wreck terrified her. She couldn't bear the thought of hurting one of the beautiful creatures.

"Now, about the property you rent. That's another exception the originals made for me. They were all really good to my mom when I got her a house here. It came with the little lake house down the hill, and I figured when I was home on leave, I could stay there. That way we each had our own space, but I'd be close."

He bought his mother a house. That seemed incredible to her, a wonderfully selfless act for a son.

"Then when the other house came up for sale, I wanted it, too. I figured it could be rental property if she needed the extra income."

Again, it boggled her mind that he'd purchased three houses, all in an effort to take care of his mother.

"Mom had the knack for winning people over. She talked about me to them, so they felt like they knew me, too. When she got sick and needed help . . ."

One glance, and Marlow knew he was struggling. With the memory, or with sharing it? The moment felt so intimate. Softening her tone, she asked, "They let you move here permanently?"

"They did. And when I asked about buying the house—the one you're in now—they had a big meeting and approved it, as long as I didn't rent it out to a group of kids or anything. You might've noticed, it's quiet on the lake at night."

"Very quiet. I love it." Once, she'd heard whispers from her covered porch, and finally realized it was two fisherman going by on the lake in a rowboat, talking softly. Sound traveled easily over the water.

"I remodeled it before showing it to anyone, and then the townspeople realized I had handyman skills, and the next thing I knew, I was doing repairs for everyone."

The urge to scoot closer to him, to touch him, nearly overwhelmed her. He was that easy to be around, and that appealing. "Do you like it? Being a handyman for everyone, I mean."

He gave his response some thought before saying, "I owe everyone here. They don't agree, but that's because they're such good people. When I moved my mother here, she was . . . fragile."

Marlow wasn't sure how he meant that, and she didn't think he needed her asking questions, so she waited.

A full minute passed before he continued. "Mom flourished here. I got her settled, but I didn't have a lot of time. I worried, checked on her when I could, but when I saw her again, she was a different woman. Healthier, happier. Like you, she appreciated everything, especially the peace and quiet but also the people." He flashed her a quick grin. "And like you, she wanted a job at the tavern."

"Your mother worked there? Seriously?" To have an affinity with his mother delighted Marlow. "See? Smart women know what they're doing."

"Stubborn women, too, apparently." His grin kept any insult from the words. "I'm glad I wasn't around when she made that decision, or I would have tried to talk her out of it."

"Like you tried to talk *me* out of it?"

He skipped past that, saying, "Turned out to be a great fit for her, a home away from home. All the regulars knew her and liked her. They became her social group, and for her, working there was like belonging to a club." He pulled into the tavern parking lot. "You and my mother are two very different people, though."

With a heartfelt groan, Marlow asked, "Is this going to be about money?"

"It makes a huge difference to a person's mindset." Quiet settled around them when he turned off the truck. The headlights faded to black, leaving them in a cocoon of shadows that the security lights around the tavern couldn't penetrate. "Mom came from nothing. It took her a long time to get used to having a house of her own. She didn't need to work—I didn't want her to work—but when I saw her in the tavern, I knew she was thriving."

Parts of him called to parts of her. Understanding, empathy. As if his thoughts became her own, she felt his consternation, and his satisfaction.

She stopped fighting the urge to touch him, and in fact, it seemed incredibly natural to settle her hand on his forearm, even when his muscles and tendons tightened beneath her palm. "Working gives us all a sense of accomplishment. In a way, it gives us self-worth and brings balance to our lives."

Briefly, he covered her hand with his own. His palm was warm and rough, twice the size of hers, and somehow that touch felt like more than it was.

Then he retreated to open his door and step out, and the moment was gone. Unsure whether she was relieved or disappointed, Marlow hurried to meet him at the front of the truck.

Cort paused. "Mom said working made her whole."

Happy that he wanted to continue the discussion, Marlow explained how it made her feel. "Working is more than labor. It's thought and effort, and reward when you're paid. It's having enough to buy someone a gift, and making sure your bills are covered. It's self-reliance. Autonomy." She thought of the big accounts she'd handled at her old job, the revenue she'd brought in. "It's a boost to confidence. And sometimes pride."

Staring down at her in the dim light, his eyes dark, his gaze intent, Cort slowly smiled. "Guess that covers it." He held open the tavern door. "Time to get your T-shirts."

Her heart jumped in excitement—for about a dozen different reasons. She could hardly wait.

CHAPTER 4

Her first week as a server was quite the experience. Her feet ached, her back felt strained, and her cheeks hurt from smiling.

Pride kept her going, and by the sixth day, she was, as Herman put it, settling in. She found a rhythm to gathering orders and moving between the tables. She learned the shortcut terms for menu items so she had less to write down.

The pay was okay, and she did great in tips.

It was a giddy feeling, getting a generous tip from a customer. It was a monetary compliment, and she liked it.

The weekend crowd was, as Cort had predicted, very different but still manageable. It was as they were closing on Saturday night, long past her recent bedtime since moving to Bramble, that she saw the framed photo on the wall.

She recognized the handsome Marine right away. Cort.

It was a younger version of him, appearing so serious, so capable. Actually, he always looked like that, but he was more somber in the photo.

Herman came up behind her. "Our local hero."

Marlow finished putting up the chair. "He said his mother worked here."

"Nora was a treat." He glanced around, saw they were alone, and propped a shoulder against the wall. "Cort was a lot younger when he brought her to us. Twenty-five or so. Nora had a bastard of a husband who'd treated her badly."

Folding her arms around herself, Marlow took an uneasy breath and wondered if she should be hearing this. Despite her curiosity, she didn't want to take part in gossip, not when she'd so hated being the subject of it. "If this is private stuff—"

"Cort doesn't talk about it, but Nora did. Everyone around here knows. See, she was pretty battered when we met her."

Her arms dropped. "Battered?"

Sad and disapproving, Herman nodded. "She'd married young, and he'd always been awful to her. When Cort was twelve, he started fighting back. Nora said he took a few beatings trying to protect her, and it nearly destroyed her. She knew she had to get out. Thing was, she didn't have anywhere stable to go. No family or anything. She and Cort moved around a lot, she worked wherever she could, went hungry a few times I suspect, but they got by. Cort worked too, but as soon as he was seventeen, he enlisted."

With a shattered heart, she whispered, "Seventeen?" That sounded incredibly young to her, but given what he'd been through, the ordeals he'd suffered, he must have been anxious for an escape. She tried to remember herself at that age, and she knew she couldn't compare to Cort.

"Got his GED, convinced Nora it was what he wanted, and off he went. Sent every dime he could back to her, because even at seventeen, that's the kind of man he was."

Honest to God, Herman sounded like a proud father. She was starting to understand why the people around here cared so much for Cort.

And why she thought about him so often.

"Nora saved the money for him, and then after a few reenlistment bonuses, he got her a place here."

What a remarkable man.

"Nora said he was always up for a challenge. If there was a B billet that needed to be filled, he was the first to volunteer."

"B billet?"

"Every Marine has an MOS—Military Occupational Specialty. That's the thing each one is specially trained for. They can take on special duty assignments, too. Those are B billets. Nora said Cort always volunteered. By the time he was thirty-five, he'd deployed six times."

Eyes widening, she whispered, "To dangerous areas?"

"He doesn't talk about it, so I don't know the specifics. All I know is what Nora shared. She loved that boy so much. Was super proud of him, too. Hell, we all are." Again, like a boastful father, Herman shared, "With recommendations from his commanding officers and a battlefield promotion, Cort was on his way to being the youngest Master Gunnery Sergeant in his battalion."

Marlow looked at the photo again. She didn't understand the ranking system in the military, but she imagined Cort could have done anything he put his mind to. "He said he'd still be serving if his mom hadn't gotten ill."

"Yeah, poor Nora. She found happiness here. We all loved her, because she loved us. You could do any little thing for her, and she was so damn grateful it'd break your heart." Herman grew quiet.

She heard him swallow, saw him glance away a moment. "Bobbi made her cookies once, and Nora cried, it made her so happy. Cookies."

"I think it must have been the gesture she appreciated, don't you?"

"Must've been, because when I changed a flat on her car for her, she tried her damnedest to pay me." He snorted. "Like I'd take money from her just for lending a hand."

Marlow smiled. "She sounds wonderful."

"Was. So is Cort. His mom found out about her lung cancer at the same time he was up for re-enlistment. We all knew how hard he'd worked to get where he was, but he opted to take an early retirement." Herman gave her shoulder an awkward pat. "If there was one thing he loved more than the Corps, it was his mama. Anyone could see that."

And yet he'd lost her. Marlow had to wipe the tears from her eyes.

"Whenever Cort was here, he was helpful to everyone. We loved how he cared for Nora, but he cared for all of us in one way or another." This time, Herman didn't hide his teary eyes from her. "He thinks he's beholden to us or something for loving his ma, but that's how we feel about him. He's a good man, one of the best, and we're lucky to have him."

"I agree."

Patting her shoulder again, Herman added quietly, "Like I said, he's our local hero."

Because of a few late nights, Marlow had missed a couple of sunrises, and she was determined it wouldn't happen again. Bleary-eyed and with badly disheveled hair, she made her way down the hill to the lake. Cort was on the shoreline but a good distance away. As she walked, she kept an eye on him, hoping to send him a wave.

He didn't look up.

Now that she knew more about him, she was even more drawn to him. He'd gone through a lot, yet he never showed any disappointment in his life. Maybe that was why she felt a kinship to him.

They'd each had their lives rearranged through no fault of their own.

Well, in her case that wasn't entirely true. She should have been more aware of Dylan's infidelity. If she'd paid as much attention to her marriage as she did to her career, everything might be different now.

Without thinking about it, she wrinkled her nose. It was a distasteful thought.

Being here, now, in this place and with her refreshed mind-set, she didn't want to be anywhere else. She was—and always would be—sorry that Dylan had died. He'd been too young, too vital, to lose his life. It bothered her that her in-laws were suffering.

But she couldn't regret the divorce. If only she'd gotten it wrapped up sooner.

Cort still hadn't noticed her, so she settled into the Adirondack chair and got comfortable.

Too late, she discovered that it was covered in dew.

Her backside was now damp. With a sigh, she sipped her coffee and thought, *Oh, well.* She didn't care. The sun rose as a blazing neon yellow ball, surrounded by orange and red rays that spread out over the lake.

"Spectacular," she whispered to herself, feeling content in a way she hadn't known was possible.

By the time she finished her coffee some fifteen minutes later, the sun was high enough to warm her face and she was so relaxed she felt boneless. She set the empty mug on the dock beside her, closed her eyes, and thought wonderful things . . . until she dozed off.

Each of his footsteps rocked the dock, and yet Marlow didn't move. Pausing, Cort took in her awkward posture slumped in the hard chair, and then he heard the low rough sound of her breathing, like a very feminine . . . snore.

His mouth twitched, and he couldn't resist moving closer.

The sun would roast her in no time. Worse, she might get burned. He hated to disturb her, especially when he'd rather just look at her a bit.

Even in his own head, that thought sounded creepy, so he cleared his throat.

Nothing.

"Marlow?"

She shifted, snuggling more deeply into the chair, which seemed impossible given its hard lines, but she managed.

"Hey." Kneeling beside her chair, resisting the urge to touch her, he said again, "Marlow?"

She briefly stirred.

"If you sleep out here, you'll get a sunburn."

Thick lashes fluttered, then lifted. For a moment, she squinted out at the lake with incomprehension before the spark of awareness entered her dark velvety eyes and she snapped her head around to stare at him.

"Oh, my gosh. Where did you come from?"

"I'll assume that's not a serious question." Cort didn't stand. Nope, he liked his vantage point right here beside her just fine. "You were out."

"How long were you there?"

"Just walked up, but even though I said your name, you kept on snoring."

"Ha!" With a luxurious stretch, she straightened herself. "Guess I was more tired than I realized."

"Late nights at the tavern?"

"Just a few." She ran a hand over her uncombed hair. "Ugh, I'm a mess." Instead of dwelling on that, she smiled. "Hi."

"Hi."

"I saw you when I first came down, but you were focused on fishing."

Not for a second had he been unaware of her. He'd felt her stare like a physical touch. Wasn't easy, but he'd reminded himself of her newly widowed circumstances. Pouncing on her the moment she stepped out the door might make her wary of him. He didn't want that, so he'd waited, letting her know that she could have her space.

He hadn't counted on her falling asleep. The plan had been to wave to her as she headed back up to the cottage, then decide his next move based on how that went. If she was receptive, he'd have joined her. If she'd merely waved, he wouldn't have intruded.

Now here he was, smiling at her while she smiled at him, and it didn't feel awkward or intrusive at all.

It felt right.

His gaze went over her face, then her hair. Here in the bright morning sunshine, flaws would have been noticeable—only they weren't, not on her. Oh, her face had character, for sure. A small worry line here, a smile line there, a lonely freckle or two.

What he really saw was the flush on her cheeks, the shine in her untidy hair, the depth in her eyes. "Not a mess," he said, belatedly correcting her. "Sloppy looks good on you."

With a quick grin, she reached for her coffee mug, tipped it up, and got only a drip. "I need caffeine if I'm expected to accept false compliments with grace."

Wasn't false, but he wouldn't belabor the point. Cocking one brow, he said, "I have coffee in my thermos."

She countered with, "I have cookies in my kitchen."

An invitation? "I'll share if you share."

"Deal." She held out her hand.

After rising, he accepted her hand and tugged her up. Given his way, he wouldn't have let go. Her small hand fit into his perfectly, her grip firm and sure, her skin soft and warm. Just as it had in his truck, her touch ignited a sexual spark, one he hadn't felt in far too long. Not that he'd been celibate. No reason for that. But this much sensation?

Few things took him by surprise anymore, but her effect on him was a shocker.

Again, he didn't want to rush her, so he let her go. "You got more mail yesterday. I knew you were working so I held it until today." At the end of the dock, he picked up the knapsack he'd left with his tackle box and rod. Two letters were inside, and both looked important.

"Did you catch any fish?"

"Nothing big enough to keep."

"Bummer."

"Fishing isn't about the catch, really." She didn't ask for the mail, so he carried the sack, mail, and thermos, and together they started up the slight incline. "Even if I fish all day and don't catch anything, I enjoy it."

"No way. What's the point if you don't succeed?"

"What's the point of sitting on the dock at daybreak even when it's drizzling and you can't see the sun?"

"Fresh air? Welcoming a new day, whether it's rain or shine."

"Same with fishing."

"So you like the sunrise, too?"

He could see the idea pleased her. "I do, but I also like the sound of the water, the breeze in the trees, frogs, and birds."

Cort heard it all, but his awareness was tempered by Marlow's nearness. When she was close, he felt her presence everywhere, like subtle static on his skin, sparking but not uncomfortable. "I like the smell of the fresh air. The sun." He smiled at her. "Or the rain."

They reached her enclosed porch, and she opened the door. "You make it sound really nice, but there's still that part where a fish gets hooked." She cringed. "And baiting the hook?"

He followed her in through the sitting room and to the kitchen. "It's easy once you get the hang of it."

She went to a cabinet and got down another mug, then uncovered a plate of cookies and set them both on the table with napkins. As she took her seat, she said, "Your turn. Pay up."

He couldn't recall ever finding a woman so amusing. He set out his thermos and her mail, then went to her sink to wash and dry his hands. Back at the table, he seated himself across from her and filled both mugs. "I make it strong."

"Perfect." She sipped, nodded, then added a spoonful of sugar from the sugar bowl. "Creamer?"

"I'm good."

For a moment, she fidgeted, then her gaze met his. "I saw your photo on the tavern wall."

Yeah, was bound to happen. The framed pic wasn't so big that it drew attention, but he knew with her working there, she'd run across it sooner or later. "It was my mom's, in her house. Private." He picked up one of the chocolate chip cookies. "Mom told me her visitors always commented on it. The next time I came home, Herman had hung a copy."

"He's proud of it. Of you."

So she'd talked to Herman about him? Interesting. "Mom thought it was hilarious to take me to the tavern and surprise me with it." He rubbed a hand over his jaw, remembering how everyone had cheered him. His mom had glowed, and it was so nice seeing her happy that he hadn't complained. "Herman's great. He looked out for Mom when I wasn't around. They all did."

"Funny," she said softly. "Herman told me you looked out for all of them."

"It's what neighbors do." Not that he'd known it before moving his mother here. As a kid, he'd experienced only survival. Avoiding his father, dying a little inside when his mother couldn't do the same. Once they'd escaped, things had still been difficult. Lying low meant avoiding neighbors, dodging questions, and scraping to get by. His mom had worked long hours in housekeeping at a rundown hotel, and he'd gotten hired for odd jobs wherever he could. They'd lived week to week, sometimes day to day.

Too many times, after paying rent and gas for their old Buick, there hadn't been enough money for food. He could still recall finishing the can of soup and half a sandwich his mom had made for him, and then realizing there was no more. She'd claimed not to be hungry, but he'd known that couldn't be true. From that day forward, he vowed to himself to be more aware, not just of meals but of everything and everyone.

Idly, he turned the coffee cup, wondering how much he should share with Marlow. He imagined Herman had already given her an earful. Would it hurt to make sure she had the facts?

"You've gone awfully quiet." She tipped her head with a gentle smile. "More so than usual, I mean."

"Thinking, actually."

"About?"

"Being here was an eye opener." He met her gaze. "I chose this place because it was obscure, private, and property was cheap."

"Then," she teased. "Not so cheap now."

"Actually, because it's watched so closely, it's impossible to buy here now. Mom and I got in at the right time."

"It was meant to be."

Yeah, as he watched Marlow, he realized a few things were starting to feel that way.

"Herman said you brought her here?"

Good old Herman. He couldn't even be bugged with the guy, knowing he'd just been reminiscing. "My father found her." It still made his heart clench when he thought of it. "It was because of him I wanted to be a Marine." When some kids watched movies about superheroes, Cort had watched videos on the Marine Corps. He'd needed money, training, a way to change his life and make things better for his mother. A way to defend. To serve. The only path he'd seen was to become one of the few. The proud. The Marines.

Reaching across the table, Marlow touched his hand, surprising him. "She was hurt?"

"He hurt her." The words seemed to stick in his throat. "He was a drunken, abusive bastard—and I wasn't around."

"How did you find out?"

"In the hospital, she gave them my info, and they tracked me down. We were stateside, thankfully, so I was granted leave, got to her as quickly as I could, and relocated her in record time."

"To Bramble?"

"Best decision I ever made." There'd been so little time to consider things, to weigh the pros and cons. For a few seconds, he turned his hand so Marlow's fit against his palm. It was nice having that connection to her as he dredged up ugly memories from his past. "I wanted to find my father and take him apart." Being a Marine, he'd learned discipline, and thank God for it, otherwise his life might be vastly different now. "Instead, I made my mother and her well-being a priority, and we ended up here."

"What happened to your father?"

As he drew in a deep breath, he released Marlow and put both hands on his coffee cup. "He'd stolen Mom's car, and he did me a favor by getting stinking drunk in an unfamiliar bar. He started trouble with the wrong people, and the next day he was found in an alley."

Her searching gaze read the truth on his face even before she said, "Someone killed him."

"Yes, and good riddance." It had saved him, and his mother, the trouble of filing charges against him and going through the legal channels to have him removed from their lives.

Needing something to do, Cort bit into the cookie, surprised again as he realized it was homemade. The cookie gave him the perfect opportunity to talk about something else. "Wow, this is good."

She saw the change of topic for the evasion it was, but Marlow being Marlow, she accepted it gracefully. "I found a recipe online."

"A recipe is only as good as the person following it."

"I haven't done much baking, but it seemed simple enough." Folding her arms on the table, she watched him. "I want to tell you something, but I don't want you to misinterpret what I say."

Going on alert, Cort gave her all his attention.

"I think you're fascinating."

Okay, he hadn't seen that one coming. He could make a lot of assumptions based on that simple statement, but assumptions were dangerous things. Instead, he asked, "How so?"

"Maybe it's the way you see things, so black and white. You're . . . Well, *accepting* isn't the right word. It's more that you seem to adapt to everything so easily."

She couldn't be more wrong. Nothing was ever easy, but he knew better than to waste his energy trying to change something that either wasn't important or was set in stone. "What is it you think I've accepted?"

Silence ticked by while she continued to scrutinize him, and he let her.

Finally, she said, "Hardship," as if that summed up a dozen different things.

And maybe it did. "The Marines taught me that you can take adversity and make it work for you. Losing my mother when she was finally happy—that was a blow, no way around it. I'm here, though, with all these people who knew her well and cared for her. The people who gave her life meaning. That counts for a lot."

"I think you gave her life meaning." Before he could find a single word to say, Marlow continued. "She lived for you, doing what she could to make your life better. When you were old enough, you did the same for her. Young people put in your situation often make a lot of bad choices. You joined the Marines. You brought your mother here and helped her to start that happy life. Now you stay here because these people care for you."

Her eyes went shiny, as if she might cry, but instead she smiled.

Cort wasn't sure what to say or do.

"Like I said, you fascinate me."

They were still staring at each other, thoughts, emotions, and possibilities arcing between them.

Until the buzzing of her phone disturbed the moment.

She glanced at the counter. "Sorry. Let me make sure that isn't Herman."

Cort tracked her as she stood and lifted the phone. That's when he saw her unopened mail. The packet was on the bottom, still sealed.

Groaning, she said, "It's my mother-in-law."

"She calls often?"

"Yes." With the press of a button, she silenced the phone. "She hasn't given up on the idea of my returning to the family business, only it's not my family. Not anymore." Grabbing up his thermos, she refilled her cup and then his.

Which told him she wasn't ready for him to leave yet. Fine by him. "You haven't opened your mail."

"I know." A wan smile gave away her thoughts. "Sandra said it's some of Dylan's things. I'm rarely a coward, I swear, but this time, I'm not sure I want to know what it is."

"Dreading something is usually worse than facing it." That had been true of his father. As a kid, he'd feared the man's rages. Then when he was big enough, when he'd grown brave enough to fight back, instead of feeling dread, he'd been empowered. "Might be easier to get it over with."

Lifting her chin, she said, "You know what? You're right." She stretched out an arm and snagged all the mail, bringing it to the table, and adding the new mail he'd brought along that morning to the top of the stack. "This, at least, looks interesting."

He'd noticed it was from a bank when he'd received it at the post office. He watched her carefully tear the envelope open, scan a few pages, and then smile.

"The sale of my house was finalized with a remote closing." She waved the paper. "I'm not going back, and I'd still like to pay you in advance. What do you say?"

"I'd say that you fascinate me as well."

She beamed at him. "I'm going to choose to take that as a compliment."

"You should." He nudged the rest of the mail at her. "Would you rather do that in private?"

"Nope." She tore open the next piece of mail, then another. When the stack dwindled, she had two neat piles—one she threw in the trash, and the other she set on the counter.

All that was left was the packet.

Drawing a bracing breath, she opened it and pulled out several documents. As her gaze went over one paper, she started to frown. By the third paper, livid color slashed her cheeks and her lips were compressed.

Cort couldn't imagine what she'd received, but he could see how it affected her. "Marlow?" he said quietly.

She jumped as if she'd forgotten about him, her gaze clashing with his.

"One thing at a time," Cort said. "Whatever it is, you've got this."

Giving a firm nod, she said, "I do. It's just . . . it doesn't end."

Keeping his tone gentle, he asked, "What doesn't?"

"The lies. The betrayal." Lifting one page, she said, "An apartment he rented that I knew nothing about." She slapped the paper on the table. "A car he purchased that I never saw."

It joined the other paper. "A credit card, probably to buy gifts for the other woman."

Damn. Pushing his coffee cup aside and sitting forward, Cort considered how to reassure her.

She spoke again before he had a chance. "I'm sorry. None of this is your problem."

"I encouraged you to open it."

She shrugged. "Not opening it was only prolonging the inevitable, so I'm glad I did." Wearily, she rubbed her forehead. "You know what annoys me the most?"

He said nothing, leaving it up to her to continue.

"Me. I'm most annoyed at myself. How could I have been so clueless? He was carrying on a separate life, and I just blithely went about my business as if everything was fine and dandy. It wasn't, I knew it wasn't, but I also didn't want to rock the boat."

If they were a little more familiar, he'd give in to temptation to leave his chair, lift her from her own, and just hold her. Sadly, he didn't have that option. "Enjoying the peace isn't a crime."

"It is when it's not real peace, when it's just . . . existence with a lie."

Cort couldn't disagree. For a long time now—since he'd turned twelve, really—his preferred method of dealing with trouble was to face it head-on. Grief, however, wasn't that easy to conquer. "How'd you find out?"

Issuing another fake laugh, one that sounded close to a sob, she dropped her head back and closed her eyes. In a small voice, she confessed, "It's almost too humiliating to share."

Dark suspicions rose, and with them, a lot of anger directed at a dead man. "You don't have to share anything if you'd rather not. But if you do, know that I won't judge." At least, he wouldn't judge her. Her dickhead husband? That man he'd already tried and convicted in his head. "I'll just say one thing."

Marlow opened an eye to peer at him.

It was the perfect reaction, one that said it all in a simple and lighthearted way. She'd listen, but she was skeptical.

Challenge accepted.

Cort gave himself a moment to think, then decided to just go with his gut, say what he knew to be true. "Sometimes talking about something makes you realize it wasn't as bad as you thought. It's keeping it in here"—he touched his forehead—"and in here"—he touched his chest, over his heart—"that makes the hurt fester and grow."

Tension eased from her shoulders, and the slight tilt of her smile was more genuine. "See, you're fascinating."

"So are you."

Her smile warmed even more. "Ugh. The awful truth is that Dylan started insulting me. I think he was bothered that I hadn't noticed, or hadn't bothered to comment on, his growing lack of interest in me. I was so wrapped up in my work, mostly because it was all I had. That sounds pathetic, doesn't it? Again, my choice, something I accepted."

"You coped—until you stopped coping."

"Well, it was tough to stay in denial when he'd tell me my hair was a mess or he'd comment that I was gaining weight. In the guise of a gift, he wanted me to go to a salon for a complete makeover. He said I looked dated and older than I actually was. His exact words were, 'You look like a forty-year-old housewife.' On behalf of tired women everywhere, I was insulted."

"You should have suggested he see an eye doctor."

Another quick grin, there and gone. "He insisted that I join a gym to get in shape and shed a few pounds." Bracing an elbow on the table, her chin in her hand, she half laughed. "I took those shots badly, I'm afraid."

It was only because he'd had a lot of practice that Cort was able to keep his thoughts contained. If her husband was sitting here right now, he'd probably punch him in the nose. "Please tell me you got in a few shots of your own."

"He already went to the gym daily—at least, he said he did—but I told him he was wasting his money." She wrinkled her nose. "I accused him of being flabby."

Silently cheering her, Cort asked, "Was he?"

"Little bit."

Cort grinned with her. He liked how she fought. "Good on you for pointing it out."

"It was hurtful of me, I know, but it was starting to dawn on me why we were arguing. So many little things came together. I started to pay closer attention, to him but also to myself. In some ways, he was right. I hadn't changed my hair in forever, and my wardrobe was always whatever the stylist said was business fashionable. But it wasn't me. It didn't reflect my real personality or my preferences. Somehow, in my marriage, I'd lost myself."

Cort had zero personal experience in the marriage arena, but he had friends—some with happy marriages, some with marriages that fizzled out, and some that imploded in the most godawful ways.

And then he had his best friend . . . who'd made the ultimate sacrifice. Cort lived with that guilt every single day. It was his burden, though, not hers, and he wanted to keep her talking about herself.

Getting to know Marlow better, seeing what made her tick, enthralled him. "Seems to me that marriage should be give and take, and both people might have to change now and then to make it work."

"That's what I thought, too. Only I didn't change in good ways. That's why, after everything that's happened, I'm most disappointed in myself."

Marlow set a high bar. From what he'd seen so far, she excelled at everything.

Except a happy marriage.

For her, that'd be a tough loss. "He sounds infantile and obnoxious, and you sound rightfully reactive, but none of that was humiliating."

"Yes, well, the worst part was the night I tried to seduce my own husband. What a fool I was."

Cort tensed. He hadn't known Marlow that long, and yet it bothered him to know she'd put herself out there for a jerk who didn't deserve it. She deserved someone who would see her for the bright light she was.

"I changed my hair," she explained, "but it was a style I liked."

"The way it is now?"

"Pretty much, minus the bedhead tangles."

"I like the look." He liked everything about her. "Go on."

For only a moment, she appeared sidetracked by his compliment. He saw the moment she decided to let it go, choosing to finish her explanation instead. "I chose a sexy dress and heels—which I didn't like, because it felt like I was trying too hard, which, clearly, I was. I waited at home for him, with a romantic night all planned."

Picturing that, Cort almost felt sorry for the man who'd thrown it all away. "Didn't go well?"

Her laugh held no humor. "What an understatement. He was four hours late. I tried calling him a few times, but the calls went directly to voice mail. When he finally got home, I was in the kitchen drinking a little too much wine. He assumed I'd be in bed and was surprised to see me, but mostly he was confrontational because he knew he was busted."

His chest tightened at the wounded look on her face. His muscles tightened, too. Resisting her was getting harder by the minute. Holding her seemed as important as his next breath.

Marlow looked away from him. "He laughed at me, at my hair and my dress, asking if I was making some feeble attempt to keep him." As she spoke, her voice got quieter until she nearly whispered. "He told me not to bother, that he'd already had better and wasn't looking for round two, at least not right then."

Fury gripped Cort. "What an asshole."

She shifted her gaze to his. "He told me I could try again the next day, that he might be willing by then. Instead, I went into the bedroom and packed. He heckled me the whole time, saying a lot of vicious things. I could tell he wanted a fight, or at least a strong reaction." Again, her chin lifted. "I didn't let him see me cry."

"Good for you," he replied with feeling.

"First thing the next morning, I filed for divorce. He didn't expect that, and he tried an immediate turnaround, saying he'd been drunk, that I'd surprised him. None of that mattered to me. It was over, and I knew it. Every day since then, right up until he crashed his car and died, it was a battle."

Which had only obligated her further, Cort knew. "Stupid men say and do stupid things." And sometimes those stupid men needed their asses kicked. "I hope you didn't put any stock in his insults."

"Maybe a little."

He sat forward. "Your hair is incredible."

"It's plain old brown."

"Not even close. It reminds me of a fawn. Golden brown and soft, with subtle reddish highlights." Color tinged her cheeks, but she said nothing. "Gorgeous eyes, too."

"I'm tempted to say they're also plain brown."

"And I'm tempted to convince you otherwise." So damn tempted. "If you stay in Bramble, I probably will."

Her lips twitched. "You probably will convince me?"

"Or at least try. And since you were concerned that I'd misinterpret your comment, let me be clear that you can interpret what I'm saying any way you want. Odds are, you'll be right." With that laid out there, he waited to see what she'd say or do.

Her mouth opened and closed, and she angled her chin. "I'm staying."

Satisfaction burned through his bloodstream. "There you go." Another special moment, one of many that were starting to add up, at least by Cort's count.

He was pretty sure they'd just taken a step past friendship and into the realm of something far more intimate. That suited him just fine.

"So all those papers you received. What are you supposed to do with them?"

"I'm assuming the apartment and car were for the woman he was seeing, only with him gone, the bills haven't been paid."

Incredulous, Cort asked, "And *you're* supposed to pay them?"

"Or at least settle the accounts. I got multiple death certificates so I could respond to situations like these. Well, not exactly like these, but for bills I expected." She fanned out the papers. "The car, apparently, was repossessed, but with money owed. The apartment has been abandoned, yet the lease wasn't canceled. The credit card is maxed out. As his wife at the time of his death, I have access to his accounts."

"Your mother-in-law sent those to you?"

"Yes."

"And she's wealthy?"

"Very."

It was manipulation of the worst kind. "She claims to want you back at the company?"

"Family business and all that. I know what you're going to say. It doesn't add up. It's an insult for her to send these bills to me, especially while she's pretending her son was perfect and all the blame belongs on Pixie Nolan."

Cort went still. "You know her?"

"I've seen pictures." Again, she wrinkled her nose. "It came up in the divorce, and at that point, Dylan was more into bragging than discretion. I almost felt sorry for his lawyer, except that he was a sanctimonious jerk, too." She paused, frowned some more, then smirked. "Of course, I imagine all women feel that way when facing an unfaithful husband and the person defending him."

"You'd have to be a saint not to."

"And I'm far from sainthood, believe me." She gave him a grim smile. "Ms. Nolan worked in one of the company's warehouses at a different location, one I never had reason to visit, but apparently Dylan did. Or maybe he met her through someone else. I don't know, or want, the particulars." Indicating the papers, she said, "I'm guessing Sandra sent the stuff to me because she wants me to see Ms. Nolan as the villain. Sandra hates her, and she likely wants me to hate her, too."

Cort searched her face, but he saw no hatred. He wasn't sure such a negative emotion was even in Marlow's DNA. "You don't hate her?"

"I don't want to be her friend or anything, but why should I hate her? Dylan was the one who cheated on me. If it hadn't been Ms. Nolan, it probably would have been someone else. Seems to me that Dylan used her, too."

That was such a kind, generous attitude, Cort was certain he lost a piece of his heart to her right then and there.

"I know," she said. "You think I'm foolish."

"I think you're . . . astonishing. Beautiful. Wise. And you have great hair."

She laughed.

"You fit here in Bramble, Marlow. Perfectly."

A bright smile lit up her dark eyes, making them even prettier. "Thank you. That is, by far, the nicest compliment yet."

CHAPTER 5

During the following week, Marlow discovered several things about herself.

First, she no longer quailed at the sight of a fish being caught. Cort wasn't unnecessarily cruel, and he ate whatever he kept.

Second, her arms, actually her entire body, were now nicely toned by the physical activity at the tavern. She liked the way she looked, even with the extra pounds she'd put on at the end of her marriage.

Third, braids were amazing. Simple, sometimes elegant and other times messy, always comfortable, far more so than a tight ponytail or topknot. While watching an online how-to video, she learned to make several different types of braids, and they were now her favorite go-to casual hair style.

Best of all, she learned that Cort was right: getting a worry out in the open also helped to get it out of your head. She stopped dodging Sandra and instead answered her calls. Pleasantly, because she didn't like herself when she got snide. She expressed her concern, sympathized, but she remained firm that she would not return.

Why go back to a life she no longer wanted when her new life was so much fun?

She'd settled Dylan's outstanding bills, either with payment or with notification of his death. After all, it wasn't the lenders' fault that he couldn't meet his obligations.

It was nearing eight o'clock on Thursday when the tavern suddenly went quiet. Arms laden with a heavy tray of empty plates, Marlow glanced from one familiar face to another, then tracked their gazes to the front door.

There stood Sandra and Aston Heddings.

The sudden appearance of a unicorn wouldn't have attracted so much gawking attention.

Quickly turning away, Marlow decided to duck into the kitchen. Not that she'd dodge her in-laws, but she didn't want to greet them with her arms full. She'd only taken three steps when she heard Aston say, "Marlow?" with the same incredulity he would have given to the unicorn.

Sighing, she pivoted back and said, "Hey, you two. Come on in and grab a seat. I'll be right back." The words nearly choked her, though she used them all the time when greeting customers.

But for Mr. and Mrs. Heddings? She felt certain that particular phrase had never been issued to them.

She was only in the kitchen a second when Cort came in behind her.

"Here." He relieved her of the tray and set it aside with a lot more ease than she would have, especially with her hands now trembling.

Their friendship—or something more than friendship—had grown since she'd shared her secrets in her kitchen. Not in physical ways, but they were definitely closer, and they'd spent additional time together over recent days, which was probably why he didn't hesitate to cup her face and bend his knees to look directly into her eyes.

"Your in-laws?"

She nodded, further words sort of stuck in her gullet. "You could tell?"

"They smell of money, so yeah, I could tell."

She caught his meaning easily enough. The way they wore their clothes, their bearing, the way they had of looking at others spoke of privilege in a way few would misunderstand.

"Any idea what they're doing here?"

She shook her head. "Other than being disruptive, I don't have a clue." The tavern was still far too silent, and as she closed her eyes, Marlow was easily able to picture the tense scene. The Heddings would stand there, eyeing the place with disfavor while the customers eyed them with distrust. There'd be no avoiding the upcoming scene, so she opened her eyes again. Might as well face reality.

At least it was a weeknight, not a busy weekend. "I have another hour to work."

Herman came rushing toward her. "Go do something with those people!"

Cort frowned at him. "Give her a second."

"No one is moving," Herman said in a near panic. "No one is eating or drinking. You could hear a pin drop. I swear I just heard Bren burp." He tucked in his chin. "Don't want to tell you what I heard Floyd do. No one is used to its being so quiet."

That was just the type of nonsense she needed to hear to get her back in focus. She smiled to reassure Herman. "I'll need a quick break to handle things."

His relief was so great, he said, "Take the rest of the night off."

"Oh, no. I'm not cutting you short." No way would she let Sandra and Aston impose on Herman's business. "I'm supposed to be here until closing, and by God, I'll be here. This shouldn't take long. I'm sure they don't want to be here any more than I want them here."

That statement got Herman puffed up with indignation. "What's wrong with here?"

"Not a thing." She patted his chest. "I *love* it here, but they won't. So fifteen minutes, okay? At that point, feel free to give me a prompt."

Cort understood before Herman did. He glanced at the wall clock. "Fifteen. Got it."

On impulse, she put her palm to his jaw. A quick, simple touch that fortified her. His gaze snagged hers and held. She knew he wouldn't budge from the place until she'd finished her confrontation. Cort was rock solid in ways other people could never manage. "Thank you."

Covering her hand with his, he turned his face and kissed her palm. "Fifteen, no more."

Curling her fingers to hold onto that kiss while ignoring Herman's wide-eyed wonder, she headed back out. Everyone looked away from Sandra and Aston and transferred their curiosity to her. Fine. Let them look.

Though her in-laws had never seen her so disheveled, and they'd definitely never seen her waiting tables, she held her head high and pasted on a smile while dusting her hands on her apron. Yes, she wore an apron, and Sandra appeared apoplectic at the sight of it. Aston merely looked disgusted.

And she *did not care.*

Breezing forward, aware of the ripe anticipation in the room, she asked, "What are you two doing here?" with a show of enthusiasm she was far from feeling. She embraced Sandra in one of those *touch-as-little-as-possible*-type hugs and then did the same to Aston.

Neither of them made an attempt to return the gesture.

Undaunted, she kept her smile in place. "I'm surprised to see you."

"We shouldn't be here," Aston growled. "Sandra insisted."

Sandra snapped, "Because *she* won't listen to reason."

Keep smiling, Marlow told herself. *It'll confuse them.* "If you mean I have no intention of returning to my old job, you're correct." She lifted her brows in mock confusion. "We settled that on the phone, Sandra. Surely, you didn't make the trip here just for that."

A murmur went through the tavern, causing Aston to scowl. "We need to speak somewhere private."

"Sorry, I'm on the clock."

Sandra gasped. "You don't mean . . ." She lowered her voice to a dismayed whisper. ". . . you work *here*?"

Showing a bit of a mean streak, Marlow said, "Yup."

Nostrils flared in outrage, Aston glared at her. "I don't believe you."

"The shirt doesn't lie." Proudly, she pointed at the logo across her chest: Dry Frog Tavern.

Covering her mouth with a trembling hand didn't quite muffle Sandra's sob. "You want to ruin us. *Why?* We've been so good to you."

Ah . . . she could disagree but wouldn't. "Sandra, that's not true." Marlow rubbed her shoulder. "I care about both of you. I would never deliberately hurt you."

"Then come home," she pleaded.

"This is my home now." She heard another murmur and quickly corrected herself. "I'm not a permanent resident because that's not allowed, but I will be a longtime renter and I plan to work here as long as Herman will have me."

Proving he'd heard every word, Herman gave a not-so-subtle "Cough, *forever*, cough," making her heart happy.

"I like this job, and I love these people."

Another murmur swept the room, this time one of appreciation.

"You can't mean that." Aston's gaze passed over the customers with disdain—but then suddenly froze.

Without looking, Marlow knew he'd just noticed Cort. She could easily envision Cort standing there, tall and proud, arms crossed, gaze unwavering.

Yes, Aston, he's on my side. She thought it but didn't say it.

"I'm sorry you went out of your way to see me." And now she needed the visit to end. Sandra was getting overset, and Aston was growing angry. Nothing good would come of extending the visit. "Unfortunately, there's nowhere to stay here in Bramble—"

Aston made a rude sound. "We have no intention of staying here."

"Then that settles that." She tried for a gentle smile. "I want only the best for both of you, but I won't be returning to my old job." Or my old life.

"We lost our son. You lost your husband. Doesn't that mean anything at all to you?"

So unfair! Sandra had made no attempt to lower her voice as she spoke those awful words. The silence had been terrible before, but now it seemed everyone held their breath.

Angry words flooded to Marlow's tongue, but she didn't release them. She gave herself a few precious seconds before reacting, long enough to find some grace.

When she spoke, she kept her tone soft and her words quiet. "I can't know what it's like to lose a child. Dylan never wanted children, and whether you realized it or not, I always tried to defer to his wishes. I'm sorry for what you're going through now, but I can't help. You have resources, more than most people could ever imagine. You'll be fine without me—I'm sure of it."

Sandra seemed to expand with umbrage. "*That woman* contacted us for a job." Again, she'd spoken loudly.

Prickles of unease drifted over Marlow's body, making her first hot with embarrassment, then icy cold with anger. She didn't need to ask whom Sandra meant. From the day Marlow had discovered that Dylan was cheating on her, her mother-in-law had used the same awful words, with the same nasty inflection. *That woman.* As if Pixie Nolan had nothing else to identify her—no name, no personality, nothing.

Just *that woman*. The one who had slept with Marlow's husband.

The woman he'd chosen. The woman who ultimately led to the destruction of their marriage.

A now familiar ache tightened her chest, making it difficult for Marlow to feign disinterest. There wasn't enough air in the room to fight off the swell of choking unhappiness. Calm detachment was her usual defense mechanism, a way to protect herself whenever the subject was brought up.

By now, it should have been easier. Except that it was brought up in front of everyone—customers, new friends. Herman. *Cort.*

With a quietly indrawn breath, Marlow reminded herself that she'd abandoned a job she loved, filed for divorce from a man she'd dedicated a decade to, helped her in-laws with the cremation and memorial service, put her house up for sale, and now she was embracing a wonderful new life.

She would not succumb to the damage Dylan had wrought. She had no reason for shame.

With feigned equanimity, Marlow stated, "It doesn't concern me."

"Of course it does! We need you back here. We have to present a united front against the gossip magazines and reporters."

Did Sandra honestly think she wanted to face the paparazzi? That she'd want to continue inhabiting the role of the dutiful wife? No, thank you. People would see her as the scorned woman, and they'd pity her. She'd rather be reviled by her in-laws.

"No," Marlow said, aware that her breathing had deepened. "We've been over this, Sandra. I've moved on." From everyone and everything associated with her old life. This was *her* time, damn it. Her chance to find happiness. To live for herself, without other obligations pulling at her.

"We can't replace you, Marlow. This is a family-owned business, and you're family."

"Thank you, but you'll need to find someone else."

"Do you know that little tramp was almost hired before my assistant got wind of it?"

The injustice of that slur irritated Marlow on a basic human level. How was Dylan a saint while Pixie was a tramp?

Full of righteous indignation, Sandra continued. "You can believe I put a stop to that nonsense immediately. I'll be happy if she's never hired for an honest job again. Let the little homewrecker sell herself if she gets desperate enough. I'm fairly certain that's what she was doing with Dylan anyway. Sleeping with him for his money."

Never mind that the entire tavern was listening in. Fury burned through her blood, stiffening Marlow from head to toe. "Is that what you thought of me?" For years, she'd known Dylan's parents didn't approve of her. For years, she'd taught herself not to care. Hearing the harsh insults brought it all back, all her determination, all her drive to succeed . . . All her desire to be accepted.

Only to have Dylan insult her in the worst possible way: by seeking out someone else and taunting her about it.

"Of course not," Sandra said. "Dylan married you. He loved you. We know that."

He'd had a funny way of showing it, not only spurning her attention but turning *his* attention elsewhere.

Disgusted that she'd even asked, Marlow wondered if this would forever be her life. Reliving the past even when she didn't want to. Forever dealing with the grief and anger that surged forth without warning. Suffering the type of hurt that constantly lurked at the edges of her mind. *Why wasn't I enough?*

No. Her life was here now, and she was reclaiming her internal peace in her own way, her own time. She didn't want to be cruel, but neither could she coddle her in-laws. She deserved her own happiness, damn it.

As if she hadn't just leveled Marlow, Sandra went on with her complaints. "I put the word out on that little gold digger. No one in the company, and none of our associates, will ever give her a position of any kind. Let her work on the street. That's where she belongs."

The vile words had an odd effect on Marlow, one she didn't want to accept, and yet it rejuvenated her spirit.

She had the surprising desire to defend the proverbial "other woman."

"I understand why you wouldn't want to rehire her at the family business," Marlow said carefully, unwilling to say or do anything that would extend the painful conversation. "But everyone needs a job, and it's not as if she kidnapped Dylan." Muscles tightening in her jaw and shoulders, she spoke the truth, a truth Sandra didn't want to face. "Dylan wasn't a victim in this."

"Dylan is dead," Aston stated coldly.

"Pixie Nolan didn't kill him. He did that to himself by driving drunk."

Sandra flinched. "Oh my God, how can you say that?" The words came on a faint breath of sound. "My son is dead and you cast blame on him?"

Staying strong, Marlow softened her tone but not her stance. "Dylan was a grown man who made his own choices. Like all of us, he sometimes chose badly."

"He didn't deserve to die," Aston growled.

"No, he didn't." She could at least agree with that. "I still can't come back. I *won't* come back."

"But there's gossip," Sandra insisted. "First because of that little tramp, and now with you disappearing . . ."

"You've dealt with gossip before."

"Not like this—not about my son!"

Marlow knew that Sandra wouldn't relent, not for any reason. She was used to getting her way, and right now she was hurting. She couldn't think about anyone else, certainly not Marlow. "I'm sorry that the divorce and the reasons for it became public. That wasn't my choice. As you can see, I'm out of the public eye. No reporters have approached me, and I can't imagine anyone will."

"You could end it if you'd—"

Refusing the request before it was asked, Marlow shook her head. "No. Please don't ask again. The answer won't change." If she had to leave Bramble someday, she still wouldn't return to Illinois.

"Selfish," Aston muttered, his eyes narrowed and mean. "I told Sandra this would be a waste of time."

So much for showing grace. "I need to get back to work."

Taking that as his cue, Cort approached. "Sorry to interrupt."

"Then don't," Aston said.

Cort completely ignored him. "You're needed in the kitchen."

She nodded, then said to Sandra and Aston, "Drive safely." She started to move away but hesitated. "I hope you both find peace."

Their angry glares proved her effort was wasted. She turned, realized Cort wasn't following, and stalled . . . until Herman frantically gestured at her. With no other choice, she had to trust that Cort wouldn't start anything.

"Sorry," she immediately whispered to Herman.

He didn't seem to hear her apology as he offered, "Want me to get rid of them?"

He was so jumpy about it, she couldn't believe what she'd heard. "How would you do that?"

"Fire alarm. There's no fire," he admitted, "but we do tests every now and then."

God love him, he lightened her mood with such a silly suggestion. "Now, Herman. Would I disrupt all your patrons like that?"

"Probably not," he said, "but I would." He peered out at the silent standoff currently taking place between Cort and the Heddings. "Might be fun."

She pulled him into the kitchen, and then into a warm hug that made him stiffen and chuckle nervously.

"Here now." Awkwardly, he patted her back. "Let's do that alarm."

"No," she said, giggling. *Giggling!* She never giggled, and until now, she would have bet that she didn't know how. "Listen." She paused for effect. "Hear that? Everyone is chatting again, so I'm sure my visitors are gone and your customers are getting back to eating and drinking. Which means I need to get back out there."

His expression softened with a goofy smile. "You're a good sort, Marlow, and a damn fine employee."

No one had ever called her a *good sort* before. She liked it. "Thank you." Pleased with the sentiment, she turned in a rush and slammed into Cort. Good God, it was like running into a boulder.

He didn't budge, but she bounced back a foot and likely would have landed on her derriere if he hadn't caught her arms. She ended up bumping against him again, this time more gently.

"Hey, are you okay?"

Dazed, she looked up into light brown eyes filled with concern and had the nearly overwhelming urge to kiss him. What would he do if she dared? Had their relationship reached that point yet?

Herman shouldered past them with a muttered, "I'll check on everyone. Take your time."

And then she was alone, somewhat, with Cort. Two people worked the long grill behind them, and on the other side of the wall customers waited.

"Subtlety," Cort said, "is not his strong suit."

"Was that an endorsement, then?"

His thumbs rubbed over her bare arms just above her elbows, and his gaze dipped to her mouth.

Her lips tingled. When was the last time her lips had tingled?

So long ago, she'd forgotten they could do that.

Pressing closer, Marlow asked, "Are you going to kiss me?"

"I'm deciding."

Instead of being insulted, she felt her mouth lift into a crooked smile. "Any chance I can tip the scales in my favor?"

"You just had an uncomfortable confrontation with your in-laws. I'm not sure it's the right time to make even a casual move."

She cocked a brow. "Because you think I'm fragile? Do I appear to be falling apart?"

Now he smiled, too. "Definitely not fragile. And no, you look fairly pleased with yourself."

Ha! She was, she realized. After all, she'd had a public dispute with Sandra and Aston and hadn't let it get her down. She'd stood her ground and, at least to her mind, managed to stay firm but kind. To top it off, Herman thought she was a good sort.

Taking Cort's face in her hands and going on tiptoe, she demanded, "Kiss me."

In the next second, his mouth settled on hers. No timid kiss from this Marine, no sir. He took her order seriously and completely dismantled her understanding of a kiss.

This was more.

This was *amazing*.

It was the type of kiss that could sweep a levelheaded woman completely away. Happily.

When he eased up, she said, "Whew. Way to excel."

He didn't tease, didn't make light of it; he just studied her as if seeing something he hadn't seen before. "You haven't been here that long."

"Long enough to know I like it here and—" She gave a stealthy look around to be sure no one was listening. "—I'd really like to stay if I can convince the originals to add one more."

"What a rule breaker you are." He leaned in for another kiss, but this one was fleeting, there and gone before she could get too involved. "You know what I'd like to do?"

Her eyes widened because she wasn't quite sure what *she* wanted to do. "Tell me."

"I'd like to walk along the lake, capture a few fireflies—only long enough to see them before we let them go again—maybe show you how nice the moonlight looks on the water."

"When?" She was ready for that right now. "I work until closing tonight, Friday and Saturday."

"Sunday, then?"

She nodded, heard the crowd getting louder, and knew she had to get back out there. "Will I see you tomorrow morning?"

"You will if you're up to watch the sunrise."

"Wouldn't miss it." Or him. She dithered, then said, "Thanks for having my back."

"Anytime." Then more seriously, he added, "Understand, Marlow, I would never intervene unless you asked me to—or unless it was to physically protect you. In a verbal confrontation, though, my money's on you."

"Really?"

"Everyone could tell you had it all under control."

His faith in her buoyed her spirit even more. "Now see, that's the best type of backup there is." It was a remarkable thing to have this man's trust.

And honestly, it helped her to trust herself more, too. She did have her life under control. Sure, there were moments when doubts crept in and that hollow ache filled her chest, as if some vital part of herself was still missing.

Yet each day, she felt more whole. Each day, she found new courage or humor or determination.

She was healing herself, proactively, on her terms, and it felt great. So great, in fact, that she floated through the rest of her shift.

Cort let her know when he was heading home, but then she'd already noticed that he rarely stayed until closing, and he wasn't always at the tavern while she worked. Like her, he enjoyed the dawn, and unlike her, he didn't have a late job to work.

She briefly wondered if that kiss would change things. She looked forward to finding out.

Over the next two days, Cort's visits to the tavern were about the same, the only difference being his familiarity in greeting her when he arrived, and letting her know when he was leaving. He didn't show up any earlier or stay any later.

He didn't crowd her, and she appreciated it.

They saw each other on the dock in the mornings, and although he wasn't overly demonstrative, they did share a few more kisses. It was both exciting and new, this fresh relationship, but it was different also. She'd married Dylan as a young woman and had allowed him to guide her—into the right home appropriate to his family name, into her profession at Heddings' Holdings, into a social whirl of movers and shakers. Why, she couldn't say, except that it had been easier than standing up for herself.

Cort's personality was every bit as big as Dylan's, just quieter and more controlled. With him, she didn't feel the need to gauge her reactions. Not her laughs or frowns, her disappointment or fascination. Talking with him at dawn over coffee on the dock, she found that she could share anything, embarrassing moments and worried thoughts, and especially things she found funny or exciting.

That was why, on Sunday evening as they strolled along a

deserted stretch of rocky shoreline, she said, "I haven't heard from my in-laws again, and I'm hopeful they've given up."

"Given up on pressuring you?" His hand opened on her back, and he steered her closer. "Careful. There's a stump."

She stepped around it, and then stayed near him because it felt right. "Actually, I wouldn't mind if they've just given up on me. On ever seeing me again." She winced. "Does that sound awful?"

He took a second to answer. "I saw you with them. They were abrasive. I don't know if grief made them that way, but I suspect they've always been a challenge for you." He glanced at her for confirmation.

Her slight shrug confirmed it. "For the first few years of my marriage, I knew they didn't approve of me. They were always polite for Dylan's benefit, I'm sure. They weren't warm or welcoming, but they didn't exclude me from things. It was more a look I'd get or the way they'd smile. Condescending, you know?"

"Yes."

"They had a certain set of friends, people in their orbit, and they always assumed Dylan would marry within that group. Instead, he brought home an outsider."

"You."

She nodded. "My family was financially comfortable, but the Heddings . . . Well, you've heard of Heddings' Holdings?"

"It's a recognizable name."

"They're into everything. Properties, restaurants, merchandise. They have more employees than I could count. It's unheard of for them to track me down here and to show up personally."

"Guess they eventually accepted you, since they want you back so badly."

She shook her head. "They're worried about Dylan's reputation. Anything and everything they do is reported and shared.

That's just reality for wealthy people. Usually, they'd brush it off, but since Dylan's gone, they're worried."

"And they think you can make a difference in how the story goes?"

"I probably could." She shot him a look. "That sounds like boasting, doesn't it?"

"Not when it's true."

A damp breeze blew her hair into her face. She shook it back, then gazed up at the dark sky. "I was given a position in public relations at the company. I don't think anyone expected much from me at first, including Dylan, but I advanced pretty quickly, meeting expectations, sometimes exceeding them, until I went from local to regional and then was overseeing all the public outreach from various departments. Through the years, my position changed and I was given more responsibility, more power, until I was dealing with some of their most important partners and handling their biggest contracts. Sandra and Aston adjusted their attitudes. I don't know that they liked me more, but they definitely respected me, and in the business world, respect is everything."

"Respect counts everywhere. It's hard to genuinely like someone you can't respect."

"True." She hip-bumped him, causing him to miss a step. "I respected you right off."

Rather than bump her back, he put his arm around her shoulders and gave her a gentle squeeze. "I don't give respect lightly. You impressed me right off, but it wasn't until I got to know you that you had my respect."

"You feel like you know me now?"

"I do." He led her to a dock that stretched out over the dark water. It creaked as they walked out, accompanied by the sound of water lapping against the piers. "You're independent and proud, with a flair for adventure."

She laughed. "Bramble being the adventure?"

He nodded. "You're fair-minded, which is why you don't like injustice."

"Because I defended Pixie Nolan? I mean, I didn't. Not her specifically. It was just the idea that—"

Touching a warm finger to her lips, he halted her rambling explanation. "You have a thing for Dior but have no problem mixing it up with comfortable jeans—and a Dry Frog Tavern T-shirt."

That made her laugh. "Hey, I love that shirt."

"Whatever you wear, you own it and make it look good."

Pretty sure her smile would remain for a week.

"You have a generous view of life."

Because she felt jaded after the past months, she tipped her head and asked, "How so?"

"You don't get insulted easily. Whenever possible, you choose to be amused instead. I've seen that happen a few times now, and I like that outlook a lot. Life has enough real strife in it that no one needs to seek it out just for the purpose of being offended. You've dealt with hardship, and you obviously know the difference."

Awed that he would see her so favorably, she confessed, "I've had an easy life. I imagine it's a lot more difficult for someone who hasn't had enough to eat or is out in the cold." She looked up at him. "Or someone defending his country abroad."

He didn't comment on that, and she really wished he would. She'd love to know more about him, but he rarely shared his feelings. Cort had to have the same needs, the same desires, as everyone else, yet he was always so stoic. Not that she wanted him to be maudlin, but she wanted him to feel comfortable enough with her to show . . . Well, everything.

It struck her how much she'd changed since coming to Bramble. It had been a little over a month, but she knew she was no longer the same person, and that meant she viewed Cort, and everyone else, differently.

For now, he seemed to want to know more about her, and she had no problem with that. His interest was actually flattering. "One of my duties while working with the Heddings was to approve our social outreach to the less fortunate. For every group or charity that we helped to fund, there were a dozen I had to pass by." It had left her heart heavy with regret. "I hope they find someone else who takes the task seriously. A lot can be done when you put your mind to it."

Voice lowering, Cort said, "I have to tell you, Marlow, it's sexy how much you care. *You're* sexy, but you don't seem to know it."

Sexy? Her? She nearly giggled again at the absurd notion.

"See?" He traced her lips with a fingertip. "I saw that look."

"It's too dark to see anything. I was promised moonlight, and instead we have a cloudy night."

"True, but the fireflies are out, and you love fireflies."

"I do." They flickered everywhere, little glimmers on scrubby bushes, randomly flitting by on the breeze. "They seem magical, don't you think?"

"I like that you think it." He tugged her closer. "Are you cold?"

"A little." The June nights could still be chilly, but Herman claimed by the end of the month everyone would be sweating. Putting her arms around Cort, she rested her cheek against his chest. "You smell good."

She heard the smile in his voice when he said, "So do you."

The way he enfolded her in his arms, she felt as if she could do anything, be anyone. She felt sheltered but also empowered. "Cort?"

"Hmm?"

"Is this going where I think it's going?" She hadn't dated or flirted or even noticed a man's interest in far, far too long. "I'm a little rusty here, so I'd like some clarity."

"If you think it's headed toward the two of us in bed, then

yeah, that'd be my preference. The thing is, I don't want you on the rebound."

Marlow immediately pulled back, but he held on.

"Careful. You don't want to step off the dock."

She frowned up at him. "I'm not on the rebound, and I'm not so awkward that I'd topple off the dock."

He grinned. "You'd be surprised how many times a misstep has taken someone off the side or end. It happens, especially at night when the moon is hiding."

Okay, she could accept all that. One point remained. "I'm not on the rebound. How could I be when things ended with Dylan so long ago? I've had months to rearrange my priorities and to get accustomed to the idea that I . . ." That she what? Wasn't enough for him? That he'd never really loved her?

That she had disappointed herself, most of all.

Cort used two fingers to tip up her chin. "Strong as you are, Marlow, you have to admit you've been through it. You said the divorce was bad and took months. Your marriage was empty before that. Then his death and the funeral and upending your life to come here. This is all unfamiliar territory for you. Wouldn't you like a chance to get your bearings?"

She'd rather get him naked, but she had to agree with his reasoning. "You may have a point. Basically, my life has been in turmoil for too long."

He smoothed his hand over her hair, then under her hair to clasp her neck. "A lot of changes hit you. You're happy here, and you're enjoying yourself."

"Very much so."

"Do you want to give it a little time before you throw anything else into the mix?"

"Anything like you? Hot sex? A relationship?"

"Me, definitely hot sex, and as far as I'm concerned, we already have a relationship."

It was the perfect answer. "You can have one more week. No more."

He gave a quiet chuckle, the sound echoing softly over the lake and coming back to her again. "Not sure I'll last a week, but I'll try."

"It was your idea."

"A suggestion because I care about you. Believe me, if you change your mind before that, all you need to do is let me know. Now, tomorrow, two days from now." He brushed his mouth over hers. "A week, or even a month if that's what you need. I'm not going anywhere."

"Seriously, you have incredible patience." She sort of wished he didn't.

"You have no idea." Together they started off the dock again. "Take whatever time you need to decide if you really want to get that involved. If so, count me in."

That involved. Why did the idea excite her? He was right that she'd only recently left her old life behind, but with Cort, everything felt different. And yes, exciting.

She gave him a huge smile. "Sunday of next week. It's a date."

At least a dozen times, Cort called himself a fool. He wanted Marlow enough that he should have just gone with the moment. She wasn't a timid person. She was smart enough to know her own mind, and he'd been an ass to suggest otherwise.

He wasn't sure he'd last until Sunday, especially now that she felt free to show him affection.

Every morning when she came down to the dock, he greeted her with a kiss and briefly held her in the fresh morning air. She used the opportunity to build the anticipation between them. Each kiss was a little longer, a little bolder. Even knowing she did it on purpose, he couldn't complain.

As she'd relaxed into her surroundings, so, too, had her outfits. She continued to add touches of Dior, small earrings with her jeans and work shirt. Sneakers with leggings and a tunic. A gold chain with a skirt and tank top.

No matter what she wore, it teased him, because he couldn't stop thinking about getting her out of the clothes.

Saturday morning he was waiting for her, wondering if he'd last another day, when she started down the hill looking incredibly sweet with her hair haphazardly pinned up. She wore a roomy T-shirt over pull-on shorts, no shoes, and carried her usual mug of hot coffee.

Immediately, he set aside his fishing rod, securing it to the bank, and headed her way. They met at the ramp to the dock, and without a word, he bent down and took her mouth. She was warm and soft, and he was in a bad way.

"One more day," she murmured, making him groan. With a secret little smile, she caught his hand in hers, and together they walked out on the dock. Instead of sitting in the chair, she settled at the end of the dock with her feet hanging over, her toes just touching the icy water. "I've been thinking."

He sat facing her, one leg bent, his arms resting on his knee. "God, me, too."

Glancing his way, she grinned. "Wonder if we're thinking the same thing."

"Doubtful."

"Okay, so I'll share. What's the plan?"

"Get you naked, kiss you all over, and enjoy each other for most of the day."

Her eyes had widened with his first words, and now she blinked . . . before snickering. "Love your plan, but I meant, will you come to the cottage, or should I meet you at your house?" Quickly, she added, "I've never seen your house, and I admit I'm curious."

He rolled a shoulder. "It's just a house, same as any other around here. I'm at the end of the road, so there's no reason for you to drive by, unless you were going there specifically. You're welcome to visit anytime, though. It's older than the cottage, not as updated, but it's bigger and it's comfortable."

"You've chosen not to update it?"

He glanced out over the water, but she deserved to know. "It was my mother's house. Maybe because I still see her there, I like it as it is."

Understanding, she stated, "Your mother was happy there."

"Very. Her bedroom was downstairs, with the living room, kitchen, and bathroom close by. It's easier for me to climb the narrow stairs that lead to an attic conversion, where there's a smaller bathroom, a big closet, and a sitting area, so I sleep up there, now. I turned her room into an office, but not much else has changed. The basement is still my work area."

"Did you finish those plans for the siblings? Wade, Gloria, and Bobbi?"

"Yes, and they all three approved, which almost never happens. They'll each get what they want, but it'll take a little longer."

"Do you have anyone who works with you?"

"Sure. Bramble boasts some really talented but retired tradesmen. We have an electrician, a plumber, and a tile setter. Whenever I need help, they're happy to take on a part-time job. The only time I have to pull a worker from outside Bramble is when we need to pour concrete. That doesn't happen often, though."

"So you're like a general contractor who just organizes the work?"

"Actually, I'm a licensed plumber and electrician, too. I could do it all myself, but that's time-consuming."

The approaching dawn reflected in her dark eyes. Smiling, she guessed, "The retired people enjoy your company."

She always saw him in a favorable light, but she wasn't wrong. "They enjoy chatting with anyone, really. Plus, they have a lot of experience—decades' worth, in fact. Almost every time I work with one of them, I learn a new trick."

She started to say something else, but a sound echoed around them, coming from near her cabin. She glanced back, as did he, but there was nothing to see.

Yet.

Suspicion, and an innate alertness, had him narrowing his eyes. "That sounded like a car door."

Lowering her voice, she asked, "You think?"

"Were you expecting anyone?"

She shook her head. "No. I haven't heard from either of my in-laws, so I can't imagine them returning. No one else knows I'm here."

"Lawyer? Realtor?"

"Shouldn't be." She set aside her mug to stand.

He got up first and helped her. "Want me to come up with you?"

Biting her lip in indecision, she glanced toward his fishing gear.

"It's fine." He picked up the empty mug and took her hand. "Might just be a neighbor who's curious about you." But he didn't think so. His instincts were usually dead-on, and he had a feeling trouble had come to call.

"Hmm. I'm not exactly dressed for company."

Yet she'd greeted him, which told Cort that she was relaxed around him. Perfect. "You didn't invite anyone, so that's on them. But I think you look great."

She sent him a quick, grateful smile as they climbed the hill. "Okay then. Might as well get this over with."

At the side yard, they could see an older blue two-door car in her driveway. Marlow hesitated, then led him into the cottage through the sliding doors. She cut through the sitting room to the foyer.

Cort saw a small frown pinching her brows as she went to answer the knock at the door. He stepped up beside her, but as she pulled the door open, she froze. Eyes flaring wide and lips parting, she drew in a sharp breath and stared at the woman on her stoop.

He wasn't sure what to do, and then Marlow whispered, "Pixie Nolan."

What? Giving the young woman another glance, he saw her white-faced expression and finally realized that she held a small bundle in her arms.

A baby.

CHAPTER 6

Pixie stared at the impressive woman standing before her. Marlow Heddings. Dylan's *wife*. God, this was the hardest thing she'd ever done in her entire life. From the inside out, she shook with fear, with illness, and with the knowledge that she would probably be cursed and hated.

How could Mrs. Heddings not hate her? She hated herself.

But . . . she loved her baby, and so she was here.

On the long, grueling, nearly impossible drive, she'd rehearsed what to say, the words repeating themselves over and over in her head, and yet now that she was here, all she could do was well up with tears. She hadn't known so many tears could be stored in one body.

Any second now, her legs would give out. She tightened her hold on the baby and waited for the lash of rage.

Instead, the woman simply stared at her as if she couldn't believe her eyes. Not that Pixie blamed her. Only the worst sort of person would show up here.

If desperation hadn't forced her, she never would have been so bold, so disgustingly shameless.

Finally, one small word, quavery with tears, breathless with worry, faint with illness, squeezed out of her constricted throat. "*Please.*"

*   *   *

Marlow couldn't seem to catch her breath. Pixie Nolan was here, in Bramble. Why?

She'd seen photos of Pixie during the divorce negotiations. God, she looked so young in person. Much younger than Marlow had realized. It was bizarre, but she heard herself ask, "How old are you?"

The girl was trembling all over, her expression ashen except for splotches of red on her cheeks. Her light blond hair was badly tangled, and still she was beautiful.

"I'm twenty."

Closing her eyes, Marlow tried to ground herself, but it wasn't working.

"I'm sorry," Pixie said, her voice quavering and high. "I don't have anywhere to go. I don't have anyone."

Marlow opened her eyes, only to see tears tracking down Pixie's face. "Why?"

"If it was just me," she said in a rush, "I swear to God I wouldn't be here."

"Dylan is dead." Did the girl not know that?

"Marlow," Cort said, his arm coming around her waist, his strength surrounding her. "She has a baby."

It took a moment for that word to penetrate. *Baby?* Gaze dropping, Marlow took in the infant sleeping swaddled in a blue blanket.

Life couldn't be so unfair! This had nothing to do with her. *Nothing.* Why involve her?

"I'm so sorry," Pixie said, openly crying now, her nose running, her voice broken. "I've been sick, and I don't know what to do."

"Christ," Marlow complained, her stomach knotting, her brain cramping—and her heart clenching hard. Pixie wavered, looking as if she might keel over. In fact, Cort had one hand outstretched, as if to catch her. Marlow's own throat closed tight, but she managed to say, "Come in."

Cort immediately supported the woman, steering her through the foyer and into the sitting room, where he helped her into a comfortable seat on the couch, then quickly plucked two tissues from the box and handed them to her. As Pixie cleaned up her face, he put his hand to her forehead, then turned to Marlow. "She's feverish."

Great. Just freaking great. If only she were numb, but instead feelings bombarded her. Strong feelings. Powerful, even. "I'm not sure what to do."

Pixie nodded, then again dashed the tears from her cheeks. She avoided Marlow's gaze. "I . . . Andy is only three months old. I could live in my car, but he can't. I'm breastfeeding." She grew silent, sniffling. "I'm almost out of diapers. I have no way to wash his clothes."

Slowly, Marlow sank down on the couch, not close to Pixie, but not that far away either. Needing a moment to decide on what to say or do next, she glanced at Cort.

Of course, he easily interpreted her look. Standing before Pixie, his feet braced apart, his hands on his hips, he asked gently, "Have you taken anything for your fever?"

Pixie shook her head.

Glad for a reason to grab a private moment, Marlow shot back to her feet. "I'll get you something. And maybe some juice?"

The hope and gratitude in Pixie's big blue eyes were enough to unravel Marlow. She spun away, anxious for a quick escape from this new reality.

Why couldn't the past stay in the past?

She wanted to be free and clear of it; instead, it was smothering her.

The neediness of her in-laws had been bad enough, but

now this? The "other woman," at her doorstep, begging her for help?

Literally begging.

She went through the bedroom into the attached bathroom. In the medicine cabinet, she found two OTC medications. Unsure which would be best, she carried both with her to the kitchen, where she poured a glass of orange juice. On impulse, she put two cookies on a napkin and, feeling like a martyr, reentered the sitting room.

Cort now sat on the coffee table, talking quietly with Pixie. He'd taken charge of the situation, thank God, because for a few minutes there, she hadn't known what to do.

But no more.

This was her new and improved life, but life was never perfect. She'd continue to deal with every blow that came her way, and no matter what, she'd stay true to herself.

That meant liking herself enough to be kind, but not a pushover.

Putting everything on the table, she turned to Pixie. "Since you're breastfeeding, are there restrictions on what medicines you can take?" It pleased her that her voice sounded strong instead of stricken, that she'd infused concern into her tone. Damn it, she *was* concerned.

Warily, Pixie peeked at her.

The girl was far too timid, but then again, she was wrecked. The color in her cheeks was a clear sign of fever, and she looked drawn to the point of collapse. The baby stirred, stretching and scrunching up his little face before settling again.

Cort lifted his phone. "I just looked it up. Let's give her this one." He picked up one of the bottles, shook out two pills, and handed them to Pixie with the juice.

Her quietly mumbled "Thank you" was barely audible. She swallowed the medicine, drank a sip of juice, handed the glass back to Cort, and then just stared down at her son.

When she finally lifted her gaze to Marlow again, there was a quiet dignity there. Yes, desperation remained, illness too, but she faced Marlow head-on. "I swear to you, I didn't know he was married."

The vow startled Marlow. It wasn't what she'd expected and was hard to believe. Pixie had worked for the Heddings. Okay, sure, a warehouse position was not a corporate job, but still, surely she'd known the marital status of the company heir?

"We can sort everything out later." Marlow offered a cookie. "Oatmeal raisin."

Pixie drew a deep breath, then started coughing, and that woke the baby.

Hurriedly, Cort grabbed more tissues to hand to Pixie.

The baby let out a scream that could peel paint from the wall, and that startled Marlow even more. Good heavens, the child had a pair of lungs!

Pixie covered her mouth as the deep, barking cough continued. The baby wailed even louder.

It was unbearable.

"Here." Marlow scooped up the baby and put him against her shoulder, jostling him lightly, patting his back, and ignoring the arrested expression on Cort's face and the panic on Pixie's.

The child was small and warm, and he smelled . . . Well, he smelled partly wonderful, at least on the top of his head where a downy thatch of hair grew. But other scents were crowding in, too.

She hadn't handled a baby since her teenage years. Thankfully, her instincts remained. "Cort, could you take that blanket and spread it out on the couch? I believe he's filled his diaper."

For the first time since she'd met him, Cort looked bemused. He moved at a snail's pace, as if fearing he'd misunderstood or wasn't quite sure what he should do.

It delighted Marlow to know she wasn't the only one at a bit of a loss in this strange situation.

"Pixie, good, you've caught your breath." Marlow rubbed the baby's back, glad that he'd stopped wailing. "Shallow breathing for now, okay? At least until I find out if you have a diaper bag or anything."

She nodded. "I left it in my car."

"Good. Cort? Yes, that's perfect with the blanket." Perversely enjoying his discomfort, she smiled at him, and asked, "Would you mind fetching the diaper bag and anything else that looks essential for, say, the next hour?"

Watching her closely, he smoothed his hand over the small blue blanket one more time, and then nodded. He rose, gave both women a glance, and said, "I'll be right back."

The second he left the room, Pixie sat forward with her head in her hands. "I'm so sorry."

"You already said that, and I believe you." Never had Marlow seen anyone so miserable. "No reason to debase yourself, okay?"

Breath hitching, Pixie nodded and more tears spilled out. "I didn't know what to do."

"You said you have no one?"

"My parents . . ." Nervously, she licked her lips. "We were never close. Dylan is gone. There isn't anyone else."

Her pallor concerned Marlow, as did the awful way she shook. "I think for now, you need to eat something. Let the medicine work. Maybe rest for a bit." She didn't allow herself to think beyond that. "I don't have to be at work for a few hours yet. We'll tackle this one step at a time."

Her promise broke the dam. Bent forward, arms crossed over her knees with her head resting against them, Pixie sobbed in earnest, and the sight broke Marlow's heart. Had she ever been that forlorn? That desolate? Even when she'd discovered Dylan was cheating, when he'd issued only insults instead of apologies, she'd known she had resources at her disposal. And she'd had her pride.

Apparently, Pixie had neither.

Cort reentered in a rush but slowed when he saw Pixie sobbing.

"It'll be okay," Marlow told him. "She's overwhelmed on top of being ill. While I change the baby, could you get her something to eat?"

He gave her another wondering look but nodded. "I can do that." He set the diaper bag on the coffee table, then crouched down in front of Pixie. He offered her more tissues. Soon the tissue box would be empty.

Quietly, Cort moved a small wicker waste basket nearer to her. After Pixie dutifully mopped her face and tossed the tissues away, Cort held up the juice. "Take another few sips." Once she'd finished half the glass, he asked Marlow, "Sandwich? Something else?"

"I have more of those delicious frozen dinners you introduced me to, but yes, I also have lunch meat and canned soup."

He returned his attention to Pixie. "With that cough, I'm thinking soup is the way to go."

"I . . . you shouldn't . . ." Pixie glanced at Marlow. "I don't mean to intrude so much—"

"If you're hungry, then you should eat."

After a searching look, Pixie nodded. "Thank you. Soup sounds incredible."

"Try to drink all the juice."

It amazed Marlow, but Cort treated the woman with the same care he'd give to an overwrought teenager.

"You're both so kind and it's killing me." Again, she swiped at her eyes, but the tears kept flowing. Her face was now blotchy, her eyes swollen and her nose red. "You can't know . . . can't imagine." With a shuddering breath, she admitted, "I'm so afraid."

"Well, no reason to be afraid now." Marlow put the baby on his back and then tried to figure out the workings of his little clothes.

"I can do that," Pixie offered, already reaching into the diaper bag to find a nearly empty tub of wipes and a lone disposable diaper.

"If you're able, that might be best." She wasn't at all sure she wanted her renewed initiation with babies to begin with a soiled diaper. Carefully, she lifted the baby and turned him, so Pixie had the business end.

Even with her hands shaking and weak, the young mother made quick work of it.

Then the two of them sat there staring at each other, a wrapped-up dirty diaper between them. Talk about bizarre scenarios you never saw coming.

Marlow got to her feet. "I'll get a bag." She darted into the kitchen and was immediately pulled up against Cort's warm chest.

Against her ear, he whispered, "How's it going?"

She honestly couldn't say. "It's . . . tricky."

Putting his forehead to hers, he said, "Remember, I've got your back. Anything you need from me, anything at all, just let me know."

His generosity left her without words, so she hugged him as tightly as she could and hoped the gesture expressed all the things he made her feel.

With his hands moving up and down her back, he said, "You could call in sick today."

She shook her head. "No, I'm determined to be the best employee Herman has ever had." It was part of her campaign to remain in Bramble. The town had four hundred and one citizens.

She wanted to be number four hundred and two.

"You," Cort said, nudging up her face so he could give her a light kiss, "are determined to do it all, but you don't have to."

"For me, I do." It was how she operated. A part of her genetic makeup. All or nothing. That mode had gotten her through life so far, and especially through the past difficult months of Dylan's cheating and subsequent death. Instead of braking, she accelerated into the twists and turns, and hopefully, she'd get to the finish line—with peace of mind her goal—all that much sooner. "How about you? Do you need to be somewhere?"

"I texted Wade to tell him something had come up and I wouldn't be over today."

"I'm sorry. My problems shouldn't interfere with your life."

After a searching look, he turned to the stove to stir the soup, then switched off the burner. Keeping his back to her, he said, "Here's the thing, Marlow. This shouldn't be your problem either. You don't own it, didn't ask for it, and aren't obligated to handle it. Except that you're a good person." He glanced over his shoulder. "And so am I."

Damn it, now *she* felt like crying. Not the same despairing tears that Pixie had wept, but tears of tenderness. "Thank you." Cort was another twist she hadn't seen coming, but in many ways, he was proving to be the best part of Bramble.

Back to business, she set out a tray. "Use this. Grab her some crackers too, from that cabinet. And then maybe refill her juice?" She opened a drawer and found a disposable plastic bag. "I need to remove a dirty diaper."

They shared a quick smile, and Marlow returned to Pixie.

The girl looked nearly asleep with the baby in her arms, hungrily nursing.

"Oh." Okay, this was something she'd never seen before.

Hastily, Pixie pulled the blanket up over the baby's face to also cover her breast, but he only pushed it away. "He was hungry."

"Does it take him long?" They both spoke in whispers. "I only ask because your soup is ready."

"He'll probably be back asleep in a minute. The drive was hard on him. I think it wore him out."

It looked to Marlow as if it had worn out Pixie, too.

Without looking up, Pixie stroked her fingertips over the baby's cheek. "That was my last diaper. My car is on empty. And I only have forty dollars left to my name."

Marlow sank to the couch again, the dirty diaper forgotten.

"I'm so ashamed," Pixie said. "My life is a complete mess, and I have no one to blame but myself. You have every reason to hate me, Ms. Heddings. Most of the time I hate myself, especially because there's so little I can offer Andy." She pressed a kiss to the baby's head. "I love him so much." When her voice broke, she squeezed her eyes shut, got herself under control, and promised, "I won't sob on you anymore. I can't believe I did that already. I just . . . I meant it when I said I had nowhere else to go."

The baby stopped sucking, and Pixie expertly rearranged herself before putting him to her shoulder. Gently, she rubbed his back until he gave a loud burp.

Cort stepped into the room. "Soup's ready," he said quietly. "Where would you like to put him?"

Pixie looked uncertainly at Marlow. "It's okay if I stay to eat the soup?"

"I insist on it." There was no way she could turn the young woman out, not until she knew what was going on and how Pixie had gotten into such a dire circumstance.

Pixie gave the briefest nod of thanks. "Then maybe we could put his blanket on the floor instead of the couch? He's not rolling over yet, but he does rock sometimes, and he often spits up." She touched a thin, pale hand to a couch cushion. "I wouldn't want him to ruin your beautiful furniture."

"It's not actually mine. It's Cort's." That struck Marlow, and she said, "I didn't introduce you. I'm so sorry. Pixie Nolan, this is Cort Easton, my landlord." *And now more.* "Let me grab a quilt." She hurried to the bedroom and back, then put the folded quilt on the floor for padding, with the baby's blanket over it.

Cort asked, "May I?" and carefully took the baby from his mother.

Marlow knew why. As Pixie stood, she wavered, looking far too frail and unsteady.

She watched, her gaze anxious, until Cort had her baby settled. "His name is Andy." She twisted her fingers together. "Could I use your restroom?"

"Of course." Marlow led her through the bedroom to the only bathroom in the cottage. "Pixie."

The girl paused.

"When did you last eat?"

Holding onto the door frame, she smiled. "Yesterday."

So many questions went through her mind. "When yesterday?"

The smile slipped, and Pixie looked away. "Ms. Heddings—"

"Marlow. You're here, so we may as well drop formality. Now tell me when you last ate. No reason to dodge the truth. As I said, you're here."

Again, Pixie met her gaze. "Breakfast yesterday. I'll admit I'm pretty hungry."

Hungry, sick, breastfeeding, caring for a baby, and without options. "Wash up and then join us in the kitchen."

Nodding, Pixie quietly closed the door.

Cort was leaning against the counter when she came into the kitchen. "I heard," he said. He pulled out a chair for her. "You want some soup, too?"

"May as well. I always eat when I'm vexed."

"This is certainly a vexing situation," he replied with enough seriousness to let her know he was teasing.

She tipped back her head. "What am I going to do?"

"I don't know, but I have a suggestion that might help and gain you a little time to think about it."

"Let's hear it."

He took the seat across from her. "I have the little lake house. It's minuscule, but Pixie is welcome to use it until we—and it is we, Marlow—can figure out how to help her."

Blown away, she covered her mouth with a hand. "Where did you come from? Men like you don't exist."

"'Course they do. Don't be jaded because of one asshole."

She gave a choked laugh and marveled that she could find any humor right now. It was a gift, given to her by Cort.

Just then, Pixie came hesitantly into the kitchen.

Cort stood and pulled out a chair for her, too. "Take a seat and we'll join you for an early lunch."

Very early, Marlow thought, since she'd just been watching the sunrise before Pixie's arrival. "He's handy in the kitchen," she said lightly. "I've already been fed by him once, though it wasn't canned soup."

"It smells great." Pixie's gaze bounced back and forth between them as Cort set bowls before all three chairs. He refilled Pixie's glass with juice and got a bottle of water for Marlow at her request.

They ate quietly for a few minutes. It seemed a priority for Pixie to consume some food. Anyone could see that she was running on her last reserves. Food first, then some rest. Cort's suggestion of his lake house was an excellent solution.

Marlow only had one bathroom here, and she didn't like the idea of a stranger traipsing around her house, especially through her bedroom, when she wasn't home.

Also, Marlow valued her privacy. This was *her* time, and while she couldn't turn a blind eye to Pixie's predicament, she also wanted—even needed—to protect her newfound peace and happiness.

When Pixie had finished her soup, three crackers, and most of the juice, Marlow asked, "Have you seen a doctor?"

She shook her head. "Not recently, not since I was released from the hospital after having the baby."

Marlow had the same feeling she sometimes got during high-pressure business meetings, when she sensed there was more to the story than what was being presented. She put on her no-nonsense face, the one that indicated she'd see through any fabrications. "And before that?"

Pixie quailed. "Um . . . right now, I hope I only have a cold, but you're right that I'm a little feverish."

"You could barely stand upright."

"That's because I'm so tired." She stared down at the table for several long moments, then looked up with resolve.

Hoping to encourage her, Marlow said, "May as well share everything, so we know what we're dealing with."

Pixie's mouth pinched before she gave up. "I had been working as a waitress after I left the warehouse job, but I had difficulties with my pregnancy, so I was let go."

Good. Plain speaking. Marlow appreciated it because knowing and understanding the issues would make them easier to sort out. "What type of difficulty?"

Shyly, Pixie glanced at Cort.

"Go on," Marlow said. "He's a Marine. He won't faint." What being a Marine had to do with the issue at hand, Marlow couldn't say, but it sounded plausible.

Pixie must have been convinced, because even though her face got redder, she said, "I was diagnosed with pregnancy-induced hypertension."

Cort said, "That doesn't sound good."

"It was . . . difficult." She pressed a hand to her stomach. "Along with high blood pressure, I had a lot of swelling in my feet and hands." Her mouth twisted to the side. "A *lot* of swelling. So much that I couldn't fit in most of my shoes. My soles and my palms itched a lot, and then there was the nausea and endless vomiting." Her shoulders slumped a little more, and her voice lowered. "I had terrible headaches that would leave me dizzy."

Marlow shared a glance with Cort. This young woman had faced all that *alone*? Apparently. "What did your doctor suggest?"

"He wanted me on bed rest, but that was impossible since I had to take care of myself."

"Your parents—"

Pixie shook her head. "My aunt raised me, but she's since passed on."

Oh, poor girl. "So you missed a lot of work and the restaurant let you go?"

"Yes, and then things got really bad."

All of that wasn't bad enough? "How so?"

"Like . . . I was passing out, I guess? Everything seemed to happen at once. I ended up in the hospital, and my doctor delivered Andy five weeks early with a C-section." Despite all she'd been through, a small smile touched her mouth. "It was my birthday, and he was the best present ever."

Marlow took the words like a blow. This petite girl had been seriously ill, alone in the world, and then responsible for a newborn? *On her birthday?*

"Thank God he was healthy." Pixie sighed. "I ended up with a hysterectomy, too." She again glanced at Cort, and practically whispered, "Because of some bleeding and stuff. In a way, it was a good thing because they kept Andy and me in the hospital a while longer."

Alone, Marlow kept thinking, brokenhearted for her. That word hammered on her brain over and over again. Alone, completely alone.

How wretched must she have felt?

"Dylan had already passed away?"

Pixie's entire face tightened, tears imminent again. "Yes, but I'd ended things before Andy was born."

"Wait, what? *You* ended things?"

"I didn't know he was married! I swear to God I didn't. I'm a nobody, and when he started paying attention to me, I was too flattered to ask questions. It wasn't until I got pregnant that he told me."

"That he was married?"

Shamed, she bit her lips, but then bravely met Marlow's gaze. "I thought, because I was having his baby, he'd want to get married. He'd . . . told me he cared, and he was so nice, I believed him. But when I told him I was having a baby, he didn't have much choice except to admit that he was already married."

What. A. Swine. "You broke things off with him then?"

She nodded. "He said it'd be okay, that he'd take care of us anyway." Gasping, she said, "I mean . . . I know I shouldn't say this to you . . ."

"It's okay." It wasn't, not by a long shot. All of Marlow's initial rage and hurt had seeped back in, and that hollow feeling invaded her chest once more, but she refused to show her distress. Pixie had been through enough. Adding to her pain now would accomplish nothing. That left Marlow with the only option of ignoring her own feelings. "He got you an apartment and a car. I know because I received the bills after he passed."

Pixie literally groaned as if in pain. She crossed her arms over her stomach and rocked a little as she spoke. "I'm sorry. So sorry."

"You don't need to keep apologizing," Marlow nearly snapped. Seeing Pixie so cowed only infuriated her more—*at Dylan.* Moderating her tone, she stated, "It's in the past." Only it hadn't stayed there. Nope, the past had come knocking, and now Pixie was sitting at her table. Sick, afraid, in serious need of help, and hoping Marlow had a solution.

Life could be so absurd, sometimes.

Cort's hand settled over Marlow's wrist, his thumb brushing against her skin. When she glanced at him, he looked proud. Of *her*?

Okay, that helped. It meant he agreed that she was doing the right thing. He didn't see her as a stooge or a sucker for a sorry tale.

Pixie's tale *was* sorry. Incredibly so. And Marlow wasn't immune to it. For now, that was all the incentive she needed to keep her going.

She was strong, but Pixie looked vulnerable.

She had endless options, while it appeared Pixie had none.

She was thirty-five, and Pixie was practically a teenager.

Seeing all that made Marlow despise Dylan so much. This was beyond the hurt he'd doled out to her. It was outright abuse. He'd used this young woman, started an affair with her when she'd been only nineteen. And when she'd needed him the most, the selfish bastard had the temerity to die.

Probably hadn't been his intent, but still . . .

"I assume without Dylan to keep up the payments on the apartment and car, you fell behind?"

"I barely scraped by when I worked at the warehouse. Dylan convinced me to quit, saying I didn't make that much anyway. And with his position in the company, it would be frowned on if we dated." Pixie scowled. "I should have known something was up then, but I still never suspected he was married. If I'd kept that job, a coworker might have told me."

"I take it things happened quickly?"

"One minute I was just me, working second shift and looking forward to the next raise so I could get new tires on my car, and the next Dylan was there, taking care of everything."

Marlow could see what a lure that would be to someone so young.

Pixie said, "I wanted to get a different job, but Dylan said the hours would interfere with things he wanted to do." She rubbed her eyes, leaving them both redder. "I know I was naïve. He just made everything seem so perfect. When he couldn't be there, he'd send flowers and other gifts."

Picturing it all, Marlow briefly closed her eyes. What had she been like at nineteen? That was more than fifteen years ago, and what stood out most in her mind was losing her father, and a few years later, her mother. Then she'd married Dylan and started working with the Heddings. During that time she'd experienced much of the world. The idealistic, eager girl she'd been so long ago had disappeared like mist beneath the sun. Instead of worrying about the newest music concert and social media trends, she'd been brokering million-dollar deals, lunching with influential people, and pushing her pet projects.

She'd thought her marriage was secure.

Pixie wasn't the only one who'd made grave mistakes.

"Then I got pregnant," Pixie continued, "and Dylan told me he was already married. I ended things, got a job working at the restaurant, and he helped with the apartment, a car and credit card . . ." Dejected, she slumped in her seat. "But you know what happened with that. I got sick, Dylan died, Andy came early . . ."

Had Dylan's duplicity surprised Pixie as much as it had Marlow? Probably more so, because Marlow had suspected that her marriage was sinking before she ever confronted him. Pixie, on the other hand, had been full of new love and hope for the future. What a blow it must have been for her.

"I made such a mess of things," Pixie said. "The warehouse job wasn't great, but it was better than minimum wage, we got small but regular raises, and there were nice benefits, like medical insurance and child care. I should have stayed there. I should never have dated Dylan in the first place. He wasn't from my world, and I should have realized he wouldn't really be interested in me."

"His actions were despicable, but you're not to blame."

That statement surprised Pixie so much that her eyes flared and she drew a sharp breath, which brought up those harsh coughs again.

Foot tapping the floor in agitation, Marlow gave her time to regain her breath. She waited while thinking about the future and the past, and most of all, the present, the right here, right now.

She knew Cort was watching her, and after a moment his foot touched hers beneath the table. She stopped tapping and, grateful to Cort for being here with her, said to Pixie, "Remember, slow breaths."

After swallowing the last sip of juice in her glass, Pixie seemed more defeated than ever. "I tried going back for my old job. The one at the warehouse, I mean, but they weren't hiring . . ." She let her words fade, bit her lip, and again met Marlow's gaze. "I got a call from someone who said if I ever came near any Heddings employee, they'd 'bring the force of their considerable legal resources against me.'"

"Wow." The audacity. Sandra had mentioned Pixie's bid for a job, but it was incredible she'd taken her objection so far. Had she bothered to learn anything about Pixie? About their grandson?

She met Cort's gaze, as unreadable as ever, and yet somehow, she knew he was as irked by the threat as she was.

"I don't know what that means," Pixie said worriedly, "but it sounded serious."

"The Heddings family has blackballed you," Marlow explained. "That's what it means." She saw no reason to tell Pixie that Sandra had discussed it with her directly. "Do they know you have Dylan's son?"

"I didn't tell anyone." She frowned. "There's no one for me to tell. I've never met his parents and wouldn't have a clue how to reach them. But Dylan's name is on the birth certificate and the person who called me seemed to know every-thing about me."

With rage simmering just beneath the surface, Marlow tipped her head and asked, "Like what?"

"How to reach me, which means they knew where I was staying." Flushing again, she said, "My phone was shut off when I couldn't pay the bill. I wasn't at the apartment Dylan had rented. I didn't even have the car that he'd bought any-more. But the call came to the motel front desk and was for-warded to my room."

"Motel?"

Pixie fidgeted. "It was an inexpensive place, the only one I could afford. Just a place along the highway, and I only stayed there a week or so, trying to figure out what to do. I didn't have enough money to stay longer."

"And so you settled on coming to me."

She looked ready to jump out of her skin, then defiantly straightened. "For Andy, yes."

"How did you know I was here?"

"I used a computer at the library and found your social media account. You shared some photos of the lake."

"Incredible." Pixie had been not only desperate but inge-nious.

"When I got to town, I asked about you and was told you were staying here."

Cort frowned, and for the first time, he interjected a ques-tion. "Who did you talk to?"

"I don't know exactly. It was an older woman." She braced herself and, as if she'd committed a mortal sin, confessed, "I lied and said I was Ms. Heddings's sister."

Oh, the irony. Marlow gave a huff of amusement.

"I had to," Pixie said in a rush. "I'm sorry, but I hoped maybe you'd have an idea of a job I could do—"

"You can barely stay upright. How would you work? And what would you do with the baby? Child care is expensive."

"I know." Pixie blinked a few times but didn't avert her gaze. "I went over and over the possibilities in that nasty little motel room. I counted my remaining money three times. Then I got that awful call and was told to steer clear of any job related to Heddings Holdings, and it . . ." Her jaw flexed. "It spooked me." Her gaze nervously flicked to Cort but came right back. "I could do telemarketing, but I'd need my phone for that. I could be a virtual assistant, but that requires WiFi. I could work in a day care or something, but only if I could take Andy with me, and that wouldn't solve the problem of needing gas money and diapers."

"And food."

Her chin hitched higher, her eyes got redder, but she didn't cry this time. "I'm not proud, Ms. Heddings."

"Marlow," she automatically corrected as she struggled to keep her emotions in check. Odd as it seemed, she wanted to reassure Pixie, to offer a quick fix. Unfortunately, that wouldn't solve the young mother's problems. It would only put them on a very temporary hold.

"I am desperate. I know I have no right to be here, and I know this is a horrible invasion of your privacy. You must hate me, and God knows you have every right to. What I did is unforgivable, and ignorance is no excuse, or at least not a good one."

"Calm down, or you'll start coughing again."

"I didn't know what else to do! I couldn't beg a total stranger for help. The only name I knew was yours, and I thought maybe since you'd cared for Dylan, you might care for his son, too."

A last prayer, that's what it had been for Pixie. Marlow saw it in her eyes. "I'd care for any baby, despite who his father might be." The moment Marlow heard the words spoken out loud, all her defenses crumbled away. She was fighting the inevitable because she knew she couldn't turn Pixie away. She certainly wouldn't leave an innocent three-month-old baby without diapers or shelter.

She could, however, lay down some ground rules.

Hopeful, Pixie asked, "Does that mean you have an idea about what I could do?"

"Rest easy, Pixie." Leaving her chair, Marlow went to the fridge and got out more juice. She stopped at Pixie's side to refill her glass. "I'll help you, but that doesn't mean you'll have an easy road ahead of you."

"I don't expect it to be easy," she swore. "I'll do anything, and I'll work as long and hard as I need to."

"Good. A single mother, especially one who is still ill, will have to be strong. That means you need to recover first." She turned to Cort. "I assume you know the nearest medical facility?"

"I do." With something bright and warm shining in his eyes, he stood. Right there in front of Pixie, he enfolded Marlow in his arms. "You're amazing, babe. You know that, right?"

If he was too nice to her right now, she'd turn weepy as well. "I have a heart. Nothing amazing in that."

He kissed her forehead, then let her step away. "I agree, a checkup with a doctor is a priority."

Horrified, Pixie said, "I don't have any money. And I'm sure I just need a little sleep."

"Better if we know what we're dealing with," Marlow said. She was in take-charge mode now, using the same brisk manner she'd utilized in her work world. She decided what needed to be done, and then she made sure it happened. "You may need medicine, or a specific diet might be necessary while you're recovering and nursing. I assume a C-section is major surgery, and with a hysterectomy?" It made her midsection hurt just to think of it. "It's only been three months, and you've had a lot on your plate."

Pixie shut down with a softly murmured, "Okay."

"So a visit to the doctor first. I'm thinking we'll start with a sick appointment to be sure you don't have bronchitis or worse. The doctor can make recommendations from there."

"There's a walk-in clinic," Cort offered, "but we should get there soon because they get busy by late morning."

Surprise brought Marlow around to face him. "We?"

"I'll be the chauffeur." His eyes conveyed a message. "Plus, it might be a good idea if Pixie had someone with her when she saw the doctor, just to hear what's said."

Meaning he didn't trust her to share the whole truth, or he was worried she was too rattled and overwhelmed to remember detailed instructions? There was also the fact that she was a stranger who'd just showed up. Marlow would bet Cort was motivated by all those considerations.

It wasn't easy for Marlow to bend her brain around the idea that her husband had been unfaithful with this beautiful, very young woman, who now had brought her husband's son to *her* for help.

Pixie was a stranger to Marlow, so Cort's suggestion made sense, and his company would be appreciated.

"Also," Cort said, "I can sit with the baby while Pixie sees the doctor."

With another show of panic, Pixie said, "I can take care of him."

"And you have," Marlow assured her. "But you came to me, and I have a way of doing things, of tackling problems. First, I need to know what I'm dealing with, and that means taking you to a doctor. Cort's suggestions are great, and he's being generous with his time—something he does often, by the way—so we should probably just thank him."

Dutifully, Pixie whispered, "Thank you."

He accepted with the barest of smiles. "And my other suggestion?"

"I think it's brilliant, if you're sure you don't mind."

"It's empty now anyway. Of course I don't mind."

Confused, Pixie glanced between them but wisely didn't ask.

It was turning into quite an eventful day.

And Marlow was still determined to work her shift.

CHAPTER 7

Cort dropped by the tavern near closing. He'd spoken with Marlow on each of her breaks. The wealth of compassion she'd shown flat out astounded him. It cost her, he saw that multiple times, but she hadn't turned Pixie away—thank God.

The young woman looked like a child, petite and far too thin, her eyes bruised with illness and her shoulders rounded by loss of pride. He believed her assertion that she'd had nowhere to go and no one to help her.

Coming to Marlow might have been the best decision she'd made in a year. His faith in Marlow surprised him, too, but he didn't have a single doubt that she'd get the girl on the right track, whatever it took. She was that amazing.

Going straight to the bar, he flagged Herman and immediately asked, "Where is she?"

Herman nodded to the back corner, where Marlow was taking orders from a group of four outsiders, all of them young men. "They've kept her jumping."

His gaze never strayed from Marlow, but Cort's tone lowered and his eyes narrowed. "Meaning what, exactly?"

"Look at her. She's cute as hell and smart, with quick comebacks, and those young fools have all asked her out, several times each. Doesn't seem to matter how many times she dismisses them. I think they've eaten and drunk more just to get her back to their table."

"Excuse me." Cort started toward her. Herman was right—she was extra cute tonight with her tawny hair in a thick braid over her shoulder, jeans hugging that lush behind, and her Dry Frog Tavern T-shirt filled out in all the right ways. Even her method of tying her apron showed flair, crossed over her waist once and in a fancy little bow near her hip.

Herman was at his side in an instant. "Now, Cort. Don't go causing any trouble."

That unnecessary request stopped him in his tracks, and he slowly turned to face Herman with a frown. "Have I ever?"

"No." Shifting his feet and running a hand over his face, Herman said, "But we've never had anyone like Marlow here, either, so I think you could, given how you're looking at her." When Cort just stared at him, he groused, "Never saw you look at anyone like that before."

Damn. He hadn't meant to alarm Herman. Briefly clasping his friend's shoulder, Cort said, "I wouldn't, unless it was absolutely necessary. You have my word."

Herman's attention shifted to Marlow, and he nodded. "If it was necessary, I'd do it myself."

Huh. She'd definitely won over Herman, and probably a dozen other originals. Marlow had that way about her, a genuine kindness no one could dismiss. "Good to know." And with that, Cort moved on, making his way around occupied tables, greeting familiar faces with a nod and ignoring the wary looks from outsiders.

He reached Marlow in time to hear one guy say, "Come on, give me a shot. I swear I'll show you a good time."

Apparently fed up, she replied succinctly, "You're a child."

"I'm not!" he said, sounding very much like an insulted boy.

"Of course you are. A man would understand the word *no*." She pulled the bill from her pad and laid it on the table. "Now, if you children don't need anything else, we're ready to close."

Struggling to hide his amusement, Cort slipped his arm around her. Instantly, she stiffened, then turned on him with umbrage.

Until she saw him. "Cort!" She gave him a brilliant smile and leaned into him. "I didn't see you come in."

Ignoring the young men, he asked, "Busy night?"

"Every Saturday is like this."

"True enough." But he was still getting used to Marlow being a part of the Saturday crowd. He took the tray from her, holding it one-handed, nodded at the gawking guys who'd all clammed up, and led her in the direction of the kitchen. "Do you have a few minutes?"

"Barely." She tucked her order pad into her apron pocket. Along the way she accepted a tip from an older couple they passed, thanking them with a smile, and grabbed three more glasses off an empty table. "I'll be glad to call it a night." The second they reached the kitchen, she asked, "How's Pixie?"

Before he answered, he took the extra glasses from her, set them and the tray by the massive utility sink to be washed, and leaned in to brush his mouth over hers.

Man, he'd been missing her mouth. She'd quickly become an addiction for him—the scent of her skin, the softness of her hair, the taste of her lips.

In a little possessive show of her own, she slid her hands to his neck and deepened the kiss, then eased up and rested her cheek on his chest.

Nice. He could get used to greetings like that. "She's okay. Settled in and resting." He sensed that it was more emotional exhaustion than physical that wore on Marlow tonight. She was a dynamo with endless energy, but her emotions had been through a chaotic cyclone.

"I feel terrible abandoning her, and it annoys me that I do."

Loving her honesty, Cort wrapped her up close and offered reassurance. "Both of those feelings are understandable and acceptable. You know that, right?"

"Maybe."

Lifting a hand to her face and cradling her cheek, he looked into her eyes and knew he'd do damn near anything for her. How that had happened so fast, he couldn't say, except that he was a natural protector, and Marlow was an exceptional woman.

He wanted to make sure she knew it, too. "Life doesn't play fair. It wasn't fair to my mom, it hasn't been fair to you, or fair to Pixie." Touching her made him want to kiss her, so he did, but he kept the contact to a soft press of his mouth to her forehead. "I wish Mom had had someone like you."

"She had you, a big, badass Marine, instead."

"Not until I was older. When I was little . . ." There were so many times he wished he could go back in time and face his father as the man he was now, instead of the scared boy he'd been. "We'd have been better off alone like Pixie than with my dad around."

She gave him a sad smile and another tight hug. "The thing about life is that it has a mean way of reminding us how good we have it. You had your mom, and she had you. Your memories of her are a gift, and she was so proud of you."

"True. Some people are completely alone in the world." He'd thought of that many times. He'd lost his mother but gained a town.

Now Marlow was here, and through a campaign of her own making, she was quickly becoming an insider.

When she looked up at him, he saw that her hair was a little sweaty near her temples, and her mascara was smudged near the corner of her left eye.

No woman had ever looked better to him.

She said, "I came here to Bramble, determined to downsize my life. Less stress, less obligation and wealth, and definitely less pretense. I was so tired of living up to other people's standards. This was going to be my time." She sighed heavily. "It's easy to live in a bubble of our own complaints. In Illinois, I felt like I was living such a sorry tale."

"You've been through a lot." He already knew where she was going with this, but she had a right to her feelings. Few would have recovered as gracefully as she had, and with a huge heart still intact.

She nodded. "But then I see Pixie. My God, Cort, she was only *nineteen* when she was going through all that alone. The poor girl turned twenty and at the same time got the biggest, scariest, most precious burden life offers. Facing the world without a job or family is scary enough, but with a tiny baby to care for?" Her dark eyes held a wealth of empathy. "And she's still so sick."

It had stunned them both when the doctor said that Pixie's blood pressure was still far too high, that she should have been on meds and possibly bed rest, and that she currently had bronchitis. Marlow had wanted to stay with her, but at the same time, Cort could see that Pixie needed some space.

So he'd offered.

"For tonight, she's fine, I promise. I made sure she ate, and she has meds for the coughing and her antibiotics. I put diapers and wipes for the baby on a dresser. Plus, I stocked up on some easy food for her."

With a tired smile, Marlow asked, "Frozen dinners?"

"And canned soup, cheese and crackers, snacks, lunch meat for sandwiches, and plenty of juice. Oh, and skim milk and tomato juice, like the doctor suggested."

"I swear, you're an angel who's landed on earth. Thank you for doing all that."

He was far from angelic, and sometimes his remorse put him squarely in hell. "It's no more your responsibility than it is mine, except that people should help one another when they can."

"Yet one more Bramble rule for neighbors?"

"No, a rule for humanity." He glanced at the time. "You want to make another trip around the restaurant before clocking out? I'll wait for you." They had a little more talking to do, and he'd rather do it tonight.

"You don't mind?" she asked.

For answer, he gave her a hotter kiss, then turned her toward the seating area and walked her out. "I'll be at the bar." *Where he could keep an eye on pushy young men.*

Fortunately, within fifteen minutes, everyone had cleared out. Herman would stay until the dishwashers finished, but he insisted that Marlow go.

"You did great today. Don't think I didn't notice. How you kept up with the outsiders, I don't know, but I appreciate it."

She glowed with his praise. "Actually, it was a nice distraction, and after the first hour, I found my rhythm." She grinned. "Take orders, pick up empties on my way to the kitchen, carry out food, handle refills, and then take more orders. It was almost like working a conveyor belt, not that I've ever done that either, but I imagine it's similar, minus all the chitchat—and the tips." She bobbed her eyebrows playfully. To Cort, she said, "I'll grab my purse and be right back."

Once she'd gone, Herman grinned. "She's a keeper."

Cort agreed but kept the words to himself.

"Are you driving her home?"

"No, she has her car, but we might sit in the lot a minute to talk."

His brows lifted. "Anything wrong? Her pushy in-laws aren't back to give her a hard time, are they?"

So Herman knew they were her in-laws? "Did Marlow tell you about them?"

"Just the basics. Also told me someone got her address from a local. She said if she got any calls, she'd need to take them. Usually she leaves her phone in the break-room locker, but she kept it in her back pocket this time. Saw her check it off and on."

Marlow returned to them in time to catch that last bit. "Thank you for not complaining about my phone, Herman."

The way she'd worded it, if Herman had been complaining, he'd have felt rebuked. But Herman blustered now, saying, "'Course I wouldn't. It didn't slow you down, not like it does some people who want to be on their phone around the clock."

"You're a terrific boss."

It amused Cort to see Herman blushing. "I have to get to the kitchen, make sure everything is cleaned up right." He started toward the door. "I'll lock up behind you."

Once outside, Cort said, "We can sit in my truck for a minute, or I can follow you home. Which is easier for you?"

"You don't mind being up this late?"

It was now after one in the morning, and he should have been tired but wasn't. "I'd love to head home with you to talk for a while, but it's been a hell of a day for you. If you need to rest, I understand."

"I won't be able to sleep anyway. How about I follow you to my house? Every time I drive home after dark, I worry that a deer will jump out and startle me."

He agreed, and luckily the deer stayed hidden. At the driveway to the cottage, he waited in his truck until she pulled up beside him.

The air was brisk, the dark night amplifying the distant croak of frogs on the lake.

As Marlow unlocked the front door, she said, "It's so peaceful here, it's hard to imagine that anything bad could ever happen."

"But you're still worried?"

"Let's call it concern." She led him into the kitchen and dropped into a chair, her elbows on the table, her head in her hands. "Pixie doesn't have a phone. She's so thin, and the baby is still so tiny. What if something happens?"

This was why he'd wanted to talk. After getting them each a bottle of water from the fridge, he sat across from her. "Actually, I reactivated her phone."

"Cort!"

"She'd previously downgraded to the most basic plan, so it wasn't expensive. She can call or text but can't access the internet, and there's no GPS or long-distance calling. That wasn't my decision; it was just the plan she'd chosen before her service was shut off."

"Trying to conserve funds, I guess."

"That's what she said. Understand, honey, she protested. She kept saying the diapers and a bed to sleep in were more than she'd dared to hope for."

Marlow groaned. "If Dylan was here, I'd beat him up."

Envisioning that, Cort smiled. He'd put his money on Marlow. "I assume he was your age?"

Her head came up with a fierce frown. "Four years older, so he was damn near forty and involved with a *nineteen*-year-old. And not a sophisticated nineteen-year-old, either."

Cort didn't disagree with her. It was unconscionable that the man had used Pixie as he had. "Knowing she was pregnant, he should have legally made sure she'd be protected." That sounded wrong, like an insult to Marlow, so he amended with, "Not that a married man should have ever touched her in the first place. All that aside, though, she's here now, and she's anxious to do whatever she can to repay you."

"And you."

Knowing Marlow as he did now, he assumed she had a plan in mind. She'd probably already plotted out the next few days, maybe even the next few weeks. Her willingness to get involved astounded and pleased him.

There couldn't be many people like her in today's jaded world.

To put her mind at ease, he said, "I gave her my number in case of an emergency and told her we'd check on her tomorrow." That was hours ago. It would be dawn soon.

"Did you give her my number, too?"

"No. That's for you to do, if you want to."

"I want to," she said firmly. "I'll feel better knowing she can reach me if it's necessary." Tapping her fingers on the table, she detailed some of her plans. "I've thought about her and this situation nonstop since she arrived."

He'd known she would. "And?"

"I have some ideas on how I can help her regain her independence. That's important for anyone, but especially for a single parent. She'll need to know that she can take care of herself and Andy, no matter what."

"So that she never again finds herself in a position like this one?"

Marlow waved that off. "Things are sometimes out of our control. That could happen to anyone."

Such a remarkable attitude for a woman as independent and accomplished as Marlow. More and more every day, she impressed him.

She did more finger tapping. "I'd like to see her better armed for success, and I'd like for her to have options. That means she needs marketable skills, and probably more savvy. I can help her with both."

How was a man to guard his heart against that type of logic? "I bet you were one hell of a sexy businessperson."

Her smile showed a load of confidence, and that was sexy, too. "Cort, would you be amenable to adjusting our agreement just a little?"

He wasn't sure what agreement she meant, not that it mattered. "Right now, here with you, I'm amenable to just about anything. But to be sure we're talking about the same thing, why don't you lay it out for me?"

Her dark eyes stared directly into his, making both promises and demands. Reaching across the table, she settled her small, warm hand over his forearm. "I know it's late, or rather early, and we've both had a full day. However, I propose we bump up our assigned Sunday date to this very minute. Well, after I have a quick shower, that is."

Pushing back his chair, Cort said, "I have one stipulation." He got to his feet and held his hand out to her. "We enjoy that shower together."

"You're a tough negotiator." Grinning, Marlow placed her hand in his. "But I'll agree to your terms."

Pixie woke disoriented, on soft sheets, with a sense of security wrapped around her. For a single moment she thought she was back in her old life, at her small apartment—before she'd ever met Dylan Heddings.

Then the baby made a grumpy sound, bringing her back to the here and now.

The second awareness hit her. She reminded herself that she was safe. More importantly, Andy was safe. Tears gathered in her eyes, but good God, she'd done too much crying already. "Just a second, sweetie." She hurried to the tiny bathroom. It was clean and fresh, without the mold she'd dealt with in the motel. The house was warm, and best of all, it was secure.

For the first time in what felt like forever, she'd slept soundly, comfortably. The meds had relieved her endless coughing and lowered her fever. This morning, she had a future she could almost imagine, instead of a nightmare she had to face.

Even Andy had slept longer than usual, but then, there hadn't been noisy people in the hallway or in the parking lot of the motel constantly startling him awake.

In half a minute, she was back to Andy. She quickly changed

his diaper and then crawled back into the soft bed, a plump pillow behind her back, so he could nurse. He was such a little glutton, and she knew she'd do anything for him. *Anything.*

Gently, she brushed her lips against the top of his head. She'd lost so much recently, most importantly her self-respect, but she had her baby, and he was a greater gift than anything she'd ever known. Compared to providing for his care and his safety, her self-respect meant nothing at all.

"Did you know people like these existed, Andy? I didn't." She drew a careful breath, trying not to cough, and concentrated on getting her emotions under control. "Now that I know, I swear to you, I'll learn to be like them. I'll get stronger and smarter, and I'll get things figured out so that you can have the best life possible." She said it aloud and sealed the promise in her heart.

Whatever it took, even if it meant more groveling, and working 24/7, she would create a better future for Andy.

Even as she made that vow, exhaustion had her yawning. It was her constant companion, weighing so heavily on her that at times, she'd felt she'd just fade away. As someone who had been healthy most of her life, she didn't know how to deal with all this illness, except to keep trying.

For Andy.

So many people suggested she rest, as if that was a simple thing, but how could she? She'd botched most of her responsibilities, but she wouldn't mess up loving her son. Until the day she died, she'd give him all the love and care she had.

When his little belly was full, she burped him and then snagged the laundry basket that was currently his bed. He wouldn't be awake too long, probably no more than an hour, two at most, so she'd wait for her shower. Putting the laundry basket in the kitchen, but keeping Andy in her arms, she fixed a bowl of cold cereal.

How novel it felt to eat a favorite cereal, not in a grungy

motel room but in this adorable little house, at a clean little table. It was so quiet, and the silence felt peaceful.

While she ate, she talked to Andy, snuggled him, blew raspberries on his little tummy, and kissed his tiny fingers and toes.

He was her precious little miracle, her reason for living. How amazing would it be if they could live forever in this house, beside a lake, near these wonderful people?

No, she had no illusions that it was possible, but it was a nice, if greedy, dream. The real plan, what she needed to focus on, was learning, surviving, and making things better for Andy. That was her goal.

And someday, somehow, she'd pay back this debt so she could like herself once again.

Outside, she heard birds coming awake with song, and when she walked to the window, she could see the most remarkable sunrise creeping over the lake.

"Nothing bad can happen here," she whispered to Andy, praying it was true. "This time, finally, I made a good decision."

Lazily, Marlow stirred awake . . . and realized her nose was against a hairy chest. Mmm, this was a delightful turn of events. When she quietly drew a deep breath, Cort's scent filled her, sending a spiral of pleasure straight through to her heart.

Her movements woke Cort, and he stretched awake, too. Of course, he knew right off that he wasn't at home in his own bed alone. She had a feeling that little would ever get past this quiet, astute Marine.

Golden brown eyes glanced down at her, and when he saw she was awake and staring back, he gave her a slow, sexy smile.

Who knew a Marine could be so dangerous just by waking up? "This is a better view than the sunrise—which I think we missed."

"There will be more sunrises." He tugged her up to rest on his chest, letting his hands settle on her behind. "Good morning, beautiful."

How something—or rather, someone—so amazingly hard could also be so comfortable, she didn't know. Not to be shallow, but Cort's body was honed to perfection . . . and it thrilled her.

Normally, getting frisky first thing in the morning would have made her worry about morning breath and tangled hair, and she would have made a quick escape to the bathroom. But not now. Not with Cort.

Her eyes were opened to a whole new perspective on life. She planned to embrace every moment, all things big and small. Astounding how her viewpoint could alter so quickly, and because of the most unusual events.

After meeting Pixie, the proverbial "other woman," and spending a sizzling night with Cort, she felt less like the scorned wife in the bizarre scenario and more like the lucky one who'd gotten away.

What if *she'd* had a baby with Dylan? What if she'd not discovered his betrayal and had gone on in blissful ignorance of his deceit?

Her gaze drifted over Cort's broad chest, his hard shoulders and defined biceps, and then lingered on his Marine tattoo. *Semper Fi.* She'd looked it up, of course, because everything about Cort fascinated her. *Semper Fidelis* was Latin for *always faithful.*

"What are you thinking?" he asked, his voice a dark, quiet rumble.

Honestly, that voice was enough to make her melt, and she wasn't a melting type of woman. Or rather, she hadn't been. Now, with him? Seemed entirely possible.

The "what ifs" were piling up, but seriously, what if she'd never met this remarkable man who'd given her such a wonderful new perspective on pleasure?

She answered honestly. "At this point, I wouldn't change a thing."

"What do you mean?"

Snuggling in and relishing the way Cort's arms came around her, she opened her recently guarded heart to him. "The cheating, the hurtful comments. Moving here." She hesitated, but then decided she might as well explain. "Meeting you."

Rather than making him withdraw, the statement had him holding her closer. "Glad to hear it."

Hmm. It wasn't exactly a reciprocal declaration, but she didn't mind. Too much. Everything was so new to her, she didn't mind relishing it alone for a while.

He nuzzled against her neck. "And how do you feel about Pixie?"

"She makes it easy for me to see how fortunate I am. I'm glad to be in Bramble, and in this position—"

"Naked against a man who wants you again?"

Happiness brought out a silly laugh. "Against *you*, Cort, and if that scares you, too bad."

"I'm a Marine, baby," he teased. "A gorgeous woman doesn't scare me."

Knowing her hair was sleep-tumbled, that she wasn't wearing a speck of makeup, and she was far from beautiful, she smiled at him, and suddenly found herself on her back with him staring intently down at her.

As if he'd read her mind—something he did often—he asked, "How can you not know how gorgeous you are?" He tunneled his fingers into her messy hair, his chest lowered to hers, giving her all his delicious weight and hardness, and he kissed her in ways that, until last night, she had forgotten were possible. When he shifted to her throat, his hot mouth dampening her skin, he murmured, "Absolutely, incredibly gorgeous."

With him, she could almost believe it.

It wasn't until an hour later, utterly satisfied, that they headed down to the dock, each of them carrying a mug of coffee. The sun had already risen, scattering golden diamonds over the glimmering surface of the lake.

They'd both brought their phones with them, just in case Pixie had a problem.

Looking off to her right, Marlow studied the tiny lake house where, hopefully, Pixie was catching up on sleep.

Instead of sitting in the chair, they sat on the end of the dock again. Marlow's toes dipped into the cold water, and she leaned against Cort's shoulder. "Life can be so hard, and then so funny, and I think if we're really paying attention, if we're absorbing it instead of just drifting through it, we can learn so much. About ourselves, and about other people."

"Philosophical," he said. "Great sex does that to me, too."

She snickered. "See? You lighten my mood so easily, not that I was in a dark mood right now. Actually, I haven't been since I came here." Again, she glanced toward the tiny house where Pixie stayed. "I hope Bramble has that same effect on her."

"I think you will be the one who affects her, but yes, the town helps."

She sipped her coffee, savoring the warmth of the morning air. "Will it be a problem for you? I mean, I'm here, and now Pixie, too."

"With Andy." He smiled. "Babies count on the census."

"Ouch. So you're basically harboring three people in a town that doesn't like newcomers."

He rested a hand on her thigh. "You're all visitors, not permanent residents."

Biting her lip, Marlow refrained from pointing out yet again that she hoped to become permanent. She'd pressured him enough already. The last thing she wanted was for him to suddenly get cold feet and stop seeing her.

She was enjoying him far, far too much for that.

No sooner did she have the thought than another followed. If things did abruptly end with Cort, she'd be okay. She'd already proven to herself that she had the fortitude and resilience to move forward when necessary.

She didn't want it to happen. She was happy here, and for now at least, Cort made her happy, too. Deliriously happy. *Orgasmically* happy, in fact, as she thought about his lovemaking.

Most of all, though, she made herself happy. There was a deep satisfaction in that realization.

She gulped another drink of coffee, set the mug aside, and stretched out on her back. The sun wasn't yet high enough to blind her, but it felt nice and warm caressing her skin, and oh, that sky was a startling, beautiful shade of blue.

Because it was a new and interesting realization, she said aloud, "I've made myself happy. Not just content but seriously happy." She turned her head to look at Cort. "Isn't that remarkable?"

He, too, set aside his coffee. "We're talking about Marlow Heddings, right? I've already seen you in action, so no, nothing surprises me where you're concerned. I think you could move mountains if you really put your mind to it."

Over and over again, he gave her the most outrageous—and wonderful—compliments. "Thank you, Cort." And since he deserved to hear it, she said, "I think you're pretty special, too."

He suddenly had that sensual look in his eyes that meant he was about to stretch out over her, but then his phone buzzed. Only the slightest disappointment showed in his expression as he lifted a hip to get his cell from his pocket. "It's Bren Crawford. He runs the boat rental." With a swipe of his thumb, he answered the call.

Marlow stayed on her back, listening to the one-sided conversation but catching the fact that Bren apparently had a leaking pipe that needed immediate attention.

Cort said, "Just a sec, Bren," and muffled the phone against his jean-covered thigh. "Do you mind? I know this was sup-posed to be our day, but it shouldn't take me too long."

"I don't mind at all. Actually, I like that you'll go to his rescue."

Skeptical, Cort said, "It's not a rescue, just a helping hand."

"And you're not a hero? Pfft. There's a whole town here that would disagree." Giving up her comfortable position on the dock, she came up on her elbows and said, "Seriously, I like that you care about your neighbors and aren't afraid to pitch in when needed. Don't worry about me. I'll use the time to visit with Pixie. You can call when you're done, and we'll figure things out from there."

Wearing a silly, slightly bemused smile, he brought the phone back to his ear and promised Bren he'd be there quickly.

Marlow went with him up to the house.

At the door, he paused to drape his arms around her. "After I repair Bren's pipes, I'll need to head to my place for a shower, shave, and change of clothes." Nudging her closer, he asked, "Any chance I can convince you to join me for that?"

"Hmm, if this was a business deal, I'd insist that you make it worth my while."

He teased, "Well, I could show you my house."

She rested her hands on his chest. "And?"

Pretending to think about it, he said, "I'll take you to lunch after."

Marlow slid her hands to his neck and tugged his head down. "And in between that?"

"We should have enough privacy to do anything you want."

"Deal." Knowing he needed to go, she patted his shoulder and stepped back with a warning. "What I want might take a while, so don't count on an early lunch."

"I do love the way you negotiate."

He gave her a firm but fast kiss, then jogged to his truck and quickly backed out of her driveway.

Ridiculous, but she already missed him.

Going back to the bedroom, Marlow smiled at the rumpled sheets and unmade bed. She, Marlow Heddings, had spent a wild night with a sexy hero, and she felt triumphant because of it, as if she'd conquered a mystery of life.

How to get over wounded feelings and lingering hurt in one mind-blowing encounter. Or maybe, *How to downsize your life and upsize your pleasure.*

In reality, she knew dealing with the turmoil of life wasn't that easy and couldn't be summarized in a catchy title. There were many puzzle pieces she was still fitting together to form an entire image, but she had the border in place, and she had a feel for where things were going.

Cort was definitely an unexpected bonus, but she was determined to finish the puzzle with or without him. And . . . her analogy was now stretching so thin, she almost laughed.

Reminding herself that this was her time, she briskly made the bed, pausing only once to press Cort's pillow to her nose so she could breathe in his intoxicating scent one more time. It'd be nice if that scent lingered. She wouldn't mind sleeping with it every night.

After her shower, a quick breakfast, and a minimum of prep, she decided it was late enough to call on Pixie. Rather than drive, she put on her tennis shoes and a floppy brimmed hat to shade her face and crossed the property on foot. The houses were spaced out enough that it was a nice walk.

When she reached the small lake house, she looked beyond it to Cort's home. Bigger, with more land, it sat on a rise and, like the cottage and lake house, it would have phenomenal views of the water.

She went down a narrow gravel drive to the lake house. Before she could knock, the door opened and Pixie stood there, looking very uncertain in her bare feet, an oversized T-shirt, and pull-on shorts.

Her hair was now neatly brushed, and her eyes were still

puffy from crying but currently clear of tears. She appeared better rested but remained far too frail.

Marlow smiled to put her at ease. "Good morning, Pixie."

"Morning." She shifted from one foot to the other. "Andy's sleeping. I saw you coming and thought you might knock."

"And that would wake him?"

"I'm not sure. This is a new place and all, and I only got him to sleep about ten minutes ago."

Still smiling, Marlow asked, "May I come in?"

"Oh, yeah. Sure. I'm sorry." Pixie stepped aside, watching her warily. "Um, is everything okay?"

"With me, yes. How about you? Were you able to sleep last night?"

"Oh, my gosh, *yes*," she said with enthusiasm. "I slept so well. Andy only woke up once, and after I fed and changed him, we both conked right back out again." Still standing just inside the door, Pixie started thanking her. "I can't tell you how much I appreciate this. I know Mr. Easton let me stay here because of you, and it's so kind of you—"

"Let's sit down for a few minutes, okay?" Somehow, she had to get Pixie to stop groveling. Being appreciative was fine, but Marlow wanted her to understand her own worth, too.

Face going hot, Pixie nodded. "Sure. Um . . ." She looked around. "Where do you want to sit?"

Marlow glanced around, too, then made a decision. "The kitchen is always a nice gathering place. Let's sit there."

"Okay." Pixie hurried in that direction, her bare feet making little sound on the cold floor.

Marlow was pleased to see that she appeared steadier today. Clearly some food and rest had done her a world of good. She still looked worn, and with the shadows under her eyes there was no doubt she was under the weather. One night's sleep wouldn't be enough for her to recuperate, and that's why Marlow was here.

The kitchen was small, but what caught Marlow's attention was the roll of toilet paper on the counter. Pixie followed her gaze and a three-alarm fire lit up her fair skin, making her look feverish again.

She snatched the roll off the counter and put it behind her back. "I don't have any tissues, and I was using it to cover my cough and—"

"I understand." Marlow added, "We'll be sure to get some tissues today. Until then, it's nice to have that on hand." She pulled out one of two chairs at a small table. "Let's sit."

Still mortified, Pixie sank into her seat.

Rather than keep her in suspense, Marlow said, "I'm all in on helping you. I haven't changed my mind, so relax."

Pixie started to speak, no doubt to express more gratitude, but Marlow didn't give her the chance. She wanted the young woman to understand what would be expected of her, the scope of Marlow's intrusion into Pixie's life. Because she absolutely planned to intrude. In a big way.

There was no better time to explain than right now.

CHAPTER 8

"Once you're well," Marlow stated, "there won't be much downtime. My ultimate goal is to see you on a better track, able to care for yourself and Andy."

"I want that, too," she said. "*So much.*"

"Perfect. Then I hope to help you learn a trade, something marketable that you can use to secure a decent job with a future. That might require education, which would involve night classes."

"I'll do anything," she promised.

Pixie made it so easy, Marlow was starting to feel like an ogre. "You say that now, but keep in mind that your days will be spent caring for the baby and working."

Eyes flaring with a look of hope, Pixie whispered, "Working where?"

"For me, actually." Marlow had given it plenty of thought and decided on a course of action. "I'm ready to move forward with my plans of starting a small business. I had been researching possible locations just outside Bramble, within a drivable distance. I'll set you up with a laptop, show you what I'm interested in, and you can continue the search until I find the perfect place."

"I . . ." Breathless, Pixie nodded quickly in agreement. "Okay, sure. I can do that."

"Then we'll need to find the right merchandiser, someone who supplies quality material that we can personalize in some way to make it unique. Clothing, home goods, possibly jewelry. We can sort that out when the time comes. I'm not entirely sure yet what I want."

Her blue eyes still huge, Pixie nodded.

"None of this will be easy."

"I don't mind," she rushed to say. "I swear, I'll work around the clock. I'll do anything, I'll—"

"You will stop demeaning yourself. That's rule number one. You're here now, with me." That likely had more significance than Pixie realized, because Marlow had always been a champion of the underdog, and she especially loved causes that helped women in need gain a better foothold in the world. "No employee of mine will grovel. I want you strong, Pixie, even proud. Not apologetic."

Tears filled Pixie's eyes, and she gulped. "Sorry." She dashed at her eyes with annoyance. "I swear I won't keep doing that."

Softening, Marlow covered one of her hands with her own. "I understand, Pixie. I really do. You've been afraid, with nowhere to turn."

She whispered, "Afraid mostly for Andy. I love him more than I knew was possible. He's so tiny, so dependent on me. He's all I have, and I'm all he has, but I've made such a mess of things, most of the time I don't know what I'm doing."

Heart breaking, Marlow cut her off. "You're an attentive and loving mother, and now you're also my assistant and under my care. Let me stress that I want you well. Your health is important so that you can be the best mother possible."

"I will be, I swear it."

"Good." Brisk now, Marlow removed her hand and got back to expectations. "We'll see the doctor recommended by the clinic, and then we'll follow a plan to get you back to perfect health. Using the doctor's guidelines, we'll introduce a schedule of work that doesn't interfere with caring for Andy. There will be no dating, no wasting money on frivolous things."

"I wouldn't, I swear!"

"No fast food. No cute new bathing suits."

Pixie stiffened, but not because she was insulted by the strict warnings. "I couldn't wear a bathing suit, anyway. The pregnancy and the C-section . . ." She settled her hands over her stomach. "I'm a mess. Pretty sure my body will never be the same."

"Does that bother you?"

Showing a little spunk, Pixie snorted. "When I would never let another man touch me anyway? Not to insult Dylan—"

"Oh, please. Insult away. Just because he's gone doesn't mean he wasn't a selfish, obnoxious jerk."

That epithet earned a fleeting smile from Pixie. "I wasn't sure how you'd feel about him."

"Well, I hope he was better to you than he was to me, but it hardly matters now. He's gone, and neither of us will miss him." On the off chance that Pixie might correct her, Marlow immediately continued. "I understand that having a baby affects everybody differently, but I'm sure you'll regain your figure. You're young, and the baby will keep you active."

"Believe me, my body is the least of my worries." She plucked at her T-shirt. "With my hips wider, my stomach not so flat, none of my pre-pregnancy clothes fit me anymore. My car was already full, so I left a lot of stuff behind."

"I did the same thing!" Amazing that they had something so basic in common. "I wanted an all-new look, though. Less business, more casual."

Pixie grinned crookedly. "You always look good. Like someone in a magazine."

Funny how the compliment warmed her face. "Thank you."

"I was just going for comfort. I couldn't stand trying to get into jeans. They hurt. And with nursing, my boobs are bigger. I was spilling out of my smaller shirts." Her eyes flared. "I probably shouldn't have said that?"

"Pfft." Marlow waved off her concern. She was enjoying the camaraderie. "If two women can't talk about boobs, who can?"

Lips lifting into a smile, Pixie said, "I honestly didn't expect much when I came here. I was just hopeful you'd help for a day or two, and maybe give me some good advice. Instead, you're being so nice." She bit her lip. "I know I don't have the right to ask for anything."

Marlow went still. Pixie looked so uncertain that she braced herself. Had she misread Pixie's sincerity? Would the big requests begin now? If she wanted money, how much? Coolly, Marlow met her gaze. "Is there something you want?"

"For you to please believe me." She leaned forward, her expression earnest. "I didn't know Dylan was married. I had no reason to think he was. He asked me out, so I just assumed he was single and never questioned it. I accept the blame for being naive, for screwing up my life and getting myself into this mess, but I swear I would never have gotten involved with a married guy."

Bemused, Marlow just stared at her. *This* was what Pixie wanted? Merely for someone to believe her, to trust her?

Compassion made her heart squeeze. "I believe you."

Pixie searched her face. "You do? I mean, really?"

"Don't forget. I knew Dylan, too. Clearly not as well as I thought I did, but I know it wasn't beyond him to deceive you. After all, he deceived me as well."

"I . . . Thank you." Pixie leaned back in the seat. "You can't know how much that means to me."

Brisk again, Marlow said, "I'm glad Cort got your phone service back on. Let's make sure you have a calendar on it, and then we'll get an appointment set up with the doctor." She warned, "I'll want to go with you, because it's important for me to know the plan. It's an intrusion—"

"I'd be glad of the company if you're sure you don't mind." Pixie couldn't quite meet her gaze now as she stammered, "This has all been so scary. For a little while I thought I'd lose Andy, or that I'd die, and then who would care for him? Understanding all the medical terms and the treatment, especially when I felt like crud, was pretty overwhelming."

Marlow's heart felt pummeled. "I can only imagine. You're not alone anymore, though."

With shaking hands, Pixie covered her face and her shoulders sank, but only seconds later she straightened again and said with strong conviction, "Thank you. For everything. I promise you won't regret it."

Marlow nodded. At this point, she was *glad* Pixie had come to her. What a strange turn of events. "We'll drive your car so I can fill the tank, but understand, Pixie. I don't want you going anywhere without telling me. I'm not going to invest in you just so you can take off again."

"I wouldn't. I barely found my way here. I don't know where the nearest grocery store is, and even if I did, I don't have enough money to spend it there."

"You'll be making wages soon enough, so that will change." One more thing to tackle. "I don't know Cort's plans, but you won't be able to stay here indefinitely. For now, though, I want you to stay put."

"Even if I wanted to leave, I don't have anywhere else to go."

That was the crux of the problem. Pixie needed options, and Marlow planned to see that she got them.

"Somehow," Pixie said, "I'll find a way to repay you and Mr. Easton." She glanced around the lake house in wonder. "This place is so beautiful. I can't believe he let me stay here last night."

Marlow, too, glanced around. The lake house was minuscule, with a combo kitchen/sitting area that had only enough room for a two-seater table. However, it had a lot of windows with lovely views, and it sat much closer to the lake than her cottage. The best feature, in Marlow's opinion, was a small but tidy covered deck off the back where she could put a chair—maybe a rocking chair, actually—so Pixie could enjoy the evening or morning air.

Unlike the guest cottage where Marlow was staying, the lake house lacked fine finishes and upgrades. The kitchen was a single row of basic oak cabinets over a sink and stove with a narrow pantry squeezed in next to an apartment-sized refrigerator. No dishwasher. There were tile countertops, and a linoleum floor meant to look like wood. The space flowed into the sitting area, where a single love seat presided over one chair, one side table, and a narrow console that held a small, older TV.

She had to remind herself that to Pixie, this was a safe haven, and more security than she had known for months.

To shake off her sudden worry, Marlow addressed the next topic. "I did some research before visiting. From what I've found, it's important to get the baby on a schedule—"

"I won't let him cry," Pixie objected, for once being firm. "It almost kills me to hear him upset."

That pleased Marlow. "Of course not. I wouldn't want you to."

Pixie went limp in relief. "Oh. Well . . . that's good."

"I only meant that it's a good idea to try to start as you hope to continue with a routine bedtime and, when possible, rising at the same time each day."

"I usually nurse him first, play with him for a while, then when he sleeps again, I shower and dress."

Feeling like a mother hen, Marlow asked, "And did you eat this morning? It's important to have food with your antibiotic."

"I had some cereal. I was going to see what else there is, try to get organized a little while Andy was napping this morning. Mr. Easton brought in stuff, but I'm not even sure what. Yesterday was . . . a busy day."

With Andy asleep, she could have been going through everything now, and instead Marlow was visiting. "I could help you if you don't mind the company." And then she could see what else Pixie might need—like tissues.

"You've done so much already."

"Would you rather I leave so you can have a little peace and quiet?"

"No! I didn't mean that." She looked around again. "I feel like this is more your place than mine, since you and Mr. Easton are together."

Hearing her say it pleased Marlow but also made her wonder if other people in the town thought they were together. Not that she'd mind, but would Cort? "It's his and his alone. He lives in the bigger house next to you and owns both this property and the one I'm staying at."

"Three houses," Pixie breathed. "Can you imagine?"

Yes, she could. The home she'd shared with Dylan was extravagant, and his parents had multiple homes in multiple locations. She'd long ago gotten used to their wealth. Thinking of his parents brought her to her next topic. "Now, one more thing."

Wary, Pixie said, "Okay."

"Do you plan to tell Dylan's parents that they have a grandson?"

To Marlow's surprise, Pixie gave the question some thought before saying, "To be honest, I haven't decided. Dylan warned me against it. He said his parents wouldn't recognize my baby as a grandchild, only a mistake, and that they could be ruthless." Her mouth screwed to the side. "He was still alive at the time, and I hadn't yet gotten sick, so I didn't think too much of it. Guess I assumed he'd still be around, and he could decide what his parents should know or not know. I was so mad at the time, I didn't really listen to him. Now, though, it worries me. What did he mean by ruthless? What could they do? They wouldn't hurt Andy, right?"

Marlow suspected Dylan had been covering his own behind more than trying to protect Pixie or Andy. If his parents had found out about the baby, they'd have been disappointed in him. Would he have suffered repercussions? Unlikely, given the way they'd pampered him, but they probably would have lectured him and Dylan had hated that, too.

The problem, Marlow decided, was that Dylan hadn't been wrong. "Knowing them, I don't disagree that they could be trouble. It's not that they'd hurt Andy." At least, she didn't think so, but she understood that there were all types of hurt. "They might try to make your life more difficult—like black-balling you, which they've already done."

"Would they try to take Andy from me?"

Seeing the horror in Pixie's eyes, Marlow decided to deflect. "I don't think we should put too much stock in anything Dylan said."

Back to being wary, Pixie whispered, "So you plan to tell them?"

"No. It will be your decision, but I'd like you to consider it. We can talk about it if you'd like, go over the pros and cons—what is easiest for you versus what is morally right." Again, she covered Pixie's hand. "Who can know for certain how they'd react at seeing such a beautiful baby?"

Pixie's expression brightened. "He really is beautiful, isn't he?"

Marlow grinned. "I imagine all mothers think the same of their children, but I happen to agree. He's adorable." There was one important point she needed to stress. "If you do decide to tell them, you won't have to face them alone."

Pixie covered her mouth. "That means so much to me."

Smiling, Marlow moved on. "Nothing has to be decided

right now. I'd like you to have at least a week of rest before we tackle any weighty decisions. You and Andy both could use a little peace and quiet. Now, would you mind if I see the rest of the house?"

Again blushing, Pixie shot to her feet. "Of course not." She looked around and frowned. "I didn't even think to offer you a drink. I'm hopeless."

Hooking her arm through Pixie's made Marlow feel large in comparison. Where she was of average height and on the sturdy side, Pixie was petite and currently so thin that she seemed delicate. She could have passed for a sixteen-year-old. "We'll work on that, too, if you want, as long as you don't feel pressured."

"I'd love to learn . . . well, anything you want to teach me, really."

Together they went through the house. Marlow tried to see it through Pixie's eyes, and that made her absolutely love it—just as Pixie did. It was tiny, no way around that, but the small size just meant it'd be easier to keep tidy. Although it lacked upscale finishes, it had a lot of charm. Like the wood-burning stove in the sitting area adjacent to the kitchen. And the curved shower rod in the minuscule bathroom.

Personally, she enjoyed a long soak in a deep tub, but the lake house didn't have a tub, and Pixie said she didn't have time for long soaks anyway.

The bathroom consisted of a pedestal sink right next to a toilet and a narrow, tiled shower. At least there was a linen closet to store towels and toiletries.

The bedroom was only large enough for a single full-size bed, one nightstand, and a narrow dresser.

There was no crib or bassinet. Instead, Andy was in a sturdy laundry basket on the floor. Marlow blinked several times at seeing him. He looked cozy enough with a quilted pad under him, his little rosebud mouth pursed and his pudgy fists resting beside his face.

As she watched him, he made a few soft sounds in his sleep. Today's outfit was a little one-piece footed garment similar to what he'd had on yesterday. Pixie knelt down to smooth the back of one finger over his cheek. Pride glowed on her face as she looked up with a smile.

This time, it was Marlow's eyes that smarted with tears, and she knew why. Right there before her was the evidence of Pixie's love, and seeing the depth of her caring made it that much harder to acknowledge what the girl had been through. Marlow smiled back, then offered a hand to help Pixie stand again.

Silently, they left the room.

Pixie didn't wait for her to ask before she explained. "I couldn't fit a crib in my car. With the car seat and a few of our belongings, the laundry basket was the best I could do. He's small enough right now that he doesn't mind, but once he gets the hang of rolling over, it'll be another story. I thought when that happens, we might both sleep on the floor or something. That'd be safer for him, especially if I put some pillows around him so he can't roll too far."

"Yes, that could work." But in her head, Marlow was making a list of everything this incredible young mother might need for the immediate future. It was a long list, and she didn't want to overwhelm Pixie with everything at once.

She'd start small and just gradually, subtly, add things. Perhaps she could claim it as partial payment once Pixie began to work for her. And thinking of that, she led Pixie back to the kitchen so they could set a doctor's appointment.

Unfortunately, she couldn't be seen for a week, but the Monday appointment was early enough that it wouldn't interfere with Marlow's schedule at the tavern.

They'd just finished adding the date and time to both their phones when a knock sounded on the front door.

Immediately worried, Pixie locked eyes with Marlow. "Who could it be?" she whispered.

Marlow gave a negligent shrug. "Possibly Cort?" Although he hadn't yet called as they'd agreed. Before either of them could stand, Andy cried out to let them know he was awake. It was almost amusing how quickly Pixie shot out of her seat. As she rushed past, Marlow teasingly said, "Fine, you get the baby and I'll get the door."

"Thank you," Pixie called back without stopping.

Definitely an attentive mother. Overall, Marlow liked her. Pixie was unpretentious, earnest, and determined. She was also a survivor, but then, she'd had no choice in that.

The cries stopped just as Marlow reached the door.

She pulled it open and found Gloria and Bobbi standing there with smiles, baked goods, and a load of curiosity.

Cort was a soaked mess by the time he got Bren's plumbing under control. The pipe had been spraying water and Bren, who was eighty and cranky, couldn't hear, and didn't have great eyesight, hadn't been able to do a thing about it.

The valve was in his basement, the floor quickly flooding, and it would have been dangerous for Bren to attempt the repair on his own.

At least the seat of his jeans was dry, Cort thought, as he slid into his truck to head home. He started the engine, pulled out of Bren's driveway, and then gave Marlow a call.

When she answered with a perky, "Hey, Cort," he heard laughter in the background.

He was curious but didn't ask. Yet. "Sorry that took so long. I had to run into town to get a few parts before I could fix the pipe."

"It's okay now?"

"Yeah. Basement was a mess. I stayed to clear out as much of the water as I could. Luckily, it's just concrete, not a finished space."

"You must be beat."

He was something all right, but tired wasn't in the equation. He wanted to see Marlow, to continue what they'd started last night, but it was now past lunchtime and she had to be hungry. "I'm fine. How about you?"

"I'm with Pixie. Gloria and Bobbi came by, and of course they love the baby." She lowered her voice. "Want to stop by and get me, then I can politely suggest that Pixie take another nap?"

"Politely, huh?" If she thought it'd be that easy, she didn't yet know Gloria and Bobbi well enough. "Yeah, I'll be there in fifteen minutes."

She disconnected with the promise that she'd be waiting.

He knew the right thing to do was to get a shower, clean clothes, and take Marlow out to eat. They'd have the rest of the day together. Not sure he could do that, though. The entire time he'd been dealing with rusty pipes and broken fittings, she'd been on his mind.

He wasn't a man to obsess over a woman—never had before, didn't want to start now—so he'd fought the inclination to dwell on her. It happened anyway. By the time he had Bren squared away, he'd readjusted his attitude.

As a Marine, he didn't indulge weaknesses. He used them to his advantage. Marlow didn't make him feel weak, though. Just the opposite. She had a way of pointing out the obvious pleasures that, far too often, people took for granted.

He smiled as he thought about the fireflies.

By the time he pulled up to the lake house, he was more than ready to grab Marlow for some private time. She met him at the door with a kiss, then asked him in.

Gesturing to his soggy jeans and boots, he said, "Better not. It was a dirty job."

"Give me just one minute, then." Leaving the door open, she went back into the kitchen and said, "Bobbie and Gloria, thank you both so much for stopping by. I need to get going now, but I want to make sure Pixie is settled first. I'm sure you understand."

Grinning, Cort propped a shoulder on the door frame and waited for Marlow to realize that subtle hints wouldn't work with the siblings.

Bobbie said, "We can get her settled."

To which Gloria said, "Look at her, poor thing. She's all faded out."

"We could stay and take care of the baby while she naps."

Pixie piped in with, "Oh, no, that's okay. I need to nurse him first anyway."

Gloria said, "Go on ahead. Nothing we haven't seen before. We won't bother you."

Silence. He could imagine the wheels turning in Marlow's head as she tried to find the right enticement to get the sisters moving.

To help, he called in, "Hello, Gloria, Bobbi."

Immediately, they came to the door to greet him. "Cort! What are you doing here?"

Bobbi swatted at her sister. "Clearly, he's here for Marlow. You've seen the two of them together."

"I wanted to hear him say it, thank you very much."

No problem. Lazily, he stated, "I'm here for Marlow." There, that'd give them something to focus on other than Pixie and Andy.

The sisters elbowed each other.

"Come on, you two. Marlow is watching over Pixie, and she needs us out of the way."

Bobbi stepped out first. "What happened to you? Take a dip in the lake?"

Not to be left out, Gloria followed. "His shirt is dry." She leaned around Cort. "So is his backside."

He shifted to deny Gloria her view. "Behave." Then he thought to ask, "Why are you two here?"

"We heard all about it," Bobbi rushed to explain. "How this girl claimed to be Marlow's sister, and then Herman said she didn't have a sister, and she—"

"—had a *baby* with her. We found that out from Jenny, who was at the clinic when you all came in. You know Bobbi used to be a nurse, and I was a preschool teacher, so—"

"—we wanted to see for ourselves what was what."

A man could get whiplash trying to keep up with the sisters. No wonder Wade, their brother, bickered with them so often. "And now you saw. Satisfied?"

Gloria leaned in close. "She doesn't have a crib for that little angel, but I'm sure someone around here must have one they're ready to part with."

Nodding, Bobbi said, "I'm glad she'll be under a doctor's care soon. Marlow made sure she got an appointment a week from Monday. Until then, I'm going to keep an eye on Pixie."

Cort managed to maintain his enigmatic expression instead of showing his alarm. "How so?"

"We brought her a casserole and a dish of brownies. Good Lord, you'd have thought we gave her the moon. Poor girl got weepy about it."

"I remember your mother was like that," Gloria said.

Bobbi hushed her. "We loved your ma. Everyone did."

In a whisper, Gloria confided, "Pixie's emotional from being so ill, that's what Marlow said. Personally, I think it's new motherhood. I saw it often. It gets the hormones in a dither and sends women on a wild ride."

"I'm glad she's here now."

Yeah, Cort was glad about that, too.

"She enjoyed the brownies so much, we told her we'd bring her another dessert in a few days."

"Marlow wants us to text first, in case the baby is sleeping."

Marlow had certainly taken control of things, at least as much as she could. Just then she appeared in the doorway, her arms loaded with two now-empty dishes and the sisters' purses. Awkwardly, she tried to get the door closed.

Taking a few big steps, Cort reached her and relieved her of the dishes.

"Thank you." She pulled the door closed behind her. "Here you go, Gloria and Bobbi. I got these for you, since Pixie was ready to nod off and she still needs to feed Andy. She asked me to thank you both."

"You washed our casserole dishes," Gloria said, bemused.

"I put the rest of the food in microwave-safe dishes so Pixie would be able to heat it up when she's hungry."

Bobbi frowned. "But now we can't come back for them."

Conniving, that's what they were, Cort thought. But also considerate. "I'm sure you'll come up with another excuse to visit."

"We promised her more desserts," Gloria reminded her sister.

"But," Marlow said, smiling, "you're going to text first, right? Pixie is still trying to get settled in."

Both sisters turned their laser-like focus on him. "Settled in?"

"For a bit," he hedged, because no one in Bramble wanted anyone staying on. Four hundred and one was still one too many.

"We'll text," Gloria promised, her gaze lingering on Cort as if she thought he might suddenly drop a clue as to what was really going on.

He kept his expression inscrutable.

Bobbi said, "Hmm. Well, I hope she'll be around long enough to get the rest she needs."

"That's the plan," Marlow said. "A summer of fireflies and sunrises and friendship. Bramble is the perfect place for a vacation."

She was convincing enough that the sisters immediately agreed. They also announced a campaign to "assist" her in any way possible. Cort knew what that meant.

Did Marlow?

Doubtful. If she did, she wouldn't still be smiling as the sisters drove away.

"Come on." With his hand at the small of her back, he started her toward his truck. "My feet are drowning in my boots."

She laughed. "Sounds like it was quite the mess. Thank goodness Bren had you to rescue him."

"Not a rescue," he pointed out again, then relented. "But yeah, if that leak had gone on much longer, it could've caused real problems." He held her door for her while she hopped up into her seat. It still amused him, the difficulty she had getting into his truck. Her car, a silver Lexus SUV, wasn't small by anyone's standards, but it was closer to the ground.

As he got behind the wheel, she asked, "Are you hungry?"

"Getting there. You?"

"I had a little of the casserole the sisters brought to Pixie, but since she seemed to like it so much, I wanted to make sure I left her plenty. I don't think she's had any home-cooked food for a while."

"Maybe when we fix meals, we could put together a plate for her."

Marlow's smile brightened another few watts. "So we'll be having some meals together, will we?"

"I hope so." He pulled into his own driveway, turned off the truck, then looked at her. "Not right now, though." Catching the back of her neck, he drew her close to take her mouth in a firm kiss. "Right now, I want a shower—and then I want you."

"Exactly what I was thinking." She hopped out of the truck before he could come around to her side.

Cort grinned as she rushed to the house, which made him take longer than usual strides to keep up. He unlocked the front door for her, but as she peeked in, he sat on the porch chair and unlaced his sodden boots, setting them aside with his dripping socks.

"Jeans are wet, too," she pointed out, looking at him expectantly as if she thought he might strip those off outside as well.

Taking her hand, he drew her inside, locked the door behind them, and then headed to the laundry. Along the way, he labeled the rooms they passed. "Living room, dining, kitchen." He stepped into the laundry and, with her fascinated gaze on him, stripped off his shirt and then his jeans, dropping both into the washtub.

She sauntered forward with a smile, reached out, and slid her open palm over the back of his boxers. "Well darn, these are dry."

Grinning at her antics, he stripped them off, too. "Want to shower with me?"

"Will it be like the shower we took in the cottage?"

"Times two."

Her eyes widened. "Then yes, I want to shower with you." She looked around. "Which way do we go?"

"We could go up the stairs to my room, but the bathroom down here is bigger."

"Will we remain down here?"

"If you don't mind making use of the kitchen table. Otherwise, my bed is upstairs."

"Small bathroom it is." She led the way, tugging him along in her haste. "At my age, tabletops don't sound fun, only uncomfortable."

He could, and would, prove her wrong on that—someday. Not just a table, but the wall, couch . . . Hell, the floor would do. He had a feeling that with Marlow, any place would be perfect for him, and since he cared, he'd make sure it was perfect for her, too.

But for now, this thing with her was still new, and she was coming off a rollercoaster of disappointments, big decisions, and determination. Her ex had done a number on her, whether she acknowledged it yet or not.

So he'd show consideration and let her call the shots. He could be generous because regardless of the where or how, he was still with Marlow. And that made it more than worthwhile.

CHAPTER 9

By the end of the week, it seemed everyone knew her business. Marlow knew Cort hadn't told anyone, and she doubted Pixie had either. But the good people of Bramble had spread the news among their ranks.

Once the sisters had met Pixie, they'd started putting things together. Herman had already corrected the assumption that Pixie was her sister, not that Marlow would have let that go on anyway. As she'd told Pixie, she wasn't ashamed of her, and she didn't want Pixie to be ashamed either.

People made mistakes. Good people did their best to correct them.

That was exactly what Pixie was doing, and Marlow wanted only to applaud her, not bring more strife to her life. Her shifts at the tavern sure were interesting, though.

"So have you and Pixie known each other long?" Butler asked.

Hard to believe this unimposing man was the mayor, but in Bramble, anything was possible. Butler wasn't tall, but he did appear fit for a sixty-something guy with thick gray hair and an impressive mustache. "Actually no," Marlow said, while picking up her empties on a sweep through the tavern. "But I knew of her, of course." There, let him stew on that.

She went on to the next table, where Joann—the woman who ran the dairy bar—was enjoying burgers and fries with a friend.

"Hey, Marlow, I heard Pixie was a distant relative?"

"No." Marlow smiled. "Can I get you anything else?" When they declined, she left the bill and said, "No hurry on that."

At the last table, Robin, owner of The Docker restaurant, smiled at her. "Getting the third degree, huh?"

"Seems so." She picked up Robin's empty plate to add to her tray.

"They know already. They're just hoping you'll confirm it."

Showing her annoyance, Marlow cocked a brow. "They know *what* exactly?"

"That Pixie needs help, and you're wonderful."

Damn it, now how could she be snide over a comment like that? Obviously, she couldn't. "I do my best."

Leaving the room in a hurry, she deliberately avoided eye contact with anyone else. It had been the same every night since the sisters had gotten involved. Poor Pixie wasn't sure what to do. Bobbi and Gloria had brought her the pieces of a beautiful white wooden crib that they said they'd gotten from a friend.

Gloria had already scrubbed them from top to bottom, and Cort stopped by to put it together.

Seeing it, Pixie cried again, but she'd been laughing, too, her face rosy with excitement. She'd known so little kindness that every considerate gesture thrilled her.

All the crib needed was a mattress, so the next morning Marlow drove to town and bought the mattress along with several sheets and a few more baby blankets.

From one end or the other, Andy soiled a lot of blankets. Poor Pixie did at least one load of laundry a day. It was a good thing the tiny lake house had a stacked washer and dryer tucked into the utility closet.

Marlow's gifts had leveled Pixie, who'd stroked each blanket as if they were made of cashmere or silk instead of cotton. She'd then claimed to be ready to work.

Marlow understood her a little better each day. Pixie felt indebted, and she wanted to begin repaying that debt as quickly as possible. "Soon," Marlow had promised her, only because she knew she'd have felt the same way. No one liked feeling beholden to someone else. It robbed a person of their power.

After the gift of the crib, the troop of visitors to meet Pixie seemed endless. It frustrated Marlow, who wanted Pixie to rest, but it was also nice that everyone was taking an interest in her.

One person brought her a plant. Others, inspired by Gloria and Bobbi, brought her food. The pastor of the local church brought a stroller.

And now they all wanted a firsthand accounting of things.

In the tavern's kitchen, Marlow set aside the heavy tray, then dropped back against the wall, unsure whether she should laugh or growl.

Herman stuck his head around the wall. "Hey, everything okay?"

"Depends on your perspective."

He cautiously stepped in. "If it's all that gossip about Pixie, well, was bound to happen."

"You think so?"

He snorted. "After your in-laws were here causing a scene? You're a focal point of interest, you know."

It was almost amusing, given that she'd come here to escape her old life. "Where I lived before this, no one really cared about anyone else's day-to-day life. We were all too busy."

Inspired by that tidbit, Herman asked, "You lived in the city?"

"My home was actually in an exclusive suburb very near

Chicago, where I worked." As if absorbed, Herman leaned against the counter opposite her and gave her his full attention.

She'd never discussed her past with him, but now, as she fought the inevitable, she couldn't recall why it mattered. Privacy be damned. These people weren't really nosy, but they . . . cared. About everyone and everything.

How unique was that?

Here, apparently it wasn't unique at all.

Just as she wanted to get pertinent information from Pixie because it would better enable her to lend assistance, these wonderful people also wanted to help.

She hoped to become a permanent fixture in Bramble, so maybe it was time she opened up a little. "Would you mind if I took a two-minute break?"

"Nah," he said. "You look bushed. Grab a drink or something." He started to walk away, but Marlow touched his arm, staying him. Herman had always been kind to her, and better still, he appreciated her. Really appreciated her. He recognized her work ethic and applauded her when she did her best.

That was better than a raise any day.

"Do you have a few minutes, too?"

His eyes went wide, but he nodded. "Sure, yeah, if that's what you want."

"I was just going to tell you a little about myself, and then if you'd like, you can share so everyone doesn't feel the need to get the scoop from me."

His brows came down. "I can tell them to back off if you want. Might not work with all of them, but some of them will listen."

A reluctant grin tugged at her mouth. Herman spoke the truth. "No, it's fine. I'll just summarize and then get back to work."

He settled against the counter again.

In the briefest terms possible, showing the least amount of emotion, Marlow ran through her reasons for deciding to move to Bramble. *Dylan cheated, I was going to divorce him, but he died instead, his parents needed me, I stayed to help them, then knew I needed to move on . . . and I ended up here.* As she spoke, the look on Herman's face was almost comical. *He* wasn't lacking emotion. Surprise, then outrage, replaced by sympathy, then anger again: the poor guy went through the gamut of reactions.

Marlow liked how it all just came together, as if she'd recited the plot to a movie that she'd found only marginally engaging. Saying it aloud like that as mere details rather than pivotal points in her life, showed her how far she'd come, and how quickly.

To wrap up the story, she explained about Pixie, again omitting details that were too personal, but really, there'd be no hiding the truth, not if she stayed here—and she hadn't changed her mind about that.

"That poor child," Herman said, his brows gathering with concern.

"She's a mother, Herman, not a child." That reminder made Marlow a hypocrite, because she often referred to Pixie as a girl, not a woman.

"To someone my age, she's a child." Still scowling, he ran his fingers through his hair, glanced at Marlow, and suddenly smiled. "Good thing she came to you, right?"

Taken aback by that sentiment, Marlow asked, "You think so?"

"Don't be modest. Doesn't suit you." He gave her shoulder a fatherly pat. "You impressed me from day one. Knew right away you were special. This proves it."

In a whisper, she admitted, "I *feel* special." Was she special enough to get to stay in Bramble? "Who knew I'd ever be in this position, as a waitress at a charming tavern, in a small town named Bramble?" *With my deceased husband's girlfriend and infant needing my help.* "Not me. A year ago, I would have considered it farfetched. But now I'm enjoying every minute." She liked this adaptable version of herself a whole lot more than the business shark version. Or the obtuse wife version.

Or the hollow, heartbroken, wounded version.

"It's nice that everyone is taking an interest in Pixie, but—" Herman shared another inelegant but accurate snort.

"She's been ill, Herman," Marlow continued quietly. "She needs to rest, so do you think, now that I've told the story—or rather, you'll do it for me—we could get everyone to limit their visits to certain days and times so Pixie isn't fatigued?"

Like the perfect co-conspirator, Herman said, "You figure out the best schedule, and I'll make sure everyone knows. Anyone who oversteps will get a stern reminder from me."

"You're the best, Herman." Her hug took him by surprise, but sooner or later he'd get used to her embraces—*if* she got to stick around.

A week later, as Pixie put Andy down for bed, she walked through the quiet lake house with a smile. She'd had a productive day with the laundry all done and put away, the floors cleaned, every surface dusted, and her dinner dishes washed and in the rack. She could dry them and put them in the cabinet—or she could take a few minutes just to enjoy the beautiful location where she'd landed.

Amazement took her breath away every time she thought of her good fortune. In the matter of a few days, she'd gone from destitute and utterly alone to settled in a beautiful house on a scenic lake with new friends who honestly seemed to care about her and Andy.

Sometimes she feared she was in a dream, and she'd wake up to an ugly reality where Andy had no more diapers and she had nothing to eat. She'd worry about next week, next month, and the coming year.

She had a lifetime of caring for her son ahead, and no clear plan of how to do that. The generosity could only last so long.

And yet, this wonderful daydream continued, with townspeople who dropped in with gifts and a landlord who took care of the lawn and often asked her if she needed anything.

Best of all was Marlow. That once-feared woman had a heart of gold beneath her exterior of elegant strength. She was savior, teacher, and inspiration all wrapped up in take-charge attitude and unbelievable forgiveness.

Walking to the back door, Pixie noted the flicker of fireflies as they drifted over the dock and lake. The scene was so beautiful it took her breath away.

Rather than turn on the porch light, as she usually did at night, she slid the door open without making a sound, stepped out to the small stoop, and sat down. Rarely did she take the time to simply breathe deeply and relax. A week ago, if she'd tried, she probably would have fallen asleep, she'd been so worn out.

However, each day had brought more recovery, and she now felt like her old self again. Physically, at least. Well, except for the fuller bust and loss of her narrow waistline. Pretty sure her hips were permanently wider now, too. She smiled, knowing Andy had done that to her body.

Intellectually, she thought she was smarter now, a little wiser in the way of the world. More cynical, too, because she had firsthand knowledge of how deceptive some people could be. Never again would she let a man strip her of her pride and reduce her to a beggar in need of help. Her experience had been harsh, but lessons were learned.

Emotionally, she was now a mother, and she had so much love for Andy it sometimes surprised her that her heart didn't burst. How did mothers of multiple kids manage? Could a heart carry that much love? Apparently so.

Pleased with her progress on all levels, she inhaled the humid air and took pleasure in watching the fireflies. Out on the lake, a fish jumped with a splash, fanning out the reflection of moonlight on the surface in ever expanding ripples.

She was enjoying it all, her thoughts at peace, until the crack of a twig put her on alert. Heart pounding, she slowly turned her head . . . and saw a shadow that didn't belong. A man-sized shadow, coming around the corner of the house.

Panic dug into her, freezing her for a moment, until her thoughts naturally shot to Andy. As silently as possible, she scrambled to her feet, eased into the house, and secured the door.

Her heart pounded so hard that it stole her breath away. Eyes wide with alarm, she flattened herself to the wall beside the door and peeked out through the window. The shadow went still for a few moments, then moved closer until the clear outline of a man was visible.

It was not Cort. It wasn't anyone familiar to her. As she stared, horrified, the body came closer—as if to look in her windows!

Ungluing her feet, she ducked away and dashed into the bedroom, where Andy slept peacefully. There on the single nightstand was her phone, on but silenced. To her, it was a lifeline.

God, how she hated to be a nuisance, but more than that, more than anything, she had to protect Andy.

She shot over to the bed and grabbed the phone, rapidly texting into it, then praying for a reply. Breath still strangled in her throat, her chest aching with terror . . . until the reply popped onto the screen.

On my way.

*   *   *

Comfortably settled on the couch with Cort, Marlow yawned and knew she'd never be able to finish the movie. Any second now, she'd doze off.

Cort, always so attuned to her, kissed her temple. "Fading out?"

"Afraid so. I'm sorry."

He lifted the remote and switched off the TV. "Trust your body when it tells you what you need."

"What if it tells me I need you?"

The question didn't make him uneasy. In fact, he smiled. "Trust it."

She smiled, too. "You're so easy."

"With you." He smoothed a hand over her hair, his fingers stroking through to her scalp where he began a relaxing massage. "Want to stay over, or should I take you home?"

Home. She really wished she could call Bramble home—for good. More and more each day, she loved the place, both the location and the people. "You don't mind if I stay?"

"I'd prefer it." He nudged her face up. "But you've had a busy week."

True. Not only busy working at the tavern and searching for a suitable building for her business but also rearranging town habits to suit her. Her ploy with Herman had worked, and somehow—miracle of miracles—she'd gotten a lot of people on the schedule that best fit Pixie and, by extension, Marlow.

"I'll understand if you'd rather go home to your own bed."

And be denied a night in his bed? "What I'd really like is—"

Just then, a text sounded on her phone. She frowned, then sat forward, their conversation interrupted as she left the cozy warmth of Cort's arms to reach her phone on the coffee table. What she read shot her to her feet.

Alerted to trouble, Cort stood, too. "What is it?"

Quickly, she texted Pixie back. **On my way.** On autopilot, she shoved the phone into her pocket. "I have to go. Someone is lurking around outside Pixie's house."

Snagging her before she could rush off, he grabbed his keys without asking a single question and said, "Of course, I'm going with you."

Marlow let out a giant breath. "Of course." If she'd been thinking, she'd have known he would, but instead she'd simply reacted.

Willingly, she stayed behind Cort as he led the way out to his truck, his gaze scouring the surroundings, although it was too dark for Marlow to see much beyond the reach of his outside lights. He clicked the key fob and unlocked his truck before they reached it.

When he hoisted her inside, she was in too much of a hurry to complain. They needed to reach Pixie.

No one was ever on this road in the evening except her, Cort, or Pixie, because there were no other houses. The fronts of the homes faced the road. Behind, the properties went down to the lake.

She supposed someone might confuse directions and drive down the road looking for an address, but Pixie's word choice—lurking—suggested that the person was on foot.

Cort backed out of his driveway, and when his headlights hit the road ahead, they both searched the landscape. Other than a few deer, and a possum scurrying across the road, she didn't see any people or cars.

She texted Pixie, **We're pulling in now**, and got an immediate thumbs up in return, meaning Pixie had the phone in her hand. The second Cort turned off the truck, she reached for the door handle, but Cort again stopped her. "Let me check first?"

Okay, that sounded ominous, as if he thought there might

be trouble. Numb with worry, she nodded. He opened his door and stepped out—and they both heard the loud sound of running feet on the road, followed seconds later by the closing of a car door. Farther down the road, near the cottage where Marlow lived, red taillights shone for a brief moment. The sight of them sent her heart into her throat. Then the car spat gravel as it raced away, turning up the road that would lead past the tavern and out of town.

Still searching the area, Cort put his own phone to his ear. "Herman, I need you to do me a favor. In a few minutes a car is going to drive past the tavern. I need you to see if you can spot it. No, no idea. It's a car, not a truck, but all I saw were the taillights." He listened, then said, "It was hanging around outside Marlow's place, and Pixie thinks she saw someone on foot by the lake house. Yeah, be careful, don't approach anyone, and don't say anything to anyone else." He nodded. "Yeah, thanks."

Her phone dinged with an incoming message, causing her to jump. She read it, then said to Cort, "Pixie sees us. Should she open the front door?"

"Yeah." He closed his door and walked around to Marlow's side.

She was now jumpy, but also in a rush to get to Pixie. Cort kept her close, his attention everywhere until they reached the overhang of the front door. It opened, and he urged Marlow inside.

She took one look at Pixie's frightened face and gathered her close. "It's okay now," she promised.

"Lock the door and stay inside," Cort said. "I'll have a look around."

There was only time for her eyes to flare wide before Pixie followed his instruction. She grabbed Marlow's hand and hauled her into the kitchen.

In a faint whisper, Pixie said, "I'm so sorry to be more of a bother, but I swear, seeing someone out in the dark scared me half to death. No one is ever around here, and if it was you or Cort, I knew you'd have texted first."

"Yes, we always will, or we'd at least announce ourselves, not sneak around in the shadows. You were right to worry." She strode to the window in the door to look out and saw nothing. "Why isn't your porch light on?"

Pixie paced across the floor. "I had my chores done, and Andy was asleep, and I saw the fireflies . . ."

"I understand. This is my summer for fireflies, too." Seeing that Pixie was frazzled, Marlow pulled out a chair at the two-seater table and urged her to sit. "Slow down and take a breath. It's okay now."

Pixie nodded, but the second her bottom landed on the chair, she started rambling. "I just wanted to sit outside for a minute. When the light is on, it draws mosquitoes and beetles and moths. I sat down on the stoop—"

Because Marlow hadn't yet gotten her that rocking chair, darn it.

"—and the moon on the water was so pretty, and there were fireflies everywhere. But then I saw the shadow, and I could tell it was a man, and I almost died of fright." She shoved her hair back as if it offended her, her movements frustrated and full of self-recrimination. "When I got inside, I was afraid that if I turned on the porch light, whoever was out there would know I'd spotted them." She rubbed her forehead as if it pained her. "I should have contacted the police. Or grabbed Andy and run for my car."

"No," Marlow said. The last thing she wanted was for Pixie to possibly expose herself to danger. "Staying inside with the door locked was the smartest move."

Defeated, Pixie shook her head. "I don't even have emergency numbers. I never thought that far ahead. I *never* think ahead. I just keep screwing up." She looked at Marlow, full of apology. "All I could think to do was get hold of you."

What a revelation, but of course she was Pixie's lifeline. In fact, for now, she preferred it that way. Marlow wanted to sit, too, but more than that, she wanted Cort to get his sexy butt inside so she could stop worrying about him. "You did the right thing." She had more to say, but she needed to think about it first. After all, she wanted to encourage Pixie to be independent. As a mother, she should think ahead, so she could protect herself and Andy. They'd work on that, though.

Sighing, Marlow figured it was one more thing to add to her to-do list where Pixie was concerned.

Again, when her phone dinged, she jumped, then issued a curse. She looked at the screen and was glad to see the message. "It's Cort. I'll let him in. You sit—"

"No way," Pixie said, already crowding in near her side. "I go where you go."

For now, that suited Marlow just fine. She led the way back to the front door, then peeked out to be sure it was Cort before she unlocked the door. As he stepped in, she asked, "Was that necessary?"

"The door was locked."

"I don't mean . . ." She huffed. "Why go out there and prowl around anyway? What if you'd found someone still hanging about?"

His reply was a kiss to her forehead and an arm around Pixie's shoulders. By silent agreement, the three of them convened back in the kitchen. He pulled out a chair for each of them, then leaned against the wall near Marlow's shoulder. "No one is hanging around now, but Marlow and I saw someone taking off when we got here. They'd parked up by her place."

Pleased that Cort referred to it as her place, she wondered if he wanted her to stay. It seemed possible. Even on a disturbing night like this, she'd count that as progress.

Pixie's alarm visibly grew, which prompted Marlow to cover her hand. "We're all fine. For all we know, it might have been someone hoping to fish off the docks and not realizing that the homes were in use right now." That theory sounded believable, and hopefully Pixie would buy into it. All this anxiety couldn't be good for her blood pressure. Hmm, perhaps that was something they should ask her doctor at her next appointment. It was helpful that Pixie now included her in the discussions after her exams.

When Pixie's shoulders loosened, Marlow knew she was considering her theory.

"You have flood lights," Cort said. "Fishermen use them when they finish night fishing, to make sure they're not leaving any expensive rods or equipment behind. From now on, I want you to turn them on at night."

"But the electric bill . . ."

"You'll turn them on," he reiterated, politely putting an end to her objection. "Tomorrow I'll pick up flood lights for the front, too." His gaze pinned Marlow. "For both of you."

To encourage Pixie, Marlow said, "Thank you. I appreciate it." Of course, she would also reimburse him, but Pixie didn't need to know that.

She didn't hear his phone, but when Cort lifted it to his ear, she knew he'd gotten a call. To Pixie, she whispered, "That's probably Herman."

Confused, Pixie asked, "How do you know?"

Instead of answering, she listened to Cort.

"Did you see anything?" His brows came together. "Interesting. Yeah, it's probably related." He listened again, then nodded. "Keep it to yourself, Herman, okay? Right. It's great that I can trust you, but you know how everyone else gossips."

Oh, Marlow thought that was a genius ploy to stroke Herman's ego. When she spotted one of Cort's brief smiles, she knew Herman was eating it up.

"I'll tell her, and thank you." After he returned the phone to his pocket, he said, "Herman wants you to call him if you need anything."

What a wonderful offer. "He's the absolute sweetest, isn't he?"

Dubious, Cort replied, "Sure, if you say so."

When he said nothing else, she asked, "Well? What did he see?"

His gaze cut to Pixie, and she had the thought that he might not want to talk in front of her. She understood his reasoning, but they'd each been remiss in thinking of Pixie as a child to be protected. She needed to be aware of any threat.

"Go on," she said. "I think Pixie should be kept in the loop since the intruder was closest to her home."

Cort stared at Marlow a few seconds longer, then nodded. "A Mercedes Maybach tore out of town. Herman said it was the slickest SUV he's ever seen, and the driver ran a stop sign."

As that information sank in, Marlow murmured, "Hopefully, he didn't encounter any deer."

Pixie asked, "What's a Maybach?"

Sending her one of those bare-minimum smiles, Cort explained, "A fancy car that probably costs over a hundred fifty grand."

Stomach sinking, Marlow said, "So in other words, probably someone sent by my in-laws."

Going white, Pixie whispered, "Did you tell them about Andy?"

"No. I told you I wouldn't, remember?" It was a friendly reprimand, but still Pixie blanched.

"I didn't mean—"

"You're worried. I understand. But I will never lie to you."

Breathing shakily, Pixie nodded.

"I haven't even spoken with them lately. A few days ago, Sandra left me a message and said she'd like to talk, but I was at work, and since then I've been ... busy." Busy looking at property, caring for Pixie, and especially spending time with Cort. Overall, she'd been busy avoiding her in-laws—and living her new, happy life.

She'd feel guilty for that, except that nothing positive ever came of their chats, and they often left Marlow annoyed. Now, she had to admit that avoidance might not have been the best approach. "I'll call Sandra tomorrow to find out if they're behind this."

Cort crossed his arms. "If it is them, they might not know anything about Pixie. It's more likely they came to check up on you, except your house was dark because you were with me, and Pixie's kitchen light was on."

"So the person they sent was drawn here." Not for a second did she think Sandra or Aston had personally come to snoop. No, a task like that would be hired out. "Well, if they were behind this snooping, I'll put a stop to it."

"How?" Cort asked. "If your in-laws were nosy enough to have someone creeping around in the dark, it's unlikely they'll just confess to doing it when confronted."

Very true. Aware of Pixie fidgeting, Marlow asked, "Something to add?"

"No."

Her denial was so adamant, Marlow had to press her. "Pixie?"

"What if they show up here?" She flung her hand toward the front door. "What if they knock?"

The worry she saw in Pixie's eyes superseded everything else. "I'll find out what they want, and what their intentions are."

Cort stepped forward. "It might be better to take the surprise out of the equation. If you don't mind a suggestion?"

Pixie stared up at him as if he had all the answers. "I don't know what to do, so I'm happy to hear it."

"Tell the grandparents about Andy—on your terms, and in your own way."

Pixie pressed back in her chair. "No, I don't want—"

He knelt in front of her. "You would arrange it."

"And I'd be with you," Marlow promised.

"I'm happy to be there too, if you don't mind." Cort waited a beat to let those words sink in, then asked, "Wouldn't it be easier to just face their reaction, instead of watching every shadow and worrying when they might find out?"

"I . . ." She looked at each of them, then cleared her throat. "Could I think about it?"

"Of course you can. The decision is yours." Cort stood again. "You won't open the doors anymore tonight, right?"

"No." Sitting a little straighter, she said, "I really am sorry for bothering you both." To Marlow, she added, "I didn't realize you were together. I hate that I interrupted."

"I'm glad you texted me. Always feel free to do that, okay? The only problem would be if you didn't."

"It is a problem, though," she insisted. "I should be learning to stand on my own two feet, and at the first little thing, I panicked."

"It's not a little thing to know someone is walking around in the dark when you and Andy are here alone. You were protecting him, as any mother would do. Under those circumstances, don't you think I would do the same?"

"No," Pixie said simply. "I can't imagine you calling someone for help."

What a way to squeeze her heart. Marlow didn't know if she should be flattered by Pixie's faith in her, or if she should laugh over the idea that she'd confront an intruder alone. "Well, I'd have called Cort."

"Damn right she would."

Marlow flashed him a smile. "But," she said, "I think it'd be a good idea for you to have emergency numbers, too. I have no idea what type of law enforcement Bramble has, but I assume Cort does. We should both know the number, and the number for a medical emergency, as well."

Just then, Andy let out a short cry. Pixie jumped to her feet, but Marlow said, "I'll get him. I can change his diaper while Cort gives you those numbers." She hurried off before Pixie could object. It'd give her a few moments more to calm down before she held the baby.

It couldn't possibly affect Marlow as strongly as it did Pixie, but the baby's fussing made her hurry her steps. The bedroom was now crowded with the crib set up, so she had to maneuver around the furniture before she could look down at Andy's scrunched face, ready to give another shout.

"Hello, sweetheart."

He went still and then stared up at her. His legs kicked a few times, and his fist found its way into his mouth for a couple of slurpy sucks.

"I guess you're hungry, huh? You'll need your mama for that, but how about I give you a clean diaper?" He appeared to be listening, so while she located the diaper and wipes, she continued to speak to him. "You won't sprinkle me, will you? I saw you do that to your mama, you know. We laughed and laughed." It was a wonderful memory to share with her new friend.

Andy grinned at her.

"Oh!" He looked so precious, Marlow glanced around, anxious for someone else to see, but of course she and the baby were alone. "You little stinker."

He grinned again, then rapidly pumped his legs.

"You really are the most adorable little guy." Remembering the process Pixie had used, Marlow put the diaper and wipes on the bed, then opened the changing pad. Carefully, she lifted out the baby.

He grabbed a big hank of her hair. "Ouch. That's not a good idea, Andy. You don't want . . ." When he yanked, she winced. "Okay, let's figure this out." She lowered him to the pad, bending with him, and then painstakingly freed her hair, making certain no strands remained in his damp fist, all the while chatting to him.

He cooed, giving her the oddest feeling, as if a sweet warmth had just invaded her chest. "You're a little heartbreaker, aren't you?" She was getting better at changing him, and after witnessing the shower Pixie had gotten, she took no chances. "You smell so nice when you're only wet. You have your own special baby scent. There," she said once she had him clean and dry. "Let's get you all snapped back up, okay? If I know your mama, and I think I do, she's anxious to hold you." Putting a baby blanket over her shoulder, Marlow cuddled Andy to her, her hold secure, and turned to leave the room.

She found Pixie and Cort standing there, both of them smiling.

Not that she minded. She was fairly proud of herself for getting all that done without a hitch. "He grinned at me. A big toothless grin."

As if to prove it, Andy wiggled and did it again.

Cort said, "He's probably gassy."

Gasping in mock affront, Marlow said, "I'll have you know that he likes me."

"Of course he does," Pixie assured her. "What's not to like?"

Marlow was just about to thank her when Andy proved Cort right.

After such a tense day, they all found that hilariously funny.

"Here you go." Marlow handed over the baby. "You may need to check that diaper one more time."

Pixie took Andy, then gave Marlow a quick, one-armed hug.

"Seriously, thank you for coming to my rescue—again. I don't mean to lean on you so much, but it means the world to me to have someone. Especially someone as awesome as you."

Well, damn. Much more of that and she'd be tearing up. "I'm glad you're here, Pixie. You and Andy both." Mother and son added new depth and emotion to her life during a time when she'd needed it. Instead of exacerbating her hurt feelings, Pixie had helped to heal them. Someday soon, Marlow would explain that to her. For now, they all needed some rest.

Together, they walked to the front door.

Before they stepped out, Marlow asked her, "Will you be okay here alone?"

"I'll be fine. I feel much better now. I promised Cort that I'd keep the doors locked, and he made sure that all the numbers I might need are in my phone."

"All right, but if anything happens, or if you just need to talk, feel free to call me." She looked down at Andy. "And you, you rascal. Get your fill, and then let your mama sleep, you hear?"

He grinned at her once more.

"I'm not falling for that again." Marlow laughed, then pressed a kiss to his downy head. He really did have the best smell, making her want to nuzzle his soft cheek. She refrained, gave Pixie a smile, and stepped out with Cort.

They immediately heard the lock click into place.

At his truck, Cort paused to tip up her chin. "I know you're tired, but would you mind staying with me, or I could stay with you?"

"You're worried about me?"

"No. I feel certain that whoever was here, they're gone now and not likely to return tonight. But I'd still like to hold you." He kissed her forehead. "And sleep with you near." The next kiss was pressed to the bridge of her nose. "And wake up with you in the morning."

That sounded perfect to her. "You've convinced me. Let's go to my place, though. We'll be closer to Pixie if anything happens." And tomorrow, she'd get hold of Sandra.

Now more than ever, she dreaded the upcoming conversation with her mother-in-law.

CHAPTER 10

Cort had a difficult time leaving Marlow. Almost from the start, she'd had that effect on him. She spoke fast and he liked it. She smiled and he wanted to smile back. Her strength impressed him. Her wit amused him.

But when she showed her vulnerability, swear to God, it was like someone reached into his chest and gave his heart a squeeze. He didn't know what to do about it, and that was disquieting. He was a problem solver, and yet, Marlow was not a problem. He could never think of her that way.

If anything, she might be the solution. For Pixie, for this town.

For him.

They'd finished watching the sunrise a couple of hours ago. Breakfast was delayed while they shared a shower.

And then shared the bed.

It was a great way to start his day. Something he wouldn't mind repeating. Often.

Like maybe for the rest of his life.

For now, he needed to get back on schedule. He carried his plate to the sink after a meal of pancakes and bacon. Marlow was still nibbling on hers while perusing the internet on her laptop.

He rinsed his plate. "What are you looking for?"

"Property."

That halted him in the process of putting his plate in the dishwasher. Cautiously, he asked, "Decided not to stay after all?"

"What?" Startled, she glanced up and said, "I'm staying. I keep telling you that."

"For the summer?" he clarified, wishing it could be different but knowing the rules of the town.

Her smile teased. "For as long as I'm allowed, actually, but that's a conversation for another time."

It wasn't the first time she'd said something similar. Others had noticed that she was extending her stay—and so far, no one had complained . . . at least not to him.

The idea of having her close indefinitely was more appealing than he wanted to admit.

His feelings wouldn't change the town rules, though. The people of Bramble didn't want to add to the population, and thankfully, no one was ready to pass away. That meant adding one more inhabitant was out of the question.

"For now," she continued, "I'm looking at buildings right outside Bramble. I want to open my own little shop, but I can't find a space I like."

Cort dried his hands and joined her, one palm flattened on the tabletop as he peered over her shoulder at the laptop screen. "What's wrong with this one?"

"The exterior is too plain. I want a building with character. Something like the unique homes around here."

Yes, knowing Marlow as he did, he could easily imagine what would appeal to her. Sliding back into a seat, he asked, "Mind if I do a quick search?"

She repositioned the laptop in front of him. "Pixie and I have exhausted all options. Feel free."

The properties she'd already pulled up ranged from low-five figures to high-six. "Your price point leaves a lot of room, and there's a small town in the opposite direction from where you're looking that might better suit you." The location would add just a few miles to the distance she'd input on the search.

"I hope you're not trying to push me farther away."

For a heartbeat, he went still as he absorbed the worry in her words. Push her away? Hardly. He'd rather have her closer. When he lifted his gaze to meet hers, he was careful not to show his surprise. "Have I said or done anything to give you that impression?"

Having the accusation turned back on her left her with a slight frown. "Well, no."

The unspoken words hung between them. He hadn't asked her to get closer, either. At least, not explicitly. He'd shown her, though, and for an astute woman like Marlow, that should have been enough—for now.

With his search complete, he turned the laptop back to her. "Are these buildings more to your liking?"

It took her far too long to drag her gaze from his to the laptop screen. Immediately her frown cleared. "Oh, these are nice."

Cort had a lot to think about, so he pushed back his chair and stood. Marlow, now absorbed in the search results, didn't look up.

There were moments when she totally confounded him, yet at all times she fascinated him, too.

Unwilling to be ignored, he caught her chin and lifted her face for a kiss. Not a quick "see you later" kiss, either. No, he made sure it was one she'd remember even after he'd gone. By the time he lifted away, she was limp in her chair, the laptop forgotten, her eyes half closed and her breath labored.

"Hmm," she said. "If that's how you react when irritated, I'll need to bug you more often."

A reluctant smile caught him off guard. "You deliberately set me off?"

"I like how you detonate," she replied with a smile of her

own. She, too, stood, and then walked with him to the front door. "Let's make another deal."

Temptation burned through him. "If it involves stripping off my clothes, I don't have time."

Her laugh was half snort, half surprise. "Unfortunately, I don't have time for that either. If I want to catch Sandra, I need to make the call in the next fifteen minutes. Assuming her normal schedule has resumed, she'll be heading out for a salon appointment soon."

"I hope it goes well."

"I just hope I can get a straight answer from her." She stepped into the open doorway with him.

He'd like to think she was as reluctant to end their pleasant morning together as he was, but he could tell that Marlow had already moved on to business. It was one more thing he admired, her ability to compartmentalize tasks. He was sure that characteristic had helped to make her effective in business, too.

Looping his arms loosely around her waist, he prompted, "The deal?"

"If you decide you're ready to move on, come right out and tell me. I can handle it, and it's what I'll do if I come to that conclusion."

What the hell? There went his good mood, not that he'd let her know it. "So now I have to loop back to my earlier question. What did I do to put this in your mind?" Or was it something *she* was doing? Was the relationship winding down for her?

No, he didn't like that possibility at all.

"You haven't done anything."

Was that the problem? Was there something she wanted him to do? Knowing the mess she'd walked out of, did she need something more of him? A declaration probably wouldn't hurt. "I like you, Marlow. I'm enjoying our time together."

"Our time has been interrupted by my in-laws, and now

Pixie, and then there's the possibility of an intruder on your property."

"None of that bothers me, and it's been my impression that you're dealing with it, too, taking everything in stride."

She laughed. "Not in stride, no. My mother-in-law is like fingernails on a chalkboard. Pixie was a punch to the heart, but now I consider her a friend. And that intruder, well, he scares me, but I'm not a faint-of-heart type of gal, you know?"

It was impossible not to kiss her. "Yeah, noticed." And he admired that quality in her most of all.

Bemused by the kiss, she licked her lips and then continued as if she had a specific point to make. "Those are my problems . . . but they're somehow becoming yours, too. That wasn't my intent."

"So you've livened things up a little." With a deliberately casual shrug, he tried to let her know he wasn't worried. "I appreciate it." And then to give her another declaration, he added, "You're worth it."

Pleasure brightened her eyes and added a slight curve to her lips. Then she stepped in close and hugged him. "You always give me the best compliments." After another squeeze, she stepped back. "Still, if it gets to be too much, I want you to be upfront with me."

Cort gave her a long look. "I'm not him, Marlow. I'm not weak. I don't play games, I don't lie." When she was with him, he didn't want her thinking about her deceased husband at all. "And I would never use you."

"You're nothing like him. I know that."

Did she? As a Marine, he'd been taught to keep himself in check. That discipline had carried over into civilian life. It was now a part of him, like the color of his eyes or his need to remain active. "I've been told I'm hard to read."

Expelling a breath, she said, "*So* hard to read."

He cupped her face. "How about I promise to always be upfront with you? On everything?"

"I would appreciate it. And I'll be the same." With a wince, she added, "That's why you should know that I don't want to leave Bramble, and I'm mounting a campaign to win over the town."

Cort grinned. Did she think he hadn't noticed? That anyone hadn't noticed? Marlow wasn't a subtle person when it came to her intentions. "The originals are pretty entrenched in their decision to keep the town from growing, but they also like you a lot." And if she didn't prevail, there were properties outside the town proper.

"As long as you don't feel pressured."

She often amused him. This was one of those times. "I know the difference between pressure and pleasure. You're pure pleasure."

"See? Another amazing compliment."

If he didn't leave now, he'd be late. "Stay on guard today, okay? Let me know if you see any strangers around. I have some work to do for Wade, Gloria, and Bobbi, then I'm getting the extra lights I want to add so you and Pixie can see anyone who comes around at night." He also planned to look into front and back door cameras. "I should finish up around six, which will still give me time to get everything installed."

"Such a long day. I'm going to call Sandra, then check on Pixie. After that, if I can arrange it, I want to look at a few of those buildings. I'll be back by six, though, so would you mind if I hang out with you?"

He'd prefer it. The more time he spent with her, the more he wanted, but now, with a possible threat in town, he'd like to keep an eye on her around the clock. Not that he'd tell her so. He knew on a gut level that she'd wouldn't like overprotectiveness any more than he would, so he said simply, "Sounds good."

By the time he pulled out of her driveway, he was running behind, but hopefully he'd cleared the air a little with Marlow.

She needed to know that he liked the person she was, the way she'd reacted to Pixie, the way she embraced the town.

And he especially liked her honesty.

So far, there wasn't a single thing he didn't like.

But there were a few things he was starting to . . . love.

Marlow returned to her kitchen chair, took a few deep breaths, and then called Sandra. It threw her when her mother-in-law answered with an enthusiastic, "Marlow! It's so nice to hear from you."

Well, good thing this wasn't a video call or Sandra would see her blank-faced surprise. The greeting sounded sincere and almost too happy. "Sandra. Good morning."

"You haven't returned my last few calls, and I was worried. I hope all is well with you."

"Yes, I'm fine, thank you." She detected no guilt in Sandra's voice, but that might not mean anything. Often Sandra and Aston did things they shouldn't and felt no remorse. This could be one of those times. "I'm working at the tavern—and having a wonderful time of it—but I get home late."

Three beats of silence passed before Sandra said, "You enjoy working in a tavern. Is that a joke?"

"Not at all." Knowing her statement had to be a shock to Sandra, Marlow made an attempt to explain. "After everything that's happened this past year, I wanted a complete and total change. New people, new scenery. Being away from city life, living in this quiet little town and getting to know my neighbors, staying busy with a job that's the total opposite of my old position . . . it's rejuvenated me."

"You're trying to forget Dylan."

There was both accusation and understanding in the words. Marlow held back a frustrated sigh. "No. That isn't even possible."

"Good! He should be remembered, now and always."

So many times, Sandra had deliberately chosen to forget just how bad her marriage to Dylan had been. There was no point in reminding her again. "Sandra, I need to ask you something and I hope you'll be honest."

"Of course, you can have your old job back." She laughed with relief. "We've been waiting, *not* so patiently, for you to make that decision. We temporarily filled the position, and young Mr. Williams is doing a fine job, but he's not you, Marlow. He doesn't breathe life into the company as you did."

Marlow thought if her eyes widened any more, they'd probably fall out of her head. Somehow, her mother-in-law had managed to completely misjudge what she'd been about to say while at the same time giving effusive praise.

The type of praise she'd never given before.

"I'm sorry," Marlow said. "You misunderstand. I'm not asking to return. I *won't* return." Her frustration expanded. "I'm not off on a lark. Not indulging a temporary eccentricity. I'm making deliberate choices that please me." Her voice rose, no matter how she tried to control it. "This is *my* time, Sandra. I have no obligation to anyone else, no other responsibilities except to enjoy my life as I see fit. I really wish you'd believe me."

"You sold his house."

"It was *our* house, and yes, I sold it. As you pointed out, that house was practically designed by Dylan. He loved it far more than I ever did. As a woman alone, I didn't need that much space"—or the painful reminder of a failed marriage—"and I didn't want to live in the area anymore. There was no reason for me to keep it."

Defiantly, Sandra stated, "I took all of his things."

"I'm glad." Marlow meant it. If it helped Sandra cope with her grief, she could build a shrine to Dylan, with all of his personal belongings on display. However, she could not expect Marlow to build it with her. "I actually called for another reason."

"Other than ripping out my heart, you mean?"

Now there was the Sandra she'd known for so long. This time, Marlow released her sigh. Loudly. "My intent has never been to hurt you or Aston. I wish you both only the best." Could they say the same in return? Certainly didn't seem so. Her happiness had never been considered, much less prioritized. She understood that, but from now on, Marlow would do what was best for herself.

That determination brought her back to the reason for her call. "I have a question for you." Wasting no more time, she asked, "Did you send someone to this town? A private detective, maybe?" Again, without giving Sandra time to formulate an answer, she said, "There was a stranger on my road, poking around and peeking in windows."

The long silence was telling.

"Sandra," Marlow repeated. "I hope we can be honest with each other."

"We're worried about you! You're having a midlife crisis or something. We've tried to be patient, but it's dangerous. For you, and for this family."

Hearing the truth was a relief. At least the nighttime visitor wasn't some shady character out to rob or worse. Just someone sent by her intrusive in-laws, overstepping as usual. "I'd like you to stop and think how *you'd* feel with a stranger peeking in *your* windows."

"I'm sure you're exaggerating," Sandra scoffed. "There was no peeking involved. He was just trying to determine exactly where you're staying, and then hopefully we can figure out why. If you need a raise, you know we'd be happy to accommodate you. It's important to support family, after all."

Marlow gritted her teeth. "I don't need you to support me. I don't need a raise."

"Or," Sandra continued, undeterred, "if you wanted a different position or to be placed in another location, you know we have opportunities all over the country and in other countries, too, although we'd prefer to keep you close so we can visit."

It was incredible that no matter what Marlow said, Sandra didn't *hear* her. She was determined to pursue her own course and blindly moved forward toward a future of her own design.

That was how it had always been, how Marlow had allowed it to be. But no more. Here in this small town, everyone listened to her, sometimes more than she'd like. She shook her head, laughing at her own inconsistency.

Cort always heard her. And Pixie, bless her heart, hung on Marlow's every word. She enjoyed it, and more than that, she deserved it.

Done with the call, Marlow said, "I'm sorry, Sandra. I've resigned from Heddings' Holdings and that won't change. Ever. What I want now is a much simpler life, without the busy social calendar and business obligations." Even knowing she shouldn't share any more, Marlow attempted to convince Sandra with a few facts. "I'll be starting my own business."

Silence again.

"I want a small boutique with nice but affordable women's clothes and accessories. Something I can manage with just a few employees, selling fashions that will appeal to the everyday person. Not for the money, understand. My financial situation is healthy, and I don't need help in that regard. This is something I've always wanted."

"Meaning you didn't enjoy working with us?"

"Of course, I did! And I hope you and Aston were satisfied with my performance." They'd better be. She'd been an overachiever for them, and for Dylan.

And honestly, for herself, too. She'd never been good at half measures.

"I'll always appreciate you both. You gave me great opportunities, and in return, I tried to give you one hundred percent. I learned so much from my time with Heddings' Holdings. Invaluable lessons that I often apply to everyday life." Like strength, independence, and the ability to confront adversity.

Sandra suddenly changed the subject. "We haven't heard any more from Pixie Nolan, thankfully. I told Aston that her name alone discredited her. What legitimate person is named Pixie? It's absurd."

The scorn in her tone made Marlow bristle. "Why do you hate her so much?"

"*Why do you not?*" Sandra all but erupted in anger. "That little gold digger tried to steal your husband! She tried to corrupt Dylan. And then she had the nerve to try to wheedle her way back in with us? *Never.*"

For as long as Marlow could remember, Dylan's parents had made excuses for every wrong move he made. It was always someone else's fault, never their baby's. It was Marlow's own anger that drove her to say, "Did you realize that Pixie was only nineteen? *Nineteen*, Sandra. If you ask me, Dylan preyed on her."

"*How dare you?*" she whispered.

"One day, I hope you'll realize that Dylan wasn't the saint you paint him to be but a flesh and bone man who created many of his own problems."

The call disconnected. Marlow waited, stunned, not only that Sandra would end the call like that, but also that she would lash out in such a way. Sandra hadn't changed. She had always put a halo on Dylan, no matter what.

It was Marlow who had changed.

But in her anger, she had just betrayed Pixie.

Sandra was a savvy woman. A woman didn't become rich and powerful by being naïve. The fact that Marlow had just defended Pixie was bound to stay in Sandra's mind. She'd chew it over until it made sense to her.

Eventually, she'd wonder if Marlow and Pixie had been in touch.

Well, damn.

Pixie sang to Andy while she did the dishes. There weren't many, so it didn't take her long. Every few seconds, her gaze returned to the baby, and each time, she got a smile. This, seeing Andy happy and being able to care for him, was all she needed to be content. He was comfortable, safe, and she didn't have to wonder about running out of diapers or being able to clean his clothes. They were undisturbed. They had everything they needed. More than was essential.

Only because others were being so generous.

It was a wonderful—but temporary—fix. Making the same mistakes over and over would be unforgivable, so she had to think about their future. She needed to plan, and then she had to work toward that plan.

Today, she would call Marlow and explain that she was ready to get to work. She *had* to work. Until she started repaying her debt, she couldn't move forward with her life.

As a realist, she knew this current situation couldn't last much longer. Just thinking about Cort supplying her with a home and Marlow covering all of her expenses made her face burn with humiliation. She wanted to be independent, to take care of herself, and she had been, at least for a little while.

Until she'd met Dylan and her entire life had derailed in a big way.

When her phone dinged, she glanced at the screen and saw it was Marlow. Quickly, she dried her hands and read the text. Oh good, Marlow planned to stop by. Perfect timing. Of course, that impressive woman always knew the right social moves, so even though Pixie was dependent on her for literally everything, Marlow asked if it was convenient for her to visit.

As far as Pixie was concerned, Marlow could wake her in the middle of the night if she wanted to. Pixie owed her too much to ever refuse her anything. Besides, she liked and respected Marlow so much, she was always thrilled to hear from her.

After sending back a quick reply, Pixie finished the dishes and scooped up Andy to head to the front door. She got there mere moments before Marlow pulled in.

The fact that she'd driven instead of walking up told Pixie this wouldn't be a long visit. She didn't mean to, but she felt . . . envy. Where else did Marlow plan to go?

Wherever it was, Pixie would have loved to accompany her. Much as she appreciated everything that had been provided for her, now that she felt better, she was sometimes . . . bored. Just a little.

Feeling like an ungrateful loafer, she concentrated on greeting Marlow with a smile.

What a blessing it was to have her as a friend. Sometimes Pixie almost couldn't believe it.

Holding the door open, Pixie said, "Come on in."

"Thank you." Smiling at the baby, Marlow asked, "May I?" and took Andy from her.

That, too, amazed Pixie. Marlow owed her nothing and had every right to despise her, but instead, she not only helped in every way possible but also seemed to truly care about Andy. Like an aunt.

Pausing, Marlow asked, "Hey, what's wrong?" Then she made a face. "Did I overstep? I did, didn't I? I asked if I could hold him and then didn't even wait for an answer." She cuddled Andy closer, nuzzling her nose against the top of his head. "I blame this cutie-pie, because he's so irresistible."

Touched by the sentiment, Pixie led the way to the kitchen. That was something she'd learned from Marlow. Lead a guest to a seat and offer her a drink. She indicated one of the two chairs at the table. "Andy adores you, so no, you didn't overstep. I owe you so much that you never could. It just struck me . . ." But how could she explain? Shaking her head, she asked, "What would you like to drink?"

"A bottle of water would be great." Settling Andy in her arms, she eyed Pixie. "What struck you?"

Worried that she'd offend Marlow, Pixie stalled while getting two bottles of water. She set them on the table and then took the chair opposite her guest. She felt silly, especially since she didn't know how to put her feelings into words.

So often around Marlow, Pixie felt like a bumbling, awkward child. "Andy and I don't have any relatives. I don't mind for myself—I mean, I'm used to being alone—but for Andy . . ." She was blundering! "You're really good with him, and I was just thinking that you're like his aunt or something. Of course, you're not, but sometimes I think of you that way."

Marlow grinned. "Remember when you first came here, you said you were my sister?"

Groaning, Pixie covered her face. "I feel so bad about that."

"Don't. I'd love to be an honorary aunt. Even though I'm not actually a blood relation, I care about you both. Babies can't have too many people who love them, right?"

Pixie had a hard time believing anyone could be that generous, and yet the proof sat before her. Seeing Marlow's carefree smile, the affectionate way she nuzzled her nose over Andy's sparse hair, she knew the sentiment was genuine. Her throat felt thick as she nodded. "The more caring people Andy has in his life, the better."

"Then that's settled." Marlow cleared her throat and said in a mock-lofty tone, "Henceforth I shall be known as Aunt Marlow." Her grin widened. "I've had many titles in my life, but I like that one the best."

Over and over again, Marlow left her completely undone. Humbly, Pixie whispered, "I'm so grateful to you. I hope you know that."

"Pfft. It's a favor to me to have this little stinker in my life, so thank *you*. You're both wonderful."

It was an effort, but Pixie got it together, and just like that, real words, better words, came to her. "I've always been glad that I met Dylan. Even when I was most afraid, when I was at my sickest and couldn't get out of bed, when I didn't know what to do, I was still glad—because I had Andy. He kept me going when I really wanted to give up. Now I have another reason, too." So many emotions welled up that Pixie was nearly drowning in them.

"It's the town, right? I agree, Bramble is wonderful."

"It is," Pixie agreed. "Everyone is so nice, and Cort is so generous." In some ways, Cort represented everything Pixie had never known: the shelter of a father's concern, the protectiveness of a big brother. It was wonderful, but it wasn't the most important thing.

Marlow watched her with concern.

Pixie's lips trembled, partly with a smile born of happiness, partly because she didn't know how her sentiment would be received. Didn't matter. This amazing woman deserved the full truth. "It's you, Marlow. I'm most grateful for you."

A little breathless, Marlow said, "Oh."

"I'm glad I met Dylan because I got Andy in the bargain. And I'm glad he didn't marry me, *couldn't* marry me, because now I've met you. All my mistakes and bad judgment have brought me here, and no matter what happens now, you've had a huge, positive impact on my life." Her lips trembled, causing her next words to emerge as a whisper. "I love you for that."

Marlow shocked her by getting red-eyed, too. "Oh, honey, I feel the same way." Sniffling, she left her seat to give Pixie a tight, one-armed hug while still holding Andy securely.

The baby broke up the emotional embrace by grabbing a fistful of each woman's hair. They were tearfully laughing as they worked to free themselves. Andy just kicked his legs and cooed at their efforts.

When they were seated again, each of them blinking back tears and still smiling, Pixie felt a contentment she'd never known before. No, Marlow wasn't family, and wasn't even a typical friend, but she was more like family than Pixie had known in years.

Sighing, she said, "I know you'll grumble at me, but I have to keep saying it. *Thank you.* I hope you know how much you've impacted my life."

Marlow reached out for her hand. "Honestly, you've impacted mine, too. I'm glad you came here, and that you trust me."

Holding hands with a woman was a new experience, too, but Pixie liked the connection. How she wished she really had a sister like Marlow. Probably she would have been a better person if she'd had someone like her in her life.

That thought brought back to mind the reason she'd wanted to talk to Marlow. She released her, took a swig of water, and squared her shoulders. "I'm ready to get to work."

Marlow blinked. "To work on what?"

"Anything you want. I've loafed around enough, and I swear I feel fine now." Mostly fine, anyway. "Andy takes lots of naps, and more and more, he's sleeping longer at night." She waved a hand at the kitchen. "It takes me no time at all to feed myself and tidy the house, so I have plenty of free time to tackle anything you need done."

A considering look fell over Marlow's face, and she nodded in that decisive way Pixie had come to know. "What do you have planned today?"

Excited, Pixie leaned forward. "Nothing. Give me any task and I'll get to it. I'm anxious to dig in."

"I'm going to look at some property. Want to come along? I could use another opinion."

A bubble of pure joy swelled inside her. "For real? You mean it?" *Marlow wants my opinion?* Then reality hit her and she knew she had to be fair. "I'd love to, but I don't know any-thing about property."

"You probably know more than you realize, and even if you don't, I could use the company."

Her heart started beating too fast and too hard. In such a short time she'd gone from absolute rock bottom to this—living in a cute little house, surrounded by comfort; visiting with such an impressive woman who had every right to hate her and instead valued her company. Laughing in sheer joy, she popped to her feet. "I would love to! Thank you."

"Stop thanking me. You'll be doing me a favor." Marlow stood, too. "Grab your shoes and anything this squirt might need, and we can get on our way. I want to get back to see Cort while he installs our new lights."

Pixie gave her a teasing look as she fetched her sneakers by the back door. "Cort's more than your landlord, isn't he?"

Bobbing her eyebrows, Marlow confirmed, "He is now, and I'm enjoying every minute."

"Of course you are. He's awesome, but then so are you. You guys make a great couple."

Marlow beamed at the praise.

In two minutes, they were heading out the door, and for Pixie, it was the first relaxing adventure she'd had in a year. For too long it had felt like life was against her, and every drive was a desperate search for help.

But now . . . life was just plain good.

CHAPTER 11

After viewing the property, Marlow realized that Pixie truly did have a good eye. She easily envisioned what Marlow wanted and shyly offered suggestions that made a lot of sense.

The second building they looked at was almost perfect. There were a few walls she'd want removed to improve the flow and available floor space for displays, so she hoped Cort would get involved, too.

Before they'd left, Pixie had sat in the back seat and nursed Andy while they chatted about potential for the business. When she'd finished, she'd changed the baby's diaper, and now he was sleeping.

The drive was peaceful, the day had been productive, and Marlow decided to push forward. "Could I ask you something?"

Immediately, Pixie said, "You can ask me anything. Heck, you have the right to ask me anything."

Getting her new friend over the idea that she was "less than" wouldn't be easy, but Marlow was determined to make it happen. "No, I don't. No one has the right to make personal demands of you. I have questions, and as your friend, I hope you don't mind answering. Whether you do or not won't change our friendship."

"I don't mind."

That simple answer didn't quite cover it, but for now, Marlow let it go. "Is Pixie your real name?" So her friend would understand, Marlow said, "I think it's adorable, and it suits you, but it is unusual."

The smile that bloomed on her face reassured Marlow, even before Pixie answered.

"My aunt helped to raise me. My legal name is Joanna, but Aunt Mary always called me Pixie because I'm small, and I guess it stuck."

"What about your mother and father?"

The smile faded. "Mom lost custody of me when I was five, so Dad had me for a while. Then he got arrested, and Aunt Mary didn't want me held by the state, so she stepped in." She fiddled with her purse strap, peeked back at Andy, looked out the window.

"We don't have to talk about it if you don't want to."

"It's not that I don't want to, but no one's asked me about it before, so I just . . . never have."

There it was again, the emphasis on how alone Pixie had always been. Of course, she'd been easy prey for Dylan. The girl had been starved for attention. "I'm sorry. I'm here, and I'm always willing to listen, okay?" More and more, this brave young woman stole her heart. Pixie had such a can-do spirit, and she was so quick to smile, to appreciate every scrap of kindness she got, Marlow couldn't help but care about her.

Maybe that was how the town had felt about Cort's mother, too. Marlow, however, wasn't at all the same. That made her frown. Would the town embrace her anyway, or would people feel she didn't need them?

She did, but maybe she hadn't shown it enough. It was something to think about, but for now, she wanted only to encourage Pixie.

Quietly, Pixie said, "My mom was an addict. Dad drank too much, but it mostly wasn't a problem."

Until it was, Marlow assumed. "Why was he arrested?"

"He got in a bar fight and it was bad. He had a knife."

Dear God. "Where were you?"

"Oh, I wasn't with him! I was at our apartment."

"How old were you?"

"Ten." She went quiet again. "Dad had gotten in trouble once before, when he was drinking and got mad and threw his car keys." At the side of her head, Pixie slid her fingers beneath the locks of her fair hair. "He didn't mean for them to hit me, but they cut my scalp and I had to get stitches at the hospital. He told me not to tell anyone how it had happened, but since he was drunk, he didn't realize how loud he was. The nurses heard him."

Dear God. Appalled, Marlow said, "I am so damn sorry."

"No, it was okay. Aunt Mary ended up with emergency custody, and that turned into permanent custody. She was awesome. She passed away when I was seventeen, but by then I already had a job and was able to live on my own."

Marlow thought her emotions had taken a beating lately, and that the hard knocks had toughened her heart.

How wrong she'd been.

So often, in completely guileless ways, Pixie proved just how tender her heart remained. For this brave young woman and her endearing son, Marlow's heart ached.

Compared to Pixie's numerous trials, Marlow's paltry difficulties hardly mattered. Realistically, she knew it didn't work that way. Heartache was heartache, each unique and difficult for different people and their situations. You couldn't compare problems or how they affected someone.

Knowing that, having a small understanding of Pixie's struggles, Marlow reached out to pat her arm. "You know what? I was already impressed with you, and now I'm downright floored. You're an incredible young lady."

Pixie stared at her in bewilderment. "But I'm not! I've made a complete mess of my life."

"Oh, honey. Nothing could be further from the truth. You took a very messy life and somehow managed to become a strong, capable, and determined woman, who I think also happens to be an incredible mother."

"You're going to make me cry again," Pixie warned with a laugh. "I swear I never used to be this weepy. The doctor said it's from having a baby and my hormones being overactive—though that's not how he said it—but seriously . . ." She fanned her face as her eyes turned red. "Don't be so nice to me."

Marlow laughed. "I'll be as nice to you as I like. After all, you're working for me and that makes me the boss. Bosses often do exactly as they please." Inspiration struck, and she said, "In fact, as your boss, I'd like to stop for ice cream."

"Ice cream?"

"Yes. I think I want a banana split. What do you say? You like ice cream, right?"

"Love it, actually."

"Good, then let's indulge."

"But . . . you've already spent enough on me."

Marlow waved that off. "Consider it payment for today, for keeping me company and helping me view properties. Your time is valuable. You'll be compensated." As she drove, she saw a department store and decided on another stop first. "An ice cream doesn't cover it, so I also want to get one of those neat baby carriers. You know, the kind you wear like a backpack? What are they called?"

Pixie stared at her. "Um, with Andy so small, I'd need to carry him in front of me."

"Of course. I should have realized. A front carrier then. We'll find one." Her thoughts seemed to skitter everywhere at once. There were many things she suddenly wanted to do, and while she could claim they weren't self-indulgent, she knew that would be a lie.

Spending the day out, pampering Pixie, and enjoying time with her in the ways she wanted were actually for *her* enjoyment—but hey, they'd benefit Pixie as well, right?

As she parked in the lot, she added, "Since you're feeling better, one night this week we'll walk on the beach. I know you've seen the fireflies."

Pixie nodded. "They're neat."

Was Marlow the only person completely amazed by the tiny creatures, then? "There are so many of them along the empty stretches of beach. You'll love it. And I'm sure Cort won't mind carrying Andy."

"Oh, um . . ." With wide eyes, Pixie lifted a hand, then let it drop. "I wouldn't want to interrupt a date between you two."

"Nonsense. He'll enjoy it." Marlow felt certain of that. "And Andy will get some fresh air. Babies need fresh air." That had to be true. "It'll be a nice evening out. Not too late, of course. I don't want to throw off your schedule." She stopped in the middle of releasing her seat belt. "Will it hurt the schedule? I have no idea."

Slowly, a smile spread over Pixie's face. She released her own belt and twisted to look over the seat at Andy. "It'll be fine, and I'm already excited thinking about it."

Such a simple thing, but the joy on Pixie's face couldn't be feigned. Marlow vowed to herself that she'd arrange more days like this one, no matter what.

She and Pixie deserved it.

And at the end of the summer, if both of them weren't able to stay, well then, she'd find permanent housing for them nearby. Living just outside Bramble would be *almost* as nice as living within it.

One way or another, she wanted to continue her relationship with Cort, with Pixie, and with sweet little Andy.

Funny that she'd left so much behind . . . but found so much more in her new life.

Not only company but shopping and then ice cream. Pixie couldn't remember the last time she'd had such an awesome day. Excited to visit the store, she started to open her car door, but Marlow reached over and touched her arm.

"You look so happy, I hate to burst your bubble, but while Andy is still sleeping, there's one more thing I want to discuss."

Pixie just knew what it would be. "You talked to Andy's grandma, didn't you?"

The funniest expression fell over Marlow's face before she grinned. "Sandra, a grandma. I can almost see her reaction to that."

Pixie felt a little sick, and all of her happiness leached away. "She wouldn't like it, would she?"

"Well, I feel certain she won't like the term *grandma*, but as to whether or not she'll enjoy being one, who knows? We won't find out until you tell her."

What a relief. "So she doesn't know yet?"

"No, but . . ."

Unsure what Marlow was getting at, Pixie asked, "It was her snooping around?"

"Someone she hired, yes. The person was supposed to be checking up on me. Sandra seems to think I'm having a mid-life crisis, and she sounded genuinely concerned about me." For a second, Marlow appeared baffled by that, but then she shook it off. "My guess is that she doesn't want me to screw up too badly, because then it would reflect back on the Heddings family, and ultimately on Dylan. She wants to protect his 'legacy.'"

"But you never screw up." Pixie couldn't imagine such a thing. As far as she could tell, Marlow was perfect.

"I appreciate the vote of confidence," Marlow said, grinning, "but believe me, I've made plenty of mistakes. Being in this town isn't one of them." Her voice softened. "And neither is being your friend."

How could she stay gloomy when Marlow said things like that? "I'm honored."

Marlow drew a deep breath. "The thing is . . ." She winced. "When I spoke with Sandra, the conversation veered a little and she made a few assumptions—about you, I mean. I'm afraid I defended you."

And that was a problem? Whether she deserved it or not, Pixie was thrilled to have someone like Marlow on her side. "Okay?" she said, making it a question because she didn't understand.

"Sandra is smart. Brilliant even. A lot of people underestimate her. I've seen it happen dozens of times. They think she's just the pampered wife of Mr. Heddings, without realizing the power Sandra has. She sees things that others don't, and that means she'll quickly realize I must know you, since I automatically defended you."

"Oh." That would definitely bring more trouble to Marlow. "I'm sorry." Her apologies seemed to be stuck on repeat. Every day, five times a day, she found reasons to say those small words that didn't begin to convey the remorse she felt for complicating the lives of others.

Exasperated, Marlow shook her head. "Pixie, we're friends now. You have nothing to apologize for, but I do. If I'd been thinking, I would have simply ended the call. Now, I'm afraid I just ratcheted up her anger at you."

"Because I was with Dylan?"

"Because you, as the woman he cheated with, are proof that Dylan wasn't perfect. Sandra's already having a really hard time with everything. This is going to put her over the edge."

Shame scorched Pixie from her head to her toes. She tried her best not to dwell on it, but she'd slept with this amazing woman's *husband*. She'd been a complete fool, believing someone like Dylan would love her. Worse, she'd had the audacity to beg Marlow for help.

Before Pixie could even think of how to reply, Marlow spoke again.

"Don't you dare apologize. It'll seriously piss me off if you do."

Hearing Marlow curse startled her enough that the awful truth of her mistakes blipped right out of her mind. "Okay," she whispered.

"I mean it, Pixie. You've apologized enough, and I don't fault you. Sandra has this skewed impression of her son, as if he was a saint. Trust me, she wasn't fond of me either when I decided to divorce him. Actually, she was never all that fond of me, and I'm not going to take that personally anymore. In her eyes, I doubt anyone would have been good enough for Dylan. As astute as Sandra is in business, she's blind to her son's failings. Or maybe she sees his failings as her own as his mother, so she can't accept them for that reason. I don't know, and I'm tired of trying to figure her out."

"I can't imagine her not being thrilled with you." What more could Sandra have wanted in a daughter-in-law?

"Thank you. You're sweet. Now, I want your word that if anyone representing the Heddings family contacts you, you'll let me know."

It would be wrong to do that, another imposition, but Pixie knew turning to Marlow would be her gut reaction, especially if she felt threatened. For better or worse, she trusted Marlow, and she relied on her. "I promise." Soon, she told herself, she'd stand on her own two feet. But not yet.

Marlow wasn't finished. "If you decide to face Sandra and Aston, if you choose to tell them about Andy, I'd like to be with you."

Such a generous offer. "I'd like that, too." She couldn't imagine facing them alone.

"Well, then." Marlow shared a relieved smile with her. "I'm glad we're past that. Let's shop!"

When Cort got to Marlow's house, he was surprised, but also pleased, to find her and Pixie fixing dinner in the kitchen together. When Marlow had called earlier to say she'd like to eat with him, her treat, he had assumed she'd order pizza, or maybe want to head back to The Docker restaurant.

Instead, after knocking and hearing her call out, "Come on in," he opened the door to the scent of seasoned pork chops baking and the sound of women laughing.

Heading through the foyer to the kitchen, he found potatoes boiling on the stove while Pixie stood at the counter making a salad with a lot of different greens, tomatoes, onions, and cucumbers. Marlow had just turned the pork chops, then returned them to the oven.

His mouth watered, and it wasn't just the food. It was this, a small family gathering, the unity and cozy warmth.

They were things he hadn't even realized were missing from his life.

Marlow glanced up, her soft brown eyes smiling at him. "Hi. Just in time. Dinner is almost ready."

He noticed the table was set for three and that Andy was on a blanket in the family room, where both women could see him contentedly gumming a new soft toy.

Cort went to the stove, where Marlow poked the potatoes with a fork. Her light brown hair, now with natural highlights from the sun, was in a thick braid hanging over her shoulder. The back of her neck was enticingly bared, so he pressed a kiss there. "Smells great." The food—and her.

She tipped her head to give him better access. "I hope it tastes good, too."

He took a soft, quick love bite near her shoulder and hummed. "Definitely does."

Pixie turned away from them, but not before Cort saw her grin.

It was overly familiar of him, but why not? This all felt like a very familiar moment, so he stepped up to Pixie next and put a peck on her temple. "Hey, Pixie."

Her face went bright pink, but she smiled hugely. "Hey, back."

He started to ask what he should do to help, but then Andy started to fuss. "Could I hold him while you finish up?"

Pixie's brows lifted. "You wouldn't mind?"

"Not at all." He quickly washed his hands, then gathered up the baby, blanket and all, and took a seat at the kitchen table. "It gives me an excuse to sit while you two work."

Marlow sent him the warmest smile he'd ever gotten from her. "You've already worked today, and you still plan to put up lights. Dinner is the least we could do."

"Everything is about done anyway," Pixie said.

"I'll mash the potatoes, then we can eat."

He loved how she and Pixie meshed, the protectiveness Marlow couldn't hide, and the hero worship Pixie displayed. "Mashed potatoes. I haven't had those since my mom last made them."

"No fair," Marlow said. "I can't compare to a mother's home cooking."

Pixie said, "Ha! Pretty sure you can do anything." Then she caught herself and sent Cort a horrified glance of apology. "Not that your mother's cooking wouldn't have been—"

"She was a good cook," Cort interrupted, to spare her. "But I agree. Pressure is on, Marlow. Pixie and I both expect excellence."

"I'll do my best," she quipped back, not at all bothered.

Of course, she wouldn't be. Overall, Marlow proved immune to pressure. Immune to stress and change. She amazed him. Bowled him over, even, and after his time serving in the Marines with some phenomenal men, that was no easy feat. "Soon as we finish, I'll have to get to work on the lights." He wanted Marlow safe, and he wanted Pixie to feel secure.

"Isn't he the best?" Marlow asked as she added butter and milk to the potatoes.

And Pixie replied, "For sure." Then more quietly, "But I hate being such a bother."

Together, they replied, "You aren't." Then they even grinned in sync.

Dinner, of course, was incredible, and they told her so. Marlow accepted their praise graciously, but then, a woman like her was surely used to accolades.

It was the little compliments he and Herman gave her, truths all of them, that she seemed to enjoy the most.

It still surprised Cort that she could be so content in Bramble. Every day, he expected her to announce that she'd be leaving, either heading back to her city life or accepting a great job offer.

Instead, each day she became more entrenched in the town. She won people over with little effort—himself included. Herman couldn't say enough good things about her. The siblings admired everything about her, especially the way she'd befriended Pixie and Andy.

He was in awe of that, too.

As a woman of means, she could have simply presented Pixie with a check and sent her on her way. Doing so would have been beyond generous. Instead, she'd gotten personally involved. She'd given Pixie a greater gift than money.

Hope. Purpose. And acceptance. She'd offered a guiding hand, had become both a resource and an emotional supporter.

In the process, Marlow had completely stolen his heart.

It wasn't easy to remember, so Cort had to continually remind himself that she'd moved here to escape the chaos of conflict and emotional pain. She was here to ground herself, to start anew. In no way did Marlow appear a victim. A little wounded sometimes, but she'd shown herself to be practical, capable, quick-witted, and fun loving. She embraced life, taking from it what she could but giving back so much more.

And she'd shared that outlook with Pixie.

He thought of his mother, how broken she'd been, emotionally, spiritually, as well as physically. Thanks to Marlow, Pixie now had better prospects, an admirable role model, and her confidence grew every day.

For years, rage would infuse Cort whenever he thought about what his dad had put them through, how badly his mother had suffered, but the Marines had helped him get that anger under control. Now when memories gripped him, which they did far too often, he gave thanks that the two of them had moved here, that his mother had had good friends who'd loved her and helped her to heal.

These people had all championed her, and it had made a world of difference.

Pixie, on the other hand, had Marlow, and Cort thought that relationship just might be as impactful as the love of an entire town.

He was so lost in thought, it took him a moment to realize that the women were smiling at him. "Did I miss something?"

Marlow laughed quietly.

Pixie said, "You cleared your plate—and you're still holding Andy."

Yes, he was, because he'd insisted. The baby was a warm, gentle weight against his chest. Eating one-handed hadn't been a problem. "I like holding him."

"You're good at it. Have you been around a lot of babies?"

What an idea. "No."

Pixie tipped her head. "You're a natural, then."

Marlow shrugged. "He's a Marine, remember."

That seemed to be her go-to explanation of his thoughts, or his abilities. True, most of his Marine brothers were strong, honorable men who'd taken to family life. His best bud . . .

No, he blocked that thought. Or tried to.

Now it was there, digging in and bringing along the familiar guilt.

Marlow touched his shoulder. "What is it?"

Usually he would play it off, avoid the truth. He didn't want to lie to Marlow, though. Not ever. So he said, "Just a bad memory."

Pixie crossed her arms on the table and studied him. "From your time as a Marine?"

Again, surprising himself, he said, "Yeah," and then he looked down at Andy's angelic face. "He has the cutest little nose." The attempt to divert them didn't work, at least not completely.

Pixie asked, "Do you have a good memory you could share?" To explain her question, she said, "That's what I do. When I start to remember how scared I was when I was sick, not knowing where to go or what to do, I try to think of a good memory instead and then concentrate on that."

Slowly, Cort nodded. It was a solid plan, so he went with it. "Good memory it is." He thought for only a second, then knew what he'd share. "When we first came here, I wasn't sure what to expect. We'd never been part of a real community before." No, they'd lived in places that forced a person to concentrate on survival—but that was another bad memory. "Everyone was quirky, open, and friendly in a way I hadn't seen before. Folks were good to Mom, and good to me." Without thinking about it, he cuddled Andy a little closer. "In no time at all, Bramble felt like home, when nothing else had before."

Pixie and Marlow shared a look, and then Pixie said, "To me, too. It confused me at first."

"You weren't used to trust," Marlow said. "Either of you. I'm glad Bramble is the kind of place that lets you trust again."

Did he trust? Cort trusted her, definitely. And Herman, who in many ways was like a father figure to him. The siblings could easily be his eccentric aunts and uncle. Letting the realization sink in, he nodded. "You're right. The people here are easier to trust."

"They're good people," Marlow agreed. "Not perfect, because no one is, but I've found them all to be genuine."

Pixie looked down for a moment. "After Dylan . . ." Her voice faded, but when neither he nor Marlow pressed her, she started again. "I felt really used, and that made me feel gullible, too. Like the biggest stooge alive."

"Pixie," Marlow started to say, ready to comfort her.

She shook her head. "I should've asked Dylan about providing for the baby, but I was just so mad at him . . . And embarrassed that I'd been so easy . . . And I honestly thought I'd be able to take care of myself." She rolled her eyes. "None of that made any sense once I started getting sick, but by then it was too late." She looked up at Cort. "That's a bad memory, I guess. Sorry."

"It was his loss," Cort put in. "He screwed up with Marlow, and with you. He spent his last days being angry and making himself miserable, and in the end, he lost not one but two terrific women."

Marlow smiled her agreement. "Perfect way to look at it."

"I came to that conclusion about my father, too." Understandably, both women went quiet again. Cort didn't share personal stuff very often, but something about sitting here with these two special women, holding an innocent baby after a delicious home-cooked meal, made it feel just right. "My father spent his life drunk and angry. Mean and abusive. Sometimes I wonder what made him that way, if he had a really hard life before meeting Mom, and maybe he didn't know any other way."

"It's possible," Marlow agreed. "But that doesn't excuse it."

"No, it doesn't. I don't mourn his death. If anything, I'm glad he died when he did, because it gave Mom a chance to find peace."

Pixie, a little lost because she didn't know his history, tried to quietly leave the table.

"It's okay," Cort told her. "If you talk to a few people around here, you'll hear about it."

Pixie shook her head. "I respect you and Marlow too much to ever pry."

"I admire that, but around here, no prying is necessary."

"It's true," Marlow said. "I need to take you to the tavern where I work. They have a photo of Cort on the wall in his uniform." She glanced at him, then added, "Looking very handsome, by the way."

"That seems like a lifetime ago." In the shortest way possible, he gave Pixie a rundown on his childhood. Predictably, tears welled in her eyes. She had to be one of the most tenderhearted young women he'd ever met, and damned if her vulnerability didn't make him feel like a very protective big brother. A novel emotion, for sure. "Hey, I got through it, and luckily, nothing like that will ever happen to Andy."

She nodded. "I'm determined that he'll have a good life."

"We'll make sure of it," Marlow said.

And that, of course, was why Cort loved her.

*   *   *

While Pixie nursed Andy in her bedroom and Cort got busy with the new lights, Marlow cleaned up the kitchen. The domestic routine was nice, especially since both of her dinner partners had tried to insist on helping. She'd been just as insistent that they were guests, and of course, she'd won in the end.

Just as she finished up, Pixie rejoined her in the kitchen with Andy now wide awake and smiling. "Thank you so much. I think that was the best meal I've ever had, especially with the great company."

"We'll do it more often," Marlow promised.

"I should get Andy home now. It's time for his bath."

"I can drive you—"

"No, I'll walk. It's not far, and it's a beautiful evening."

Marlow glanced at the clock. It'd be light for some time yet. "You're feeling strong enough?"

"I feel amazing, inside and out."

Wonderful! Watching Pixie bloom was one of the most satisfying things Marlow had ever experienced. "All right, if you're sure." She walked with her to the door, where Cort, on a ladder, was adding the new, brighter lighting.

When he heard the plan, he glanced up to Pixie's house, then apparently came to the same conclusion as Marlow. "I'll be up in about an hour to change your lights, too. Will that disturb Andy?"

"No, we'll be fine. And Cort? Thank you. For everything."

"I'm the landlord," he said, already back at work.

Pixie didn't give up. "I meant for the conversation over dinner, too. Being here with you two, almost like a family . . . it's a meal I'll always remember." Holding Andy in his carrier with one hand, the diaper bag over her shoulder, Pixie headed off across the lawn.

"She's overloaded," Marlow fretted.

"She's fine," he corrected. "She doesn't have that far to go, and she's feeling steady again. I bet she's enjoying a little independence, being able to do for herself. It's how you or I would feel."

Very true. "She appreciates everything." Marlow didn't want to think she'd ever taken her life for granted, but had she truly appreciated each and every special moment? "I want to be her family."

Cort glanced down at her. "Is that so?"

"An older sister, and an aunt to Andy. We discussed that today, before a fun shopping trip."

His brows lifted, then he smiled and got back to work. "Glad to hear it."

"I can only imagine what my mother-in-law will think, once she finds out that Pixie and I are friends."

"I think it's a blessing Pixie found you."

"A blessing for her—and for me," Marlow agreed.

"Might as well count me in there, too." He started down the ladder. "I'm enjoying it all as well."

Marlow moved out of his way, but when he reached the ground, he dropped his tools and gathered her into his arms. "Pixie is right. Dinner was great, not only delicious but incredible company, too."

"Like family?" she asked, searching his gaze. Had Cort had many family meals? From what she knew, it was just he and his mom, and after an awful childhood, he'd spent a lot of his time serving in the Marines.

His broad chest expanded as he inhaled a slow breath. "I never knew much about family, really, other than my mom. She and I ate a lot of meals together whenever I was home. It was nice, but in a totally different way."

Thrilled to have him open up a little, Marlow silently waited.

His forehead touched hers. "My best bud in the Marines was a family guy."

Was. Her heart thumped heavily, and her stomach clenched.

She could tell this was a bad memory, maybe the one Cort had been thinking of at dinner.

From the day she'd arrived, he'd been there for her. She wished she could have been there for him, too.

Lightly, she kissed him, then without a word, she wrapped her arms around his waist and squeezed. She waited for his usual inscrutable reaction. Maybe he'd hug her and then get back to work. Whatever he chose to do, or not do, she wouldn't pressure him, because he'd never pressured her.

Then suddenly, he held her closer with her face tucked under his chin so she couldn't look at him. "There was a deadly Osprey accident when I was stationed in North Carolina. I was supposed to be there, on that flight, but I'd left earlier that day to be with my mother."

Marlow's throat tightened with dread. She nestled against him, which was all she could do in her current position.

His voice was still strong and steady, but she felt the pain in the words as he spoke. "Mom's doctor had called, saying she might not make it through the night, so I was granted emergency leave."

Tears welled in her eyes. "You had to be with her."

He gave a single nod. "I was by her bedside when the Osprey left for Pensacola. Along the way, there was a catastrophic mechanical failure, and it went down." His throat worked as he swallowed heavily. "Everyone on board died."

Marlow didn't mean to, but a gasp escaped her, prompting him to kiss her temple.

"Twelve Marines died, including my best friend, Nathan." Silence stretched out. "He left behind a wife and two little kids."

Breathing was difficult when all she wanted to do was sob. "I'm sorry, so sorry," she managed to choke out. Good God, this was painful. She felt Cort's agony, and his undeserved guilt.

"It should have been me, Marlow. I was supposed to be on that flight."

"*No.*" Somehow she got out of his arms and glared up at him, furious that he would say such a thing. His expression was severe, yet wounded, softening her reaction. "No, Cort," she whispered.

"My mother died that night, too. I didn't have anyone else, but Nathan had a family who needed him."

I need you, she wanted to shout, but it wouldn't be fair to put that on him. "Everyone in this town needs you. Don't you know that?"

He started to turn away, but she knotted her hands in his shirt and did her best to bring him back around. She succeeded only because he let her. "I'm not a badass Marine, so I can't pretend to know how you feel. But I know it hurts, I swear I do."

His gaze veered from hers, but she brought it right back with a gentle touch to his cheek. "How is Nathan's wife now? His kids?"

"She remarried a few months ago. She seems happy. The kids are doing great. They've all . . . adjusted." He crushed Marlow against him. "They're both girls, cute as hell. Everyone is okay. I see that, and I'm glad." His mouth firmed, and his nostrils flared on a ragged breath. "I'm also aware of what he lost."

"It was tragic," she said, wishing there was a way to ease him. "All those heroes—"

"Brothers," he said. "Good men."

He was a good man. She had to make him see that. "That describes you, too, Cort. You are the finest man I've ever known."

He made a sound of disgust.

"It's true!" With one hand still knotted in his shirt, she thumped his chest. "This town is amazing, but you're a big part of what makes it that way. Your mother's life started out awful, but it ended happily because of you." She released him just long enough to swipe away her tears. "Don't you dare downplay your worth." Her voice broke. "Not to me."

Brows coming together, he whispered incredulously, "You're *crying*?"

"So? I'm allowed." She swallowed heavily, and more tears welled up. Damn it, now she understood why tears frustrated Pixie so much. But if there was ever a reason to cry, this was it. To see this strong, capable, caring man suffering such awful guilt . . . She'd cry buckets for him, whether he liked it or not.

"Babe, don't." Gently now, he cuddled her to his chest. "I'm sorry. I shouldn't have unloaded on you."

"Gah!" Taking him by surprise, Marlow shoved him back, nearly tripping herself in the process. She saw his shocked face, and it only angered her more. "I *want* you to unload on me!" She pressed a fist to her chest. "I want you to share with me. Trust me. *Include* me."

"Marlow?"

"Don't you dare look confused! There's no way you don't know that I'm . . ." *Falling in love with you.* She sucked in a startled breath. They stared at each other, both of them silent.

She wasn't falling. Oh, no.

She was flat on her face, completely and thoroughly in love with Cort Easton.

And she didn't even know if she'd get to stay in Bramble.

"Good God," she breathed, feeling as bewildered as he looked. Hastily, she stepped up to him again and tried to sound like a logical woman as she—nicely this time—embraced him. "Thank you for telling me, Cort. I mean that. I love that you shared with me. Please, always feel free. I want you to."

Cautiously, his hands came to her back.

The poor man probably didn't know if she'd explode on

him again. "Of course, I'm heartbroken for you, too, and for the men who lost their lives." To think he'd been carrying this burden all alone. That was the worst part. "The thing is, Cort, I'm so very, very glad you're still here. Not just in this town but in the entire world, because I swear, it's better with you in it."

He stroked his hands up and down her back as if to soothe a wild animal. "I'm glad you're here, too, in Bramble."

"With you." She tipped her head back. "Say it."

For long moments he just stared down into her wet eyes, then he growled, "With me," and punctuated the words with a kiss that seemed to put everything right.

His hands cupped her face as he deepened the kiss. He let up long enough to reiterate, "I'm glad you're here with me." Then he took her mouth again.

Marlow groaned. God, it felt good to be wanted by Cort. So good that she wouldn't have stopped, but he was a responsible guy—a Marine, she reminded herself—so when he gradually eased up, she slumped against him, trying to catch her breath.

His thumb brushed her cheek, then her damp bottom lip. "I'll make you a deal."

"I live for deals," she quipped back, feeling a little unsteady on her feet.

His mouth curled in one of those small smiles she cherished. "How about you stop trying to conquer the world, and I'll try to deal with my guilt?"

"Or," she said, loving him so much it almost hurt, "we could just be imperfectly human together." *For now. Tomorrow. Possibly . . . forever.*

"See. You always have a solid plan."

Wasn't easy, but she managed to stand upright entirely on her own.

He bent to pick up a tool. "Marlow?"

"Hmm?"

As he started back up the ladder, he said, "I care a hell of a lot about you, too."

Her heart floated. It wasn't a declaration of love, but for a man like Cort, it was a lot.

And as he'd said, she didn't need to conquer the world—just this small part of it. As far as she was concerned, she was making excellent progress.

CHAPTER 12

With the brighter flood lights installed, Marlow could see the surroundings of the cottage at night. The back flood lights had already illuminated the dock and quite a bit beyond. Now the front lights shone over her entire driveway, all the way up to the road. Could someone still lurk about? Sure. With the large trees and hills, there were enough shadows to hide in, but no one could get close to the house without being seen.

Cort had also set up cameras at the front and back of each house, with signs that stated the property was monitored. It seemed silly now because a week had gone by without incident. She truly believed Sandra was behind the snooping.

For now, Pixie's secret was safe. However, the young mother was happy to have the added security. The incident had clearly left her shaken. Cort had even added a timer to the lights. When it got dark, they automatically came on. Pixie was content.

The only thing that bothered Marlow was that Cort wouldn't let her repay him. Stubbornly, in that quiet way of his, he'd stated that the houses were still his and would remain so . . . even after she and Pixie had moved on.

"I'm not moving on," she muttered to herself while refilling a tray with drink orders. She loved that he'd opened up to her, but now she dwelled on how badly she'd handled it.

She'd *cried* on him. Then *yelled* at him. And she'd even tried to manhandle him, not that a breathing boulder like Cort could be physically moved.

Privately, he'd explained that he'd like for both of them to stay, but it wasn't up to him. The town had lived by the same set of rules for a long time.

"Stupid rules," Marlow said to herself. She checked her order, then grabbed the appetizers that were now ready, along with two burgers. For a weeknight, the tavern was awfully busy. Fortunately, she got off in an hour.

Leaving the kitchen, Marlow got back to work. She delivered the ordered food, then darted between tables to refill drinks. She was still stewing on her campaign to remain in Bramble when Cort arrived. Usually he sought her out right away, but today he found a seat and pulled out his notebook and pencil. Hmm. Perhaps he had a new job request and he needed to jot his thoughts down while they were fresh in his mind.

For Marlow, it was impossible to concentrate with him nearby. He had a presence that dominated a room. There were other men his age in Bramble, but they weren't Cort. They didn't have his magnetism, his appeal. At least not to her.

June had come and gone, and the July weather boasted plenty of sunshine and humidity. Herman had air conditioning in the tavern, but with the door always opening and closing, the air felt warm. The back of her neck was damp, as well as the bridge of her nose. Leo, a regular at the place who owned an arcade in town, was talking to her, but then Leo was always talking. It became impossible to follow along, not that Leo minded. Even if he asked a question, he didn't wait for an answer.

Marlow interrupted him to say, "Sorry, Leo. I need to refill my pitcher," and she hurried away.

Joann, from the dairy bar, waved her over. Marlow could tell by the woman's expression that she had gossip. Thankfully, it shouldn't be about her. Sandra and Aston hadn't returned, and everyone already knew about—and adored—Pixie.

After Pixie had come into the tavern one day, everyone now asked about her. Some visited her, others called her, and some offered help. People instinctively recognized Pixie's shyness, and they admired her dedication to Andy. She was a very likable person in many ways.

Marlow greeted Joann with, "Did you need anything else? Dessert? A refill on your cola?"

Shaking her head, Joann said quietly, "They're having a meeting about you."

Taken aback, Marlow asked, "Who? About what?"

Rolling her eyes, Joann said again, "About *you*. You've been at Cort's guesthouse so long now, no one believes it's just a vacation. It was bound to happen."

"What, exactly, was bound to happen?"

"Everyone thinks you're trying to be permanent."

Plunking the empty pitcher on the table and grabbing hold of the back of a chair, Marlow steadied herself. "When?" She drew a deep breath. "When is the meeting?"

"Wednesday night."

"But I have to work Wednesday! I won't be able to attend. I—"

"Shh. I shouldn't be telling you this." Joann gave a furtive look around. "The meetings are public, but they're set up in private."

Marlow's gumption flooded back. "They're hardly private if you know, and now I know, and all the eavesdroppers in here probably know, too." When she glanced at different customers, they all pretended to be busy.

Except for Cort.

He didn't shy away from her gaze. She doubted he shied away from anything. Things had changed between them. They were closer now. She felt it, but if she was forced to leave, what would happen?

Nothing, she assured herself. So she'd live in the next town over. So what?

So it wouldn't be Bramble, and now that she'd dug in, she wanted to stay.

She'd still see Cort, she assured herself. All week long, he'd made it clear just how much he cared. It was there in his touch, in his every word, in the way he sometimes stared at her, as if trying to figure out a puzzle.

"What time is the meeting?" Marlow asked.

Shrugging, Joann said, "I honestly don't know. It changes. The members figure out what works, and then they get together and make decisions."

"That doesn't seem fair!"

"Other people can weigh in—*if* they know about the meeting and attend."

Someone cleared their throat, and when Marlow looked back, she saw grumpy Ben Crawford with an empty coffee cup lifted toward her. He had a few bites of pie left. She was on the clock, so she needed to get back to work.

"Thanks for letting me know, Joann." And now that she knew, she'd figure out a way to attend that meeting. To fight for herself. To cement her citizenship in Bramble.

"I'm rooting for you," Joann said.

"You are?"

"Pretty sure we all are. You're one of us now."

She heard murmured voices saying, "That's right," "One of us," and "She's not going anywhere." Tension eased from her shoulders; affection lightened her worry. Turning to face her curious audience, she held up a fist, like a championship fighter, and got a few laughs with mingled applause and whistles.

She loved this town. She loved these people. Most of all, she loved Cort. With that much love going around, how could she lose?

Cort watched her work. For a moment there, Marlow had looked devastated, then defeated. For only a moment, though. He knew she'd heard about the upcoming meeting.

Did she think he wouldn't fight for her?

Probably, because he hadn't yet told her the truth: that he was in love with her. She'd *almost* told him, and if she had, he'd have declared himself on the spot. But she'd pulled back, and that made him think she wasn't yet ready for such a big step.

Though her marriage had been rocky for years, it hadn't officially ended that long ago. Conflicting feelings probably still plagued her. He believed she'd fallen out of love with her husband, *if* she'd ever truly loved him in the first place.

But divorce and death were two different things, both of them devastating to the emotions.

The last thing she needed was for him to try to tie her down with commitment.

He knew that, and he'd still unloaded his biggest issue on her. It shamed him. Not because he was human enough to care, but because of his priorities. When he had nightmares now, they weren't about his abusive father or his mother passing away. He'd grown up with those realities. His dad had always been a mean bastard, and his mother had always suffered. Cort had despised his dad, loved his mom, but he'd lived with the reality that she could be gone at any time, because his father might go too far and kill her. When it came to his mother, what ate at him the most was that she'd finally found happiness, and then lost it to ill health.

If he could have saved her, he would have. He'd have done anything for her.

Yet those were all familiar feelings, ones he'd grown accustomed to and had learned to deal with.

Having twelve of his brothers die unexpectedly . . . that was the kind of shock that took out a guy's knees. And Nathan . . . Cort closed his eyes.

Nathan had been the best of them. A comedian when you needed one, a listener when someone had to talk, quietly supportive no matter what. He'd had so much to live for.

"What are you working on?"

Cort opened his eyes to see Marlow at his table, a cautious smile on her face as she set a glass of water and a cup of coffee before him.

He turned over his notebook so she couldn't read it. "Joann told you about the meeting." A statement, not a question.

Tucking the tray under her arm and frowning at him, she said, "Apparently, everyone knows. Why didn't you tell me?"

"Because I'm handling it." The look on her face almost made him laugh. She'd been all geared up to be mad, and he'd deflated her anger.

Suspicion brought her brows together. "You're handling it how?"

Now there was the issue. If he told her, he could just imagine how she'd react. She wouldn't like it—that much he knew for sure. Marlow was the type of person who wanted to handle things on her own. But if they were going to be a couple—*and they were*, as soon as she was ready—then she'd have to get used to his help.

Just as he'd have to get used to her crying every now and then. *For him.*

That still felt like a kick to the heart. Terrible and wonderful, both.

She'd gone through her own traumas dry-eyed and focused.

But for him, his strong, beautiful, take-on-the-world Marlow had broken down in tears. It humbled him as nothing else could.

"Cort," she warned.

"You've inspired me," he replied honestly, knowing it was true. From the day he'd met her, she'd been inspiring . . . well, everyone. Him most of all, though. "The way you got on with your life despite everything." Things that would have emotionally crippled a person without her iron resolve. "You knew what you wanted, and you went after it full force."

In a mere whisper, she asked, "What do you want?"

"Peace in my own life. Happiness." *Love*. That meant having her—here, or anywhere else. "Instead of continuing to kick myself for not doing enough—"

"That's not true," she interjected desperately, quickly taking the seat next to him. "You did everything you could and—"

He touched a finger to her lips. When Marlow decided to defend someone, it took her a little while to wind down. "I think I've lost enough. I'm going to start celebrating the life I have and the people who matter to me." *You most of all*.

Her dark gaze searched his. "Will you tell me what, and who, that is?"

Soon—when she couldn't thwart his plans. "You have a customer waiting."

Her frown returned. "I have another half hour to work. Will you still be here when I'm done?"

It was one of the few days when she was scheduled to get off at eight, instead of eleven. He planned to make the most of it. "Can I convince you to come to my house for a late dinner? I have steaks to grill."

"I'm famished, so I'd love that." She leveled a stern look at him. "And then we can discuss some things."

He loved her stern, serious moods. Not in the least threatened, he gave her a crooked smile. "I'll be waiting."

Watching Marlow hustle off to work was a distinct pleasure. She moved with purpose and grace, accomplishing so much without looking rushed.

He'd just gotten back to his task when Herman plopped down in the seat across from him. "What's the plan?"

Pretending confusion, Cort cocked one eyebrow. "Plan?" Of course he had one, and Herman would be part of it. Fortunately, he was already playing his role.

"Don't give me that." Not bothering to hide his irritation, Herman thumped a hand onto the table. "There's no way you'll let Marlow be run off."

"She wouldn't go far anyway," Cort stated quietly. "She's looking at property in Lankton."

"Lankton!" An imminent implosion was evident in his gaze. "No! It'd be too far for her to drive here every day to work."

"It wouldn't be ideal, but knowing Marlow, she'd manage. The property is nice, though. I checked it out for her yesterday." As if he didn't have bigger things on his mind, Cort explained, "She wanted to know if it'd be possible to take out a few interior walls. Good news, it is. Pretty sure she'll put in an offer."

Red-faced, Herman muttered, "You live here. She works here."

Glancing over, he saw Marlow laugh at something Leo said, then while the man was still gabbing away, she patted his back and moved on. "I didn't make the rules."

"What about Pixie?"

"Knowing Marlow, I assume she'd take Pixie with her." She was like a mother hen, and Cort loved that about her, too.

Suddenly Herman loomed closer, so close that Cort felt his breath. "You're bullshitting an old bullshitter. You're in love with her."

"Yeah, I am."

Herman drew back. "You admit it?"

"I wouldn't lie to you." It was past time for him to own up to his feelings. "I probably should have said this sooner, but you're the closest thing I've ever had to a father figure. Everything you did for my mother, and then for me." Yeah, seeing the look on Herman's face, he knew this talk was long past due. "I appreciate it, and I especially appreciate you. You're the one I've always talked to when I needed to work something out." Or when he'd just needed someone who cared.

Completely taken off guard, Herman flushed. "I . . ." He cleared his throat, twice, and his words emerged with reverent gravity. "I'm honored, especially since I've always thought of you as a son. I couldn't be more proud of you if you were my own. You're a good man, Cort, the best."

That was almost identical to what Marlow had said. He certainly tried to be a good man, but the best? If he pleased Marlow, and Herman, too, that was good enough for him. "Thank you."

"You have to fight for her, son. You know that, right?"

For one of the few times in his life, Cort knew he was a lucky man. Yes, he'd lost people who were vitally important to him. His mother, best friend, guys who were like brothers . . . as Marlow had pointed out, everyone had their share of difficulties, some more than others.

But he'd also had incredible blessings. His mother had loved him enough to sacrifice for him, and the people in this town had accepted him as one of their own. As a Marine, he'd learned the best life had to offer, and he'd met incredible men who'd shown him what his father hadn't—the meaning of honor, loyalty, and bravery. How to be responsible, to work hard, to meet and exceed expectations.

Now he had Marlow, and she was a bigger gift than he'd ever dared hope for. She was the kind of sunshine that cut through a cloudy day, a grin when his thoughts turned dark, and a warm hug when he didn't know he needed it. There was Pixie, and Andy. And a future to embrace.

"I plan to fight for her, but it'll take more than me to cause change." Cort watched him, waiting to see if he'd take the bait.

Herman didn't hesitate. "It's not just you. I'll fight, too."

"Marlow wouldn't want strife," he warned. "You know her well enough to understand that. Doesn't mean we can't sway the town with logic, right?"

Grinning, Herman tilted closer again. "What's the plan?"

And just like that, everything fell into place.

Pixie was busy on the laptop Marlow had loaned her, searching through various merchandisers and making notes. Andy had fallen asleep thirty minutes ago, and she wanted to make the most of the time she had.

Next to the laptop was a stack of her sketches, with her favorite one on top. She didn't know if Marlow would like it, and she was incredibly nervous about showing it to her, but if Marlow could be brave, then so could she.

Her simple rendering of a firefly, with flourishes, had turned out really cute. Delicate black lines, a few decorative swirls, and a yellow glow at the tail. Pixie had made several copies, and then experimented with font around it to create a logo for Marlow. No one had asked her for a logo, but she'd doodled while nursing Andy, so it wasn't as if she'd taken time away from the tasks assigned to her.

When the knock sounded on her front door, she went utterly still. Ridiculous, that she was still so jumpy over a visit. There was no threat, had never been a threat, really. Marlow had handled her in-laws.

Still, before Pixie moved, she snatched up her phone and checked the small image from the camera feed. Two men were at her door.

Her first instinct was to call Marlow in a panic. But no, she immediately rethought that. Marlow trusted her to work, to become more independent.

It was time to get started on that.

Straightening her shoulders with resolve, Pixie tried to think logically. It was still light out. Her doors were locked. She and Andy were safe.

She needed to ask who was visiting.

The second, slightly harder knock, jolted her to her feet. She didn't want the noise to awaken Andy, so she hurried into the living room and peered out the window. "Who is it?"

A big, official-looking dude dressed in khakis pointed her out to another, older guy. They both stared at her for a moment, and then the older man asked, "Pixie Nolan?"

The double-time beating of her heart stole the strength of her voice. "Yes?"

His brows came together. "I'm Aston Heddings. We need to talk."

Dark spots danced before her eyes. Gasping, Pixie straightened away from the window, one hand blindly finding the wall for much-needed support. Her legs felt like rubber, her lungs strangled. Forget double-time; her heart launched into a frantic race that threatened to bring on a faint.

Dylan's father. *Here.*

The knock came again, this time more of a pounding, and predictably, Andy woke up with a startled cry.

At least that sound sent new strength through her system.

Pixie demanded through the window, "What do you want?"

"Only to make you an offer."

She shook her head. "What offer?"

"Considerable payment—if you'll go away."

Go away? To *where?* This place was home. Marlow and Cort were family.

Only . . . it wasn't really her home, and though she could pretend all she wanted, they weren't her family.

The truth settled heavily in her soul. "Just a minute," she said, wishing she could go numb instead of feeling so much. Still carrying her phone, she rushed to the bedroom and picked up Andy. His face was red, big tears filling his eyes.

"I'm sorry, sweetheart." Pixie cuddled him close, murmuring apologies in between kisses to soothe him. "I didn't mean to make you wait. Everything is okay." Only it wasn't. "Shh, shh. Mommy's here."

His cries turned to hiccups, and he pressed his face to her shoulder.

She'd promised Marlow that she'd call if she heard from Dylan's family, only she hadn't heard from them. Finding them at her front door was different.

If she could get rid of them, she'd tell Marlow all about it afterward.

More pounding made her jump. They weren't giving her time to make a call anyway.

If it was anyone other than Dylan's father, Pixie might've been able to figure out what to do. But this was her baby's grandfather. Worse, he was a ridiculously wealthy, influential man.

But did that excuse bad manners? No, it did not. So how dare he just drop in on her? And why keep banging on her door like that? So rude.

Disgruntled now, she snatched up a diaper and wipes and returned to the front room to another hard knock. *Thank God for sturdy locks.*

Andy cried anew, and that did it. Through the window, Pixie snapped, "Stop making so much noise! You're upsetting my baby." The second she said it, she sucked in an appalled breath, and then quickly retreated so they couldn't see her.

Oh, no. Why had she said that? Their silence was deafening.

Andy, however, could no doubt be heard squalling.

She didn't dare peek out again. Holding Andy closer, trying to soothe him, Pixie wondered what to do next.

She filled her lungs with a deep, slow breath. Her heartbeat slowed. Her spine stiffened.

Sooner or later, Dylan's parents were bound to find out about Andy. They'd somehow located her at a motel, so of course they'd learn about a grandchild. She should have listened to Marlow and Cort, should have arranged a better meeting . . .

Too late now.

As calmly as possible, she returned to the window. The older man was pale and grim-faced; he almost looked in pain. The other guy was rigid with anger.

Pixie said, "I need five minutes."

"You can't keep Mr. Heddings waiting," the angry dude growled.

Wanna bet? "Wait or don't wait, but I need five minutes." Without another word, Pixie went to the love seat to change Andy's diaper. He continued to fuss, kicking and anxious to be nursed. She'd have to make it a very quick visit with Mr. Heddings so she could feed her son. If the man wanted to get to know Andy, it would need to be on another day, when he was polite enough to call in advance and make appropriate arrangements instead of dropping by unannounced.

Now was not a good time.

Once Andy was freshly diapered, his fist in his mouth, Pixie smoothed her hair, gave a tug to her loose T-shirt and, carrying Andy close to her chest, went to the door and turned the locks.

The second the door swung open, Mr. Heddings stared— first at her, and then at Andy. Sweat beaded on his temples, and his eyes appeared red.

Pixie braced herself, for what she wasn't sure.

Until his gaze met hers and he stated, "I'll give you twenty-five thousand dollars to leave and never come back."

When Cort slowed in front of the lake house, then came to an idling stop, Marlow's thoughts veered from her intention to first get Cort naked, love him silly, and then grill him on his so-called plans. She'd been figuring out everything she wanted to say, and how to say it, when he stopped.

One glance at Pixie's place and she saw why. A Mercedes

Maybach sat in her driveway, the same car that had driven away when Pixie had spotted her nighttime intruder.

Worse, she recognized Aston Heddings with another man, standing at the open front door.

It took all she had not to leave her car right there in the road and run to Pixie. She thought about blasting her horn to get Cort moving when he slowly, as if undecided about what to do, pulled his truck into the driveway.

Parking behind him, Marlow grabbed her purse and started to get out. Cort opened her door but blocked her in. "Stay put a minute."

Her brows shot up, but she didn't have time for this. "That's Aston."

Staring at the men, Cort said, "I don't care if he's Santa Claus. This feels off."

She was even more alarmed—for Pixie. "It'll be fine." As she scrambled out past him, she said, "Behave, okay?"

Given the incredulous look on his face, no one had ever told Cort to behave before.

She snagged his hand. Whatever was about to happen, she wanted him with her.

Trotting forward, Marlow called out, "Aston, hello." From behind the men, she could see Pixie, her eyes dazed and her body frozen, and the sight put Marlow into a killing rage. Not that she'd show it. Yet. No way would she give Aston the upper hand. "What are you doing here?" She glanced around. "Where's Sandra?"

"She's at home." Turning his back on Pixie, Aston directed all his anger at Marlow. "*You knew.*"

Oh, this wasn't good. Mustering a show of bravado, Marlow thrust up her chin. "Knew what, exactly?"

"That Pixie Nolan is here, that she has a child she claims is Dylan's."

Still clinging to Cort's hand, Marlow said, "Yes, I've known Pixie for a little while now."

Aston's voice rose an octave. "And you didn't see fit to tell us?"

He might as well have shouted *traitor*! The accusation was there in his florid face and the bunching of his eyebrows.

There wasn't much she could say. He and Sandra should have been notified, but then again, it wasn't her place to do that. "If you want to speak to me, you'll lower your voice." Releasing Cort, Marlow stepped around Aston to reach Pixie. In a near whisper, she asked, "Are you all right?"

Pixie's mouth opened, but nothing came out. Andy was starting to fuss, and when Marlow glanced back at Cort, he appeared far too grim.

She cleared her throat. "Pixie? Would you like to invite them in?"

"He . . . he offered me money." Pixie seemed to have a hard time replying. "A lot of it."

"Oh?" As she turned to face the men, Marlow stepped in front of Pixie so that she mostly blocked her from their view. "Trying to buy her off, Aston?"

"Dear God," he breathed, his hands in fists at his sides. "This is low even for you, Marlow."

Well, that stung. "Even for me?"

Aston took an aggressive step forward, and Cort was there, blocking his way. "I wouldn't."

Appalled, Aston stepped back, then remembered himself and turned to the man with him—who took that look as permission to press forward.

Marlow stood her ground but said, "Cort?"

"Yes?" he growled.

"If he doesn't behave, you don't have to either."

Cort slowly smiled, and now he was the one stalking forward, effectively backing both men farther away from the door.

Marlow had no idea what she might have unleashed, but she had faith that Cort could handle the situation, one way or another. He was a calm, capable, peaceful man, she reminded herself. He wouldn't escalate the confrontation.

Needing a moment, Marlow said, "If you gentlemen would all wait here, I'll discuss this with Pixie." She started to close the door—not completely, just enough for privacy—but the man with Aston reached out to stop her.

Cort said, "No." Just that, calmly stated, but wow, it had impact.

"Who *are* you?" Aston demanded.

Oh, Lord. Marlow realized things had just gotten even more complicated.

"You first," Cort said with a nod at the guy Aston had brought along.

"He works for me."

Cort nodded. "Marlow is a tenant."

"More than a tenant," Aston sneered.

"More than an employee," Cort countered.

Well. Clearly, Cort had this under control. She touched his arm. "Just a few minutes, okay? If they choose to leave, that's fine."

"Sure." Cort stationed himself on the front stoop, an immovable object standing in the way of anyone who tried to rush her timeline. "Let me know when you're ready." Then he pulled the door shut. Completely.

Well darn. Now she'd have no idea what was happening out there. That was impetus enough for her to hurry the discussion along.

Releasing an unsteady breath, she quickly turned her attention to Pixie. "Come on." She led Pixie to the love seat and urged her to sit.

"I . . . I need to feed Andy."

"Do you want privacy?"

She grabbed Marlow's hand. "No. Don't leave me."

In that moment, Marlow knew she'd fight dragons—or

angry in-laws—for this wounded young woman. "I'm right here." Andy started to fuss, knowing what was to come, so Marlow said, "Go on. We can talk while you nurse him."

With a nod, Pixie got the baby settled, but she wouldn't meet Marlow's gaze. After a moment, she said, "He offered me twenty-five thousand dollars to go away."

"Bastard," Marlow replied mildly, but the offer worried her. "What do you want to do?"

"It's so much money. I could repay you and Cort."

It was incredibly hard to know how to respond. She wanted to grab Pixie and tell her not to go. But more than that, she wanted Pixie to *want* to stay. She wanted her to look to the future and think about plans and consequences. "Neither Cort nor I have asked for any payment."

"I know, but it's still a debt." She faced Marlow, her blue eyes full of doubt. "I feel it, in my heart." She didn't falter or look away. "I want you to be proud of me."

"Oh, Pixie." Marlow smiled through her sadness—and her pride. "Don't you know? I already am."

As if she didn't believe her, Pixie continued. "Mr. Heddings threw that out there, and my head's been swimming ever since." She reached for Marlow's hand again. "It's selfish of me, I know."

Bracing herself, Marlow waited.

"But I don't want to go. I don't want to leave you, or Cort, or this town."

The relief was enough to wilt Marlow. "Then don't go! Stay. We'll build a fantastic future together."

Pixie breathed harder. "You mean it?"

Nodding quickly, Marlow said, "I know Cort will agree."

Pixie's smile was a beautiful thing, but then, she was a stunning young woman. As her health had returned, and her color improved, she positively glowed. Especially when she held Andy.

"Cort's pretty awesome, isn't he?"

"The most awesome." In every way. That's why Marlow loved him. "We may not be able to stay right here in Bramble, but we will stay close. This is home now. For both of us."

"Home." Pixie squeezed her hand tighter. "And family. God, that means so much to me!"

"Definitely family, because I've grown used to being a big sister and aunt."

Reassured and no longer panicked, Pixie grinned. "I want to learn to be independent, like you. I want a stable future for Andy. And I want him to have good people around him. You and Cort are the best people I know."

Marlow's heart turned over. "Thank you. I'm sure Cort will be as flattered as I am." He'd lost his mother and his best friend, all in a twenty-four-hour period. Knowing that helped her to understand Cort a little better.

He protected the people he cared about.

He went out of his way to help them, and she was so glad he had a town full of people who embraced him. Without a doubt, he would want to protect and nurture Pixie and Andy, too.

But when it came to Marlow, would he feel the same? She knew he cared. She felt it every time he held her, each time he encouraged her and applauded her. It was there in his secret little smiles, in the way he sometimes watched her when he didn't think she'd notice. Especially at work. Or when he thought she was still sleeping beside him.

Yet he would feel different about her because she wasn't in need. She was self-reliant, empowered, with money and re-sources. She had choices, had always had choices, so how deep did Cort's feelings for her go?

It wasn't an answer she would get today, not now with big trouble right outside Pixie's door. She knew her in-laws, knew how they liked to take over. Even if they did accept Andy as a grandchild—and there was no guarantee of that—would they accept the boundaries Pixie would impose and respect her for the amazing mother she was?

With their shared history, Marlow didn't think so.

When Andy finished nursing, Marlow knew they had to plan. "So, to start building that independence, what do you say I let Mr. Heddings in? We can introduce him to Andy, you can politely turn down his offer, and we'll go from there."

Tentatively, Pixie said, "I could maybe invite him back, him and Mrs. Heddings, I mean." She hurried on. "You were right. I should have told them already. It's just that everything was so nice here, I wanted to enjoy it in peace for a while."

"Understandable, after what you'd been through."

Once Pixie had burped Andy, Marlow took the baby. Together, they went to the door.

Cort still stood there, arms crossed, one shoulder leaning against the door frame, relaxed but immovable.

Aston paced in the yard while his bully boy glared daggers at Cort. In that moment, Marlow made a decision. She touched Cort's shoulder. "We're ready," she said quietly.

He straightened, glanced at Pixie, and asked, "You're okay?"

Smile shy, Pixie nodded. "Yes, thank you."

Cort moved to the side, saying to Marlow, "It's your show."

Actually, it should have been Pixie's, but to get things started, she called out, "Aston?"

His head jerked up, and he glared at her.

"Would you like to come in for a few minutes?" When he agreed, she would stipulate that his aggressive friend should wait outside.

Aston surprised her by locking his gaze on Pixie. "Fifty thousand."

Pixie sucked in a breath.

Cort's enigmatic expression never changed.

"She doesn't want your money, Aston." Marlow put her hand on Pixie's back. "Now, do you want to meet your grandson?"

He breathed harder. "One hundred thousand."

Stumbling back, her eyes wide as saucers, Pixie looked at Cort, then at Marlow.

Say no, Marlow silently urged her. *Say no.* Pixie was so stunned, it was a wonder she didn't faint.

Then Pixie took a step outside the door, her head held high, her chin elevated. Only shaking a little, she said, "I appreciate the offer, Mr. Heddings. I really do. It's incredibly generous. More money than I've ever even dreamed of."

Aston said, "You and your child can have a whole new life— somewhere far from here."

"No, I can't. This is the only life I want." She reached for Cort's hand, and he willingly gave it. Then she put her other hand on Marlow's shoulder.

Oh, it felt good to be united like this. Cort's expression didn't change, but Marlow knew the gesture pleased him. She'd gotten to the point that she could sense what he wouldn't say, and standing there with her and Pixie felt right to him.

But then, he was a man of strong convictions and honor. She couldn't say the same for Aston. Honestly, she wasn't sure what Aston was thinking, or what he was doing.

Voice strong, Pixie said, "I'm sorry to disappoint you, but I can't take your money."

"I'll—"

She shook her head. "Doesn't matter what you offer. I'm staying. Oh, and Marlow wanted me to contact you and Mrs. Heddings. I asked her for a little time. It's not right for you to blame her."

Unappeased, Aston said, "She should have contacted me herself. Then we could have already proved what a fraud you are."

Pixie didn't waver. She didn't shout or cry. She said simply, "Since you're not interested in meeting Andy, and you're only being rude, you should go."

"*Andy*," he sputtered in rising tones. "That was my father's name!"

"Really?" To Pixie's credit, she didn't flinch from his anger. "I didn't know that. Before he died, Dylan suggested the name if I had a boy. From that day on, I thought of the baby as Andy."

"It's outrageous!"

"I sincerely wish you could discuss it with Dylan. I wasn't aware of the significance."

"I demand a paternity test. Immediately."

Pixie nodded.

"Until then, you won't get a dime from us."

"I wouldn't accept money from you anyway. Have a good day, Mr. Heddings."

Marlow was in awe of the graceful and kind way Pixie had just handled herself. When she glanced over at Cort, his inscrutable expression had been replaced by a small smile of satisfaction.

Together, the three of them went inside. Marlow first, followed by Pixie. Of course, Cort made sure he was last to protect their backs.

Andy, the little sweetheart, kicked his legs, cooing.

Cort hugged Pixie right off her feet. "Bravo. You handled that well."

"Yes, you did," Marlow agreed. "It was perfect." Currently filled with love—all kinds of love—Marlow felt extreme pity for Aston. Because of his attitude, he'd never know anything like this. And that, truly, was a shame.

CHAPTER 13

By silent agreement, Marlow and Cort decided to have dinner with Pixie rather than leave her alone. She'd made them both proud, but anyone who knew her could see that it had cost her to confront Aston that way.

He wasn't just Dylan's father, he was an affluent man of power, and he'd been incredibly ugly to Pixie. His offer to buy her off, the equivalent of hush money, had been an insult, a clear indication that he thought she was lying about Andy. Would he not even consider the possibility that the baby was his grandson?

Well, he had mentioned a paternity test, so maybe he had doubts.

Cort was being extra gentle with Pixie, his protectiveness in full force, and Marlow loved it.

Later, when she had him alone, she'd mention how much she appreciated his emotional support, while politely explaining that *she* could take care of herself. She couldn't recall Dylan ever standing up for her like that, but then, it had never been required. The only angry men Marlow had ever faced were in boardrooms negotiating massive deals with execs and assistants present, and more recently, Dylan and his hateful lawyer.

Not to pat herself on the back, but she'd always held her own.

As Marlow pondered, she walked back and forth with Andy so that Pixie could get some baby supplies together before joining them at Cort's house.

Then she spotted the sketches. "Oh, wow." She lifted the top sheet to look more closely. "Are these our fireflies?"

Cort cocked a brow. "Did you adopt some specific fireflies that I don't know about?"

"You know what I mean. Bramble fireflies." She shot him a smile. "They're special."

Coming around the corner with a freshly loaded diaper bag, Pixie caught her looking at the sketches and flushed bright pink.

Her reaction prompted Marlow to give the sketches closer scrutiny. "These are stunning. Where did you find them, Pixie?"

"I, um . . ." She practically shuffled her feet. "I did them."

"You did them?"

"Drew them, I mean. Sketched. Quickly." She hurried toward the back door to get her shoes.

"No way." Marlow tilted the paper so Cort could better see as he looked over her shoulder. "They're incredible." She went through a few more drawings, then noticed the stack of notes Pixie had compiled for prospective products. She'd certainly been busy! And better still, the items were exactly what Marlow had been looking for.

"Very nice," Cort agreed. "You have real talent."

"It's just a simple sketch—with a little glowing butt." Pixie inched closer, too. "I added your name."

"I see." Bouncing Andy a little, Marlow read aloud, "Marlow's Whimsy." She grinned at Cort. "Isn't that clever?"

"What exactly do you plan to sell?"

"Pixie and I talked about it, and I'm thinking casual clothes like T-shirts, tanks and halters, maybe some loose, flowing skirts, sundresses, things like that. Summery clothes but also custom jewelry that's affordable. Coffee mugs and sun hats." The more products Marlow mentioned, the more she wanted. "Seasonal stuff for holidays and some kitschy things, like maybe coasters, little birdhouses. Oh! Maybe firefly houses."

Getting into the spirit, Pixie said, "She's talked about beaded pouches, pot holders, maybe custom puzzles made from photos of the sunset over the lake."

Cort's smile went crooked. "I think it all sounds great. And yeah, Marlow's Whimsy is perfect."

"Pixie, what you've done looks great, and I love that you incorporated a firefly. Could we use this as our logo?" Not giving her a chance to get flustered, Marlow said, "I'd pay you well."

"What? No. I mean, sure, I made it for you, so you can do whatever you want with it. But it's a gift. I can't take money for it."

"Of course, I'll pay you." Marlow couldn't stop admiring the design. "I want you to create a few more, slightly different from this one, to use as prints to sell."

"Great idea." Cort took the diaper bag from Pixie. "Your work is worth something, and Marlow is a good businesswoman. You can trust her on this."

"Of course I do! It's just . . ." Now, with Aston gone, Pixie looked ready to cry, but they were happy tears. "You guys are the best." She gave Colt a big squeeze, then without lifting her face, turned to do the same with Marlow, enclosing both her and Andy in the embrace.

Marlow heard her sniff and patted her back. "You're going to be okay, Pixie."

She nodded, looked up with a big smile and tears in her eyes, and laughed as if the weight of the world had been lifted from her shoulders. "You know what? I finally believe it."

Hours later, after a wonderful meal with wonderful people, Pixie felt stronger than she ever had. Amazing how standing up to a bully would do that. Seeing the disdain, the disbelief on

Mr. Heddings's face had made her want to shrivel up and die. She understood the man, because she'd often felt that same way about herself.

The thing was, she hadn't set out to sleep with a married man.

She hadn't planned on getting pregnant. Or sick.

She'd certainly never planned on needing charity.

Life had a way of throwing unwelcome surprise parties that could leave a person completely defeated.

Marlow claimed that everyone made mistakes, because everyone was flawed. She said Pixie had no business thinking she could avoid every pitfall, since no one in creation ever had. It was so funny how Marlow could be both assertive and compassionate, blunt but kind. She suggested that instead of beating herself up over mistakes, Pixie should move forward with determination to do better. And when she tripped, as she was likely to do, she should learn from the mistake and get going again.

Those suggestions seemed attainable. She *could* be a better person. A more independent woman. The best mother she was capable of being.

And she'd be a good friend, too.

It honestly wouldn't have mattered if Mr. Heddings had offered her a million dollars. She owed Marlow her loyalty, and she owed Cort her appreciation.

She owed them so much, and all they expected was for her to do her best.

Careful not to wake Andy, she lowered him into his crib and changed his diaper.

Oh, to sleep the sleep of the innocent.

When she finished, she brushed her teeth and changed into loose shorts and an oversized T-shirt—her version of pajamas—and went out back to watch the sunset. Cort had told her that the most important day was today. She couldn't change yesterday and didn't know what tomorrow would bring, so she should put her all into today.

And she had. She was planning for a better future, trying her best, and she wanted to make the most of today.

Over steak and potatoes, a few laughs, a little worry, and amazing company, she'd enjoyed the day to the fullest. She didn't feel like an interloper. She felt appreciated. She felt like family.

For the first time in a very long time, she liked herself.

Cort could feel Marlow gearing up. She was trying to be sly about it as they put away the dishes after taking Pixie home.

Home. The girl really did have a home now, regardless of where she actually wound up living. If she couldn't stay in Bramble—though he was hoping she could—she'd still have Marlow, she'd still have him. That's what home was all about. Not the building you lived in but the people in your life. The ones who filled you up and understood you, who questioned you and laughed with you. People who sometimes frustrated you but didn't stop caring.

Pixie had that now. To Cort, she was like a little sister, only better, because he was better. He was in an emotional place where he could be the type of supportive big brother Pixie deserved. Marlow had gotten him there.

He'd always tried to show the town his appreciation, but now he accepted that living here meant more than that. It wasn't just what folks had given his mother but what they'd given him, too. He loved Bramble, loved Marlow, and he loved Pixie and Andy as well. All different types of love that fed his soul, making him whole in a way he'd never been before.

As they finished up in the kitchen, Cort asked, "Something on your mind, Marlow?"

"Actually, yes." She turned from the sink, her hands braced

behind her, her look challenging. "This plan of yours. Are you going to tell me about it?"

Inside he smiled. Outside, too. Hell, he felt like smiling all the damn time lately. "How about you try trusting me, instead?"

"Dirty pool!" Huffing a laugh, she pushed away from the sink to confront him. "I do trust you, but I really want to know."

It was the most natural thing in the world to pull her in close, hold her pressed against him in blood-heating ways, and to kiss her. "I'm a Marine," he teased. "I use whatever tactics I need to."

"Well, you were great with Pixie." Slipping out of his hold but taking his hand, she led him around the house to double check the doors. "Are all Marines so nurturing?"

Putting a hand on her ass, he countered, "Are all businesswomen so sexy?"

She grinned over her shoulder at him. "You know what? With you, I feel sexy."

He gave a low growl, nuzzled her neck until she giggled, then got her started up the stairs. Along the way, he did more teasing. Touching. Making suggestions that had her hurrying her steps.

In the bedroom, she pulled her shirt away from her body, fanning herself a little. "We sat outside and it's been warm. Maybe I should shower real quick—"

Knowing he wouldn't last that long, Cort backed her up to the bed. "Let's shower after." And he removed his shirt.

On a slow breath, she removed hers, too. "If you're sure."

"I'm completely sure—that you're perfect." Absolutely perfect—for him.

An hour later, physically relaxed, Cort turned his head toward Marlow. Her hair was spread wildly over the pillow, her skin dewy as she sighed, and he knew he wanted to spend the rest of his days like this, making love to Marlow, teasing her and planning the future. Watching her sleep and being with her when she woke up. Sharing sunrises and sunsets, fireflies, and life.

"Now I really need a shower."

"You're still perfect," he said, meaning it.

She glanced over at him. "Do you think we could interrupt this pleasure coma for something a little more . . . serious?"

From one concern to another, Cort's thoughts jumped around. Would she grill him on his plan to keep her in Bramble? Would she announce that she'd decided to move to Lankton? Was she concerned about Pixie? Concerned about something else?"

"Hey." She grinned at him, then half crawled over his chest. "It's not a big thing."

"Okay." So then what?

"With Aston and his goon . . . I appreciate that you were there. And I know I sort of used you as a threat."

The way Marlow had said, so enticingly, that he didn't have to behave had put caution in the other men's eyes. Both Aston and his fancy-ass bodyguard had gone alert. Rightfully so. Of course, Cort knew Marlow wouldn't want him jumping the gun and demolishing anyone. He wasn't a loose cannon. The opposite. He was completely in control of himself. Except maybe where Marlow was concerned; from day one she'd kept him off kilter.

"I just want to make it clear," she said. "I can take care of myself."

"Believe me, I'm well aware. You could take care of yourself, a business, and this entire town, and no doubt look hot doing it. Your point?"

Her lips twitched. "I love the way you see me. Before you, no one would ever have accused me of being sexy."

"You hung around with a bunch of businessmen, right?" They might have been uptight and too polished to show it, but there was no way Cort would believe they'd been unaware of her earthy appeal. "Trust me, they saw it."

"Before you," she said again, "I'm not sure I'd have wanted anyone to think it. With you, I like it—a lot." She smooshed a smiling kiss to his mouth. "The thing is, unless I specifically ask you to intervene—"

Whoa. He levered himself up to an elbow. "Don't expect me to stand by, waiting for permission, when some asshole is threatening you, because that's something I can't do."

"Cort!" Surprised by his language and his vehemence, she frowned. "There were no threats—"

"Bull." He cupped her face. "I get that you were fine with your father-in-law. Totally trust your judgment on that. You know him, and people like him, in a way that I don't." In a way he never would. That kind of money and prestige were well out of his world. "But the guy who was with him? That dude I know. He was there to intimidate, and your father-in-law would have allowed it, because he's the one who brought him along."

"Hmm," Marlow said in a thoughtful way. "You could be right—though I still think I could have handled him."

God love her, the woman thought she was invincible. Honestly? He thought she might have handled the bodyguard, too—not physically, but with cutting intelligence that would have put the guy in his place. Only Cort wasn't willing to risk it. "When it comes to someone like him, doesn't matter if he's a drunk who's pissed himself or a guy in a thousand-dollar suit." Cort kissed her soundly. "As a kid, I had to stand by and watch my mom get battered." Just saying it still had the power to tighten his guts. "There's no worse feeling in the entire world than seeing someone you care about going through that hell."

"I'm sorry," she whispered softly. "I hadn't thought of it from that perspective."

Cort needed her to understand. "I won't overstep, babe. You've got my promise on that. I don't throw first punches, I don't escalate situations. But when they start, you can bet your sweet ass I'll finish them."

Her eyes grew wider with each word he spoke. In a deliberate and obvious bid to lighten the mood, she said, "I'm glad you think my ass is sweet."

He went along with that, cupping her lush behind in both hands and saying, "It's the truth."

Growing somber again, she nestled down against him. "It tortures me, thinking of what you went through as a kid."

"No, don't do that."

Of course, she didn't listen. "I can't imagine how you must feel about it."

Cort sighed, but here with Marlow, in the quiet evening, naked in bed together . . . talking about it didn't seem as brutal as usual. "I used to hide in my closet and cover my ears. That's what Mom taught me to do, always while promising that we'd get away soon. Only I knew she didn't have anywhere to go. No family to help her, and she wasn't allowed friends. Then one day I was brushing my teeth, looking at myself in the mirror, when he got home and started on her again. Just like that, I knew I couldn't take it anymore."

The kiss she pressed to his chest, right over his heart, encouraged him to keep going.

"I knew if I went down that road, it was going to be bad. He'd knocked me around before, but Mom would always step in. Even knowing she'd take a beating. She always protected me as much as she could."

"How old were you?"

"That last time? Twelve. A big twelve, tall but scrawny . . ." He could recall that ordeal as if it was yesterday, all the emotions, fear and pain, desperation and horror, and ultimately, pride. "I did what I could, used what weapons I could find, like a bottle, a book, even a lamp." Normally, remembering would be awful, and talking about it impossible. It was Marlow who made all the difference. "I hurt him. I know that, because he staggered, and God, he cursed up a storm. I think he planned to kill me, or at least hurt me as much as he could."

She squeezed closer, and without her saying a word, he knew she was crying again. Amazing Marlow, the woman who only cried for others, never for herself.

"I caught him in the head with the lamp, and that did some damage. He started out drunk, but then he was disoriented, too." The scene spread out in his mind, a bright, gruesome visual. "He was bleeding everywhere before he fell. Mom kept sobbing." That had been the worst part. Her terror. Her uncertainty about what to do. "To this day, I can't bear to hear a woman sobbing. It rips me apart."

"I swear to never sob," she said tearfully.

That vow prompted a small smile. Cort tipped up her face. "I swear to never give you reason to sob." Using both thumbs, he brushed the tears from her cheeks. "But if you ever need to, for any reason at all, I'll hold you. I'll fix what I can for you, and otherwise just be there for you."

Her lips trembled. "Thank you."

"Do you know, you're always thanking everyone?"

She dipped her chin in a small nod. "Because I appreciate all the wonderful people in my life, and Cort? You're the one I appreciate the most."

That vow sounded mighty sweet to him. He hoped she felt the same after the Wednesday meeting, because he was betting everything on it.

Smoothing her hand over his chest, she asked, "You and your mother got away then?"

"No. There were a few more beatings while she tried to save

enough so we could. The thing is, I realized I preferred getting beaten to cowering. I felt a hell of a lot better facing my dad than standing back and being a victim or letting my mother face him alone. It wouldn't be the same for everyone, I know that, but I learned that facing my problems head-on rather than trying to hide from them allowed me to like myself more." Casually, as he spoke, he trailed his fingers through her hair, detangling it, smoothing it. Just enjoying touching her. "It wasn't long before we were able to leave. Mom worried about everything, though. Would we have enough food, enough heat in the winter. Men. Strangers." Those had been trying times. "We both worked."

"At twelve?"

"You'd be surprised how much a motivated kid can do. Mom did housekeeping at a little roach-infested motel, and the owner paid me to get the trash from the public areas, to sweep the entrances, and keep the lot cleared. Every time he handed me an extra five bucks, it felt like a step forward. Occasionally, someone would order pizza and give me a slice." He smiled, remembering how much he'd loved food back then. Like many boys his age, he'd been a bottomless pit. "Overall, it was tough, but sometimes an adventure. I learned a lot about myself."

"You learned you wanted to be a Marine?"

"Real life heroes, that's what they were to me. Then I signed on, and man, if you think I loved it all, you'd be wrong." He didn't say it, but becoming a Marine had carved him, taking him from a block of cement and turning him into steel. "I loved what it did to me, how it taught me so much. I enlisted with a lot of rage. I used to dream about finding my dad and taking him apart. Literally. That image in my mind was what got me through. Well, that and my mom. I'd always thought she was soft and frail, because Dad hurt her so easily and there didn't seem to be anything she could do about it." Remembering that shamed him. "Now I realize she was the toughest woman I've ever known."

"She had to be. And she had to have a huge heart, too. I think she must have loved you the way Pixie loves Andy."

"Strongest thing in the world," he agreed. "A mother's love."

Marlow smiled sadly. "A dad's love is the same. I'm so sorry you never got to feel that."

Cort didn't mind saying, "Herman is close. I have massive respect for him. Gratitude, too. He represents the best parts of this town. Hardworking, honest, open, and caring about others."

"Herman is terrific, I agree. He has great management skills. When one customer is trying to monopolize too much of my time, Herman has a smooth way of interrupting. He can be stern with anyone acting up but extra friendly to the locals who seem to need a little more attention."

"With the aging population, that's a lot of people."

Stacking her hands on his chest and resting her chin there, Marlow asked, "As long as we're talking, will you tell me more about your friend Nathan?"

For the first time ever, Cort felt like sharing those memories. Nathan had been an incredible guy, and it seemed a shame he hadn't boasted about him more. Now he could because Marlow had given him that gift. "What do you want to know?"

"Anything." Her gaze searched his face, then settled on looking into his eyes. "Everything."

So he talked. Cort shared funny stories and heartbreaking stories. Times when Nathan had kept him going and when he'd repaid the favor. They'd been so close, Cort missed him daily. The things they'd shared guaranteed a lifetime of memories. He'd be thinking of Nathan, just as he thought of his mom, until he left the earth.

But in between those bittersweet memories, he hoped he'd be enjoying every day with Marlow and making new, wonderful memories—together.

The meeting was at the tavern! Marlow couldn't believe it. She heard from Robin, who heard it from Butler—he was the mayor, after all—that Cort, with Herman's help, had arranged it that way.

Everyone knew everything, and she'd been kept in the dark.

The word going around was that Cort wanted Marlow to have her say. Well, if she hadn't already loved him, that would have done it.

She'd been busting her butt since her shift started, partly in an effort to distract herself from the possibility that these people might not accept her, and partly in hopes that she'd get a chance to steal away and pitch her case. Then the crowd had started arriving, and she couldn't understand why a Wednesday should be so blasted busy. Her hopes of attending the meeting had faded, until she'd spoken to Robin.

Now that the meeting was coming to her, nervousness gripped her. In the way of an internal pep talk, she told herself that she was in her Dry Frog Tavern T-shirt. Her hair was in a high, tidy braid. Her only Dior accents were tiny earrings that made her feel good, and she was sure no one would notice them.

She was "one of them." Surely, they'd see that.

Wade, Gloria, and Bobbi—the siblings, as they were called—came in with Pixie and Andy in tow. Pixie waved to her, but Marlow saw her tension, too. The two of them had so much on the line.

In a relatively short time, Bramble had come to represent hope, happiness, and a better future. Logically, Marlow knew she could find happiness anywhere. It came from within her, not from a location. But it was here that she'd rebuilt her damaged pride, recovered from a brutal divorce and the disappointment of betrayal. Here, she'd been the happiest.

Depositing her tray of drinks to the appropriate tables while deftly avoiding conversation, Marlow made her way to Pixie.

"I didn't expect to see you here."

"*I know*," Pixie said in hushed, almost excited tones. "Bobbi said that Cort told them to bring me in."

Uneasily, Marlow glanced around. Everyone was watching her, so she did her best to act blasé. She didn't want to give anyone warning of her intent to insist, if necessary, that she and Pixie be allowed to make Bramble their permanent home.

Whispering, she said to Pixie, "No matter what happens, we'll be fine."

Pixie's smile was soft, her gaze understanding as she noted Marlow's nervousness. "I know. You need to know it, too." Her attention wandered around the room, taking in all the people present. "Like you, I'd rather be fine here, but Cort said family isn't where you live, it's who you love."

That sentiment left Marlow undone. "He is one wise, wise Marine."

"I think he's your wise Marine," Gloria said. Then she went back to cooing to Andy in the most outrageous way. Baby talk, it seemed, was not Gloria's talent.

Herman called out, "Everybody find a seat. Let us know what you want to drink, then settle down so we can get to it."

"Oops," Marlow said. "I think that means I have to get back to work."

Pixie hugged her. "You've got this."

Such faith!

Marlow made several quick trips before all the locals were served. She kept looking for Cort but didn't see him, yet Herman repeatedly gave her sly looks, as if he was in on a secret. Well, Herman would be an easier nut to crack than Cort, so she started in his direction, only to be pulled up short as the official meeting got underway.

Jumping the gun a little, Marlow cleared her throat to draw everyone's attention. "I'd like to state my case for permanent—"

"We have a protocol," Butler interrupted, "and you're out of order."

Of all the nerve! "But I need to—"

Cort spoke from the break room as he made his way forward. "I believe I'm first on the docket."

"And then me," Herman said, popping up from his seat.

Butler turned to the clerk, who happened to be his wife, for verification.

She nodded. "That's correct. Cort and then Herman."

"All right, fine," Butler said. "Put Marlow after them."

His wife did some quick writing, and said, "Done."

Marlow couldn't take her eyes off Cort. What was he up to?

Butler said, "Come up front, Cort, so everyone can hear." To the mayor's credit, he wasn't snarky or rude, just determined to follow procedure. She'd never quite seen him like this. Usually when Butler was around the tavern, he was just another one of the guys, easygoing, funny, and a nice tipper.

It was Cort who had her most confused of all. She wished he'd clued her in so she knew what to expect.

Silent anticipation kept everyone rapt as Cort walked up to join Butler. All over again, Marlow admired his presence and the way he held a room. Cort was their hero.

Her hero, too, though she hadn't yet told him how much she loved him.

When her chest burned, she remembered to draw air into her starving lungs.

Cort got things started by saying, "I officially propose that the population rule should be changed." A murmur swept the room. "We could limit new housing, instead of new people."

Marlow felt all eyes on her now. She lifted her chin.

"It makes more sense than restricting human beings, when neighbors might marry and originals might have grandchildren, or in my case, when someone has a relative who lives with them."

Leo said, "Marlow isn't your relative."

"Yet," someone added with a chuckle.

Herman jumped up again. "But his mama was, and I won't believe a single one of you didn't want her here."

The room fell silent until Robin, from The Docker restaurant, stood. "My father is getting older. What if I needed to bring him here to take care of him?"

Joann shot out of her seat. "Someday I want to have kids."

Butler's flustered wife, acting in her capacity as clerk, pointed out, "Offspring are already allowed."

"I know," Joann countered. "And how ridiculous is that? To allow or disallow children?"

Wade got to his feet. "What if one of us had a family emergency? Like Cort and his mom, most of us have kin. Would we have to leave town to help our families?"

Another murmur made the rounds as everyone considered his point. Given the way things were going, Marlow kept silent. She hadn't expected this show of support, and she was overcome with gratitude.

Cort regained the floor. "What we're all trying to say is that the population is going to change. It's out of our control." He looked at each council member. "As long as we don't add new residential or commercial real estate, we can keep growth under control. Bramble won't become a busy, crowded town, because none of us want that."

"No," Bobbi said. "But we do want Marlow to stay."

Robin added, "And Pixie. We want them both."

"The three of them," Gloria called out, while cuddling Andy.

"They're part of us now." Joann smiled at her. "They have to stay."

Others weighed in with agreement until the whole room was talking, and Marlow could barely breathe. These wonderful people were openly championing her. She'd badly wanted to be here, but she hadn't realized that they wanted her, too.

Cort met her gaze while speaking to everyone. "If you can't see your way clear to approve that, I understand." Grumbled complaints ensued as others made it clear that they did not understand. "I'm prepared to sell my properties."

Marlow's heart shot into her throat, then dropped into her stomach. "*What?*" She forgot about everyone except Cort. "No, you can't—"

"Sell?" Herman shouted theatrically, startling Marlow because he was not a good actor. Anyone could see that he was speaking a rehearsed line. With a gasp for effect, he demanded with flair, "Why ever would you sell?"

Oh, this was like a terrible play that delighted you anyway.

Cort, however, delivered his lines with true conviction. "Because if Marlow moves to Lankton, I'll be moving to Lankton, too."

Happiness bubbled up, threatening to burst until she couldn't hold back her grin. Of course, she'd never let him do that. Cort and this town were intrinsically tied together. Could she stop him? Yes. Somehow, she'd find a way.

Wade pushed back his chair and stood. "You're still working on our addition."

Cort said, "I'd drive back to finish it."

Bobbi shook her head. "But we need you *here*."

Gloria pointed at the back wall. "Herman has your photo hanging. You're *our* hero, not Lankton's."

And with firm conviction, Cort said, "I go where she goes."

Incredulous, Marlow covered her smile with a hand. No

matter how her housing situation worked out, she was so very glad she'd met this remarkable man.

Uncaring that much of the town looked on, she said clearly, "You're the most wonderful man, Cort." She couldn't keep the smile off her face. "Thank you for backing me up."

"I told you I would." His gaze locked on hers, and he added with some significance, "Always."

The way he said that, infused with such meaning, made her think impossible things. Amazing things. "You . . . Does that mean . . . ?"

Everyone started chuckling, even the mayor.

Good God, she couldn't ask him to clarify his feelings right here, right now, with an audience all around them.

Pixie called out, "FYI, I love you both."

That got more laughter and some agreement.

Slowly, Marlow got it together. In a voice unlike her own, she squeaked, "Ditto," to Cort, to Pixie, to all of Bramble.

Knowing everyone waited to see what she'd do, Marlow stepped up to Cort's side. He put his arm over her shoulders and gave her an encouraging squeeze.

She faced the mayor. "Bramble is special. I would never want to do anything to change it. That's why Pixie and I want to stay, because it's perfect as it is. But Cort is right. One way or the other, we'll respect your rules."

The mayor let out a groan. He leaned in to talk quietly with his council members: the postmaster, fire chief, head of maintenance, and the owner of a house museum, as well as his wife.

In no time at all, they turned back, and the mayor announced, "We like the idea of simply restricting the buildings. That regulation should ensure that we don't grow too large. Since the houses Cort owns are already here, and you and Pixie live in them, your permanent residency shouldn't be a problem. However, we'll discuss a limit on how many can dwell in a single-family home." He raised a hand. "But we'll leave room for extenuating circumstances. Of course, the new ordinance will have to go up for a town vote, but we don't foresee a problem." He grinned at Marlow. "Welcome to Bramble."

Her legs went weak. Oh my God, for months she'd been quietly campaigning to gain citizenship here and it had turned out to be easier than she'd ever hoped.

Shocked, she turned to Cort, who hugged her off her feet.

Everyone loved that, too. She felt certain that Cort could do just about anything and they'd adore him for it.

After a lot of cheering and celebrating, everyone gradually settled into enjoying meals and drinks, which meant Marlow needed to get back on the clock.

With her heart still thumping double-time over the astounding news, she smiled up at Cort. "I didn't come here looking for someone like you."

"I know that."

"But I'm so glad you're in my life." In case that was presumptuous, she said, "I hope that will continue."

"I hope so, too." Keeping his arms around her waist, he kissed her. "But there's no rush. You can go on enjoying the sunrises and the fireflies." He glanced down at her chest. "And your Dry Frog Tavern T-shirts. No pressure, okay? I'm happy that you're happy. I'm surprised that I'm so happy, because until you, I didn't realize what I was missing. Most of all, I'm glad I found you."

Relief that she hadn't misinterpreted brought back all her confidence. "I think *I* found *you*, but I suppose Marines like to take all the credit."

He treated her to that gorgeous, crooked grin.

"I should get to work." A glance around the tavern showed several empty glasses. "I think this is the busiest we've ever been."

Before she could move, Herman tugged her away from Cort to give her a long, tight, make-everything-right kind of hug that she felt clean down to her heart. Cherishing the moment, Marlow squeezed him back.

When Herman eased up, he said, "You're a good one, honey. Now remember that I'm the boss and don't argue when I tell you to take the rest of the night off." He flashed a grin at Cort. "I'm sure you two have things to discuss."

Before she could even think of disagreeing, Cort said, "Appreciate it, Herman." He caught her hand and started toward the front door.

She resisted. "I can't go. Herman will be swamped."

The mayor interrupted their progress. "Not so. A bunch of us will help out. We've done it before, so go and enjoy yourself."

Cort said, "Thanks, Butler." The two of them shook hands. "For everything."

Butler winked. "It's what neighbors do."

She'd heard that before. It could be a Bramble slogan, maybe on the shirts she'd make. Marlow decided to ask Cort what he thought about the idea—as soon as she got him alone. "We need to say goodbye to Pixie."

"I'm right here," Pixie said, having somehow snuck up on them. She held Andy, who was awake and smiling at everyone. "I'll walk you both out, but I'll stay another hour or so. Gloria ordered burgers and fries for all of us, and Wade said if Andy got fussy, we could pack the food up for home." Sheepishly, Pixie said, "They treat me like a granddaughter."

Cort asked, "Do you mind?"

"I love it."

Happiness followed them out the door, until they came face to face with Aston and Sandra, who were just leaving their car to come in.

It was a toss-up who was more surprised.

"Sandra," Marlow said. "What are you doing here?"

Sandra scowled at her, then narrowed her gaze on Pixie. Her color faded, and she breathed harder. "*You.*"

Pixie blanched.

Shooting Marlow a killing look, Sandra said, "I can't believe you've hidden her here! From *us.*"

Well, hell. The day had been going so nicely and now this. There were other people in the lot, some hurrying into the tavern, likely to share the news of yet another standoff.

"No one is hiding," Marlow said calmly as she stepped down to meet them on the gravel lot. "In fact, we were having a small celebration."

Fury brought Sandra forward until she and Aston stood right in front of Marlow. "It's a betrayal of Dylan, of everything he ever meant to you."

Murmuring voices came closer, meaning they now had another audience. Poor Herman. She'd brought a lot of unexpected excitement to his establishment.

"Would you like to follow me home to talk?" Anyone could see that Sandra was hurting, but to Marlow's mind, that didn't excuse such an ugly public display.

Without looking at Pixie, Sandra demanded, "Is she staying with you? Living off you?"

"No. Pixie has her own place."

"Because of *you.*" Sandra's voice broke. "Because you're helping her behind our backs."

Aston kept quiet, and for once he looked a little unnerved.

Using a quieter tone than Sandra had, Marlow asked, "Would you rather she and your grandson suffer together?"

Silence stretched between them, then somehow ignited with tension that grew tighter and tighter . . .

The slap snapped Marlow's head to the side, the sound of its impact loud and obscene, penetrating her ears before the burning pain registered.

Suddenly Cort was stationed in front of her, his body rock

hard and practically vibrating with controlled rage. "Back. The fuck. Off."

Marlow wanted to tell him she was okay, but she was still too stunned to get the words out.

Herman stepped to her right side, his hands fisted and his angry breath audible. Pixie stationed herself at Marlow's left. Andy, bless his innocent little heart, cooed with interest but thankfully no fear. He was a very secure little boy.

It seemed that dozens of people emptied out of the tavern to stand beside or behind her.

As what had happened sank in, Marlow could only gape at her mother-in-law. Disbelief seemed to be her overriding reaction, but a fresh torrent of rage rushed in behind it.

CHAPTER 14

Stepping around Cort, Marlow faced off with Sandra at close range. "How *dare* you!"

Hand over her mouth, Sandra swallowed convulsively as huge tears filled her eyes. "Oh God, Marlow," she whispered brokenly. "I'm so sorry." She started to reach out, but as Marlow tensed, Sandra slowly withdrew. "I can't . . . I don't . . ."

Marlow watched her fall apart.

Gulping, nearly gasping for air, Sandra stared in horror—and then openly sobbed. As if her legs gave out, she sank down to the dusty step near Marlow's feet, uncaring of her designer slacks or the many people surrounding them. "I'm sorry." Arms clutched around herself, she rocked forward. "I'm sorry. So, so sorry."

Aston stood there, his expression aghast before he lowered himself down to sit beside his wife. When he looked up at Marlow, she saw that his eyes, too, were suddenly wet. "Deepest apologies, Marlow. We've both been overwrought . . . It's no excuse, I just didn't realize." He put his arms around Sandra, saying softly, "She's always so strong."

For the first time that Marlow could remember, Aston seemed to genuinely cherish his wife. Sandra buried her face in his neck, her wracking sobs heartbreaking.

Cort clearly wasn't appeased, but his fury lost that dangerous edge. He looked back at everyone else, murmuring something that encouraged them all to go back inside.

Marlow felt their retreat but didn't see it because she couldn't pull her gaze away from her in-laws.

They were broken people, doing things they normally wouldn't do. Belatedly, she understood what the loss of their only son had cost them. Their never-ending arrogance, their secure position in society, had blinded her to the fact that love was love, period.

These people had deeply loved Dylan, flaws and all. He was their flesh and blood, the baby they'd once held just as Pixie now held Andy. They'd watched him grow, had encouraged him endlessly, and despite his many issues, they'd been exceedingly proud of him. Knowing Dylan was gone forever had taken a terrible toll.

Unsure what to say or do, Marlow turned to Pixie, who had remained at her side. "You're okay?"

Holding Andy protectively close, her gaze on Marlow's cheek, Pixie nodded. "But your face . . ."

"I'll be fine." *In a few more minutes.* "Maybe you should wait inside—"

"No." Pixie kissed Andy's head. "They're here because of me. It's past time I faced them."

Marlow couldn't really argue with that, so she turned to Cort, offering a small smile despite the sting it caused. He needed to know that she had a firm hold on her emotions.

His hand, large but gentle, settled over her cheek as if to heal her. A fire of rage glowed in his warm brown eyes, but Cort was not an unrestrained man. He always controlled his reactions, especially when dealing with others.

It was but one of the many things she loved about him.

Quietly, he asked, "What can I do?"

He was already doing it, sharing the difficult moment, and as he'd promised, not escalating things.

From the step below them, Aston said, "What happened is unforgivable, but I can promise that we won't bother you again."

Marlow leaned into Cort, and together, they peered down at the older couple. They appeared utterly defeated, and she couldn't be immune to their pain, no matter what.

She couldn't pretend that nothing had happened, but she could proceed differently. "You're forgiven, but Sandra, you will never again lay a hand on me or I'll file charges."

Sandra nodded. "I wouldn't blame you. I don't know how it happened this time." The words shuddered out uncontrollably. Digging a tissue from her purse, she patted her cheeks, but the damage to her makeup was done.

Aston took the tissue from her and gently cleaned around her eyes.

Sandra looked at him with gratitude before lifting her face to address Marlow. "I've never struck anyone before." She glanced at her hand as if she didn't recognize it, then cradled it to her chest. "I love you, Marlow. I know you don't believe that, but it's true. We haven't been fair to you, and you owe us nothing, but . . ." Her voice broke. "You're all we have left of Dylan."

Gently, Marlow said, "No, I'm not." She reached out a hand to Pixie, who reluctantly joined her. "If you'll open your heart just a little, you'll see that Pixie is a wonderful person who simply made a mistake, same as Dylan did, and the same as the rest of us do."

Cautiously, Sandra's gaze moved to Pixie, and then as if drawn by a will of its own, to Andy . . . where it lingered.

The baby kicked his legs and grinned.

The little stinker seemed to be doing his best to thaw

Sandra's heart. It would surely work, because who could resist him?

Of course, Andy surprised everyone with a little gas, which made him grin even more.

Pixie chuckled nervously and kissed him again. Even Cort cracked another grin.

Sandra appeared mesmerized, her own lips tilting a little.

"You see, Sandra?" Marlow smiled. "You have a beautiful grandson. He's healthy and well-cared-for and loved. Not just by Pixie but by Cort and me, too."

Both Sandra and Aston glanced at Cort. He stepped closer and put a possessive arm around Marlow. She didn't mind; she loved him and didn't care who knew it, including her in-laws.

As soon as she got Cort alone, she'd make sure that he knew, too.

For now, she had other issues to settle. "Whether or not you get to know Andy is up to you. I hope you give that a lot of thought." Having said her piece, Marlow led Cort and Pixie back inside. No way could she leave just yet.

After watching them drive away, Cort closed the tavern door.

"I'm sorry, Marlow." Sadness and regret showed in Pixie's blue eyes, but the baby was still fascinated with the lights and sounds of the tavern.

Cort drew Marlow into his arms. He, too, was somber.

By God, this was a celebration. Marlow wasn't about to let anything, or anyone, destroy their happiness. "Let's focus on the fact that we've been accepted, and we get to stay in Bramble, okay?"

"I'm so glad I have you in my corner." With the slightest smile, Pixie said, "My hamburger is ready. I think I'll go enjoy it."

"You're going to stay?" Marlow asked.

"Yes, because no matter what, I'm happy now, and like you,

I'm determined to stay happy, to concentrate on the good stuff."

"A sound plan," Cort said.

"Please, you two don't need to stay."

Marlow said, "But—"

"But nothing. Andy and I are enjoying the time out, and everyone is super nice. I'm not worried, and I don't want you to worry either. Go, relax." Her gaze flicked to Marlow's cheek. "You two deserve some downtime." This time she smiled at Cort. "Together."

Giving a nod, Marlow allowed exhaustion to steal over her. Her mind was weary, her thoughts fractured. Resting her face against Cort's chest helped, as did the way he coasted his hands up and down her back. "That was so awkward."

"As usual, you handled it well, better than anyone else could have."

Enjoying the feel of his cotton T-shirt and the scent of him through it, she asked, "Is everyone staring at me now?"

He smiled against her temple. "They're always staring at you. You fascinate them."

"Like a strange object?"

"Like a woman who never fails to surprise them. They care about you, and right now they're trying not to applaud you."

The very idea made her snort. "No, they're not."

"Wanna bet?" His lips pressed lightly to her cheek. "Turn and face them and see what happens."

Holding him tighter, she said, "Soon." She was plenty comfortable just like this.

"We could just go home."

"That would make me a coward."

His hand cupped the back of her neck. "No one would ever think that of you."

"I don't want to think it of myself, either." When another,

not-as-large hand settled on her shoulder, she knew whose it was. "I'm fine, Herman."

"Do you need some ice, honey? A drink? Or would you like a bunch of us to go out there and run them off?"

Seriously, she was not the type to hide, so Marlow released Cort and gave Herman her attention. "They've already left."

He gasped at the sight of her cheek, and then several others did, too.

Marlow didn't know what it looked like, but the sting was already receding, so she faced the roomful of people and stated with conviction, "My mother-in-law is overwrought. What just happened . . . well, it was unlike her." Such an understatement. Usually, decorum ruled Sandra's every decision. "It will never happen again, I promise."

Silence.

Marlow tried again. "I'm fine, and I'm also grateful that you're all my friends. Thank you for accepting me to Bramble."

Wide-eyed, they looked at the mark on her face, then at her, and it wasn't just applause she got but a standing ovation.

Speaking softly near her ear, Cort said, "Told you so."

Herman cleared his throat. "Maybe you should take tomorrow off."

"Absolutely not. I don't even feel right about leaving you now."

"Too bad, because I insist, and don't think you can talk your way around me like you usually do."

Relenting, she said, "Only tonight then. Tomorrow I'll be here and that's that."

Herman shook his head, but he looked relieved that she was acting more like herself. He leaned in to whisper. "Go let Cort pamper you. He still looks ready to commit murder."

"He's more controlled than that."

"Not with you." Herman winced again at her red cheek and added, "For my sake, go rest."

Cort helped settle her indecision by asking him, "You'll keep an eye on Pixie? She might need to feed Andy soon."

"Got it covered. We'll all look out for her."

It pleased Marlow that Pixie's world was expanding to include so many wonderful people. Now in a hurry to be alone with Cort, she gave a friendly wave to everyone. "Thank you all. Coming here was the best decision I ever made!"

She left to the sound of more cheering. The townspeople were in a cheering mood today, for sure.

Outside, she saw that her in-laws were indeed gone, and she wondered if she'd ever see them again. For their sake, she hoped they would soften their stance.

"Want to just ride with me?" Cort asked. "We could get your car tomorrow."

It was sweet that he wanted to pamper her. No one had done that since her parents passed away. "Nope, I'm good, but as usual, I'll follow so you can be the deer spotter."

Fortunately, though they did see a few deer, the beautiful animals bolted away from the road rather than into it.

Once they were inside Cort's house, he locked the door and then carefully gathered her close. He studied her cheek again, his scowl fierce but his hold tender. "For an old woman, she packed a hell of a wallop. I think you might bruise."

The slap seemed to have hurt Cort more than it did her. "Did you see Sandra look at her hand? I bet her palm was smarting." Her attempt at humor fell flat. Marlow wished she knew what to say to him, but she was at a loss. Never before had she faced a situation like this. Never had she expected to. "It's over, Cort. I'm fine, I get to stay in Bramble, and I'm with you. Overall, the day has been amazing."

His mouth tightened. "I've never in my life hurt a woman, but I swear to God, I wanted to pick her up and stuff her into her car and tell her never to return."

Marlow understood that. At first, she'd been equally incensed. "I think in the long run, it'll be better and easier for Pixie if Sandra does come back—as long as she contains herself."

Cort ground his teeth before taking her hand and leading her up the stairs. "It'll probably be good for Mrs. Heddings, too. I don't like your in-laws, and I won't pretend that I do. But I know what it was like to lose a mother, to face the awful reality that there will be no more phone calls, no visits, no disagreements or jokes. The smiles, the hugs, the everyday conversations are gone . . . forever. With my mother, I knew she was ailing. I knew it was coming." Inside his bedroom, he drew her to the bed and sat beside her, his hands braced on his knees, his shoulders rigid. "Your in-laws had no warning they were about to lose their son. I'm sure they assumed they'd die before him." Again, his jaw flexed. "They're not nice people, Marlow."

All she could do was nod, but she clarified, "They're not usually this bad. In all the time I've known them, the worst treatment I ever received was icy politeness." That didn't feel fair, so she added, "They were never unkind to me."

"You're so special, I don't know how anyone could be."

"I'm as imperfect as everyone else."

Ignoring her comment, Cort said, "I accept that even Sandra and Aston suffer heartache. It was pretty obvious that your mother-in-law shocked herself, and I think her apology was genuine."

"I do, too." She leaned against him. "Thank you for not stuffing her in her car."

Reluctantly, he nodded, then cast her a look. "If she ever touches you again, I make no promises."

"She won't." Marlow pushed him back on the bed, then crawled over him. "So, Cort, I was wondering . . . What are we doing?"

He didn't pretend to misunderstand. "You blindsided me." His fingertips brushed her cheek. "I've tried to be prepared for anything life might throw my way." He touched her lips. "No way could I have prepared for you."

Like a verbal nudge, she reminded him, "You said you cared about me."

"I love you."

There it was, and still she repeated, "You love me?"

"Don't panic," he said, far too seriously. "I love you, but it doesn't mean you have to—"

She crushed her mouth down on his, and it was an odd kiss because she was laughing and maybe crying a little.

He pressed her away. "Marlow?"

"I love you, too, you silly Marine." She forced her way down for another kiss, then grinned at him. "How could I not love you?"

"I hope that's a rhetorical question."

"I've never known anyone like you. And you want to talk about blindsided! Holy smokes, you bowled me over. *Constantly*. Somehow meeting you took the worst period of my life and turned it into the best. Believe me, I was not looking for another romance. I wanted the freedom to be me, to live life any way I wanted, to make my own choices without having to consider anyone else."

A small frown showed Cort's worry.

Marlow put her hands on his cheeks. "With you, Cort, I've felt more like myself than I have since before my marriage. I like the person I am now a lot more."

"Good, because I would never ask you to change."

"I know that, and it's just one of the many reasons why I love you. Bramble is special, and I want to stay, but I could be happy anywhere as long as I'm with you."

He turned them so she was on her back, and he was over her. "I know you, Marlow. With or without me, you'd find a way to be happy, because that's who you are. A survivor, an upbeat participant in life, a gentle soul with a backbone of iron and fierce drive. I'd rather you be happy with me, but no matter what, you'd find a way." He kissed her carefully, mindful of her bruised cheek. "I love you enough to do things your way."

She stalled. "Um, what does that mean?"

"I'm an old-fashioned guy, and as you know, Bramble is an old-fashioned town. Eventually, I'd like us to get married."

Her heart started tripping wildly.

"I know you've been down that route without the best results. I'll understand if you want a lot of time. If you prefer to go on living in the guest cottage, if you want us to slow down a little—"

"I don't." When he appeared confused, she tried again. "You're right. I'd rather wait a while before getting married, but not too long. Maybe we could shoot for next summer?" That would give her heart time to settle down, so she was only thinking with her head. "And I love the guest cottage, but I'd also love to be with you more."

Cautiously, he asked, "Would you like to live here?"

"Yes," she said too quickly, so she politely tacked on, "If you don't mind."

He smiled. "The sunrises look the same from my dock, I promise."

Thinking about spending a lifetime with this man had her blood pumping and her entire body too warm. "I'll need some office space, too."

He nodded. "We'll look at the house and figure out what works best."

"I still plan to work for Herman," she warned.

"He'll be thrilled to hear it."

With Cort being so agreeable, her thoughts and plans hit Mach speed. "I still plan to open a shop in Lankton, too."

"The building you looked at will be perfect."

So much happiness couldn't be contained in one body. "God, I love you."

He gave her another, deeper kiss, one that signaled more was to come.

"Can Pixie stay at the lake house?"

Taking his kisses to her neck, Cort murmured, "On one condition."

Oh, heavens, his lips felt delicious, nearly sidetracking her. She managed to breathe, "What is it?"

"You can't keep paying for her."

"I have to."

Pausing long enough to make his one and only demand, Cort said, "It's something I want to do. I like having her here where we can help her when necessary. I want to watch her grow and learn from you, and maybe she'll learn a few things from me, too."

Marlow put her palm to his face. "She'll learn many things from you."

"Then that's settled." He tugged at the hem of her shirt, then slid his hand underneath. "Now let's move on to more important things."

Breathless again, she asked, "Like loving each other?"

Sliding down in the bed to kiss the bare skin of her midriff, he growled, "That's the perfect place to start."

Two weeks later, the whole town was aware that she'd moved into Cort's home, intended to keep working at the tavern, and had made a bid on the building in Lankton.

Their plan right now was for Pixie to be her manager. She was an organizational guru and had already impressed Marlow with how quickly she accomplished tasks.

Marlow had fifteen minutes before she'd start her shift. She knew once she stepped out to the floor of the tavern, there'd be questions galore. It didn't bother her, but she didn't want the talk to impede her work. Herman counted on her.

The end of August had brought grueling heat, with the sun

beating against the windows. She'd pinned up her usual braid and wore her tavern T-shirt knotted at the side.

Cort already sat at a table. He often stopped by for dinner when she worked, and sometimes he brought Pixie, too. Right now, though, Andy was cutting a tooth, and the poor little guy was miserable, which meant Pixie walked with him a lot. He was still breastfed, but now it was supplemented with bottles, so Marlow and Cort could regularly give her a break.

Suddenly Cort showed up at the break-room door. One look at his face, and Marlow knew something was up. "What is it?"

"Your mother-in-law is here."

She groaned.

"Want me to tell her to leave?"

"Would you?"

He turned to go. Laughing, Marlow snagged him back. "Okay, okay. You would—but I don't want that. I have a few minutes before I start, so I'll just go see why she's here."

Cort's expression said it all: he would have preferred to send her away.

Every day, Marlow had wondered when, if, Sandra would return. She had to be curious about the baby. "How about I introduce you?"

"Yes," Cort said with satisfaction. "Let's do that."

Grinning at him, Marlow took his hand and stepped out of the room. There by the door stood Sandra. Everyone, especially Herman, eyed her critically. Marlow didn't see Aston, but that didn't mean he wasn't close by. It would be a long drive for her mother-in-law to make on her own.

Going first to Herman, Marlow said, "Stop it."

"Why? She deserves the stink eye."

Cort agreed. "She does."

The phrase almost made her laugh. "She might, but this is still a public place, and it appears she might be a customer."

"Doesn't have to be. I can refuse her."

Marlow patted his shoulder. "I'd rather not cause a scene."

His gaze shot to her. "Does that mean you plan to talk to her?"

"Of course I will." Not that she particularly looked forward to it. "I still have a few minutes."

He just stared at her.

Softly, Marlow said, "She wasn't herself that night. I've never seen her so broken. Please, let's try to be kind."

He gave one sharp nod. "For you, I will. Just know that if it looks like she's bothering you, I'm setting off the fire alarm."

The grin got away from Marlow, but she quickly forced her lips into a more sedate line. "I won't be bothered, so don't do anything." When he frowned at her, she added, "You're a charmer, Herman. I hope you know how much I care for you."

He turned his frown to Cort. "You going to introduce yourself to her?"

"Marlow is taking care of that for me. Don't worry, okay? She knows what she's doing."

With that vote of confidence, she sauntered over to her mother-in-law.

With each step, she felt the eyes of customers on her—Sandra's included. Tension thickened the air, making her wonder if her mother-in-law actually felt nervous. For Marlow, it was like facing a tough client. She'd be professional, polite, but to the point.

When she reached Sandra, she said, "Hello, again."

Sandra glanced at Cort, then away. "I hope you don't mind, but I wanted to see you again."

"I don't mind." She smiled up at Cort. "Sandra, this is Mr. Easton. Cort, this is my mother-in-law, Mrs. Heddings." Bracing herself for an explosion, Marlow stated, "Cort and I are together now."

Sandra hesitated only a second. "I see." She glanced away, and then her gaze lifted. "I'm pleased to meet you, Mr. Easton."

How about that? Progress.

Cort nodded. "Mrs. Heddings."

"I should apologize to you as well," Sandra continued. "The way I behaved on my last visit . . ." Words failed her for a moment. "I won't make excuses. Just know that I regret it a great deal."

Visibly relaxing, Cort said, "I assume this visit will be different."

Marlow appreciated his compassion. "If you don't mind, Cort, I'd like to talk to Sandra alone."

He said, "I'll sit right over there." Meaning close, and where he could see her.

Marlow indicated a table to Sandra. "I have a few minutes before I start my shift. Should we sit?"

Letting out a breath, Sandra drummed up a strained smile. "Please."

So far, everything seemed to be going well. After Sandra took a chair, Marlow settled across from her, keeping her back to everyone else. This would be easier if she didn't have to see everyone gawking at her. Again.

Pleasant expression in place, Marlow rested her hands on the tabletop. "Is Aston with you?"

"I left him at a bar outside of this little . . . village. I wanted to see you alone, to talk personally, woman to woman." Faint lines bracketed her mouth. "If there was anywhere nice to stay overnight, I'd have come alone. Instead, we'll drive back to Louisville for the night, then head home tomorrow."

A lot of explanation—that told Marlow very little. "How are you, Sandra?"

Seconds ticked by, emphasizing the silence of the tavern, until finally Sandra whispered, "A mess, actually." Her spine seemed to droop, her head bowing. "I don't have the words to tell you how sorry I am."

It was an olive branch, one Marlow accepted. "I understand. I know that losing Dylan has been difficult."

"Impossible, really," Sandra admitted softly. "I can't imagine anything worse. Not losing Aston. Not losing the business." Her nostrils flared, her lips trembling. "It would have been easier to give up my own life."

Marlow felt her pain as an ache in her own heart. "I'm so sorry." Her whispered words weren't adequate, but what would be?

Again, time stretched out. Murmurs began in the tavern, and slowly conversation returned. Herman came by, so Marlow guessed he was the reason everyone was attempting to carry on. Bless the man, she really did adore him.

Looking only at Marlow, he asked, "Would you like a drink?"

Grateful for the interruption of the awkward, emotionally laden moment, she smiled. "Since I have ten minutes left, I would. A cola with plenty of ice, please." She addressed Sandra. "You?"

"I'll have the same." Her hands clenched together, but she said to Herman, "Thank you."

With a nod, Herman meandered away, his reluctance to leave her alone apparent to everyone. Hoping to lighten the moment, Marlow said, "That wasn't so difficult, was it?"

Sandra cracked a small smile, too. "I didn't think he'd leave us otherwise."

"Probably not. He's protective. Everyone here is—even though I don't need protecting."

"Not from me," Sandra assured her, and she sounded as if she meant it. "Even before that . . . mistake, I didn't make a very good impression."

"You were verbally aggressive," Marlow agreed. "I understand that you were hurting, but these people don't know you. They may seem laid-back, but they're all loyal to each other."

"And to you?"

"Apparently so. It pleases me."

"And Mr. Easton? He pleases you, too?"

"He pleases me the most." For the first time since leaving everything and everyone behind, Marlow thought that she might enjoy peace with her in-laws. Not a close continuing relationship, but maybe a congenial one, without all the animosity. "Understand, Sandra, when I came here, I couldn't have imagined getting involved again. My marriage with Dylan ended long ago. I just hadn't realized it. Then the divorce dragged on . . ."

"And his death," Sandra whispered.

Seeing it through Sandra's eyes now, Marlow kept her tone soft instead of defensive. "All I wanted was to start over. To be free and happy again."

Sandra straightened. "I know Dylan strayed."

Just then, with uncanny timing, Herman returned to their table. He set out two tiny napkins and placed tall, icy cold drinks on them. From his tray, he retrieved two straws.

Again, looking only at Marlow, he said, "If you need anything else, anything at all, just give me a nod." His gaze cut to Sandra, and then he walked off.

Marlow made a quick scan of the room and saw everyone ready to jump to her aid if necessary.

She was an authoritative woman who could navigate high-stakes situations on her own, yet it was nice to have others who cared. She smiled at Cort, and he smiled back.

Sandra had spoken her mind, so Marlow would do the same. "Yes, Dylan strayed." What a vague way to say that her husband had repeatedly slept with another woman. "I found it unforgivable. He betrayed not only me but the life we had and the commitments we'd made to each other. He destroyed my trust." And in ways that Sandra would never know, he'd been deliberately cruel.

"He apologized," Sandra pressed, "and still you went ahead with the divorce."

There was less accusation in Sandra's tone and more of an appeal to understand, so Marlow tried to explain. "You know it wasn't an amicable divorce. Not because he loved me and didn't want to lose me, but because it angered him that I would dare call him out on his bad behavior." Something his mother and father had never done. "He expected me to turn a blind eye, to accept his quickly given, offhand excuses. Not once did I think he was sincere." Because he hadn't been. "I was so angry and so hurt, I knew I couldn't move beyond it, and that would have only made us both more miserable. Divorce was the only way."

"It crushed him."

"No." She'd come to the realization that Dylan had never truly loved her. The bigger realization, however, was that she'd stopped loving him, too. He'd been angry, yes, but then so had she, and she'd allowed her anger to dictate her every move. "He was probably embarrassed because his friends found out. He didn't like that he couldn't control the situation. He was frustrated and furious that I wouldn't relent." She met Sandra's gaze. "He blamed me for it all."

Unable to hold her gaze, Sandra looked down at her hands.

"But never, at any point, was your son heartbroken." That was the absolute truth. "I want you to know that."

Sandra slowly nodded. "You still can't forgive him."

"And so you can't forgive me?" Marlow saw the stiffening of the other woman's shoulders. "Actually, I have forgiven him. Not necessarily because he deserved it, but because I do. He hurt me, Sandra, far more than I'd like to admit." Largely it was her pride that was wounded, so in one way, she was no better than Dylan. "Now that I'm here, living in an entirely different atmosphere, I'm so content and happy that I realize I hadn't been happy with Dylan, not for a very long time."

Sandra looked aghast. "You can't mean that."

It wasn't her job to convince anyone of her happiness, so Marlow didn't try. "I forgive him, but I won't ever forget."

"I understand," Sandra whispered. "Aston has strayed several times, too."

Marlow went utterly still. Her mother-in-law knew about Aston's affairs? She'd always assumed . . . But of course, she shouldn't have. Sandra was a sharp-witted woman. In her position, she had to be. "I'm sorry."

Sandra shook her head. "That's what he always said. That he was sorry. Until I stopped mentioning it, and he stopped apologizing. Now that he's older, I don't think it happens anymore." Her gaze lifted to lock with Marlow's. "Life was easier when I just ignored his infidelity, so I couldn't understand why you didn't."

Something wounded inside her own heart reached out to this indomitable woman who'd forged her own path in a shark-infested business world. "I couldn't. It's not in me to do that."

Sandra's gaze fell away again. "And yet, I did."

"I wasn't criticizing, I promise. Your marriage, your relationship with Aston, is your own business, not anyone else's." When that didn't seem to reach her, Marlow tried again. "You fit in that world with Dylan and Aston, more than I ever could. I tried, and I think I was successful."

"You did an amazing job, and we'll always appreciate you."

"Thank you, but it was never a part of me, not like it is with you. No one would expect you to give up that life, regardless of what anyone else does."

Sandra's hands tightened on the tabletop. "I made that business what it is today."

Relieved to see her mother-in-law returning to her old self, Marlow nodded. "Yes, you did. Others might have done business with Aston or Dylan, but they knew you were the one with the final say." Whereas Aston could negate or approve

Dylan's moves, he'd never had that power with Sandra. Just the opposite. "You are, and always will be, a force in Heddings' Holdings."

"Damn right."

They shared a smile, a sign of the first genuine camaraderie between them in all the time they'd known each other.

"Were you really not happy with us?" Sandra asked.

"For a long time, I thought I was." Her mother-in-law deserved nothing but the truth. "If things hadn't happened as they did with Dylan, I'd be there still. Now, though, living here, I realize that this is the place I'm truly meant to be. I do the simplest things, like walking on the shoreline or watching the sunrise, and it . . ." Marlow felt silly saying it, yet she knew it was true. "It fills me up."

Sandra glanced around with skepticism. "If it pleases you, then I'll try to be happy for you."

"Thank you." As the old bitterness faded away, Marlow said with sincerity. "I'm so glad you came by."

"I am, too." After a slight hesitation, Sandra admitted, "I've missed you."

Shocking, and yet Marlow believed her. Despite all the strife that had been between them, she knew Sandra saw her as a link to Dylan. After all, for nearly ten years they'd been mother-in-law and daughter-in-law.

This place, Marlow realized, really was magical. It had changed her, softened her edges and breathed fresh life into her dreams. It had opened the door to new possibilities. Could it do the same for Sandra? In this particular moment, Marlow believed it could.

Reaching across the table, she touched Sandra's hand. "Have you ever seen fireflies?"

Sandra blinked. "The insects?"

"Yes. The ones with the glowing butts."

Sandra's lips twitched. "Years upon years ago, I used to go

out with my sister at my grandmother's house. There were fields around her home, and we would play for hours. Mostly we'd find crickets and butterflies, but I recall seeing fireflies toward evening a few times. The entire field lit up, and my sister told me they were fairies, but I knew better." Sitting back with a sigh, Sandra whispered, "I'd all but forgotten about that. I think I was only four, maybe five."

"Well, I'm thirty-five and I still love seeing them."

A peaceful expression settled on Sandra's face. "Perhaps sometime I could see them with you."

The perfect opening! "I'd enjoy that. Let's plan on it."

Reluctantly, Sandra slid back her chair. "For now, I should get going. It gets dark early here, with all the trees and hills."

When she opened her purse, Marlow stopped her. "Drinks are on me this time."

Instead of debating, Sandra smiled. "Next time will be my treat."

"So there will be a next time?"

"To see the fireflies." Seconds ticked by, and then Sandra met her gaze. "And I'd like to meet my grandson."

There were numerous ways Marlow could reply. She could point out that it was up to Pixie. That it was about time. She could warn Sandra that she'd have to be on her best behavior. For now, none of that felt necessary.

Instead, she asked, "How long did you know about him?"

"I had no idea," Sandra swore. "I knew Pixie was around and I despised her. I blamed her for everything—and yes, now I realize that was unfair." She closed her eyes as pain pinched her features. "To think I tried to drive her away, to keep her from being able to work . . ."

While Sandra seemed so receptive, Marlow briefly explained everything Pixie had gone through. "She could have lost the baby, and she could have died."

"Dear God."

"She literally had no resources, no place to turn—so she came to me. I know it angered you that I helped her, but Sandra . . ." Praying Sandra would understand, that she'd accept the reality of the situation, Marlow asked softly, "How could I not?"

"Indeed." Brisk now, she folded her hands on the table in a businesslike way. "Aston told me what he did. I think he was caught up in the moment and then he regretted it. He said . . ." She chewed her lips a moment. "He said he was afraid to believe the baby was our grandson. His heart was still shattered, he—we—are still hurting over our loss. I don't think he was ready to take on more."

"I'm glad he told you about it. He offered Pixie a lot of money, but she wants a real life, with friends."

"Like you?"

Marlow nodded. "I care about her. Cort and I both do."

"Then she must be a lovely young woman." Sandra met her gaze. "I should have thanked you instead of shouting at you." She shook her head. "I should have helped Pixie myself."

"You didn't know."

"I swear I didn't—but I should have found out."

"You were, and still are, grieving."

Pride kept Sandra's head high. "I will always grieve. Dylan is lost to me forever. But you're right that I have a grandson, and what a wonderful link that will be."

Leaning closer with a smile, Marlow asked, "Isn't he the cutest little guy ever?"

Huge tears welled in Sandra's eyes, forcing her to blink fast and swallow hard. She pressed her hands to her heart, and her lips curved. "I thought he looked like Dylan. Aston noticed that, too, and now he has to apologize to Pixie."

"It'd be nice if the animosity could be resolved."

"He said he was trying to protect me, when I didn't think he'd noticed how devastated I was. But then, I didn't pay much attention to him, either. We were both a little lost, and in some ways, we're closer now."

Glad that the two of them were finding each other again, Marlow gently steered the conversation back to Andy. "He's a big baby, isn't he?"

"He is, but he wasn't at all fussy. He smiled at me."

Marlow didn't remind her about the gas.

"Dylan was so fussy, but he had colic, you know. Weighed over eight pounds when he was born. And he cut teeth early."

"Andy is cutting his first tooth now."

Awed by that news, Sandra breathed, "Just like his father. I should warn Pixie that Dylan was slow to walk. The doctor assured me that was normal, and he certainly made up for it once he started. He was always on the go."

Seeing all that enthusiasm made Marlow enthusiastic, too.

As she walked out of the restaurant with Sandra, Cort followed. She understood. He didn't intrude, just stood in the doorway, there if she needed him.

Sandra turned at her car door. "You forgive me? Really?"

"Yes, of course."

With only the briefest hesitation, Sandra embraced her. "Thank you, Marlow. I mean that. I hope we can visit more often."

"If you call first, we can make time around my work schedule."

"Yes, of course. And I hope, if you ever feel like visiting us, you'll let us know."

That wouldn't happen, but Marlow nodded.

Sandra looked up, then nodded at Cort. "Goodbye, Mr. Easton."

"Drive safely."

As she left, Cort stepped out and wrapped his arms around Marlow from behind. "Always so bighearted. For your sake, I'm glad that's resolved."

"I am, too." She leaned back against him. "Assuming you heard everything, will you update Pixie for me?"

"She'll be . . . surprised." He kissed her temple. "And maybe pleased."

Marlow smiled. The fireflies were all around, twinkling on the hills behind the parking lot, flitting across the air. "I should get to work."

Everything was okay now.

How could it not be in the town of Bramble? She'd found love, true friendship, family . . . and fireflies.